THE VENGEFUL WIFE
AND OTHER BLACKFOOT STORIES

THE
Vengeful
Wife
AND OTHER
BLACKFOOT STORIES

Hugh A. Dempsey

UNIVERSITY OF OKLAHOMA PRESS • NORMAN

ALSO BY HUGH A. DEMPSEY

Crowfoot, Chief of the Blackfeet (Norman and Edmonton, 1972 and 1989)
Charcoal's World (Saskatoon, Lincoln, Toronto, and Berlin, 1978)
Indian Tribes of Alberta (Calgary, 1979)
Red Crow, Warrior Chief (Saskatoon and Lincoln, 1980)
History in Their Blood: The Indian Portraits of Nicholas de Grandmaison
(Vancouver and New York, 1982)
Big Bear, The End of Freedom (Vancouver and Lincoln, 1984)
The Gentle Persuader: James Gladstone, Canada's First Indian Senator (Saskatoon, 1986)
(with Lindsay Moir) *Bibliography of the Blackfoot* (Metchuen, N.J., 1989)
The Amazing Death of Calf Shirt and Other Blackfoot Stories (Saskatoon and Norman, 1994)
Tribal Honors: A History of the Kainai Chieftainship (Calgary, 1997)
Tom Three Persons: Legend of an Indian Cowboy (Saskatoon, 1997)
Indians of the Rocky Mountain Parks (Calgary, 1998)
(with Colin F. Taylor) *With Eagle Tail: Arnold Lupson and 30 Years among the
Sarcee, Blackfeet and Stoney Indians on the North American Plains* (London, 1999)
Firewater: The Impact of the Whiskey Trade on the Blackfoot Nation (Calgary, 2002)

This book is published with the generous assistance of
The McCasland Foundation, Duncan, Oklahoma.

Map facing title page shows the hunting grounds in southern Alberta, Canada, as well as
the present Indian reserves and reservations in the area. Map has been adapted from one
used as the frontispiece in *Crawfoot, Chief of the Blackfeet*, by Hugh A. Dempsey (Norman:
University of Oklahoma Press, 1972). The Treaty No. Seven area and High River have
been removed and Elkwater Lake, Fort Walsh, and Sun River have been added.

Library of Congress Cataloging-in-Publication Data

Dempsey, Hugh Aylmer, 1929–
   The vengeful wife and other Blackfoot stories / Hugh A. Dempsey.
      p.   cm.
   Includes bibliographical references and index.
   ISBN 0–8061–3550–6 (hc. : alk. paper)
      1. Siksika Indians—History.   2. Piegan Indians—History.   3. Kainah Indians—
History.   4. Oral tradition—Alberta.   5. Oral tradition—Montana.   6. Tales— Alberta.
7. Tales— Montana.   I. Title.

E99.S54 .D45 2003
978.004'973—dc21

                                                                              2002043178

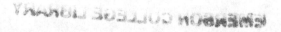

Contents

Illustrations

Illustrations

Introduction

The tribes of the Blackfoot Nation that I discuss in this book are the Bloods, Blackfoot, North Piegans, and South Piegans, who today call themselves the Kainaiowas, Siksikas, Pikunis, and Blackfeet respectively. Today they reside on reserves in Alberta and a reservation in Montana. To avoid confusion I refer to the Blackfoot tribe as the Siksikas, while I call the nation Blackfoot. Allied to them as part of the Blackfoot Confederacy are the Sarcees, or Tsuu T'inas, and, until 1861, the Gros Ventres, or Atsinas. These tribes inhabited the northern Great Plains from the Missouri River in the south to the Battle River in the north and from the Rocky Mountains on the west to the Cypress Hills on the east. It is a vast region of prairies and foothills occupying some seventy-five thousand square miles.

In the nineteenth century the plains were black with buffalo and abounding with antelope, elk, deer, bear, wolves, and other creatures that ran, walked, and crawled. Overhead flew stately eagles and hawks, noisy crows and magpies, and a multitude of other birds that flitted through the prairie grass and darted among the cottonwoods in the river bottoms. And far above the birds were the clouds drifting across bright blue skies, joined at night by a canopy of glimmer stars.

This was the land of the Blackfoot. It was a physical place where people constantly searched for food and protected their hunting grounds from a host of enemies. It was also a spiritual place where animals spoke to men, birds foretold the future, and visions guided and directed the course of people's lives. It was a place where women owned the lodges, raised the children, provided spiritual guidance through their secret societies, and offered beauty through their artistic skills. It was a place where young boys played at war before experiencing it and where girls learned at an early age the drudgery of collecting firewood and water, tanning hides, and preparing meals. Occasionally, some girls broke out of that mold to become warriors and were ultimately accepted in their chosen roles. Similarly, a few men opted out of the war games, donned dresses, and helped the women with their chores.

Warriors went to war, chiefs went to council meetings, youths courted girls near watering places, and women gathered to share the tasks of making new lodges. And they traveled. Whenever the buffalo moved, they moved. During summer they might be in the shadow of the Cypress Hills, watching for enemies, butchering buffalo, drying meat, gathering berries, and performing the rituals of their secret societies. In winter they might be huddled for weeks at a time in the wooded valleys of the Bow, Marias, or Oldman Rivers, the men venturing out to hunt whenever the weather permitted. When they were snowbound by blizzards, the women broke out prized bags of pemmican to provide sustenance to the family until the next supply of fresh meat arrived in the lodge.

The winter was also a time for storytelling. Gathered around the fire, the old men taught the children about being a Blackfoot Indian. They learned how Napi had created the world and then did foolish things while traveling through it. They learned how great warriors had fought for the land and protected it from strangers, sometimes dying gloriously in battle. They learned how young boys performed daring feats of bravery and how a woman had brought the Sun Dance to the people. And they learned that nothing happened by accident, that there were a myriad of spirits, both good and bad, who guided people, threatened them, took pity on them, and brought them good luck on the war trail or bad luck on the hunt. These spirits, the known and the unknown, were recognized as a reality of Blackfoot life. As a result of storytelling, a rich folklore emerged—heroic tales, star myths, legends, and the stories of brave men and women whose lives could well be emulated by the young listeners.

The Blackfoot were generous with their stories and did not mind sharing them with others. When explorer David Thompson spent the winter of 1787–88 in the valley of the Highwood River, the elderly Saukamapee spent hours telling him the history of the Piegans and the legends of the tribe. In the winter of 1792–93, trader Peter Fidler wintered in the same area and also found the Blackfoot, as well as other tribes, willing to recount their stories. He wrote in his journal that he had collected a large amount of information about their customs and languages and that these "I have collected together into another Book." Sad to say, that book has never been found.

In the nineteenth century travelers and writers found the Blackfoot willing and anxious to tell their stories. James Willard Schultz, who went among them in 1877, later wrote numerous books of children's fiction based on these accounts, while in 1892 George Bird Grinnell published the classic work *Blackfoot Lodge Tales*, which is still in print today. Similarly, Walter McClintock's memorable book *The Old North Trail* was the result of stories told to him by Mad Wolf and others. In later years anthropologists and writers made major contributions to the preservation of Blackfoot lore. Foremost among these was John C. Ewers, longtime ethnohistorian with the Smithsonian Institution, who interviewed many elders on the Blackfeet Reservation in Montana and reserves in Canada in the 1940s. Others in that era included Esther Goldfrank, working with the Bloods in 1939; Jane Richardson Hanks and Lucien Hanks, who worked among the Siksikas from 1938 to 1942; and Claude E. Schaeffer, curator of the Plains Indian Museum at Browning, Montana, who was active from 1947 to 1954. The Hanks and Schaeffer papers are now in the Glenbow Archives, Calgary, Canada, where they are frequently consulted by Natives and non-Natives alike, while the Goldfrank papers are in the Smithsonian Institution in Washington, D.C.

Most important were the few Native historians who acted on their own, recording the stories as they knew them. Prominent among these were Mike Mountain Horse, Joe Beebe, Anthony Pretty Young Man, Joe Little Chief, Jim White Bull, and Bob Black Plume. Sometimes using scribblers (lined copybooks) or scraps of paper, they put their residential-school training to good use, preserving a part of their history and culture.

As a young reporter I was following a well-worn trail when I first started asking questions of the Bloods and Siksikas in 1951. And the elders were just as generous in sharing their oral history and traditions with me as their ancestors were with earlier writers. It all began when I met a lovely Blood Indian girl named Pauline Gladstone, whom I later married. At that time tuberculosis was the great scourge of Canadian Indians, and a special hospital had been opened for them in Edmonton. On weekends Pauline and I visited such Blood and Siksika patients as Jack Black Horse and Albert Wells. As we sat with them, they began to tell stories and, as a dutiful newspaper reporter, I began to write them down. We spent many pleasant afternoons hearing about warriors and great chiefs, the real and the supernatural.

My foray into pure research began as the result of a question that puzzled me. I had read everything available on the Blackfoot and particularly on the great chief Crowfoot, who had died in 1890. One day, at a meeting of the Indian Association of Alberta, I asked Frank Medicine Shield about the chief. How, I asked, could the Blackfoot have such a high regard for Crowfoot when everything he did seemed to be for the benefit of the white man? He became friends with the fur traders, signed the Blackfoot treaty, stopped young people from going to war, permitted the Canadian Pacific Railway to pass through their lands, and kept the tribe at peace during the Riel Rebellion. How could the Blackfoot, who were great warriors, have confidence in a chief who seemed to be catering to the whites? Frank's only comment was that if I was not his friend, he would beat the hell out of me for saying bad things about his chief.

Puzzled, I started on a voyage of discovery to find out how there could be two such opposing opinions of the Blackfoot chief. I spoke to Crowfoot's grandson, to a woman who had been a teenager in the chief's lodge when he died, and to others who had known him personally. I found my answer, and it was a simple one: whatever Crowfoot did, it was for his people. If their goals happened to be the same as those of the white people, well and good, but they were not his motivation. With the superiority that seemed to them to be inherent in their race, however, many whites assumed that Crowfoot had taken his various actions to please them. He had not done so, and in the end I wrote a book to tell this story about him. Entitled *Crowfoot, Chief of the Blackfeet*, it was first published in 1972 by the University of Oklahoma Press.

That research project led me to many other writing projects, and many productive hours were spent in the homes of elders and in their lodges at the Sun Dance. I was inducted into the Magpie Society and painted during the transfer of the hailstone tipi, and in 1967 I became an honorary chief of the Blood tribe. During these years I asked questions, listened to stories, and conducted research in Ottawa, Washington, D.C., and Helena, Montana, as well as in the vast collections of the Glenbow Archives in Calgary, Canada. I found that oral history from the elders blended easily and smoothly with government reports, newspapers, and other sources if one could view it all from a Native standpoint. With the help of my wife, my father-in-law, and my many friends among the Bloods and Siksikas, I was privileged to have this opportunity.

Introduction

I learned, for example, that a storyteller, reciting the incidents of a century earlier, could include the actual conversations that had taken place. At first this seemed to be almost fictionalizing the events, until I realized that oral communication was the only way the Blackfoot had to pass on their history. Each storyteller was careful to relate the tale just as he had heard it; consequently, after being repeated by two or three generations, it still maintained the integrity of the original story. In passing along the stories in this book, I have followed the Blackfoot practice of including the conversations just as they were told to me or to other recorders by Native elders. I was pleased to find that in the many instances where Blackfoot stories could be checked against newspaper or government reports of the day, there was a high degree of consensus, the differences often arising from the interpretation of events from the recorder's own background or culture.

This book is the second volume of Blackfoot stories that I have collected over the years. The first, *The Amazing Death of Calf Shirt and Other Blackfoot Stories*, published in Canada in 1994 and reprinted by the University of Oklahoma Press in 1996, has proven as popular with Native students as with the non-Native public and has been used in such institutions as Red Crow College on the Blood Reserve. I hope that this second set of stories will be as well received as the first.

Hugh A. Dempsey

THE VENGEFUL WIFE
AND OTHER BLACKFOOT STORIES

I *The Vengeful Wife*

The summer of 1775 was a good time for Blackfoot women to pick the succulent figlike fruit of the prickly-pear cactus.[1] The weather had been warm and the fruit plentiful. Although primarily meat eaters—and more particularly buffalo-meat eaters—the Blackfoot also enjoyed fruits of the land such as prickly pears, saskatoon berries, and wild turnips. The tribe was at war with the Snakes, the Crows, and the Crees, but its members still found time to gather such food when it became ripe.

Calf Looking, Onista'miwa, was a subchief of his band. He had a beautiful wife, Elk Woman, Ponoka'ki, and two young children. His band was camped south of the Little Bow River, and although enemy war parties had been seen in the area, the women had been anxious to pick prickly pears. After repeated requests Calf Looking finally agreed to take his wife to a place about twenty miles from the camp where the fruit was known to be plentiful. When other women heard they were going, they joined the two, making a happy cavalcade of horses and riders.

When they arrived at the site, Calf Looking rode to the top of a nearby hill to watch for enemies. From his vantage point he could look across the rolling foothills to the Rocky Mountains in the distance and, to the south and east, to the open prairie. After a short time he noticed something in the distance. At first he thought it might be a small herd of buffalo moving quickly along the grassy valley, but as they came nearer, he saw that it was a mounted war party at full gallop. Their scouts had obviously seen the pickers and had told the warriors to attack. It would be an easy kill: plenty of women and only one man.

Quickly, Calf Looking signaled the danger to the women, who immediately discarded their bags and rushed for their horses. Most of the older women had their own ponies, inferior little mounts that usually pulled travois when they were on the trail. They were no match for the magnificent horses of their enemies, for the attackers were soon recognized as Shoshonis, or Snakes, who possessed some of the finest horses in the Rocky Mountain region. As the fleeing women galloped towards their distant camp, one by one the slower ones lagged behind and were ruthlessly killed with a blow from a war club or the thrust of a spear.

Calf Looking was mounted on a fine buffalo runner, but his wife was not so lucky. Her travois pony could not keep up with the faster horses, so she cried to her husband for help. As he swung his horse around, Elk Woman jumped on behind him, clasping her arms tightly around his waist. But Calf Looking's horse, as good as it was, could not carry a double load and stay ahead of the Shoshoni pursuers. Finally, the young man turned to his wife and shouted, "Get off. The enemy will not kill you. You're too young and pretty. Some of them will take you, and I'll get a big party of our people and rescue you."[2]

The woman pleaded with him, begging that they should die together, but heedless of her cries, Calf Looking shoved her from the horse and she tumbled to the ground. Then, with a burst of speed, his horse raced ahead, soon catching up with the others and outdistancing their pursuers.

No one had seen the young chief's actions and he told no one what had happened. Instead, like the other men who had lost wives, he painted his face black and wailed and lamented her loss. Later, when a relief party had been assembled, they rode back along the tragic route, each family stopping to pick up the slain and scalped woman who was their wife or mother. When the party reached the prickly-pear cactus field, Calf Looking's wife was the only one unaccounted for. As her husband had predicted, because of her beauty she had been taken prisoner instead of being killed. When they returned to camp, the chief dressed in his finest clothes, mounted his best horse—a coal black buffalo runner—and rode through the village, crying and announcing to all that he was going in pursuit of his missing wife.

When he went back to his lodge, Calf Looking cut off his hair in mourning and dressed in old rags—he was a pathetic figure as he sat and wept. Many people came to share his grief and to offer to join him in rescuing Elk Woman. The chief then invited his three brothers and his wife's three brothers into the tepee, where they all smoked, thus signifying their willingness to go with him. One of his wife's brothers included in the group was a young boy still in his teens, a handsome lad who had the longest hair of anyone in the camp. When the ceremony ended, the young chief took the pipe outside so that others who wanted to join the war party could also smoke.

Siksika elder Joe Little Chief recalled that after everyone had smoked, Calf Looking told the people, "Here is what I will do. My three brothers, also my wife's three brothers, and I will go and look for my wife. When we come back, if we do not come home with her, then all of you can go with me."[3]

The following morning, Calf Looking and his six relatives picked up the trail of the Shoshoni raiders; they followed it south for many days across the open prairies until at last they came to a big river. On the far bank they could see the smoke rising from the Shoshoni camp. The Blackfoot party found a grove of trees on the side of a hill from which they had a good view of the land around them and the enemy camp across the water.

"I'll go down tonight and try to see my wife," he told the others. "You just stay here and wait. If I don't come back, you start off for home."[4]

The young chief swam the river and then, with his robe wrapped around him to shield his face, he boldly walked into the enemy camp just as the shadows of evening were creeping over the land. He wandered from tepee to tepee, glancing inside if the door was open and always watching for a glimpse of his missing wife. At last he came to a large tepee in the center of the camp. By this time the village was in darkness, and peering through a narrow slit at the top of the doorway, Calf Looking saw his wife sitting quietly on the left side of the lodge.

Until then, he had not known for certain whether she was alive or dead. They had not found her body as they followed the Shoshoni trail, but if she had been killed it could easily have been carried away by wolves or other prairie beasts. But in fact, when Elk Woman was pushed from the horse, she landed unharmed and was quickly claimed by one of the triumphant warriors. He was immediately challenged by another, and in the end they agreed to present the girl to their chief. Upon seeing her, the chief decided to take her as his wife rather than as a slave, so she had been treated kindly.

Slipping away from the camp, Calf Looking searched for a place where he might intercept his wife without being discovered. Near the river, he found the path where the women went to get water, and along the shore was a cut bank with a hole large enough for him hide within it. Crawling inside, he pulled the earth around him until only his eyes showed through a narrow crack.

Next morning, he watched as the women came for water. They arrived in twos and threes, often laughing and joking as they dipped water from the turgid stream. There were young girls who were glad to be away from the eyes of their watchful mothers; old women who paused only briefly before returning to their labors, and even a few young men who casually strolled to the water's edge as though looking for missing horses but were actually trying to catch the attention of a particular girl. All day they came and went, but the young chief's wife never appeared. Then, in the late afternoon, a lone woman came for water. It was Elk Woman. Quickly, Calf Looking pushed the earth aside, jumped from the hole, and grasped his surprised wife by the arm.

"I came for you," he said. "Our children are very lonesome, so I came with three of my brothers and three of your brothers to look for you."[5]

He told her that the others were hiding in the trees on the nearby hill and urged her to hurry so they could cross the river before he was discovered. But the woman drew back, saying, "Wait. These people have given me a great many pretty things. Let me go back. When it is night I will gather them up, steal a horse, and cross over to you."[6]

Nothing the young man said could change her mind. She insisted that she should capture some trophies from the Shoshonis so that she could return to her people with pride rather than as an escaped prisoner. At last Calf Looking reluctantly agreed to wait for her across the river until she slipped away during the night.

As Elk Woman was returning to the lodge with her water, she picked up some black ashes from an old fire and put them in her mouth, as though she had been eating them. She threw herself on the ground, twisting and moaning as if demented, and then fell into unconsciousness. The Shoshoni chief carried her into the lodge and called for a medicine man to treat her. When she recovered, she used sign language to explain what had happened, for she could not yet speak her captors' tongue, nor could they understand Blackfoot.

With signs, she said that the Sun spirit had struck her down and given her a vision. This caused a stir among the people who crowded the lodge, as visions were an important part of their culture. She said the Sun spirit had told her that seven enemies of the Shoshonis were hiding in the trees across the river. One was a chief who was very powerful, while another was a young man with long hair. She told them that the life of the chief should be spared, that he should be brought to the camp and offered as a sacrifice to the Sun spirit.

The Shoshonis believed everything the woman said, for they had great faith in visions. The war chief organized a raiding party, which quickly surrounded the grove of trees just before sunset and attacked the Blackfoot hiding place. Calf Looking and his followers did not have a chance. As the arrows began flying into the trees, the chief's oldest brother shouted that they had been betrayed but that he would claim the honor of being the first to die. Brandishing his knife and war axe, he dashed from the trees but was slain before he reached the Shoshoni lines. The second brother said he would follow, so that his older brother would not travel alone on the road to the Sand Hills, the land of the dead. He too was killed.

When Calf Looking was the only one left alive, the Shoshoni leader called for his warriors to seize him and, after a short struggle, he was taken prisoner and brought back across the river. As the Shoshonis rode triumphantly into camp, they waved the bloody scalps in the air and displayed the war trophies of knives, bows, and axes taken from the bodies of the dead Blackfoot warriors. Especially prized was the scalp of Elk Woman's youngest brother, its the long black hair waved about in triumph before the scalp was presented to the Shoshoni chief.

Calf Looking was taken to the chief's lodge, where he was bound hand and foot. Elk Woman calmly sat in front of him and mockingly offered him food, but the angry Blackfoot retorted, "You have no heart, no pity. I came looking for you because our children are so lonesome for you. Look what you have done. Your brothers and my brothers have all been killed."[7]

"What does he say?" the Shoshoni asked in sign language.[8]

Elk Woman replied that the man had called the Shoshonis cowards and claimed that no torture could hurt him. He dared the chief to pour hot coals from his pipe onto his chest.

During times of war a dare could not be ignored or denied, so two men threw the Blackfoot on his back and pulled up his shirt, and the burning ashes were scattered on this chest. In spite of the searing pain and the smell of burning flesh, Calf Looking refused to cry out and would not give his wife the satisfaction of seeing his agony.

"You have no pity," he snarled at his wife. "Look what you told them to do to me."[9]

The Shoshoni chief again made signs to Elk Woman, asking what the prisoner was saying. She replied that he was still defiant, and now he dared the chief to pour boiling water over his head. Again the chief could not refuse, so he instructed a woman to boil some water, and when it was ready, she poured a little of it on the prisoner's head. Calf Looking writhed in pain but refused to cry out, even when his hair began to fall out in chunks. He refused to ask for pity, and so the woman continued to pour the boiling water until all his hair was gone and he had lost consciousness.

When he was revived, he was in such pain that he wanted to die quickly. "Pity me," he said to his vengeful wife. "I have suffered enough. Let them kill me now. Let me hurry to join those who are already traveling to the Sand Hills."[10] Again the chief asked the woman to translate, and she said Calf Looking wanted to be given to the Sun spirit, just as she had predicted in her vision. The chief agreed and said that next morning the Blackfoot prisoner would be tied to a tree and left to starve to death as an offering to the Sun.

Throughout Calf Looking's ordeal, the lodge had been filled with warriors who came to enjoy seeing the prisoner suffer. Near the entrance crouched a poor old woman whom everyone ignored. Her husband was dead, and she had survived on handouts of food from her neighbors and the chief. She lived in a tattered little lodge, with only her travois dog as her companion.

Her husband had been a Shoshoni; he had found her among the Crees many years earlier and had married her. Most people assumed that she was Cree, but she was really a Blackfoot who had been captured by the Crees when she was just a little girl. She had forgotten much of her original language, but she remembered enough to know that Elk Woman was lying when she translated the prisoner's messages. She felt sorry for the man and was determined to help him.

Next morning, the chief announced that they were moving camp and that the prisoner would be left behind as an offering to the Sun. The bark was stripped from a cottonwood tree, its trunk painted black, and the man tied securely in place. His face, too, was painted black to signify that he was to be left for the Sun spirit to claim.

Meanwhile, the old woman took her travois dog into the woods, tied a strip of leather around his jaws so that he could not bark, and left him tethered to a tree. When it came time to leave, she called for the dog but he did not appear. She cursed him, saying, "Wait till I find him, and I'll break his neck."[11] As she stomped around the camp, the others laughed and ignored her and no one tried to help her. She was not surprised, for she was still considered to be a foreigner, even though she had been in the camp for many years. At one point the chief rode by and asked her why she was not ready. When she explained that her dog was missing, he offered to provide one of his own to pull her travois, but she refused, saying she would not leave her dog behind. The chief was not prepared to delay their departure for the sake of a crazy old woman, so when their horses were packed, everyone left.

As soon as they were out of sight, the woman released her dog and cut the cords that bound the unfortunate man. He collapsed to the ground, too weak from the tortures to move. Carefully, the woman bathed his head and placed a buckskin covering over it to protect it from the rays of the sun. She gave him a little water, and when he revived sufficiently she shared her small supply of pemmican with him. She had never had children of her own, so she told the young man that she was taking him as her son.

When he had regained some strength, Calf Looking thanked the woman and accepted her offer to become his mother. "I am a chief of the Blackfoot," he told her. "Now I will go back home to my people. I know when they see me and hear my story, they will have pity on me. You see all that grass? I will have an army as thick as the grass. I will have my revenge for what my wife has done to me."[12]

He rested for a moment to catch his breath. Then he told the woman to pitch her tepee slightly apart from the others so that he would recognize it. Also, if the camp divided and went in different directions, she was to remain with the chief and plant a green stick in the ground, bent to point the direction they had gone. "Now I am going home," he said. "When I come, I will see you at night time and tell you what to do."[13]

With a pair of moccasins and a small supply of dried meat supplied by his new mother, Calf Looking made his painful way back to his own territory. Many days later, as he approached his camp, he went to a nearby hill and sat there until one of the scouts noticed him. When the man drew near, the chief began to cry and wail, bemoaning the fate of his family and himself. Others came and saw his pitiful condition—his scalded head, burned chest, and lack of hair. He was escorted down to the camp, where he stopped in front of the lodge of his wife's parents.

"My friends and relatives," he shouted, "come forth from your tepees, come forth and see my piteous plight. Come hear my tale of woe and listen with horror to what I have to say." Then, speaking to Elk Woman's parents, he said, "You gave your child to me for a wife, but learn now that it was no woman that you brought into this world, not a woman but a savage beast."[14]

As he told of the terrible events he had suffered at the enemy camp, great cries of anguish and anger arose in the village. Elk Woman's mother went to sharpen her axe and told everyone what she would do if she met her daughter. Others rounded up their horses and selected their finest weapons for an attack on the Shoshoni camp.

The most formidable type of assault against an enemy was the revenge raid. When the people experienced a defeat that brought them disgrace and humiliation, their honor demanded that it be avenged. Everyone in the camp, even the young men and women, were invited to take part in the action. Such was the torture of Calf Looking and the killing of his brothers and brothers-in-law. The offence was not simply the killing of some Blackfoot by the Shoshonis, for such incidents were common. No, the crime was Elk Woman's betrayal of her people, which resulted in the callous extermination of her own brothers. Even while she had directed the torture of Calf Looking, the long bloody scalp of her youngest brother had been hanging from a nearby tepee pole in all its gory splendor.

Calf Looking refused to return to his lodge or to enter any lodge until the betrayal had been avenged. Camped under a bower, he was treated with poultices and medicines until he was fit to travel. Then more than three hundred people—almost the entire camp—girded for war. Only a few old people, young children, and guards stayed behind. The others set out across the plains, following Calf Looking's tortuous trail southward to the big river. When they arrived at the battle scene, they found the melancholy remains of their companions, partially devoured by animals and scattered near the grove of trees. These were gathered and placed on burial scaffolds amid much wailing and the renewal of promises to avenge their deaths.

Across the river the Blackfoot found the abandoned Shoshoni village. The chief showed the others where he had lain in hiding near the watering place, where he had been tortured, and finally, the blackened tree where he had been left to die.

Next morning, two scouts went ahead of the revenge party, following the trail and watching for signs that their enemy might be near. On the third day they found another campsite, where the Shoshonis had stayed for some time. When they left, they had split into two groups, one going south and the other west. Within the abandoned camp was a green willow twig stuck in the ground, the top broken and pointing to the west. The break was near the top, indicating that the enemy had planned to travel only a short distance before making a new camp.

The scouts traveled ahead cautiously on foot, and in the late afternoon they signaled that they were returning. As they came down a hill, they ran in a zigzag fashion to show that they had made a discovery. As Calf Looking and his leading men stood in a row, the scouts gave the call of a crane, indicating the success of their foray, and kicked over a pile of sticks representing an enemy camp. They told the chief that the Shoshoni village was in a valley just beyond the second ridge. Both ridges had trees and bushes along their slopes that provided excellent hiding places.

Leaving their horses behind, the leading warriors went to the first ridge and into a secluded spot along its slope. They also found a coulee that led directly to the second ridge, and when they followed it, they camped deep in the bushes where no one could see them. As they crept to the top of the ridge, they saw the Shoshoni camp spread out before them in the next valley. Calf Looking told them about the old woman and said, "Her lodge is at the outskirts of the camp, and she has a large black dog with shaggy hair always with her."[15]

After nightfall, the rest of the revenge party came to the coulee, bringing their horses with them in readiness for the attack. Meanwhile, Calf Looking announced that he would go ahead to warn the old woman so she would not be harmed. Some of his men argued with him, fearing that she might betray him. "No," said the chief, "it will not be so. That old woman is almost the same as my mother."[16]

Quietly, he entered the camp, and when he reached the tiny tepee that had been set apart from the others, he looked through a crack above the door and saw the shaggy black dog almost asleep by the fire. "Hairy One," he called softly.[17] The dog looked towards the door and began to growl, but the old woman told him to be quiet. Now that the occupants were alerted, Calf Looking stepped inside and kissed his new mother.

"We are going to have revenge on this camp tonight. Is my wife here?" he asked.[18]

The old woman nodded. She explained that since the killings, people believed that Elk Woman possessed strong powers and showed her great respect. She still lived with the chief in the largest tepee in the camp. She pointed to the center of the village, where the poles of the chief's lodge were visible in the moonlight. The woman insisted on feeding her new son, after which she packed her few meagre belongings and followed him back to the ridge.

Before the raid, Calf Looking announced that he wanted his wife taken alive. His only surviving brother, Wolf Leading Along, Makoyi'estapisitan, mounted his horse and rode in front of the revenge party, singing his war song. "I will capture your wife and bring her alive," he promised, adding that he hated the woman as much as his brother did.[19]

Just before daybreak, the Blackfoot swept down from the ridge and into the Shoshoni camp. Caught completely by surprise, many men were killed as soon as they stepped outside their lodges, and the slaughter became general. Some of the lucky ones, women and children in particular, darted into the bushes and ran to safety while the Blackfoot attackers concentrated on the men who tried to oppose them. Using war axes, clubs, knives, arrows, and lances, the angry raiders vented their fury on the tribe that harbored the woman who had betrayed her people. In a short time all the Shoshonis who remained in the camp were dead.

As soon as the raid began, Wolf Leading Along and a companion had raced directly for the largest tepee in the camp. They caught the Shoshoni chief at the door and killed him. When they entered the lodge, Elk Woman cried out, "Don't hurt me. I'm a Blackfoot. Are any of my people here?"[20]

"Many of your relations are here," said Wolf Leading Along, then he added sardonically, "They will protect you."[21]

As soon as they grabbed her, the two men bound Elk Woman and kept her secured until the brief battle was over. Their first task was to keep the woman's mother away from her. Armed with an axe, she rushed forward, shouting, "*Hai yah!* There is my Snake woman daughter. Let me split her head open."[22] She was restrained, as were others who wanted to wreak vengeance on the one who had betrayed them. Instead, she was brought before her husband and a council of warriors to decide her fate.

The Shoshoni tepees were pulled down and their poles gathered into a huge pile. When these were set afire, Calf Looking stripped his wife's dress from her body, hung the scalp of the dead Shoshoni chief around her neck, and told her to dance the Scalp Dance in the fire. Instead of cringing, the woman stepped defiantly into the woodpile, then turned to her husband and spat, "You cowardly dog! Do you think you are a mighty warrior this day because you have beaten a woman? After you thrust me from your horse and left me to the fate you know, did you think then that you were doing a brave deed? I am not afraid of death, for I have already had my revenge, coward that you are."[23]

The fire was lit, and as the flames curled up around her Elk Woman tried to get away, but each time she did so, the people laughed and threw her back on the pile. At last she fell down in the funeral pyre and died. By this action the Blackfoot had accused and convicted her of the greatest crime known to the tribe—greater even than murder. As a Blackfoot once told a missionary, "On no account betray your friend."[24] She had broken that rule and suffered the consequences.

Calf Looking invited the old woman to return north with them and be his mother. When she agreed, they heaped many gifts upon her, and she remained with her nascent tribe until her death many years later.[25]

2 *Medicine Pipes and Fur Traders*

In their constant raiding of each other's camps, the Blackfoot, Crees, Assiniboines, and other tribes sought to gain war honors by capturing valuable war and religious trophies. Among the most desirable articles worthy of taking were the medicine pipes. Crooked Meat Strings, a Siksika, ranked such pipes along with guns, bows and arrows, and shields as items eagerly sought during a raid. He described the shield as important because it was "very scarce," while medicine pipes were "very choice."[1] A Siksika named Sleigh said that if a man captured a medicine pipe, he was entitled to wear a shirt trimmed with weasel tails.[2] During the nineteenth century there were at least two occasions when the loss or recovery of medicine pipes involved traders of the Hudson's Bay Company. Since that time, in telling and retelling the stories, these events have gained an element of mysticism that may not have been present at the time of the original occurrence. There was a tendency on the part of storytellers to attach a supernatural significance to any event that was out of the ordinary or that concerned a victory involved with religious objects. This was the situation for fur traders and medicine pipes. In at least one of the stories, fur trader John Rowand was seen to have spiritual powers that were quite contrary to his tough, no-nonsense approach to the company's business dealings.

John Rowand was born in 1787, the son of a Montreal medical doctor. He joined the North West Company in 1803 and was immediately posted to Fort Augustus, which was located adjacent to Fort Edmonton, of the Hudson's Bay Company. Rowand was known to the Blackfoot Indians as I'kaki, or Short Man, while his nickname among the fur-trade employees was "One Pound One," because he walked with a limp with one foot striking harder the ground than the other. When the North West and Hudson's

Bay Companies amalgamated in 1821, Rowand took charge of Fort Edmonton and was the main trader dealing with the Blackfoot tribes. According to his biographer, the fort had previously been losing money, but "within a few years, because of Rowand's superior management, it had become one of the most profitable in the Indian country. Much of his success lay in his ability to deal with the Plains Indians who frequented his post, no easy task since the prairies were constantly in a state of unrest due to the warfare between the Blackfoot confederacy and the Crees and Assiniboines."[3] Rowand himself admitted, "No one will say that I ever spoilt Indians. . . . I give them due but they must do their duty."[4]

Rowand was in charge of Fort Edmonton from 1822 until his death of a heart attack in 1854. During those years he came to know all the chiefs of the Siksikas, Bloods, Piegans, and Sarcees and constantly counseled for peace among the warring tribes, as much for the benefit of the fur trade as for his personal friendship with the people.

Rowand's involvement in recovering a medicine pipe occurred during the trading season of 1824–25.[5] In October 1824 a war party of Crees from the Beaver Hills near Edmonton traveled southeast and attacked a large Blackfoot camp at Nose Hill that was under the leadership of The Feather. The men were away hunting at the time, so it was an easy victory for the Crees. They killed almost four hundred women and children and took about twenty more as prisoners. The Crees culminated their raid by scalping their victims, looting the camp, and taking anything they wanted, including one or more medicine bundles. One of these bundles belonged to Big Plume, O'muhk-sapop, a Siksika chief.[6]

According to Siksika patriarch Many Guns, when Big Plume returned to camp, he found the bodies of the victims, the tepees either stolen or destroyed, and some of his people taken prisoner. The chief had two children kidnapped, while the rest of his offspring and all his wives but one had been killed. The one surviving wife had escaped and told him the story of the Cree raid.[7]

Fearing revenge, the Beaver Hills Crees fled eastwards, the straggling families arriving at Fort Carlton (in the present central Saskatchewan area) a week after the attack. The first visitor told of the attack and displayed a scalp he had taken in the massacre. By late in October quite a number of Crees were camped near the fort, begging for supplies to "enable them to pass the winter in the Strong Woods, being too much afraid to return to the plains after having massacred so many helpless women and children."[8]

John Stuart, the chief trader at Fort Carlton, was disgusted by the action of the Crees in killing the helpless victims. He wrote:

> These Crees considering them as a tribe are the most miserable set of people I ever seen in all my travels on either side of the mountains. Few of them have the courage to look a man in the face and yet when an opportunity occurs without endangering themselves, they are for war, murdering defenceless women and children, and no sooner a massacre is committed than they fly to the Strong woods where the Plain Indians cannot follow them and then remain starving until the approach of the Stone Indians to whose camp they resort for Protection of themselves. They dare not venture into the Plains nor can they subsist in the woods, otherwise than in a starving condition and if we had not assisted them in the articles of Provisions many of them this very winter would have starved to death.[9]

Stuart was concerned both for the detrimental effect further warfare would have on the fur-trade business and for the possibility that the Blackfoot might take revenge on the traders, many of whom were intermarried with the Crees. Through the presentation of gifts, the trader managed to gain the release of nine Blackfoot prisoners—seven women and two children. "I intend to send [them] up to Edmonton," he wrote, "to be returned to their relations in hopes it may have some effect in preventing them in their war excursions from molesting such of the whites in this quarter as they may fall in with, for the present they consider them equally inimical as the Stone Indians and Crees."[10]

Because virtually everything had been taken from the women, Stuart provided them with buffalo robes so they could make their own clothing. One of the released captives was a sister of The Feather, and as she could speak some Cree, she acted as a go-between for both her captors and the traders. Once the clothing was finished, the women and children were escorted to Edmonton, where a happy reunion took place among at least a few of the families.

The goodwill engendered by this action was immediately evident, for when a Blackfoot war party arrived at Fort Carlton in November 1824, they met some Cree hunters and took their guns and clothing but spared their lives. Among the Blackfoot party was the brother of one of the rescued women who had been sent to Fort Edmonton.

Over the winter of 1824–25, starvation forced the Beaver Hills Crees to leave the protection of the woodlands around Green Lake and camp near the Eagle Hills to hunt buffalo. As soon as the Blackfoot learned of their presence, they began to raid their horse herds, even though winter war parties were rare. In January they ran off two bunches of Cree horses in separate raids and killed two Assiniboines. In the following month they took thirty Cree horses and killed two more Assiniboines.

In the spring of 1825 Big Plume went to Fort Edmonton, where he met John Rowand and told him he was organizing a revenge party that was going to wipe out the Crees. "You'd better not," Rowand advised him. "Just go home [for the sake of] your two children that are captured with eight others. Some men of mine are going to the Crees, and they'll buy back the captives and your medicine pipe."[11] Big Plume agreed to wait and returned to the prairies. Later he learned that Rowand had sent a message to Fort Carlton saying that he wanted the prisoners and medicine pipe returned, that he wanted "them all back, not just one of them."[12]

Chief Factor Stuart at Fort Carlton, whom the Blackfoot called Ksis-tuki'poka, or Beaver Child, invited the Cree leaders to a meeting. According to a story told by the Blackfoot, once they were inside Stuart locked the doors and told the Crees, "Bring the ten women and pipe in here, and I'll give you a big keg of whiskey."[13]

The chiefs refused, saying, "The Blackfoot do the same to us, so we're not going to give them up."

"Then this summer we won't give you any bullets or powder and nothing sharp, like a knife or an axe. Then we'll send a message to Big Plume to attack you and he'll kill you off like a stick killing ducks. We're going to lock you chiefs up here because it is your fault, not giving these women up."[14]

The story goes that the Cree chiefs became frightened by this threat, so they sent a messenger to the camp instructing the people to bring the prisoners and medicine pipe to the fort. Later, nine women and the pipe were delivered, but the tenth woman was held by Willow People Crees and had been taken farther east. The chief factor was satisfied and said that he would rescue the other woman and the children later. As a mark of goodwill, he then gave the chiefs their promised keg of whiskey.

According to Hudson's Bay Company records, the medicine pipe was returned in March of 1825. According to Stuart, "Mr. Heron got one of the Pipe Stems of the Feather's, Blackfoot Chief, which he sent me. I requested him in winter to get that pipe stem from these Indians, that conformable to the desire of Mr. Rowand it might be sent up to the right owner."[15]

In the spring of 1825 the medicine pipe was ultimately taken to Edmonton, where ten young Blackfoot happened to be trading at the time. They immediately took a message to Big Plume to come and get his pipe, which he did. "Now Rowand was a great friend of Big Plume," recalled Many Guns. "Of course, Big Plume was head chief of the whole Blackfoot Nation. Rowand then gave Big Plume a drink. Big Plume got drunk so Rowand had to put him to bed upstairs. He treated him just like a brother."[16]

When the chief had sobered up, the chief factor told him he was going to return the medicine bundle and give him a large Hudson's Bay Company flag to cover it.[17] He said the chief should fly this flag whenever his tribe was at peace with their enemies, but when they were at war, he should use the flag to cover the pipe and protect it.

According to the Blackfoot, "Rowand had Indian powers; he had strong dreams. He had a song that went with the flag. He stood by his friend and sang the words: 'White man above is hearing me.'"[18] Rowand commanded Big Plume to stand up, then draped the flag around him like a shawl and sang the song again. After that he took the flag and covered the pipe with it. Ever since that time, medicine pipes have been covered by a red shawl or blanket representing the Hudson's Bay flag given by John Rowand.

The trader knew he could not touch the pipe until he was purified, so he waited while Big Plume had two of his men make a small fire and sprinkle some sweetgrass on it. While the incense was rising, the fur trader placed both of his hands in the smoke and used this to purify his body. Then, according to Blackfoot tradition, the fur trader gave the following prayer: "May all of us live long and walk on our ground for a hundred years with all our children, all their children, their wives, their relatives. May you live long and walk on the ground where you get your herbs, sweetgrass, and all the things that you need for your ceremonies."[19] When this was finished, Rowand went into the next room, brought out the pipe, and presented it to the Blackfoot chief. He also gave many gifts to the chief and his followers before they returned to their own hunting grounds.

Some time later—in 1832 according to the Many Guns winter count— Big Plume decided to transfer his medicine pipe to a new owner as part of his strategy to revenge the Cree massacre. He wanted a younger man to help execute his plans for revenge, so he looked for a young bachelor who could become the new custodian of the pipe. In exchange he wanted to become the owner of the best racehorse in the nation. Accordingly, he rode through a huge combined camp of Siksikas, Bloods, and Piegans until he saw the animal he wanted. The custom was that a pipe owner could go to anyone and "capture" him by offering to smoke with him. The person could not refuse, and shortly thereafter he had to present gifts to the pipe owner in exchange for the pipe and ceremonies.

Big Plume decided to find out who owned the racehorse that he so admired. He stopped to examine it then spoke to some young boys who were loitering nearby.

"I have lost a horse like this. Whose is it?"

"It belongs to Somebody, a Blood."

"Well who?"

"Somebody. That's his name, Somebody."[20]

Big Plume returned to his camp and summoned four old men who had been medicine pipe owners; they in turn recruited another nine drummers and singers to help with the "capture." Ten of them surrounded Somebody's tepee so that the Blood could not escape. As soon as he heard the drums beating outside, he knew that he had been trapped and there was nothing he could do but willingly submit. Big Plume and three former pipe owners entered the tepee. One carried the pipe, another a weasel skin, and the third an owl skin. Somebody then accompanied the procession back to the Blackfoot camp for the transfer ceremony. There, instead of asking for many horses and gifts, Big Plume said he wanted only the racehorse. The Blood agreed, but when his relatives heard about the transfer, they also came forth with gifts of horses and clothing.

During the transfer ceremony Big Plume told the young man, "I'm going to give you a good name, because you don't have one now. You are going to receive my name of Big Plume, and when you invite me to your lodge this evening you will call me Nina'piksi, Chief Bird, which will be my name henceforth."[21] Then followed four days of ceremonies, during which the young man was taught how to conduct himself in daily life as a medicine-pipe holder. He had to learn what he was permitted to drink, what to wear, how to dress his hair, and how to avoid things that were taboo. For example, he could no longer speak the word *kyi'yo*, or "bear"; instead, he had to use a synonym, *paksik'oyi*, or "sloppy mouth."

When the transfer was completed, Chief Bird announced that he was going to war against the Crees. He invited several Siksika, Blood, and Piegan chiefs to accompany him, but only Big Plume (the former Somebody), one Piegan chief, and a number of Siksika chiefs and their followers agreed to go. After several days' travel they found a Cree village, and that night Chief Bird sent four scouts into the camp, instructing them to use buffalo dung to mark the best trail for the others to follow when they attacked.

At dawn, as soon as it was light enough to see the rows of dung, they crept close to the camp and began making noises like snorting buffalo. Soon they heard their enemies cry out in Cree, "Come! The buffalo are near! Come and chase them!"[22] As the hunters dashed from their lodges, a Blackfoot shouted, "Here, my friend, I'm here!" and then opened fire. The enemy tried to repel the raiders, but they had been so caught by surprise that they could not mount an effective defense.

In the Cree camp were two Blackfoot women, sisters who had never been rescued. One was named Matsinam, Nice Looking, and the other Kinski. As soon as they heard the gunfire, they ran outside and hid in the bushes. There they were seen by a Blackfoot warrior, who was about to shoot them when he suddenly recognized them as his own sisters. So he hurried them from the camp and into a safe place behind the Blackfoot lines until the fighting was over.

As the battle wore on, it was apparent that about half the Crees had fled the camp while the remainder had stayed behind to fight. These were slain one by one, until all that were left were dead bodies and a few prisoners. During the battle Chief Bird killed an enemy and then called on the young medicine-pipe holder to fire a shot into the dead man's body and take the scalp. During any future coup-counting sessions, Chief Bird would say, "I killed a Cree," and Big Plume (the former Somebody) would say, "I, Big Plume, killed in an imitation fashion a Cree, through Chief Bird and the medicine pipe."[23]

Only one Cree man was captured. He had fought particularly bravely and had killed several Blackfoot in hand-to-hand combat. He was taken to the Blackfoot camp and there, during the Victory Dance, was killed by a Blackfoot named Apstsapo, or Humpback (likely to revenge the death of a son or relative who had died in the battle).[24]

Thus Big Plume, now called Chief Bird, had obtained revenge and had seen his medicine pipe transferred to a younger man who would give it the attention and care it required. This pipe, known as the Longtime Medicine Pipe, became famous among the Blood tribe, and its ownership can be traced in an unbroken line for more than a hundred years. According to Jim White Bull, it went from Big Plume to Somebody and then to Eagle Head, Crop Eared Wolf, Sleeps on High, Heavy Shield, Wolf Tail, Big Wolf, Jack Sun Dance, Shot Both Sides, Big Sorrel Horse, Jack Weasel Head, Bobtail Chief, Stephen Fox, Calling First, Arthur Soop, Henry Standing Alone, John Red Crane, and Charlie Davis. It then went back to Red Crane, who sold it to the Provincial Museum of Alberta in 1968.

The second account of a fur trader's being involved with a medicine pipe also occurred at Fort Edmonton. The Blood and Sarcee[25] accounts of this incident also involve Native mysticism and ritualism relating to medicine pipes in general. The actual story is probably that two young Sarcees, Spotted Eagle and Hanging Crow,[26] were engaged at the fort to assist in taking the winter supply of furs by boat to the Hudson's Bay Company's depot far to the east. While en route, Hanging Crow was left behind on an island in a lake when the boat stopped for the night. This may have been an accident or perhaps (as the story goes) it happened because he had become involved with the trader's wife. When the others reached their destination, Spotted Eagle was detained for a while then given a medicine bundle by a senior fur-trade official before returning to Fort Edmonton. En route home, he joined his friend on the island, perhaps willingly, perhaps not. The traders presumed both of them had drowned or been killed, which they reported to the men's families. Meanwhile, the two men were able to get off the island, and after weeks of travel they successfully made their way to the prairies. When they arrived back home, the traders apologized and gave them presents.

That may be the general idea of what actually happened, but the Sarcee and Blackfoot versions of the story, told from a Native perspective, are quite different. Their story begins when the Sarcee tribe, including Spotted Eagle and Hanging Crow, went with others of their tribe to trade at Fort Edmonton.[27] According to one account, "Halting near the fort, [they] sent four or five scouts ahead to inform its factor that their chiefs, councillors and warriors proposed to trade with him. The factor gave the messengers some tobacco in token of his good-will, where upon the whole tribe entered the fort and traded its furs."[28]

The Hudson's Bay Company had already packed its winter catch of furs and was preparing to take them downriver when the Sarcees arrived. According to an elder, Spotted Eagle and Hanging Crow were good friends of the chief factor, so he hired them to accompany him.[29] When they agreed, Spotted Eagle was placed in one boat with bales of furs and Hanging Crow in another boat that formed part of the flotilla.

Hanging Crow was a very handsome man, and as they traveled downstream, the Native wife of the chief factor became attracted to him and spent every spare moment with the young Sarcee. The interpreter warned Hanging Crow that the woman was in love with him and there might be trouble, but the young man just laughed and ignored the jealous scowls of the trader. An elder recalled, ". . . as they travelled down a big river [the North Saskatchewan] to a great lake [Lake Winnipeg], he let his glances rest on her so often that the factor became angry and ordered his men to maroon him on an island."[30] When they stopped to cook a meal, one of the fur-trade employees asked Hanging Crow to go and pick some berries. While he was gone, the others packed up their gear, and the last boat was already out in the water before he returned. Hanging Crow rushed to the shore, calling for the men to stop, but his friend Spotted Eagle shouted, "It's your own fault. I told you not to be crazy about that lady. Now her husband doesn't want to take you along with us. Don't try to get away; stay right there until I come back."[31]

The chief factor believed that Hanging Crow would be killed by one of the bears or other wild animals that inhabited the island. The young Sarcee was also afraid, and after the boats had disappeared he began to cry and to pray for help. When it began to get dark, he searched for a place to sleep and found an empty cave on a nearby hill. In the early morning, while he was still asleep, a large bear entered the cave, which was his home. He walked over to Hanging Crow and began licking the man's hands. This awakened the young Sarcee, who was so frightened that at first he could not move or talk. Then, as he noticed the bear was being friendly to him, he began talking to him, asking him to protect him from the other wild animals and to give him food. The bear seemed to understand, for he walked out of the cave and came back later with the carcass of a deer. Hanging Crow was very happy; he made a fire, cooked some of the meat, and was now confident that the bear was indeed his friend. That night, Hanging Crow had a dream in which the bear came to him, saying that he would give him some of his powers and protect him from the other animals.

Meanwhile, Spotted Eagle continued his journey with the fur traders. When they arrived at their destination several weeks later, the white man in charge of the depot was not pleased to see him. Tony Pretty Young Man said this white man was a "king," (that is, a very important man). The first night Spotted Eagle was locked up in a place where the white man kept wild animals. He was afraid the animals would attack him, but he spoke quietly to them, telling them he was their friend, and they lay down and slept. The second day he was put in a different room, and again the wild animals did not bother him. "Even a spotted lynx obeyed his word," said an elder.[32] On the third night the white man took Spotted Eagle to a tall building that had no windows. He put him in the attic, where it was so hot that most men would have died, but the Sarcee had the power to make cold water and drank it to stay alive. In the morning the white man came for him and tried to push him down the stairs, but instead of falling, Spotted Eagle just floated down like a feather and was unhurt.

At this point the white man realized that the Sarcee had strong super-natural powers, so he tried to become friends with him and invited him to come and eat with him. "No," replied Spotted Eagle. "When I came you should have come and shaken hands with me and given me a big dinner. Instead of that you wanted to kill me. You did not know that I have special powers. I do not want to stay here. I want to go."[33]

The white man said he wanted to give Spotted Eagle a present before he left, so he invited him to come to his house. On their way over Spotted Eagle met another Indian who told him that the house contained many objects once owned by Indians. He was advised, "if the owner asked him what he wanted he should request, not the fine things around the walls, but a certain bundle that hung upon the door."[34]

When they entered the house, Spotted Eagle saw that it did indeed contain many fine Indian things—clothing, religious objects, and war trophies. The white man gave the young Sarcee some rum to drink and then asked him to choose something as a gift. Spotted Eagle said that he wanted the bundle that was hanging on the door. The white man tried to dissuade him, urging him to pick something more beautiful and valuable, but Spotted Eagle just shook his head. "Those things are too good," he said. "You have asked me what I want. Well, all I want is that bundle and nothing else."[35]

The white man said that the bundle belonged to his house and he did not want to part with it. He said it was not worth carrying home and urged him to look around and find something else. Spotted Eagle stayed in the white man's house for four days; each day the white man asked him to pick something, and each time he picked the medicine pipe. On the fourth day the white man finally agreed. He wrapped the medicine pipe in a red Hudson's Bay Company flag and gave it to him.

A number of canoes were going back to Fort Edmonton, so Spotted Eagle joined them, and a few weeks later they reached the island where Hanging Crow had been abandoned. Spotted Eagle was positive he had been killed by wild animals, but he had to find out for sure. The canoes would not stop, so Spotted Eagle asked the man in charge to pull close to the beach so he could jump off and wade to the island. When he first got ashore, Spotted Eagle could not see Hanging Crow anywhere, but at last he found him near the cave, sitting under some trees with his friend the bear.

"Don't be afraid," said Hanging Crow. "This is my godfather. He has saved me from the wild animals ever since you left."[36]

Spotted Eagle ran up to his friend and hugged and kissed him, and they both started to cry as they thought of their wives and children, who were so far away. Hanging Crow explained how the bear had protected him during the weeks he had been a prisoner on the island. Spotted Eagle in turn showed his friend his medicine pipe and told about his adventures with the white man. Hanging Crow then asked his friend, "Have you ever been granted a vision that gave you medicine power?"

"Yes," replied Spotted Eagle. "I am a medicine-man. I can take you home. Cut a hole in my neck and close your eyes."[37]

Hanging Crow did as he was instructed, and when he opened his eyes, he found that Spotted Eagle had taken them to another island that was closer to the shore. In this way they moved to a third island, and a fourth. Finally, they reached the mainland in a swampy area near the mouth of the Saskatchewan River. From there they began walking, picking berries and living on anything they could find. They almost starved, but they traveled for many weeks until at last they reached the open prairies. In one place they saw a camp that they thought belonged to their allies, the Blackfoot, but it proved to be enemy Crees, and they barely escaped with their lives.

According to an elder, "One morning the Sarcee looked up from their camp and, seeing two men with a flag on a neighbouring hill-top, sent out a rider to investigate. The rider quickly recognized Spotted Eagle and [Hanging Crow], and, springing from his horse, kissed them. He then signalled the news by waving his blanket, first to the east, then to the west, and preceded them down the hill to the camp."[38] Everyone was surprised to see the two men, for they had been told by the chief factor that they had died during the trip to the east.

That autumn, Spotted Eagle and Hanging Crow accompanied the rest of the tribe when they went to Fort Edmonton to trade. As was the usual custom, the Sarcee chief sent two messengers ahead to tell the traders they were coming. The messengers also reported that Spotted Eagle and Hanging Crow were in the party, but the chief factor did not believe them, as he thought they were dead. When the Sarcees reached the North Saskatchewan River, they camped on the south side and waited for the rowboats to take them across to the fort.

The boatmen were surprised to see Spotted Eagle and Hanging Crow. They shook hands with them and said they never thought they would see them again. Then they began to ferry the Indians across the river, but Spotted Eagle and Hanging Crow refused to accompany them. Instead, they instructed the boatmen to inform the chief factor of their presence and tell him to come with his wife to the bank of the river to meet them. When this message was given to the chief factor, he still refused to believe that the two men were alive.

"All right," said Spotted Eagle, "I will make him believe me."[39] He told some fellow Sarcees to pitch a tepee beside the river, and when it was ready he went inside and began to sing one of his sacred songs. Immediately the sky became black and a high wind swept through the valley, blowing down buildings and causing great havoc at the trading post. Spotted Eagle sang the song a second time, then told the boatmen to take him and Hanging Crow across to the north side. In the boat he sang his song again, and the waves in the river were so high that they threatened to upset them. But they arrived safely on the other side, and by the time Spotted Eagle sang for the fourth time, the chief factor had become convinced that the men were alive.

As the trader went down to the river, he said to his wife, "Go and kiss your sweetheart and tell him to stop the wind and I will give him goods, and his people too."[40] The woman did as she was instructed, and as soon as she kissed Hanging Crow the winds stopped and the darkness disappeared. The chief factor then apologized to the two Sarcees and invited them to the fort, where he gave them many presents. He also took Spotted Eagle's medicine pipe, removed the flag that had become tattered and torn during the weeks of travel and replaced it with a new one, and put fresh tobacco in the bundle to renew its powers.

The pipe, said an elder, was not harmed by the chief factor's handling it and adding tobacco to it, because "the bundle had been derived from a white man."[41] Thereafter, whenever the Sarcees brought the medicine pipe to the fort, the factor's first actions were to renew its tobacco and provide it with a new flag.

The medicine pipe remained with the Sarcee tribe long after they settled on their reserve on the southwestern outskirts of Calgary. Because of its association with the fur traders, it became known as the Peace Pipe Bundle. In the 1930s it was owned by Big Knife, who explained to anthropologist Diamond Jenness the daily ritual that he followed:

> The blanket-wrapped medicine-pipe bundle hung every day on a travois behind the tipi, that is to say on its west side, since the entrance always faced the east. [It was] taken down at sunset, or when rain threatened, and hung inside the tipi, the bundle directly over its owner's head . . . ; certain accessories of the bundle, such as the food bowl and the fan used in the sweat-lodge, hung on top of

According to ancient tales, the Sarcee peace-pipe bundle was obtained by Spotted Eagle from a fur trader in the East. It was covered with a Hudson's Bay Company flag at the time of presentation; ever since that time, when the bundle is not in use it is covered with a red shawl representing the flag. The bundle in seen here on the Sarcee Reserve, about 1930.

Courtesy Glenbow Archives, Calgary, AB, cat. no. NA-667-818

the . . . back-rest. Since the mouthpiece of the pipe had always to face the north, the two ends of the bundle were distinguished by differently coloured cloths.[42]

This bundle was later sold to the Provincial Museum of Alberta, but in the 1980s there was such a concern expressed by the Sarcees about the loss of this sacred object that it was returned to the tribe and placed in the Sarcee People's Museum, where it rests today.

3 *Massacre at Sun River*

By the 1830s the Blackfoot tribes had been at war with the Crows for generations. Sometimes there were periods of peace, but more often they were raiding each other's horse herds and killing one another at every opportunity. Each spring, young men planned their raids as soon as the grass was green and the horses had grown fat. Traveling on foot for hundreds of miles, the warriors—whether Piegan, Blood, Siksika, or Crow—entered enemy country and carefully scouted the coulees and river bottoms until they found an encampment rich in horses. Then, during the darkness of night, they crept silently forward, seeking the prized horses that were tethered to their owners' tepees or hobbled nearby. Carefully cutting the thongs, they led the animals out of the camp and then galloped off towards their own hunting grounds.

But if the snapping of a twig, the growling of a dog, or any other noise awoke the owner, then the results might be different. Gunfire, screams of rage, and defiant war cries might echo through the still night as the raiders rushed for the safety of darkness. If they were lucky, they escaped. If not, their scalps adorned the lodges of their adversaries.

Sometimes, if there were too many deaths and too many women with their hair cut short in mourning, the chiefs might sue for peace. A messenger bearing tobacco would be sent to the enemy with an invitation for them to come together in friendship. If it was accepted, the wise leaders met in council, the pipe was smoked, and promises were made that there would be no war. The older chiefs kept their promises, but the young warriors, thirsting for adventure, ultimately ignored the peace agreement and slipped away at night to make the long walk to an enemy camp. When they returned, the peace pact was effectively shattered and the tribes resumed their hostilities until the next treaty could be made.

That was the situation early in 1833, when winter began to shrug off its mantle of snow and crocuses started to poke their fuzzy heads through the brown prairie grass. As soon as enemy ponies had shed their shaggy coats and put a little weight on their skinny bodies, they would be able to survive the long journeys to their new owners' lodges. But the chiefs were growing tired of war. They wanted to hunt without fear, to trap in the foothill and mountain streams, and to take their catches of beaver and muskrat to the traders on the Missouri or Saskatchewan River. But while they were at war, the raiders could come and go as they pleased.

Early in the year, a group of Piegans under Big Snake Person set out from their winter camps to raid the horse herds on the west side of the Rockies. Big Snake Person was a veteran warrior, a member of the Grease Melters band, and a brother of its leader, Bear Chief. He was a proud man with long hair that was beginning to show tinges of grey but was always neatly groomed and had abalone shells for decorations. He chose to raid the mountain Indians—Flatheads, Kootenays, or Nez Perces—because spring came early on the Pacific slope and those tribes were famous for their Appaloosas, pintos, and other fine horses. As soon as the raiders entered the mountains, Big Snake Person said that he wanted to turn north to attack the Kootenay camps in the Windermere valley. The other members of the war party disagreed, saying they preferred the Flathead camps, so they split and went their separate ways. A few weeks later, those who had raided the Flatheads returned with captured horses and exciting tales of their victory. Big Snake Person was still away, but no one was worried, as the mountain passes to the north were likely still choked with snow.

As the warmth of spring spread over the land, the Piegans began to move from their winter villages toward the open prairies. Some had camped on the upper waters of the Teton River, others on the Two Medicine and the Marias. From there they traveled to Sun River, with some continuing on to the valley of the Missouri. A few families from the Grease Melters band, consisting of four lodges, were the last to leave. These tepees were occupied by two chiefs, Eagle Flag and Bear Chief, and by the families of Many Dust and Lone Medicine Man. Although the weather was mild on the open plains, winter had been slow to leave the foothills, where the snow was still deep and the weather cold. On their first day the small Grease Melters clan traveled from their campsite, where the town of Choteau now stands, and went as far south as Freeze-out Lake.[1]

Next morning, three of the lodges were struck and were moving along the snow-choked valley when Many Dust saw a war party of Crows hiding behind a ridge of snow. Presumably they were waiting to ambush the Piegans while they were on the trail. Alerted to the danger, Eagle Flag turned back to the campsite with his comrades, and all three again pitched their lodges beside Bear Chief.

Realizing that they had been discovered, the Crows tried to present themselves as a peace-making party. A Sarcee Indian who lived with the Crows and could speak Blackfoot came forward and said, "Your chief is invited by the chief of the Crows to come over and make friends."[2]

Bear Chief watched as five Crows cleared a place in the snow, put their weapons aside, and sat down to meet with the Piegans. When he saw this, Bear Chief prepared to go down the hill to greet them, but Lone Medicine Man stopped him and said, "If you go down there you'll die. We all know what the Crows are."

Bear Chief replied, "No, our people will hear of this. I must go."

"I want to know why you feel you must go to them?" persisted his companion.

"My friend, I must make peace with them."[3]

When Bear Chief arrived at the meeting place, the two Crow chiefs arose and greeted him. One was named Painted Wing and the other Spotted Lip. Speaking through the Sarcee interpreter, Spotted Lip said, "This summer we are going to make peace with the Blackfeet. At that time I will make you a present of six horses and a mule."[4] Painted Wing also promised him the same.

Bear Chief returned their greeting, and after they had smoked a pipe of friendship, he invited the Crow chiefs to come to the Piegan camp, saying they had plenty of back fat cooking with the meat. There was an anxious moment while Bear Chief was speaking, for he had a revolver hidden under his shirt, and when he sat down it accidentally fell out. Bear Chief later recalled, "It was still cocked. I was so excited it's a wonder I hadn't shot myself." As the revolver dropped to the ground, one of the Crow chiefs said, "You saw us put our arms down. This doesn't look very good."⁵ Bear Chief made the excuse that he had come to their parley in such a hurry that he had forgotten to leave his gun behind. They probably didn't believe him, but they decided not to press the issue.

After some discussion the Crows agreed to come to Eagle Flag's tepee and then travel with them to the main Piegan camp on the Sun River, where they could further discuss the treaty. When they all gathered at the camp, Eagle Flag saw that there were more than fifty Crows in the war party. While they were eating, the chief called Many Dust to his side and quietly told him to go to Sun River to warn the others that they were coming and that there might be trouble. Then, in a loud voice, he asked the young man to go for water. Picking up a pail, Many Dust left the tepee without arousing suspicion, saddled his horse, and hurried down the trail toward Sun River. Some of the Crows saw him leave and tried to pursue him, but he got away safely and later arrived at the Piegan camp on Sun River.

The messenger had expected to find a large encampment of Piegans, but there were only ten lodges of the Skunks band there, under the leadership of Young Bull. The others had gone south to the Dearborn River to hunt for mountain sheep. The main camp of Piegans under Big Lake, chief of the Worm band, was only a few hours away on the Missouri, so another messenger was sent to his camp, telling him that the Crows were coming and that they said they wanted peace.

Meanwhile, Eagle Flag, Bear Chief, and the others struck their tepees and joined the Crows on the ten-mile trip to the Sun River camp. The Crows believed that the Piegans had no suspicion that they wanted to kill them, while the Piegans were confident that their warning had reached the other Piegan village. As the groups rode along the trail, both sides were suspicious yet confident.

When they arrived at Sun River, the Crows saw how small the camp was and realized that they could have an easy victory. But a show of goodwill was exhibited by both sides, as the Crows were welcomed into the camp for the peace-making meeting. According to Little Plume, "The council proceeded without even so much as a sign of the hostility of the past, and as to the course to be pursued in the future, it was to be one that would make the Crows and Blackfeet as one nation. Everything had progressed to the satisfaction of all. The council had adjourned to give place to feasting and dancing during the night."⁶

While the visitors were seated in Eagle Flag's tepee, the chief's little girl went over and sat on the lap of the Sarcee interpreter. He quickly became very attached to the child, and when the Crows were busy eating, he whispered to the chief, "I have a daughter at home. My companions have announced they will kill you people tomorrow. Get your things together. I'll take you away so you and your family can escape."[7] But Eagle Flag refused, saying that he would not desert his comrades.

At dawn the Crows were dismayed when Big Lake and his entire band arrived and pitched their lodges farther up the river. According to Split Ears, "Spotted Lip didn't believe there were many camps along the river, but soon he heard many Piegans coming. Young Bull said to him, 'You thought Bear Chief and I had lied to you. You hear the people coming and that isn't all. There are many more Piegans farther below.'"[8]

With this sudden change of events, the Crow chiefs decided to continue with their story about a peace treaty. Big Lake, the head chief of the entire tribe, greeted them in a friendly fashion and invited them to a feast in his lodge. There they visited and promised to conclude a formal treaty when all the chiefs of both tribes could be brought together.

Meanwhile, the Piegan scouts kept a vigil over the rest of the Crow war party as they lazed around the camp and prowled around their horse herds, but as long as they caused no trouble, they did nothing to interfere with them. During this time one of the Piegan scouts decided to follow the back trail of the Crow war party, and when he was some distance from the camp he noticed something unusual at the side of the path. It was almost covered over with snow, but on closer inspection it proved to be a buffalo robe decorated with porcupine quills. He recognized it immediately as the one belonging to Big Snake Person, the man who was late in returning from his excursion across the Rockies. As he looked closer, the scout saw a bullet hole that went through the middle of the robe. Right away, he knew that Big Snake Person was dead and that the Crows had killed him.

As he hurried to spread the news, another dramatic event was taking place at Big Lake's camp. The Crows had left their personal belongings and storage bags in one of the tepees while they visited the Piegan chief. While the women busied themselves around the lodge, preparing food for their visitors, a tiny dog sniffed at the Crow bags and became very excited. Split Ears recalled, "A woman looked into one of the bags and found a scalp. Everyone recognized it as that of Big Snake Person because of the gray hair and decorations."[9] Big Lake was called outside his tepee on a pretext, and he was told about the grisly discoveries of the scalp and buffalo robe. His response was to tell his warriors to pour grease into the pans of the muzzle loaders and to ready their bows and arrows. "Let's make a trade," he said—Big Snake Person's life for the lives of the Crows.

While the Piegans prepared their weapons, Big Lake went back inside and announced that he had a surprise for his guests. He told them that Bear Chief, the man the Crows had first met and the first to smoke a pipe with them, was camped farther down the valley and had invited them all to another huge feast. As such an invitation could not be refused, the Piegans and Crows set out for the Grease Melters camp. It was bitterly cold outside, so after riding for a short distance, the Piegan chief suggested that they get off and walk. Along the trail they met Bear Chief, who knew nothing about the plan nor his supposed invitation. Quickly, Big Lake drew him to one side and told him that the Crows had killed and scalped Big Snake Person. Now they were going to kill the Crows.

Bear Chief was saddened that his brother had been killed, but he told Big Lake that he did not want to start a fight. He wanted to avenge his brother's killing, but he also wanted to save the lives of the Sarcee interpreter and the two chiefs who had smoked with him. He called the Sarcee to join him, but when the man tried to leave, Spotted Lip raised his bow and arrow and stopped him. This triggered an attack by the Piegan warriors, and the battle was on. In the first onslaught several Crows fell, but only two shots were fired by them before they fled into a coulee. There they made an entrenchment at a site known as the "Breaks" and held the angry Piegans at bay.

As the Crows lay surrounded in the coulee, an old Piegan holy man named Sitting on Top of Glass decided to teach a lesson to a young warrior in his tribe. Some time earlier, the man had come back drunk from a trading post and had started a fight with Sitting on Top. Now the holy man found the young man, seized him by the hair, and dragged him within sight of the Crow lines. Then, in front of the whole camp, he dared the young man to attack the entrenchment with him.

This was a serious matter. A dare made during a battle could not be ignored or the person would be branded a coward and expelled from the camp. Without hesitation the young warrior proved that he was no coward, joining the holy man as he crept and crawled through the snow to the edge of the fortification. When they looked inside, they saw that many of the Crows had been wounded, while others were freezing in the cold. The young man immediately called to his comrades and told them that it was a good time to attack. He was the first to jump into the trench and captured a gun from a Crow warrior. Later he presented it to the holy man, apologizing for his earlier actions and asking him to become his friend.

According to Little Plume, "then commenced one of the most bloody battles ever fought between two nations."[10] The Piegans succeeded in dislodging the enemy and driving them down the river. Little Plume said that "After resting until evening, the Piegans again started in pursuit and overtook the Crows at what the white men now call the 'Middle Bridge' which is about two miles above the town of Sun River."[11] Here the Crows made another stand, but again they were dislodged. In their final stand at a cut bank a few miles below the present town of Vaughn, the last of the enemy were slain. The site of their demise was named by the Piegans, The Place of the Painted Wing and Spotted Lip Massacre.

According to Split Ears, the Crows were either killed in battle or were wounded in the trenches and froze to death. "The only casualty among the Piegans," he said, "was a man who was stabbed in the foot."[12] Years later, the Piegans learned that the Crow war party had lost its way. It had been going to raid the All Medicine Men band's camp farther north but had accidentally stumbled across the four lodges of Grease Melters. It was a fatal mistake.

4 The Revenge of Bull Head

Bull Head, Stamixotokon, was remembered as a kindly old man who gave his name to Col. James F. Macleod in 1874 and permitted the North-West Mounted Police to build a fort in his hunting grounds. Yet this was the same Bull Head who, eight years earlier, had wiped out an American government farm, killed a nephew of the famous Kit Carson, and forced the closure of a Jesuit mission and had been declared a "hostile" in the United States.

Bull Head was chief of the North Piegan tribe, which usually wintered in the Porcupine Hills and along the upper waters of the Oldman River west of the present Fort Macleod. In summer the tribe ranged far out onto the plains in search of buffalo, often camping within sight of the Cypress Hills. They were a part of the great Piegan Nation, which consisted of the North Piegans, Aputohsi-pikuni, and the South Piegans, Amiskapi-pikuni. No one knows when they split into two tribes, but by the time the first fur traders arrived they had already divided. In 1811, for example, trader Alexander Henry described the North Piegans as "30 or 40 tents who seldom resort to the plains, either in summer or winter, unless scarcity of animals or some other circumstances obliges them to join their countrymen. This small band generally inhabit the thick, woody country along the foot of the mountains, where they kill a few beavers, and, being industrious, they are of course better provided for than those Piegans who dwell in the plains."[1]

The North Piegans began trading with the British when the Hudson's Bay Company established posts along the North Saskatchewan River in the 1790s. Later, when American entrepreneurs first came up the Missouri into what is now the state of Montana, they tried to open trade relations with the entire Blackfoot Nation, but they failed for two reasons.

First, the Lewis and Clark Expedition in 1806 had killed two Piegan Indians, so the tribe did not look kindly upon visitors from the south. And then there was the American method of gathering furs. While the Hudson's Bay Company encouraged the Indians to hunt and to bring their catches of beaver and robes to trade for knives, kettles, and other goods, the Americans preferred to do their own trapping. Independent trappers, known as mountain men, invaded Blackfoot territory and took their catch of beaver pelts out to a rendezvous point where merchants bought them. To the Blackfoot this was theft, and the interlopers were killed whenever they were found.

A major change occurred in 1831, when the American Fur Company came to the Upper Missouri to trade in the same fashion as the British. A treaty was made, and Fort Piegan was built at the confluence of the Missouri and Marias Rivers. This widened the gap between the North and South Piegans, for now the southern group tended to trade with the Americans while the North Piegans stayed with the British.

Sometime during this period—probably in the late 1830s—Bull Head became a member of the tribe. He was not born a North Piegan but was from the southern branch of the nation. His daughter married a North Piegan, and when he went to visit her, he liked the people so much that he decided to stay. He was soon joined by a number of other South Piegans, including the families of Little Leaf, Big Bull, Meat Face, Elk Head, and Pretty Face. Bull Head eventually became leader of the Seldom Lonesome band, one of the four bands that made up the northern tribe. The head chief was a man named Rising Head, while other family leaders included Big Lake, North Chief, and Little Grey Head. Bull Head had previously belonged to the Blood band of the South Piegans (not to be confused with the Blood tribe), who were under the leadership of Mountain Chief and wintered in the St. Mary's Lake region, just south of the present Waterton National Park. This band was the closest one to the North Piegans, and Mountain Chief and Bull Head were good friends. Over the years Bull Head became recognized as a leading war chief of the North Piegan tribe, and by the 1840s—likely after the death of Rising Head—he became its head chief.

The first white man to record actually meeting him was Methodist missionary Robert Rundle. The fur traders at Fort Edmonton and Rocky Mountain House undoubtedly knew him, but his presence was not recorded in their journals. This was not unusual, for individual chiefs were seldom mentioned unless they did something particularly note-worthy while visiting the fort.

In 1847 Rundle left Fort Edmonton to visit the Blackfoot tribes along the foothills. After he crossed the Highwood River, he came to a camp of twenty-four lodges and visited "Bull Head's tent, principal chief of this party of Peagans."[2] During the next two weeks Rundle stayed in Bull Head's camp and learned something about the chief's fierceness in pro-tecting his hunting grounds. He was told that a year earlier, Bull Head's warriors had been involved in a battle with a mixed war party of Koote-nay and Pend d'Oreille Indians. After some fierce fighting, the Piegans had driven their enemies back and killed two of them. The mountain Indians withdrew, but the Piegans pursued them the next day, and another fierce battle took place. When it was over, another four of the enemy were slain while the Piegans lost four men, including a chief.

Bull Head was reputed to be a capable and powerful man who pro-vided wise leadership and was relentless in war. One elder commented that Bull Head "was a great warrior. The tribes across the Rockies greatly feared him. He was known as a great leader in war and was hated by the other tribes."[3] This aggressiveness was not limited to his dealings with enemy tribes. In 1854, when James Doty was sent out to encourage Indi-ans to attend a forthcoming treaty with the American government, Bull Head made it clear that he could not attend. As Doty explained, "He would like to go to the Council but there was an old quarrel between himself and the Iron Shirt, a South Piegan, and if they met there would be murder committed."[4]

The treaty with the American government was negotiated in the fol-lowing year and, true to his word, Bull Head was not present. Instead, Little Grey Head and Mountain Chief represented his tribe. Interestingly, at the same time that his fellow South Piegan chiefs were speaking with U.S. government officials, Bull Head was negotiating a peace treaty at Fort Edmonton with enemies from the Cree tribe.

Missionary Thomas Woolsey described the arrival of the Plains tribes: "Two of their chiefs (one being a war chief) arrived first, to intimate their approach, as the Crees, with whom they are at war, were encamped near us. . . . They at length reached the river's edge, unburdened their horses, and prepared to come over, firing off their guns as a signal. The large boat then crossed for their men, women, children, and luggage, &c., the horses and dogs swimming over."[5]

Once everyone had crossed, the mixed party of Piegans and Siksikas marched in procession to the fort, all wearing face paint, singing, and jingling bells. When they reached the palisades of Fort Edmonton, the officers of the fort came out and two shots were fired from the company's cannon as a form of welcome. After further welcomes the trading began. Said Woolsey:

> Before they left the Fort, they formed a treaty of peace with the Crees. For this purpose the different tribes assembled in the hall, when energetic addresses were delivered by the Blackfeet, which were made known to the Crees through an interpreter, who had a suitable reply. Each tribe then placed the calumet (or sacred pipe) upon the table, forming an angle, after which the pipes were lighted and handed round by one of the Blackfeet to each of the Crees. Then followed another, giving to each Cree a piece of lump sugar, first touching his own lips with it, and then applying it to the lips of the other. Then followed a third, who kissed each Cree; and then a fourth, who shook hands with them. This was followed by a recognition on the part of the Crees, three or four of whom presented several small parcels of tobacco to the Blackfeet chiefs, as presents for other chiefs of their tribe, with whom they expected to meet shortly. All these acts were preceded by a very expressive oration. The Blackfeet expressed themselves most enthusiastically and eloquently.[6]

This treaty would last as long as the young warriors of each tribe would permit. But someone was sure to be tempted by their enemy's horse herds, and in the raid blood might be spilled. Warfare would then begin again in earnest until the next treaty could be negotiated. Bull Head, like all good chiefs, fulfilled the terms of the treaty as long as it was in effect. He did his best to prevent his young men from going to war but was merciless if he discovered any Crees trying to raid his camp.

In the following spring of 1856, presumably knowing that his enemy Iron Shirt was far away, Bull Head took his followers to trade at Fort Benton, just east of the present city of Great Falls. On March 25 the clerk reported "Bulls head and party N Piegans arrived to trade."[7] At this time Bull Head met his fellow chief, Little Grey Head, and undoubtedly learned the terms of the treaty signed with the Americans. When the treaty commissioners had met with the Blackfoot the previous autumn, they duly noted the absence of Bull Head with the comment, "Of the 57 lodges of Piegan absent, all agreed in the conferences with Mr. Doty in his trip north, to be bound by the treaty, but did not attend the council."[8] The treaty provided for the Blackfoot to surrender their hunting grounds south of the International Boundary, established a large ninety-nine-year hunting ground for all tribes who would live at peace with each other, and provided other benefits. The clause that ultimately affected Bull Head stated that the government would "build houses for agencies, missions, schools, [and] farms."[9]

One of the government's ideas was to teach Indians how to farm so that they could be weaned away from their nomadic life based on following the buffalo. In 1858, partly in fulfillment of its treaty obligations, the government established a farm on the Sun River about fifteen miles west of the present Great Falls. By the following year it was producing wheat, corn, and various kinds of vegetables. Virtually no Piegans, however, showed any interest in agriculture, for as long as there were buffalo on the plains, the tribesmen had no desire to scratch the earth.

Although he was friendly with the American traders, Bull Head usually wintered on the British side of the border and often took his trade to Edmonton rather than Fort Benton. In 1864 the U.S. Indian agent, Gad E. Upson, commented that Bull Head and his followers had not even bothered to attend the distribution of annuity goods of cloth, blankets, flour, and other items. "I learn," he reported, "there are some twenty lodges with the North Piegans that were not here, and, I am informed, seldom favor this place with their presence."[10]

During this period relations between the Blackfoot and Montana settlers were becoming increasingly unsettled. With the discovery of gold about 1860, miners flooded the mountain areas and invaded Blackfoot hunting grounds on prospecting expeditions. Traders found that they could make better profits doing business with the miners and no longer catered to their Native customers. To add to the problem, the Blackfoot tribes lost their Indian agent at the outbreak of the Civil War because of his Southern sympathies. He was not replaced for a year and a half, and when a new agent did arrive in 1863, he failed to deliver the promised annual annuities.

The strained relations erupted into open warfare in 1865 when the Blackfoot were decimated by a measles epidemic and blamed the white people for its introduction. In April of that year a war party of Bloods took forty horses from the village of Fort Benton, and the angry frontiersmen promised vengeance against the first Blackfoot who dared come into town. Unaware of these events, Blood chief Sitting on an Eagle Tail rode into the fort and was promptly shot and killed by Joe Spearson. The Bloods responded by organizing a revenge party. On their way to Fort Benton they encountered a party of ten woodcutters and killed them all.

The response of the government was to demand a new treaty that drastically cut down the size of the Blackfeet Reservation. The major chiefs of the nation did not attend, but the commissioners went ahead anyway, took the signatures of the lesser chiefs who had appeared, and declared that the treaty had been approved. This may have pleased local residents, but it did nothing to improve the worsening relations between the Blackfoot tribes and Montanans.

In the autumn a war party of nine Piegans and Bloods met two prospectors on the Yellowstone River and offered to travel with them. While they were riding along, the Piegans shot and killed them. A few days later, Blackfoot Indians encountered a number of enemy Gros Ventres and attacked them. Among the enemy party were two white traders, Hunicke and Legris, and they were killed as well. On the day after New Year's 1866, a Piegan Indian stole a bay horse from a trader and took it to his camp on the Teton River. The trader followed him; when he demanded the return of the horse, he was defiantly told to try and take it. In the following month South Piegans attacked a work crew constructing a road from Helena to the Musselshell River. One Piegan was killed and a road worker was wounded.

Bull Head, now spending most of his time in the Porcupine Hills area, may have believed that he was too far away to be affected by the strained relations that existed on the Montana frontier. However, he had not taken into consideration that his followers, particularly the young men, liked to cross the border into the United States, either to raid the Crows or to trade at Fort Benton.

During the winter of 1865–66, a rumor was spread that gold had been found along the Sun River in the heart of the South Piegan hunting grounds. Five hundred prospectors flooded the region, built a village near the government farm, and spent the winter killing game and driving off the Indians. By late winter, however, they realized that there was no gold, and only a few diehards stayed on.

In mid-March 1866, four young North Piegans arrived at Sun River and went to the government farm looking for food. The manager, John J. Healy, was away on business and his brother, Joe, was reluctant to let the armed men enter his quarters. However, when they agreed to surrender their weapons to him, he let them in. After they had a big meal he allowed them to stay the night, and "next morning [they] departed without touching a dollar's worth of property."[11]

From there, the North Piegans went to the home of John B. Morgan, who lived nearby and was married to a South Piegan woman named Catherine Armelle.[12] According to Lt. James H. Bradley, "It chanced that a party of prospectors, numbering eleven men, was then camped in the vicinity and some of whose members had indulged in bombastic bravado and boastings directed against the Indians whom they might encounter in their gold-seeking rambles. Morgan, leaving the four Indians in his house, went to this camp and told them that there was a chance now to put some of their threats into execution, as there were four Piegans in his house."[13]

Delighted by the prospect of killing a few Indians, the miners immediately went to Morgan's place and took the North Piegans prisoner. The Indians offered no resistance, possibly believing that the white men were having some fun at their expense. But when they were led outside and the men were carrying ropes with nooses at the end, they knew it was no joke. On their way to a hanging tree, about a mile and a half from Sun River Crossing, one of the North Piegans drew a knife and slashed at a guard in an attempt to escape. However, he was shot and instantly killed by one of the miners walking behind him. The remaining three were taken to the tree and hanged.

Unknown to Morgan and the miners, five other North Piegans had witnessed the execution and promptly rode off to inform their people of what had happened. Not only the North Piegans, but the entire Blackfoot Nation was incensed. To kill someone in battle was acceptable, but simply to hang these young boys was to give them an ignominious death.

The Bloods responded on March 28 by running off the horse herds of a number of settlers along the Sun River valley; on April 5 a wagon train heading for Fort Benton, but still some fifty miles away, had all its horses and mules stolen. In the train was Hyram Upham, deputy Indian agent for the Blackfoot tribes. "Since learning of the killing and hanging of the four Indians at Sun River," said a Montana newspaper, ". . . they will rob and murder every white man they can find."[14]

It is quite possible that one of Bull Head's own relatives was among the four who had been killed, for he was swift to organize a revenge party and head south for Montana. By this time, following the abortive gold rush, there were only a few people left along the Sun River. Even the government farm was almost deserted, occupied by only two employees, Cass "Tex" Huff and Nicholas Sheran.[15] The manager, John Healy, was in Fort Benton, and his brother Joe was taking a load of lumber to Helena.

Bull Head, with a party of thirty North Piegans, swept into the Sun Valley on April 22, 1866. When they were spotted by an Indian woman—perhaps Henry Morgan's wife—she rode to the farm headquarters, obviously in a state of great excitement. She shouted a message to the men, but neither of them spoke Blackfoot. As she made signs for them to follow her, they suspected that she was leading them into a trap and refused to comply. She was, in fact, trying to warn them of their imminent peril. At last, concluding that they would not listen to her, she wheeled her horse around and galloped away.

Some time later, Bull Head and his revenge party came down the trail leading to the Sun River farm and slaughtered seven head of oxen grazing in a nearby field. At that moment Tex Huff was down by the river getting a pail of water, so he did not see the Indians arrive. As soon as Nick Sheran sighted them, he opened a trapdoor to the roof and tried to signal his companion, but he was too late. The North Piegans had already discovered him.

"The poor fellow was soon shot down," said Healy, "but evidently not killed outright, as he crawled upon his hands and knees towards the brush of the river bank and had disappeared from sight before Nick left the roof."[16]

Turning their attention to Sheran, the North Piegans rode toward the main farm buildings. The frontiersman remembered that the front gate had not been barred, so he rushed from the roof and bolted it just moments before the Indians arrived. Back on the roof, he observed the attackers gathering branches and wood to burn down the buildings. Over near the river, he could now see Tex Huff's scalp suspended from a pole.

According to an official report:

The Indians then set fire to the buildings, which, being perfectly dry, burned like tinder. Shannon [Sheran] remained in the house until the heat became so intense that it fired off the loaded guns in the house. There were in the house, at the time, two boxes of shells for a 12-pound howitzer. Shannon [Sheran] remained until the flames reached these and then jumped from the window on the opposite side of the house when the ammunition exploded, filling the air with logs and timbers and completely demolishing the whole house.[17]

He timed his escape just as heavy smoke was rolling over his position and moments before the explosion took place. Sheran jumped fifteen feet to the ground then dashed into the bushes along the river. The Indians did not see him escape, nor did they search for him, as they believed he had been killed by the explosion. Creeping away from the scene, Sheran traveled on foot for three days and nights until he reached the ranch of Paul Vermet, which by that time had also been raided by the Piegans.

From the government farm, Bull Head and his revenge party went eight miles along the river to Henry Morgan's house, but he had already heard of the attack and had fled to the territorial town of Helena, dropping his wife and children off at the nearby St. Peter's Jesuit mission. The Piegans butchered the man's cattle, took his herd of eighteen horses, and followed his wagon trail. When it led to the mission, they believed that Morgan was hiding there. As they approached the mission, they came upon eighteen-year-old John Fitzgerald looking for cattle about a mile and a half from the buildings. He tried to escape, but the Piegans ran him down and killed him. When it was found later, his scalped body was peppered with four bullets in the back and a number of arrows in the chest.

The Indians did not attack the mission itself, but while Fathers Anthony Ravalli and Francis Kuppens watched helplessly, the attackers slaughtered five head of cattle and drove the rest away. A short time later, the missionaries abandoned the place and retreated across the mountains. Meanwhile, the Piegans again picked up Morgan's trail and followed it to Paul Vermet's ranch on the Dearborn River. When they arrived, Vermet and Charles Carson, a nephew of the famous Kit Carson, were rounding up their horses. Carson noticed some Indians near the herd, so he walked over to chase them away. As he did so, other North Piegans hidden in ambush shot and killed him. Vermet escaped and fled to his ranch house. A short time later, two Piegans approached the ranch with Carson's body and left it near the buildings. The Piegans then took the rancher's horse herd and disappeared.

The revenge party was satisfied, even though Bull Head had not caught the instigator of the entire tragedy, Henry Morgan. He lived for many years and later settled on the Blackfeet Reservation with his South Piegan wife and family.

The reaction of the Montana press to the raids was vitriolic. "They . . . invade the sacred domain of the church," proclaimed the *Montana Post*, "flout Fitzgerald's scalp in the very face of the benevolent missionaries, each strand of the gory locks flinging out its message to the whites, 'you are women.' They burn the government property, kill one of its employees, and attempt to roast the other alive, defying even the Government itself. They shoot down in cold blood Charley Carson, compel all the whites throughout a hundred miles of country to seek safety in flight."[18]

After these incidents the North Piegans were designated as "hostiles," which meant that they could be attacked without warning or provocation if they ever appeared again on American soil. So they remained north of the boundary, along the Oldman River, where they were beyond the reach of the American army and the vengeful Montanans. Immediately after the attack, the Indian agent commented that ". . . most of the North Piegans are at open war with the whites, as well as with all other tribes of Indians. They live for the most part in the British possessions, and only come here to receive their annuity goods or to commit some depredations. Many of them have never been here at all."[19] Four years later General Alfred Sully commented, "A portion of the Piegans, under Bull's Head, an old chief, are hostile, and are still north of the line."[20]

The troubles in Montana did not end with the Bull Head raid. The army established Fort Shaw next to the government farm and tried to pacify the frontier, but the Bloods, Piegans, and Blackfoot continued to have confrontations with miners and settlers. As the Indian agent explained, "There are many young men in the camp who are continually on the war path against other Indians, and who, in the course of their excursions, are continually meeting with whites. In such cases a collision generally occurs, thus keeping up hostilities between the whites and young warriors, while the chiefs and old men are trying to keep the peace."[21]

And the aggressiveness and violence was not all one-sided. In September 1866, five months after the Sun River incident, eleven South Piegans started to cross the Missouri at Fort Benton when they were noticed by twenty miners and townspeople. The settlers immediately set up an ambush and opened fire on the Indians as they landed on the shore. One Piegan was killed and three wounded before they retreated back into the water. The attackers then scalped the dead Indian. The next day, this same group of white men learned of another party of Piegans about six miles upstream. They attacked, killed six of them, and brought their scalps back to the fort.

This type of killing and retaliation continued until the cold wintery day of January 23, 1870, when Col. E. M. Baker attacked a defenseless camp of South Piegans, mostly women and children, and left 173 dead on the frozen prairie. That singular tragic event ended any major hostilities between the Blackfoot tribes and the Americans for all time.

As for Bull Head, he stayed north of the line, living in his traditional lands along the Oldman River. He traded with the Hudson's Bay Company at Rocky Mountain House and then with Healy & Hamilton when they built Fort Whoop-Up in 1869. He continued to patronize them until the Mounted Police arrived in the West in 1874. In his old age Bull Head took the name Towipee, variously translated as "Walking Forward," "Sees First," or "Scout."

There is a tradition among the North Piegans that when the North-West Mounted Police selected the site for their headquarters, they knew they had to get permission from the chief in whose hunting area it was located. This was Bull Head, now an old man. "Colonel Macleod asked Towipee for permission to use the site for his fort," recalled an elder. "Towipee refused him. Then Colonel Macleod gave him a high silk hat and a coat with epaulets on it. Towipee's attitude softened and he gave Colonel Macleod permission to stay in the district for the winter. At the same time, he gave him his other name, Stamixotokon, Bull Head."[22]

According to the elders, Bull Head died that winter of 1874–75, so the Mounted Police never left and Fort Macleod became their permanent headquarters. At the time of his meeting Colonel Macleod probably had no idea that the elderly leader he saw before him had once inspired fear and anger throughout the Territory of Montana and among enemy tribes that dared to encroach upon his hunting grounds.

5 *They Acted Like Women*

Four Bears, Nisu'ks-kyiyo, was a poor young man in the Piegan camp. He wanted to go to war, but unlike others his age, he did not have doting parents to provide him with a horse, extra moccasins, and the ceremonial objects he would need for the journey. So in order to seek spiritual power he traveled alone into the Rocky Mountains, where he found a secluded place to fast and pray. There the Sun spirit came to him and told him he would be granted special powers if he fulfilled certain obligations. When Four Bears agreed, he returned home and, in secret, made a woman's dress and two elk-tooth bracelets, just as his spirit helper had instructed him.

On a day when ceremonies were taking place in a lodge, Four Bears entered wearing the women's apparel. "My children," he said to the assembled leaders, "I will show you why I wear this dress. The Sun gave me this power."[1] He then began to sing a song that had been given to him by the Sun spirit and performed rituals that showed he had received holy powers. At that moment everyone knew that Four Bears had become an *A'yai-kik-ahsi*, a man who "acts like a woman."

This happened about 1830, and from that time on Four Bears wore women's clothing whenever he was involved in religious activities or went to war. For ceremonies he also wore a cap made of fisher skin and had a willow branch attached to his back with two magpie feathers on the end of it. When he performed rituals, the feathers waved towards the sun and caused sun dogs to appear. Four Bears was said to have had the power to control the weather—to create or stop rain and snowstorms.

People soon began coming to him for prayers or guidance. When young warriors asked for a prediction of future raids, Four Bears would hand them a pipe and ask them to make a wish. Most asked for a successful expedition to capture enemy horses. He would then tell a warrior to go to a particular place in an enemy camp, where he would find a horse of a certain color that he should take. According to anthropologist Claude Schaeffer, "He would then add, 'If you can stand to come to me, I will nurse you like a woman.' Then the youth would approach Four Bears and place his lips to one of Four Bears' nipples. The act was thought to connect the suppliant as if by an invisible cord to his mentor and thus insure a safe and successful return."[2] A few days after the warrior had left, Four Bears would don his female attire and go to the center of the camp circle. There he painted his face and directed the people to look upward as he prayed to the Sun spirit for the safe return of the warrior.

When another warrior asked for spiritual protection just before setting out with him on a raid, Four Bears said, "Here's a pipe. Smoke it." As the pipe was being smoked, Four Bears prayed, "Give us either fog or rain so that the enemy won't overtake us."[3] He then offered the warrior an eagle feather that would bring fog if it was needed to cover the raider's escape.

When preparing to go to war, Four Bears put on a dress and wore the elk-tooth bracelets on each wrist. Then he raised his arms to the sun and prayed, "Look at my elk tooth bracelets. I'm going on the war path."[4] He raided the Crees, Assiniboines, and Sioux, showing exceptional bravery. Wearing his dress, he would enter an enemy camp, untie horses that were tethered to their owner's lodge, and make his escape. If people saw him, they paid little attention because they thought he was a woman.

As he grew older, Four Bears became chief of the Worm band and was the camp crier, who announced the decisions of his fellow chiefs. Many people were convinced that he was also a prophet who could not only predict the future of a war party but could even foretell the future of the Piegan tribe. An elder stated that when "Four Bears was at Fort Benton in 1864 he prophesied that future generations would live in padlocked boxes [houses] and travel around in black bugs [automobiles] and chiefs would be like branches of a tree and would travel around in sky-like ducks [airplanes]."[5]

This man was one of those unique Plains Indians whom the traders called "berdache," taken from the Arabic work *bardaj*, meaning "male concubine." A berdache was defined by one anthropologist as "an individual of a definite physiological sex (male or female) who assumes the role and status of the opposite sex."[6] This all-encompassing definition included homosexual males and lesbians, transvestites, and those simply showing strong characteristics of the opposite sex. However, like other terms borrowed from alien cultures, the word could not adequately cover the wide variations in Native sexual roles or take into consideration the complexity of Native practices and beliefs. For example, there were "manly hearted" women who became warriors; women who disguised themselves as men to be with their male lovers; men who dressed like women but were great warriors; and men who cowered with the women in times of danger. And there were a few men like Four Bears, whose involvement was not sexual, but religious. Four Bears was not a homosexual but wore women's clothes because his spirit helper told him to do so. He went to war, married, had children, and lived like any other man in the Piegan camp.

Significantly, the war stories remembered about Four Bears are usually humourous rather than heroic, implying a certain intolerance, either because of the man himself or because of his male-female role. For example, while still a young man he admired the religious leadership of Mad Wolf, a medicine man whose powers were said to prevent him from being killed by an enemy. On one occasion, just as the Piegans were preparing to raid an enemy camp for horses, Four Bears saw Mad Wolf go to a nearby rock to pray for courage and success. When he was finished, Four Bears decided that he should go to the same rock to see if he could obtain the kind of powers held by his friend. When he came down, he was certain that he had become invincible.

When the Piegans silently entered the enemy camp, Mad Wolf whispered to Four Bears that they should take some horses tethered to a nearby lodge. Instead of speaking quietly, Four Bears was so convinced of his newfound powers that he said in a loud voice, "No, I'm going to take that white horse," and to the sleeping camp he added, "Here's Four Bears going to take your horses!"[7] Surprised by the outburst, the Piegans grabbed the first horses they could find and scrambled away. Afterwards, Mad Wolf said, "I almost cried. I believe I did cry. I know I cried."[8]

In another story Four Bears was in a large war party. When he fell behind, some young boys stopped in the tall grass to wait for him. As Four Bears came up, he was talking to himself, muttering that when they entered the camp to get horses, he should get some of his friends to help him. "I'd get this fellow to go around to the right, this one to the left," he said.[9] He sounded as though he already had the horses in his possession, so one of the boys jumped up, laughed, and said, "Brother, give us some of your horses."[10]

Four Bears was embarrassed, knowing that he would be the butt of many jokes when they joined the other warriors, so he told the boys to say nothing and that all they had to do was to look at him and he would give them his food. For the next few days, each time they stopped, the boys stared and the food was given. Soon Four Bears was so hungry that when the boys looked at him again, he said, "Ah, you can tell it if you want to. I'm pretty nearly starved to death."[11]

A third incident took place in the summer of 1870, when the Piegans were hunting near the Cypress Hills. They determined that their enemies, the Assiniboines, were nearby, so Four Bears volunteered to act as a lookout. According to an elder who witnessed the incident, "Four Bears went to the top of a hill with his spy glass to watch for enemies but he was so busy looking at us that the Assiniboines came close to him without being seen. Just then his horse got nervous, and when Four Bears looked around, he saw the enemy party coming after him. He threw down his glass, jumped on his horse, and rode away just as they fired at him."[12]

The stories are good natured, indicating a fondness for Four Bears, but they are not heroic. At the time of his death about 1883 the entire tribe mourned his passing, and on that day, out of respect for him, no one built a fire or ate any food.

There appear to have been relatively few berdaches among the Blackfoot tribes. Elders could remember less than a dozen such men and women during the course of the nineteenth century among a population of some thirteen thousand people.

Besides Four Bears, one other well-known berdache among the Piegans was a man who was variously known as Piegan Man, Pikunikwan, or Piegan Woman, Pikunaki. His mother began dressing him in women's clothing when he was just a child, and he never changed. There was a belief among the Blackfoot that a child's sex was determined before it was born, but sometimes a mistake was made and a child that was born a boy was supposed to have been a girl. One instance was recalled in which a midwife delivered a baby and said, "It's a boy!"[13] The next day, the family announced that it was a girl. In that case the family believed a sex change had taken place immediately after the birth. In any event if the mother believed her male child had been intended to be a girl, she might dress him in girl's clothes and raise him as a female.

This practice was followed fairly consistently by several families whose children later became known berdaches. Rather than showing signs of femininity on their own as they grew up, they were treated as women by their parents from birth and were expected to fulfill the role that had been laid out for them. Perhaps the action was taken by the parents because they sincerely believed that the child was a male by mistake, or possibly they observed that berdaches were not necessarily expected to risk their lives by going to war and that they could fill a unique role in the camp without being accused of cowardice.

As a child, Piegan Man played with girls, spent most of his time with them, and adopted the female form of speech. He wore bracelets, earrings, and necklaces and had his hair in two braids in the style of women. When he was about fifteen, he began going on horse raids but continued to wear a dress, even on the war trail.

As a young man, he was taken as a mate by Short Robe and performed the women's chores of cutting and drying meat, doing quillwork and beadwork, and cooking. At this time Short Robe already had two female wives, Charges on All Sides and Going After Water. Short Robe's niece recalled that Piegan Man "was a good housekeeper, tanned hides, made lodge covers of hide. He was kind-hearted. He wore much jewellery, woman's leggings, and a wide leather belt studded with brass nail heads. Sometimes he would start crying, saying that his husband was beating him and would complain to his husband's mother. Everyone ridiculed him behind his back."[14]

He was described as tall, good looking, and well built, with large hands. Like some other berdaches, he was physically stronger than most women and therefore more easily able to perform heavy chores around the lodge. He was also highly skilled as a bead worker and quill worker.

Like Four Bears, Piegan Man was the butt of humourous stories. For example, Fish Wolf Robe recalled, "Pikunikoan [Piegan Man] took a number of women along to gather firewood. It was raining and he made a big bonfire and he put his legs over the fire to burn off the hair on his legs. He burned off the hair and caught fire on his legs."[15]

One of the most outstanding berdaches was a man named Tongue Eater, Matsinoi, a member of the Siksika tribe and a son of Holy Sitting.

He dressed like a woman and created excellent beadwork, and his war exploits were very impressive. Like Piegan Man, his introduction to the female role began shortly after birth when his parents dressed him in girl's clothes. Not only that, but when his younger brother, Matsii-sikum, was born, he too was raised as a girl.

According to one man who knew Tongue Eater, he "acted like a woman, dressed like a woman, yet went on war parties and was very brave. He was dressed as a woman [on the war path] and had to tuck up his skirt to run. He married boys and did glorious bead work. He was not called *he* or *she*, but just by his name."[16] At first no one was aware of the fact that Tongue Eater was a male; everyone thought he was a girl. His parents knew, but they did not tell anyone. They called him a girl, and he grew up that way without anyone's knowing what he really was.

One day, Tongue Eater went to his father and said, "I am going to battle."[17] His father agreed and suggested that he go with his uncle, Calf Robe. When he joined the warriors, Tongue Eater was still wearing a dress, but Calf Robe explained that his nephew was really a young man who was "acting like a woman."

The party of about twenty men left their camp on foot and traveled to the confluence of the South Saskatchewan and Red Deer rivers. From there they went east into the bush country where, instead of finding an enemy, they were discovered by scouts from a nearby Cree encampment. No sooner had the Siksikas made a camp and begun to cook a meal than they were attacked by a Cree war party. As they ran for cover, a man named Black Eagle killed a Cree and took his horse. Meanwhile, Calf Robe kept charging the enemies and holding them back to give the others a chance to escape. When he was shot in the arm, Black Eagle picked him up and carried him to safety.

As they fled on foot, Tongue Eater's brother-in-law, Big Fish, was cut off from the others and harassed by the enemy. One of the Siksikas saw this and called out to Tongue Eater, "Why don't you save your brother-in-law?"[18] As soon as he realized what was happening, Tongue Eater handed his blanket to a friend, tucked up his skirt, and rushed back to help the besieged man. When he arrived, he saw that Big Fish was exhausted and that the Crees had gathered around him in a semicircle and were shooting at him.

"Don't be alarmed," Tongue Eater shouted to him.[19] "Walk as fast as you can. I'll stay behind."[20] Armed only with a bow and arrows he ran around the semicircle, forcing the enemy to retreat. As he rushed them a second time, he told Big Fish to walk as far as he could toward their friends, who were entrenched some distance away. As the exhausted man stumbled toward freedom, Tongue Eater kept shooting arrows and moving around, keeping the Crees as a respectful distance. They fired many shots at him with their muzzle loaders and bows, but he got away unscathed. After the two Siksikas had successfully escaped, one of the Crees is said to have remarked to another, "My, how strong that woman is. She chased us back just with a bow and arrows."[21]

On another occasion Tongue Eater went with a war party under the leadership of Eagle Ribs to raid the Crows. They walked for many days south to the Missouri River and then on toward the Yellowstone. After crossing the Missouri, scouts were sent ahead until they finally discovered an enemy village. After nightfall the war party approached the camp and found a herd of horses on an open plain. They decided not to risk creeping into the camp but to be satisfied with taking these animals. Two of the horses were so big that the Indians could not get on them without being boosted. Skunk Meat and Dog Chief each took one of these, while Tongue Eater picked out one he could easily ride.

Eagle Ribs said the herd was too big for them to take everything, as it would slow them down on the trail. Instead, each man was told to pick a few animals and head out. This way the raid was made without their being discovered. Before morning, they killed a buffalo and each man cooked his own food. Even though Tongue Eater was wearing a dress and normally performed women's duties, on the war trail he was treated like a man. The war party traveled rapidly northward, and Tongue Eater returned safely to his father's lodge on the Red Deer River.

Tongue Eater was very good looking, and so a man in the tribe, Singing Bird, arranged to take him as a mate. Tongue Eater continued to dress like a woman and wore bracelets up to his elbows and rings on his fingers. He tanned hides, made moccasins, and, when moving camp, stayed with the women. According to a friend, "Tongue Eater was married to Singing Bird for some time, and Tongue Eater was his only wife. Singing Bird had girl friends and was good looking but after his marriage he was faithful to Tongue Eater."[22] They remained together until Singing Bird died of an illness in the early 1870s.

According to one elder, men who married berdaches didn't care if their mates weren't women. They knew they were good workers, maintaining the tepee, making clothes, and doing beadwork. "In every way," he said, "they treated these men just like other women."[23]

Tongue Eater's younger brother, Matsii-sikum, followed in the moccasin steps of his older brother. He was raised as a girl by his parents, and at first no one knew he was a boy. A friend said, "His parents made him that way. They wanted to make him act that way so he kept acting like a woman."[24] As a child he played with girls and performed female duties, but when he became a teenager he told his friends that he was really a boy. A "marriage" was arranged between him and a man named Pino, and when Pino's mother complained she was sent away. However, Matsii-sikum did not remain faithful; he became involved with other men, and the two split up. He died in the late 1870s.

Another Siksika berdache was named White Backfat, Apioh'suk. As he was born about 1862, he was old enough to have experienced life in the buffalo days but almost too young to have a war record before his tribe was confined to a reserve. This was probably a good thing, for all indications are that White Backfat was a timid person who preferred household tasks to warfare. He came from a large family including his father, Weasel Bear, and his mother, grandmother, an aunt, and two uncles. One of the uncles was Singing Bird, the man who took the berdache Elk Tongue as his mate. They were all members of the Moccasin band, led by the great chief Crowfoot.

White Backfat loved his mother, but he adored his father, who doted upon him. The boy became a favorite child, a minipoka, and his father encouraged people to give him presents. When someone presented the boy with an otter-skin wristlet, his father gave the man two horses. When another gave White Backfat a buffalo stone amulet, his father gave the man a horse. The boy also received a Sun Dance wristlet (a gift for a woman), an otter-skin neck piece, and other presents.

From the time he was born until he was thirteen, White Backfat slept with his father. This was most unusual, for children normally slept with their mothers until they were about seven, at which point boys began to sleep by themselves. In White Backfat's case, his mother was the one who finally insisted that he sleep alone. On the first night White Backfat said, "I cannot go to sleep," and Weasel Bear complained to his wife, "Why do you want my son to sleep alone?"[25] But the mother was adamant, and the boy finally became accustomed to sleeping by himself.

When he was old enough, his uncle, Spotted Eagle, sometimes took White Backfat to visit his camp. He and his wife had no children, and they liked the boy. However, whenever this happened, Weasel Bear became impatient after a few days and rode out to search for his brother's camp. When he found it, he told the boy, "You've been away long enough. I want you to come home."[26]

As a young child, White Backfat wore girl's clothes and assumed a female role. For example, when children were playing a tepee game— comparable to "playing house"—he wanted to take the part of a woman and have a friend as his husband. Once when they were playing war, the boys divided into two teams, while the girls gathered separately. White Backfat stayed with the girls. The two teams had a war, one attacking a camp and the other defending it. The attackers won, captured the horse herd, and took the girls and White Backfat prisoners. While they were pretending to sleep, some of the girls decided to escape and took the boy with them. Later, when the other team won back the camp, the girls and White Backfat returned home. Throughout the whole "war" White Backfat's role had been an entirely passive one, while the rest of the boys were pretending to be warriors.

White Backfat continued to wear dresses until he was about fifteen. He used the female form of speech and combed his hair like a woman. When he was old enough to ride, his father bought him a pony and had a saddle specially made for him. As a teenager, he was taken in hand by an uncle and taught to look after the family's herd of twenty horses. Each day he got up before sunrise, gathered the horses, then drove them to water before bringing them into the camp. A short time after he had started this routine, the camp's horse herd was raided by the Crows. White Backfat became very frightened when he realized the danger of his work and would not herd the horses anymore. This timidity pervaded most of his activities. When the band went to Fort Edmonton to trade, he was frightened by the sight of white men and would not leave the camp. When someone offered him a gift during a ceremony, he was afraid to go forward to receive it. When a Blood was killed in a drunken fight with a Siksika, White Backfat was afraid to go to look at the body even though almost everyone else in the village went.

His first personal experience with the violence of Plains Indian life occurred when he and a party of twenty people went buffalo hunting. His duty was to hold the legs of the slain buffalo while the women did the butchering. On one such hunt they were observed by Crows and immediately took refuge in a wooded hollow. There they made a barricade of dead trees, and everyone lay flat on the ground. When the Crows approached, the Siksikas opened fire and charged them. Even though White Backfat was fifteen and well within the age to be a warrior, he stayed with the women inside the shelter while the other men counterattacked their enemy. In fact he did not even have a weapon.

Though White Backfat switched to men's attire when he was about fifteen, he continued to speak in women's style and perform women's duties. He lived at home with his parents until he finally married a woman at the age of forty-two, but he had no children. The gossip was that he had male lovers and that his wife stayed with him for eighteen years because she could run around with other men and he did not object.

In White Backfat's case his behavior as a berdache appears to have been motivated by his father's affections. It is significant that the young man changed from women's dresses to men's clothes when he was no longer sleeping with his father. Yet his early years had an impact upon his actions for the rest of his life. He continued to act in a feminine fashion and was known throughout the tribe as an *A'yai-kik-ahsi*, a man who "acts like a woman." People made fun of him behind his back but seldom to his face. As a friend remarked, "If you mention this to him, acting like a woman, he will be surprised and won't like it. He is a member of the Elk Society, and goes to dances. He is a pretty good sport. He used to be a jockey. . . . He acts like a woman and man together."[27]

Anthropologists have applied the term *berdache* to women as well as men, although the Blackfoot made a distinction by calling a female berdache a "warrior woman," *awau-katsik-saki*, or a "manly hearted woman," *ninauh-oskitsi-pahpyaki*. As was the case with men, there were wide variations within these terms. They could apply to a woman who dressed as a man, went to war, and took female mates but were equally applicable to a woman who simply henpecked her husband.[28]

No doubt the most famous female berdache was a Piegan woman named Running Eagle, Petau-mahkan, who was immortalized in a dramatic fictional novel by James Willard Schultz[29] and has a waterfall in Glacier National Park, Montana, named after her.

She was a member of the Blood tribe who was born with the name Empty Valley, Naps-stikum. While she was still a young woman, her Piegan husband was killed by Crows and she swore revenge. She had a dream in which the Sun spirit came to her and said, "I will give you great power in war, but if you have intercourse with any other man, you will be killed."[30] She went to war after her vision and succeeded in capturing many enemy horses. After she exhibited bravery on the war path and killed an enemy in battle, she was given the man's name Running Eagle. She was said to have been the only woman in the history of the tribe so honored.

Most of the time Running Eagle raided the Crows as her own form of revenge for the death of her husband. On one such expedition, she called her men together just before they reached an enemy camp and sang, "Be all brave and do your best/ It's a good thing to hear each other say/ I have good luck in battle."[31]

Described as being a large woman, on the warpath she wore a woman's dress, men's leggings, a blanket coat, and "a sort of undershirt doubled over like a diaper."[32] Because of her success men began to follow her, and soon she was organizing her own war parties. However, she always insisted that she was a woman; while she was on the war trail, she did the cooking for the men and repaired their moccasins. When a man protested that their leader should not be doing such menial repair work, she replied, "I am a woman. Men don't know how to sew."[33]

She also raided the Flathead Indians on the west side of the Rockies, and when that tribe learned she had been responsible for the attacks, they were determined to kill her. One day, a Flathead guard saw an unfamiliar woman leading some horses from the herd. When he challenged her, she began to back away. Aware that he had trapped the famous Running Eagle, he shot and killed her on the spot. Some Piegans believed that she had lost the spiritual protection of the Sun spirit when she had an affair with one of the men in her war party. "That," said an elder, "was why she was killed."[34]

Fur trader John Rowand may have been referring to Running Eagle when he wrote to a friend in 1844, telling of his family's adventures. He said that his son John had been traveling on a well-worn trail in Cree country near Fort Pitt. "It is a war road," he said. "John met face to face with a war party of 1,000 men who had upwards of 200 women with them, and at their head the Queen of the Plains. The latter with her army were very kind indeed to John. He was two days with them."[35] No other record exists of this incident, but it is obvious from its size and composition that this was a revenge party, organized to punish their enemies for some insult or indignity. The fact that a woman should lead such a party was a great tribute to her leadership and ability.

Another female warrior among the Bloods was named Trim Woman, Isis-toni-miyaki. She dressed in women's clothes but lived a man's life, refusing to tan hides or do women's chores. Instead, she hunted, looked after her horses, and raided enemy camps. Trim Woman never married.

On one occasion when she was leading a war party that was going to raid the Crows, a man asked Trim Woman to sleep with him. She said, "If you capture a horse at the door before I do, I will consent."[36] Before she gave the order to start the raid, she told everyone to gather afterwards at a rendezvous point deep in a timbered area. She was the first to arrive at the site, bringing with her two race horses that she had taken from the front of an enemy's lodge. The prospective lover, on the other hand, had failed to take anything from the Crow tepees and was ridiculed for having to settle for a poor horse from the herd grazing outside the camp.

"That kind of woman is always respected and everyone depends on them," recalled a Blood elder. "They are admired for their bravery. They are lucky on raids so the men respect them. An approach of the kind [by the young man] could only have been made by a very young kid who wanted to be smart."[37]

Another incident in which a Piegan woman dressed as a man was the result of love, not war.[38] The primary figure in this drama was a married woman with two children. She had taken a lover, and together they plotted for the woman's escape from an unwanted union. She faked an illness, then a friend convinced her husband that she had died. Her body was wrapped in a robe and placed on a burial scaffold, but that night her lover came and released her. Together they went to his lodge, where her lover fitted her out with a pair of men's leggings and a shirt. He also trimmed her eyebrows in a straight line, in male fashion, and gave her false braids to wear. Then the couple slipped away and traveled to the camps of the Siksika tribe far to the north.

The next day the husband went to her burial scaffold to grieve and was surprised to find that the body was gone. He believed that it had been stolen and scalped by an enemy tribe, and the matter was not pursued. A few months later the lover returned to the Piegan camp, bringing along his new friend, a person named Young Man, Manikapi. The husband was amazed at how much the young Blackfoot resembled his late wife, but he dismissed it as a coincidence. After all, his wife was dead.

The young Blackfoot seemed to fill the male role to perfection. He accompanied his Piegan friend on horse raids and proved to be a fearless warrior. However, after a time the resemblance of Young Man to his dead wife caused the Piegan husband to become suspicious. When he discussed the matter with his children, he found that they, too, believed that the Blackfoot might really be their mother in disguise. Emboldened by their assurances, he took the opportunity to stop her accidentally on the trail. When he looked directly into her eyes, he knew she was his wife. He did not say a word; instead, he walked away and then made plans to kill both his wife and her lover.

That night, the husband crept over to their lodge, gun in hand, but when he looked inside, it was empty. His wife knew she had been exposed and that her life was in danger, so as soon as it became dark, the woman and her lover had fled. Later, the husband learned that they had returned to the Siksika tribe. He never saw them again.

There was another manly hearted woman among the Bloods named Snake Child, who was the wife of Chief Calf, leader of the All Tall People band. She went to war with her husband, and whenever there was a battle, she would dismount and recover the weapons of the slain foe. On horse raids against the Crees and Crows, she went right into the enemy camps with her husband to cut the picket ropes and take the horses.

Before using a buffalo jump, Snake Child's husband would call the people to his lodge, where he and his wife had been painted for the buffalo-calling ritual—a male role. Snake Child started the ceremony by singing that they had found the buffalo and then continued the male role by leading the rites that called for the killing of many cows.[39] Although she was manly hearted, Snake Child never pretended to be anything but a woman, and did not adopt the male mode of dress or speech. She was simply a woman with a strong and dominant personality.

Among the Blackfoot, the wife of Good Old Man dressed as a woman but carried a gun when moving camp and actively hunted buffalo. Her name was First at War, Itomosksi. One time, when traveling with her family, she suddenly raised her gun, aimed, and fired. Then she turned to her boy and said, "My son, go over there. I killed a jack rabbit."[40] Sure enough, when the boy looked in the bushes, he found a rabbit that had been shot through the neck.

First at War also participated in at least two serious intertribal quarrels. Recalling the incidents, her stepson said, "In the two fights where my father was, she had a gun and did everything but shoot. In the fight, there were my father, mother, a Blood and a Piegan. The two Piegans and my father did all the fighting. The other fight was when two other men and my mother went to another man to kill him. When they got there, the others killed the man first. That is why she didn't do any shooting."[41]

The Blackfoot knew about female berdaches not only because they existed in their own tribe, but because they were to be found among their enemies as well. For example, there was a famous Kootenay warrior woman named Grizzly Bear Sitting in the Water, Qánqon kámek klaúla, who dressed as a man, took a female mate, and was well known to fur traders. The traders called her Bowdash or Bundosh, both variations on the term berdache. In the 1820s she introduced the Prophet Dance—a ceremony that spread all across the mountain country—and became a prominent holy woman. She was killed by Piegans in 1837, while she was trying to mediate a peace treaty between them and the Flatheads. According to one account, after her death a Piegan ripped off her breech-cloth, and that was when they learned she was a woman.

The Blackfoot also were familiar with Woman Chief, a Gros Ventre who was raised by the Crows. One of her initial acts as a warrior was to kill a Blackfoot and wound two others outside a trading post. Her first war expedition was against the Blackfoot, at which time she killed two men, scalped one of them, and ran off the band's herd of horses. She was killed by Gros Ventres in 1854.

Speaking of warrior women, ethnohistorian John C. Ewers states, "What is known of these woman warriors does not suggest that they were sexual deviants. They did have to be powerfully motivated to assume a warrior's role in a culture where the great majority of women did not."[42] The death of Running Eagle's husband, for example, was believed to have been a strong motivation for her actions in becoming a warrior.

It is evident that the roles of male and female berdaches in Blackfoot society were considerably different, and that women who took a male role commanded much more respect than their male counterparts. This in part can be explained by the fact that Blackfoot culture was male dominated and that people would have had more respect for someone who forced her way into a dominant role rather than someone who opted out of it. Male berdaches might earn praiseworthy war records, but they still insisted on doing those things that the tribe considered menial—cooking, looking after the lodge, tanning hides, and so forth. The concern, therefore, was cultural and not sexual. Women, on the other hand, could prove themselves by going to war, hunting buffalo, and creating their own horse herds. Even if they retained some of the women's practices, their war records were enough to give them a high status in their tribe. Either way, such men and women were uncommon features of Blackfoot culture, which provided a clear delineation between male and female roles; nevertheless, that culture was democratic enough to permit persons to find their own roles in its society.

6 *The Battle at Elkwater Lake*

The years 1863 and 1864 were frustrating ones for the Piegans, as they were bombarded from all sides. To the east they were involved in several bitter conflicts with the Gros Ventres, and both tribes vowed revenge. In the north some Assiniboines had attacked a party of Piegans who had gone to Fort Edmonton to trade. Even the Sioux who were camping south and east along the Missouri River were harassing the Piegan camps. The plains of southern Alberta and northern Montana were in a state of turmoil, leaving the Piegans angry, bitter, and anxious to punish anyone who trespassed on their lands.

On the west side of the Rocky Mountains, the Kootenay Indians were planning just such an incursion. During the winter of 1863–64 they had subsisted on deer and any game animals they could find along the Columbia and Kootenay Rivers, but by spring they were ready to cross the mountains and hunt buffalo on the open plains. This was a practice that had been going on for generations. Sometimes they sent advance messengers to make a temporary peace pact with the Piegans and other Blackfoot tribes, and when this happened, the two groups hunted amicably together—or at least coexisted on the same buffalo range. Sometimes, however, the Kootenays did not bother to seek permission, for they knew that in midsummer the prairie tribes usually hunted near the Cypress Hills, a good two hundred or more miles east of the foothills. The Kootenays were satisfied to search for buffalo along the upper waters of the St. Mary, Belly, and Marias Rivers, sometimes extending their range as far east as the present city of Lethbridge. They always sent scouts ahead to make sure that the Blackfoot had really gone east then kept a constant watch during the entire time they were on the plains. After they had

The Kootenays sometimes made a pact of peace with the Blackfoot tribes before venturing onto their hunting grounds. This Kootenay camp on the Oldman River was painted in the summer of 1875 by Richard B. Nevitt, North-West Mounted police surgeon. The Kootenays had made peace with the Piegans and were traveling eastward to hunt.
Courtesy Glenbow Museum, Calgary, AB, Glenbow Archives, cat. no. NA-1434-20

concluded their successful hunts, they dried the meat, packed it on their horses, and returned to their own lands.

These two factors—the anger of the Piegans and the hunting practices of the Kootenays—resulted in a dangerous and deadly combination during that summer of 1864. The South Piegans had spent the previous winter on the upper waters of the Marias River in Montana, while the North Piegans had camped within the friendly confines of the Porcupine Hills and along the Oldman River. In the spring the Montana bands traveled northeast to the Belly River, where they met their northern friends, and from there they prepared to venture together into enemy territory on the east side of the Cypress Hills. There were plenty of buffalo in their own region, but a vow made a year earlier by their Holy Woman obliged them to travel to an area infested with Gros Ventres, Crees, and Assiniboines. The vow had been made because of a failed Sun Dance.

In the summer of 1863 the Piegans had suffered a defeat at the hands of the Crees and had gone into their enemy's hunting grounds east of the Cypress Hills on a revenge raid. They had arrived just as the saskatoon berries turned ripe, so the Holy Woman decided that they should have their Sun Dance right there in the valley of Maple Creek. However, this ceremony had no sooner started than it had to stop.

Two Piegan warriors—Heavy Crop Eared and Double Runner—had gone on a scouting expedition and had not traveled far when they discovered a Gros Ventre village. That night they gathered up a herd of enemy horses and returned to their own camp in triumph. Learning that the enemy was so close, the Piegans decided the time was ripe for revenge.

A war party was formed under the leadership of Red Old Man, and only the women and old men were left behind at the Sun Dance camp. A short distance from the Gros Ventre village, the Piegans stumbled upon two men and a woman. The men were killed, but the woman escaped and raised the alarm that the Piegans were near. Her tribe immediately went on the attack, driving the Piegans back and forcing them to retreat to their own camps. As soon as they arrived, the warriors switched their tired horses for fresh ones and then rode back to confront the enemy. The superiority of the Piegans with their fresh horses quickly turned the tide of battle. One of the first enemies to die was Star Robe, a leading chief of the Gros Ventres. Under the Piegan onslaught the attackers became a disorganized mob, fleeing for their lives. According to a Piegan warrior, "it became an awful slaughter,"[1] until the Piegans finally called a halt to the pursuit and the battle was over.

After the fight the Sun Dance was halted and the Piegans moved to the north side of the Cypress Hills, then back into their own hunting grounds. In the fall the South Piegans went south to the Missouri River and the North Piegans to the foothills.

All this had happened a year earlier, so in the spring of 1864 the Holy Woman announced that the Sun Dance must be completed at the same place where it had started the previous year. This meant a return trip to Maple Creek and to enemy territory. In accordance with her wishes, the main Piegan camp, under Mountain Chief, moved slowly past the north end of the Cypress Hills, its members hunting buffalo as they went, until they came to Maple Creek. Scouts soon determined that there were no enemies in the region.

Meanwhile, another small camp of Piegans, under the leadership of Big Nose, was following several days behind the others. Big Nose decided to stop north of the hills, where the hunting was good, but as soon as they camped they were observed by a Cree war party. The enemy waited in the thick brush nearby, then they surrounded the camp that night and attacked in the morning. Bullets, arrows, and even large rocks rained on the camp, but Big Nose rallied his men, who forced the Crees to retreat into quickly dug rifle pits. At one stage Big Nose even climbed a tree so that he could shoot down into their pits. When it was over, nine Piegans had been killed and the entire Cree war party, except for one man, had been slain. The warriors did not try to pursue the man who escaped, for he would carry the message that the Piegans were not to be harassed.

Realizing that there was strength in numbers, Big Nose hurried eastward to join their fellow tribesmen at Maple Creek. After he reached the east side of the Cypress Hills, virtually the entire tribe was together, far from their usual territory on the open plains north and east of the Sweetgrass Hills. This time the Sun Dance went off without interference. Not only were the saskatoon berries ripe enough to be made into broth for the sacrament, but the valley was so lush with raspberries that the year's ceremony became known as the Raspberry Sun Dance.

Buoyed by a successful Sun Dance, the camp at last withdrew to its own hunting grounds. However, the Piegan chiefs, still angry for the harassment they had experienced in the previous months, were bound and determined to punish any enemies they found within their hunting grounds. They camped at Elkwater Lake then fanned out towards the Bull Head and Eagle Butte to continue their summer hunt.

Meanwhile, the Kootenays had decided to conduct their summer expedition without the formality of a peace pact with the Blackfoot tribes. This decision was made after scouts determined that the Piegans were far to the east, even beyond the Cypress Hills. The chief of the Kootenays, Back Showing, Kaka-wits-kiyuta, came from the Tobacco Plains. Like others in his tribe he had been converted to Christianity, and he was better known by the name Edward. Chief Edward had assembled all the bands from Tobacco Plains, Columbia Lakes, Kootenay River, and St. Mary's River into one large force so they would be less likely to be bothered by any enemy war parties that they might encounter. The mountain tribes were always prime targets, for they had some of the finest horses to be found anywhere in the plains and mountain regions.

The Kootenays moved cautiously from the west into the mountain passes and through Red Rock Canyon to the present Waterton National Park. From there Chief Edward sent scouts to search for buffalo. Although they found a few herds, these had already been hunted, perhaps by small bands of Flatheads or Pend d'Oreilles who had also come from the west side of the Rockies. After a few days of hunting Chief Edward said, "Get ready! We'll move! The game looks like it's been picked over by another hunting party."[2]

The Kootenays moved to St. Mary's River, near the present town of Cardston, but they found few buffalo, so they kept moving east past the Milk River Ridge. From there they went north of Pakowki Lake, until they found a cool freshwater spring and a plentiful supply of buffalo within sight of the Cypress Hills, which were known to them as the Copper Mountains. As they thought the Piegans were still on the east side of the hills, they had no qualms about penetrating so deeply into Blackfoot territory and so far from the protective slopes of the Rocky Mountains. Unknown to them, however, the Piegans had returned and were now only a few miles away on the shores of Elkwater Lake.

After they were comfortably settled in camp, the Kootenay hunters went out to the buffalo herds. A man named Abel picked out a fat cow, and even when it broke free from the herd and dashed over a hill, he stayed with it. The animal traveled a long distance on a circular path, until at last Abel killed it and set to work to butcher it. By this time he was all by himself. He packed some of the meat on his horse and, instead of following the meandering route he had taken in pursuit of the animal, he set out in a straight line for his camp. Riding to the top of a nearby hill, he saw scattered groups of people butchering their kills. As he calmly rode through them—thinking they were fellow Kootenays—he began to notice that they were strangers with strange horses. He saw a Piegan (whom he later learned was named Stingy) make three cuts with his knife, which was not the Kootenay method of butchering, and suddenly knew that he was riding among his enemies. When Stingy called out to Abel and he did not answer, the Piegan became suspicious.

"That fellow riding that gray horse is a stranger!" he shouted.[3]

All the hunters stopped work and stared at him. Abel quickly untied his packs of meat and dashed off at a gallop. Before the Piegans could organize a chase, the Kootenay came within sight of his fellow hunters then rode his horse back and forth in a zigzag manner on a nearby hill to signal that the enemy was close at hand. A messenger was despatched to the main camp, while others rode back along the trail of dead buffalo, warning the other Kootenays of the presence of enemies. Within a short time the mountain Indians had assembled their forces and were ready for war.

Meanwhile, Mountain Chief, the head chief of the Piegans, was having trouble of his own. He had borrowed his brother-in-law's horse and had been unable to control the animal. After Mountain Chief had shot and wounded a buffalo bull, the beast had turned on him and the horse had not moved quickly enough to avoid it. In a thrice the horse was gutted and Mountain Chief had to leap to safety. He became exasperated at this piece of bad luck, and to vent his frustration he shouted that he wished an enemy would show up so that he could shoot him. As if on schedule, a large war party of Kootenays appeared; instead of taking them on single-handed, Mountain Chief promptly forgot his threat and dived into some nearby bushes. He was not noticed and safely made his escape.

The alarm was given at the Piegan camp, and they too called in their hunters. Then the war chiefs mobilized their warriors and set out en masse to strike at the Kootenay camp. But the Kootenays had not been idle; they had also assembled their fighting men and prepared to do battle. The two forces came within sight of each other in a hilly area of prairie and brush at the edge of Elkwater Lake, and each waited for the other to make the first move. Some young Kootenays, inhibited by the fierce reputation of the Piegans, were apprehensive until their war chief, Big Eagle, or Isadore, reassured them that their enemies were made of flesh and blood and could die just as easily as anyone.

A Kootenay named Dodger rode to the top of a nearby hill, dismounted, took careful aim at the enemy, and fired the first shot in the fight. As he was reloading his gun, a Piegan named Many Swans galloped up the hill. Dodger's comrades tried to warn their friend, but the wind prevented their voices from being heard. The Piegan reached his enemy, stared at him in surprise for a moment, then shot and seriously wounded him. He had paused because he recognized the man as his half brother. Many Swan's mother had at one time been married to a Kootenay. As the Piegan rode away, a Kootenay picked up Dodger and carried him to safety, but he soon died of his wounds.

After the first shot the fighting became general. Red Old Man directed the battle for the Piegans, while Big Eagle led the mountain tribe. The Kootenay war chief shouted to his followers, "All you people know me as Big Eagle. Today we're going to have a good fight. Try and do your best."[4] As the lines converged, the Kootenays made derogatory signs to their enemy. One man in particular—Moko'es, who was a prankster—made fun of the Piegans and insulted them. Infuriated, the Blackfoot charged, and in the onslaught Bull Chief claimed the credit of being the first to kill a Kootenay—a man riding a magnificent white horse. Big Eagle then called on his warriors to retreat as he bravely rode between his own lines and the Piegans to keep the enemy at bay.

Farther away, Eneas Tallow was being harassed by another group of Piegans, so Big Eagle rode over and helped to drive them back. The war chief then galloped forward to rescue a young Kootenay who had lost his horse and was being pursued by the attackers. Quickly he scooped up the young man, then dropped him safely behind his own lines. Next he saw an old man in trouble, but when he tried to save him, the Piegans drove him back and the man was slain. Eneas Tallow also saw an old man in trouble, but he too was unsuccessful in making a rescue.

By this time both sides were penetrating each other's lines and shooting at close range. An unarmed Kootenay holy man, Raven, rode right among the Piegans, shaking his rattle and singing his war songs. Several Piegans shot at him, but he returned to his line unscathed.

Among the Piegans was a nineteen-year-old warrior of Kootenay-Flathead descent who had been raised by the Piegans. His Flathead name was Kunsa. He dashed towards the Kootenay lines, but when he drew near Big Eagle rode out and chased him back. As the two men entered the Piegan lines, Big Eagle shot at him, missed, then warned the young man not to try such a foolhardy stunt again. Several years later, Kunsa moved to the Kootenays and gave them the Piegan version of the battle. He estimated that a thousand Piegans had gone up against three hundred Kootenays. The Piegans staged a second charge, trying to force the Kootenays into a tight bunch so they could be surrounded and killed, but the mountain tribesmen retained their positions even though several were killed or wounded. Then the Kootenays dismounted so that they could shoot with more deadly accuracy; as the Piegans withdrew, the mountain Indians switched their tired horses for fresh ones. One of the first to change was Big Eagle, who abandoned his blue grey stallion and mounted a brown horse.

In the next attack a Kootenay named Tsa'nwats, or Cut Nose, jumped from his horse to take a better shot but was confronted by a young Piegan who raised his knife to stab him in the back. Just then Cut Nose turned around, and when the Piegan saw that the man's face had been horribly scarred in a fight with a grizzly bear, he was momentarily in shock. But before Cut Nose could take advantage of his enemy's delay, Red Old Man swooped down on the Kootenay and sent him fleeing. Cut Nose ran through the bushes and waded into Elkwater Lake, but there was no escape. The Piegan war chief followed him into the water and killed him. Meanwhile, another Piegan mounted Cut Nose's blue horse, but he too was shot and killed.

At sundown the fighting ceased as the Piegans withdrew to their camp with their dead and wounded, while the Kootenays did the same. That night Four Bears made an announcement to the Piegan camp. "We break camp early," he said, "follow the enemy and give them all the fighting they want."[5] Next morning the warriors set out, while the women broke camp. Their scouts, riding ahead, found that the Kootenay camp had been hurriedly abandoned and that a great many objects had been left behind.

The Kootenays, who had fled immediately after the battle, traveled all night. The next day they camped on the open prairie in a large circle to defend themselves in case of attack rather than taking refuge in the confines of the river valleys. For the next two days they camped by day and traveled unobserved by night, passing the present city of Lethbridge and reaching the Rocky Mountains the following day. From there they followed the mountain passes to the sanctuary of their own lands.

As in any battle, both sides claimed that their losses had been few and their enemy's losses large and that they had been the victors. The Kootenays said that thirty Piegans had been killed and sixty wounded, while the Piegans claimed that they had lost only three men—Back Axe, Throwing Water on Them, and White Eagle—and only one wounded, Bad Boy. For their part the Kootenays admitted to only six fatalities. These were three old men—Ki'wakumkake, Tsanwats, and Rising Wolf—as well as Dodger, Wolf Coming Up, and the father of a boy named Dippy. They also said that only Tuma and another man were wounded. On the other hand Many Tail Feathers, a Piegan who took part in the fight, claimed that "many of the enemy were killed."[6] Probably the truth lies somewhere in between. However, the casualties must still be considered low in view of the hand-to-hand combat and the bravery shown on both sides. The battle went into the Piegan winter count (their calendar system) as the year of the "fight with the Kootenai in which many were killed."[7]

One of the interesting casualties was a Kootenay Indian named Wolf Head. When they were gathering up their dead, the Kootenays could not find the young Indian and presumed he had been slain. In fact he had been struck down by a Piegan, scalped, and left for dead. When the battle was over, he had crawled into some bushes, and he successfully hid from the enemy when they searched the area the following day. Then he slowly made his painful way back to the mountains, traveling by night and hiding by day. When he finally appeared in his own camp on the Tobacco Plains—minus his scalp—the people said it was a miracle. And when the Piegans heard about it, they agreed. From that time on, the Piegans called him a ghost and avoided him.

There can be little doubt that the chiefs on both sides were badly shaken by the fight. While not allies, the Kootenays were not bitter enemies of the Piegans—not like the Crees, Assiniboines, Crows, and Gros Ventres. During the winter of 1864–65 both sides had time to ponder their future actions, and both agreed that they wanted peace.

During the following summer the South Piegans and Kootenays met, and a pact of peace was concluded. Ambrose Gravelle, a Kootenay historian, concluded his account of the battle with the comment, "Peace was made. . . . This was our last big battle with the Plains Indians."[8]

7 *Ghosts*

One day while a few Blood Indians were in camp, the chief sent out a crier at dusk to invite them to his lodge for a feast. As the people were walking casually toward the tepee, one of the men seemed to be holding back. He wore a long blanket and his face was hidden from view.

One of the other warriors noticed the stranger. He was aware that Cree war parties had been seen in the area and suspected that this might be an enemy coming to steal horses. He called out to the blanket-clad figure, "Why are you so slow to enter the lodge?"[1]

The stranger did not answer but stood all alone in the center of the camp. The man asked him again, "Why are you so slow to enter the lodge?" When he still received no answer, the Blood picked up a stick and hurled it at the man. But instead of striking him, it went right through him and hit the wall of a tepee behind him. At that moment the Blood knew that the stranger was not a real person but a ghost.

All the Indians rushed into the chief's tepee and stood in fear, wondering what the apparition would do next. It followed them to the lodge, then stood outside and said, "I came here to smoke. Instead, you try to hit me."

A pipe was quickly prepared, but no one was brave enough to take it outside. At last the chief instructed one of his wives to pass the pipe to the ghost. She handed it through the doorway, but as she did so, the ghost grabbed her by the wrist and pulled her outside. As it began to drag her away, the men tried to stop them, but the ghost was too strong for them. Then a man picked up a burning stick from a nearby fire and struck the ghost on its bony hand. Instantly, the specter released the woman and disappeared.

The woman fell to the ground unconscious; when she was revived, the people discovered that she had been rendered insane by the terrifying experience. She was carried to the lodge of a holy man, and through his prayers and incantations she eventually regained her sanity. She was then given the name of Sta'apiaki, Ghost Old Woman. From that time forward she possessed powers that enabled her to cure people, particularly those afflicted with mental problems.

This is one of the many stories about ghosts told by members of the Blackfoot Nation. To them, ghosts were real and were part of their concept of life and death. The Blackfoot believed that when a person died, its spirit went to the Sand Hills on the eastern edge of their hunting grounds. There the dead lived as they had before but without the gaiety of their former life. They dwelt in villages, hunted ghost buffalo, and used the personal possessions that they had with them when they died.

But not all Blackfoot spirits immediately went to the land of the dead. In fact some never left but remained where they had perished; they were the ones who had died in a horrifying or unexpected manner. They had not accepted the fact that they were now of the spirit world, so they stayed near their bodies and showed no desire to leave. Other ghosts were angry that life had been taken away from them and vented their feelings on the living. These were malevolent spirits that were greatly feared.

Some were so attached to their families that they did not want to go to the Sand Hills. Instead, they stayed nearby to help and protect their loved ones. In some instances the family actually encouraged such a spirit to remain by taking a bone from the body, often a finger joint, and keeping it in their lodge so the spirit would not leave them.

Most spirits, however, stayed in the area of their death for only about two months, as though becoming accustomed to the fact that they were no longer alive. Once they had reached that acceptance, they left for the Sand Hills and were never heard from again.

The general term for a ghost is *sta-au*, meaning "fearing something unseen." A person who had just died was called *akasta'auasi*, or someone "turning into a ghost." A kindly ghost might simply be called *ksisapsiw*, "nothing," or *tsiktumspikoan*, "fleshless person." An unfriendly ghost was *sokataksapini*, "large hollow eyes."[2]

The malevolent ghosts were the ones most feared, particularly at night, when people were sometimes afraid to travel alone. "Go home quickly, do not travel at night, hurry up," an Indian told missionary Jean-Louis Levern. "It's late and you live far from here, beware of the dead."[3] If a

When the head of a Blackfoot family died, his body was sometimes left in his fully furnished tepee together with his personal possessions. Such a place was avoided because of the Blackfoot fear of ghosts. This particular "death lodge" was photographed in the 1880s. The canvas has rotted, and a willow backrest can be seen at the right.

Courtesy Glenbow Archives, Calgary, AB, cat. no. NA-670-28

person died during the night, people often would say, "The dead, *stahex*, killed him."[4]

According to one observer, "Outside in the dark they do much harm, especially the ghosts of enemies who have been killed in battle. These sometimes shoot invisible arrows into persons, causing sickness and death. They have hit people on the head, causing them to become crazy. They have paralysed people's limbs, and drawn their faces out of shape, and done much other harm."[5]

Such was the fear of ghosts that when a person died, his or her name would not be spoken again. The belief was that if anyone spoke the name, the ghost of that person might think it was being invited to stay. Instead, people would find synonyms they could use, such as "the person we loved," "the old man," or "the one who has left us." When the great chief Bull Back Fat died, they referred to him as "he who was buried by women."

If a child was sick, the mother feared that ghosts of their relatives might come to take the young one from them. In these instances a holy man might be invited to stay near the sick child to keep such spirits away. One young man recalled sleeping alone in his parents' tent, when he dreamed he was surrounded by old people who had died many years before. They were singing and kneeling beside a body that was covered up. One of the ghosts began to give instructions to the young man, but he struggled to get away. When he awoke, he was paralyzed for a few minutes. Finally, he went outside and prayed to the spirits not to take him away. He was convinced that the covered body he saw in the dream was his own.

Partly because of this fear of ghosts, young children under the age of seven were taught the meaning of fear. One of the first words a child learned was *na'nan*, or "danger." If they heard it, they immediately ran to their tepee or to their mother. Some of the things they were taught to fear were practical, such as fire, knives, horses' hooves, deep water, and snakes. But they also learned to avoid burial places and going out alone after dark. To reinforce the fear of ghosts, a member of the family would sometimes dress in a fearful disguise and peer into the lodge at night, frightening all the little children inside. Interestingly, after the age of seven the teaching was reversed and children were taught to be brave, the belief being that they were now old enough to be aware of the dangers and would be able to cope with them.

Sometimes people thought they were ready to die, but the spirit world would not accept them. This happened to a Blackfoot named Going Home First. He had been sick for some time and could barely move around, so during the winter he decided it was time to die. At his request his family cleared a patch of snow, made a bed for him, built a big fire, then dressed him in his finest clothes. Beside him they placed his pipe, tobacco, and a pail of tea. At sunset the man told his family that if he did not return home the following morning, they should mourn for him.

After dark Going Home First heard a ghostly voice calling out the names of chiefs who were being invited to a feast. They were all chiefs who were dead. The man had a feeling that someone was near him, so he lit his pipe and held it out. It was taken by unseen hands, then passed around in a circle surrounding his resting place. After smoking the pipe the ghosts began to dance, and soon the man could see the feet of the dancers. Someone asked him for another smoke, so he refilled the pipe and passed it around. He also passed around the pail of tea.

After each dance the man could see more of the ghostly dancers until they were completely whole, and on the third song they invited him to participate. Because of his illness he had not danced for a long time, but he arose and joined them. For hours he danced, and all that time the fire kept burning and never went out. When they paused after the third dance, the ghosts talked to the man and told him stories.

"When the dance is finished," one ghost said, "go home and see your parents. You'll be all right."[6]

After the fourth dance the sun was beginning to rise, so the ghosts took him home. As he passed through the village, his ghostly friends accompanied him and dogs barked in fear. People looking out from the lodges noticed that the fire beside the man's resting place was still burning, even though no fuel had been added to it all night. When the man reached his own lodge, the ghosts disappeared and his relatives came out to greet him. He purified himself with incense, then told everyone to leave him alone, as he had been dancing all night and was tired. Next day when he arose, he was completely cured.

"This is no fairy tale," said Pretty Young Man. "It really happened."[7]

One of the classical stories about a ghost took place in the present Fort Macleod–Lethbridge area in the 1850s. Seven Blood Indians had gone on foot on a raiding expedition to the Cypress Hills, but they had been unable to discover any enemy camps and began to return home. Their leader was a man named Heavy Collar.[8] One day, when they were camped on a hill near Seven Persons Coulee, the leader announced that he would go ahead to locate the Blood camps. Once they were found, he could bring horses back for the others.

Following the river, Heavy Collar discovered three old bulls resting near a cut bank. He crept close and succeeded in killing one of them. He butchered it, left some of the meat where his comrades would find it, then went down into a coulee to make a camp and roast a piece of meat for himself. One of the strategies used by warriors on a raiding expedition was to set up camp, build a fire, then move away after dark. This way, if their presence had been observed, the enemy would surround the abandoned camp and attack it at daybreak. They would find it empty and their enemies, carefully covering their tracks, would be safe in another hiding place. Heavy Collar was aware of the dangers of traveling alone, so he decided to move farther upriver after sunset. Traveling by the light of the moon, he entered another coulee close to the present city of Lethbridge and found a nice patch of buffalo grass that would make a comfortable bed.

Heavy Collar was very tired, but he could not sleep. He would doze off, hear something, then wake up. Sometimes the noise was close and at other times far away, but he could never quite figure out what it was. At first light he looked around and was shocked to see the bones of a skeleton nearby. They were the remains of a Blackfoot woman who had been killed a year earlier. Frightened, Heavy Collar left immediately, forded the river, and traveled upstream until evening, never forgetting the woman's skeleton that had been his companion all night.

Meanwhile a storm came up, so Heavy Collar decided he should make a shelter for the night. Crossing to an island, he found a tree that had fallen down, leaving a high stump as a natural protection against the elements. He placed poles against the fallen tree and covered them with green branches, then made a bed of grass beside the tall stump. He lit a fire, cooked some of the meat he had carried with him, and was relaxing in comfort while the thunder and lightning raged over head. Suddenly he heard an owl hooting in the distance, then closer, then closer again. Heavy Collar was frightened, as the owl was a messenger of death, and ghosts sometimes used its cry as they wandered through the night.

As he hid his head in fear, Heavy Collar heard the sounds of something being dragged through the bushes. At first he thought it might be an enemy, but then he realized that no enemy would be that noisy. The dragging sound continued right up to the edge of his campfire, and there the noise seemed to move about, as though trying to attract the Indian's attention. He recalled: "Turning my head, without moving my body, I saw what looked to be a ghost seated on the far side of the fire. It was clothed entirely in white, with white blanket—coat and leggings. There was a hood over its head, which completely hid its face. It was very tall, with long bony legs, which it kept stretching towards the fire, as if it were cold."[9]

Fearfully Heavy Collar spoke to the ghostly figure, saying that if it was human, it should tell him its name. If it was not a living person but a ghost, then he prayed that it have pity on him and go away. He repeated the question, but the figure continued to sit silently by the fire. Instead of answering, it stretched out its bony feet as if trying to touch him. Each time it did this, Heavy Collar drew away.

At last the Indian became angry at the ghost's refusal to answer his questions. "Well, ghost," he said, "you do not listen to my prayers, so I shall have to shoot you to drive you away."[10] With that, he picked up his gun and fired directly at the specter. It fell over backwards into the darkness, and a few moments later he heard it crying, "Oh, Heavy Collar, you have shot me, you have killed me! You dog, Heavy Collar! There is no place on this earth where you can go that I will not find you; no place where you can hide that I will not come."[11]

The man could not stay in the fearful place any longer, so in spite of the darkness and bad weather, he left the island and fled upriver. At dawn he could see the friendly slopes of the Belly Buttes, where he hoped he might find a refuge from the terrible specter. Comforted by the familiar surroundings, he lay down beside an old cottonwood tree and slept soundly for several hours. He was not bothered by the ghost, so when he awoke he felt refreshed and believed the frightening experience was over.

When he had separated from the war party, Heavy Collar had told his companions that if he could not find the Blood camps, they should meet at the base of the Belly Buttes. He knew they would probably go directly to that place while he followed the river, so he expected them to arrive before him. He was correct, for they were camped at the buttes while one of the men remained on a hill as a lookout. After a while the man signaled to the others that two people were coming; as they drew near, he could see that one of them was Heavy Collar, while the other was a woman.

When the scout returned to the others, he laughed and said that their leader had probably taken a prisoner and now they should decide who would get her. As they were joking, they all saw Heavy Collar approach a coulee with the woman hurrying to keep up with him. But when he emerged from the other side, he was alone.

"Heavy Collar, where is your woman?" one of the men asked.

"Why, I have no woman. I don't understand what you're talking about."

One said, "Oh, he has hidden her in that ravine. He was afraid to bring her into camp." Another said, "Where did you capture her, and what tribe does she belong to?"[12]

As the men continued to laugh and probe, Heavy Collar at last realized what had happened. The ghost woman was still with him, even though he could not see her. So he told the others what had happened. Some believed him, but others did not; they went down into the coulee, looking for signs of the missing woman. They saw the place where Heavy Collar had crossed the muddy bottom; there was only one set of footprints, so they all accepted his story.

Later that day the war party located a camp of seven Blood tepees, and Heavy Collar hoped that he was now safe from the ghost. But that night the woman came to him in a dream and said, "Since you shot me last night, from here on, until you die, you will never get a rifle from your enemies when you fight. You will never be hit by a bullet, no matter what. But no rifle."[13] This was intended as a curse, for capturing a rifle was a high war honor. In addition the spirit woman told him never to return to the place where she had been killed.

The curse proved to be true. Until this time Heavy Collar had been considered a great warrior and a leader of war parties. But now his luck changed. Whenever he went on a raid, either the war party could not find an enemy camp or they were discovered and forced to flee. After a time Heavy Collar got the reputation of being an unlucky leader, and no one would follow him to war. If he had continued to be victorious, perhaps some day he would have become a chief, but because of the ghost woman's curse, he went through life as an unlucky warrior.

Many years later, when Heavy Collar was an old man, the Americans built log trading posts along the river and sold whiskey to the Indians. One day, Heavy Collar's band camped in the valley not far from Fort Whoop-Up, and only later did the man realize that this was the same coulee where the ghost woman had died. "Oh well," he said. "I'm old, so I suppose it doesn't matter what will happen."[14] That night, a bunch of drunken Bloods were celebrating and shooting their guns into the air. One of the stray bullets struck Heavy Collar in the back and killed him instantly. Everyone knew the ghost woman had had her revenge.

While ghosts were feared, there were other stories about their helping people, particularly if they were in danger. It did not necessarily need to be a family ghost nor one that was familiar to the people it helped. Here is one such story.

One day a Piegan named Lazy Boy and his wife, Little Fool, went hunting. When they came to a hill, the husband told the woman to stay there until he had killed a buffalo. He said he would call her to help with the butchering. While she was waiting, she saw two strangers approaching on horseback. She tried to run away, but the men overtook her and made her a prisoner. They were Pend d'Oreilles from across the mountains.

Little Fool was taken to the Pend d'Oreille camp and was turned over to the warrior's mother. All her bracelets, her belt, and her beaded dress were taken away from her, and she was given an old, worn dress with a rope for a belt. Then the man who had captured her gave her as a gift to another man, and she was taken to his tepee.

"Since there are enemies about," the new husband said, "you, my wife, better sleep with my sister."[15] He tied the two women together and left them alone. Late that night, when the Pend d'Oreille woman was asleep, Little Fool untied herself and crept outside. It was raining, and during lightning flashes she saw someone else leaving the camp. She hoped it might be another captive who had also escaped. She hurried in the same direction as the other traveler, but she could never catch up with her.

After a while she realized that the figure was a ghost. It said nothing but indicated by signs that the woman should follow it. Little Fool was frightened, but she concluded that the ghost was there to help her, so she did everything she was told. When the ghost lay down in a hollow place, the woman did the same. A few moments later the Pend d'Oreille husband rode by, calling for his captive. When the danger had passed, the ghost arose again and kept leading the Piegan woman across the prairie, through coulees, but always in the same direction.

At daylight the ghost disappeared, and Little Fool sat beside a large rock not knowing what to do next. A short time later she heard a man singing and crying, and she recognized the voice of her older brother. She ran up to him and hugged him and told him of her miraculous escape. She said, "I followed the ghost first as a person; then I knew it was a ghost. I was more afraid of the enemy than of the ghost, and I knew the ghost was there to protect me."[16]

In another incident a Piegan named Young Bear Chief went with his wife to raid the Assiniboines east of the Cypress Hills. After traveling for several days, they found an enemy camp on a little creek that flowed past Buffalo Lip Butte. While his wife waited in hiding, the man crept into the camp and cut two horses loose from their tethers; with these, he and his wife rounded up another sixteen animals grazing on a hillside.

As they rode away, a fog rolled in and became so thick that Young Bear Chief had no sense of direction. He and his wife rode for a long way, but the man feared that they might be going in circles, for there were no landmarks to follow. After traveling for some distance, Young Bear Chief dismounted to fix his belt, then turned to his wife and said, "We don't know which way to go." At that moment a voice came from the fog behind him and said, "It is well; you go ahead. You are going right."[17]

As Young Bear Chief later explained, "When I heard the voice, the top of my head seemed to lift up and felt as if a lot of needles were sticking into it. My wife, who was right in front of me, was so frightened that she fainted and fell off her horse, and it was a long time before she came to."[18] Following the advice of the voice, they traveled all night through the dense fog. Next morning, they saw that they had passed the Cypress Hills and were approaching the Sweetgrass Hills, well within Piegan territory. They never saw the ghost that helped them, but they felt they owed their lives to its advice.

In their travels the Blackfoot avoided any places where many people had died, either from disease or in a battle. Probably the most well known of these was near a site of Fort Whoop-Up where hundreds of Indians had perished during the smallpox epidemic of 1837–38. As a result of this catastrophe, the area became known as Akai'niskui, or Many Died. Another forbidden site was at the forks of the Waterton and Belly Rivers, where there were many tree burials.

Cecil Denny, an officer in the North-West Mounted Police, unknowingly camped near such a ghost village in the summer of 1875. He had gone hunting upstream from Fort Macleod and was returning by boat, when he encountered a violent storm about fifteen miles from home. Seeing a good stand of timber, he decided to stop there. He was no sooner settled in place than he heard Indian drumming and singing. Looking for shelter, he walked through the woods toward the sound, while the thunder crashed and the lightning flashed through the sky overhead. "Coming out into an open glade of quite an extent," he wrote, "I saw before me the Indian camp not more than two hundred yards away. I could see men and women, and even children, moving about among the lodges, and what struck me as strange was the fact that the fires in the centre of many of the tents shone through the entrances, which were open. This surprised me, as you do not often find the Indians moving about in the wet if they can help it."[19]

Suddenly a bolt of lightning struck a nearby tree, followed immediately by a loud crash of thunder. The lightning lit up everything around him, momentarily stunning the Mountie and knocking him down. When he arose, the Indian village had disappeared. "I stood for a moment almost dumb with astonishment, seeing and hearing nothing," he said, "when suddenly an overwhelming sense of terror seemed to seize me, and almost without knowing what I did, I ran towards the bank overlooking the river, which was about a quarter of a mile away, dropping my gun as I ran. . . . Here I managed to gather my wits together, and to think of what had taken place."[20]

Denny abandoned his boat and supplies, for they were too close to the mystery village, and walked the rest of the way to Fort Macleod. When he arrived at midnight, he immediately turned in. Next morning he told his brother officers about the incident, but they just laughed at him. Determined to solve the mystery, he returned to the site with a Blackfoot Indian and an interpreter. Denny said that "On questioning the Indian he stated that the Blackfeet had surprised and slaughtered a camp of Cree Indians at that place many years ago, and in fact we came across two bleached skulls lying in the grass."[21]

This incident was unusual, for the Blackfoot believed that Indian ghosts did not bother white people. In fact one Blood Indian at the turn of the century, finding that he had to pass through a burial ground after dark, called aloud the few English words he knew so that the ghosts would think he was a white man.

The Sand Hills, found in southwestern Saskatchewan and known today as the Great Sand Hills, were another place that the Blackfoot avoided. According to Morning Owl, a Blood Indian:

> In the olden days our ancestors were travelling in the south and fighting all the time, when one day they came to camp near a big sand hill. One night the people could not sleep for all night they heard human voices—men, women, old men, old women, children—people talking, conversing together. The Indians scouted all around the area, trying to see these people but go as they may in every direction, they could find no one. They also heard horses neighing, dogs barking, but there were none. Then one man finally guessed the mystery: "Wait a minute," he says, "it is here the souls of people that have died have come!" And ever since then it is said of someone who dies, "He has gone to the sand hills."[22]

There were a few instances of people visiting the Sand Hills, sometimes by accident. For example, a Blackfoot war party going eastward intended to skirt the area but came closer than they intended. That night they heard two boys singing and shouting as they drew close to the camp. Then there were the sounds of other young men and of a woman beating a dog. Finally, they heard the voice of a great chief named Many Swans, long since dead, who shouted, "Boys, keep quiet! Let those men who have come sleep. Don't bother them!"[23] The Blackfoot raiders gave up all thoughts of sleep and immediately returned to their home camps.

Then there was a woman who had been sick for some time and decided it was time to die. That night she had a dream in which her spirit left her lodge and went to the Sand Hills, where it was stopped by an old man leaning on a long stick.

"Why are you here?" he asked.

"I'm to live here."

"Your body is too strong," he said. "It's not your time."[24]

She insisted that she be permitted to enter, but the old man barred her way, so she ran back home. When she awoke, she was bathed in sweat and her sickness was gone.

The belief in ghosts took two ritualistic forms among the Blackfoot. The first was the performance of the ghost dance, which was believed to have been given to a young man by the spirits. The second was the existence of the ghost medicine-pipe bundle, which was said to have come directly from the land of the dead.

The ghost dance came to the Blackfoot through a young man who was camped alone on the prairie with his wife and baby boy. His wife died and, knowing he could not feed the boy, he left him beside his mother's body. Then, grief stricken, he sewed up the doorway of the lodge and left them there. He traveled all that day, and in the evening he came to a lodge beside a stream. At first, when he looked inside, he thought it was empty; but then he heard a voice calling him to enter. This was followed by the sounds of drumming and singing.

When he looked around, the man saw human bones scattered around the lodge and a fire burning in the center. Then a pipe was passed from one ghostly hand to another, and when they had smoked four times, the skeletons took their human form. The ghosts were glad to have bodies again, so they sang, danced, and recounted their war experiences. But they noticed that the man was sad and did not join their merriment. When he explained that his wife and child had been left behind in a death lodge, the ghost leader asked the man if he would invite the ghosts to his lodge.

"There is no woman in my lodge to prepare for you," he replied simply.[25]

Four times the ghost leader asked, and finally the man agreed. They all went back to his death lodge, where they smoked and sang until dawn. Then they went away, only to return the following night. On their fourth visit the man's wife arose and prepared a meal for them, and the baby boy became alive and well. The ghost chief then instructed the man to copy the dance he had seen during the four nights and to perform it for good luck and for the well-being of the Blackfoot people. It became known as the Night People's Dance, *Sipi-i'tapi-puska*. During the ceremony the use of the word *Sta-au*, or "ghost," is taboo.

I witnessed such a dance on the Blackfoot Reserve in 1963. After going through ceremonies of prayer and purification, the participants began in a kneeling position, holding their fists in front of them. As the ghost song was performed, they arose and moved their bodies up and down in rhythm to the music. Various other actions took place, including passing the pipe and offering prayers. One of the prayers stated, "May they not be afraid of the Night People [ghosts] when they go home."[26]

When the third dance began, two "ghosts" entered the room, dressed in masks and old clothes. They performed the same dance as the others,

During the Ghost Dance, held on the Blackfoot Reserve in 1963, two "ghosts" wearing masks have joined the dancers, but everyone pretends they are not there. At the center is Edward Axe, who directs the ceremony.
Courtesy Glenbow Archives, Calgary, AB, cat. no. P-74-7

but no one acknowledged their presence. It was as if no one could see them. After the dance ended, they slipped out into the darkness. Later in the evening, when people were fed beef tongues and saskatoon-berry broth, some of the food was taken outside and left as an offering to ghosts.

As for the ghost medicine-pipe bundle, it came from the villages of the dead in the Sand Hills. Like the ghost dance, it involved a man who had lost his wife, but in this case he decided to go to the Sand Hills to find her. He left his children with their grandparents and traveled eastward for four days and four nights, until he was well within the bleak confines of the Sand Hills. There he met a boy who was only a shadow and a voice. When the man explained that he was looking for his wife, the ghost led him to a lone tepee. As he entered, he heard a voice tell him where to sit. A shadowy figure picked up a pipe, filled it, and began to smoke. Gradually the ghost's hand and arm became visible. The pipe was passed to the next wraith, and it too became partly visible. When the pipe was empty, it was refilled and the ceremony repeated. At the end of the fourth smoke, all the ghosts were visible to the young Blackfoot.

"My son," said the ghost chief, "what are you looking for? What is the reason for you to journey into this land? It is unusual for us to see a living person in these Sand Hills."[27]

"I am looking for my wife," said the young man.

The ghost chief nodded his head. "You can sleep here tonight. Tomorrow we will look for your wife."

The next day, the ghost explained that there were four villages of ghosts in the Sand Hills. The first was nearby, so the ghost chief called the ghost of an old man to his side and said, "Old man, go to the first camp and tell all those women who have recently come from the west to leave their lodges and pass in a single line in front of this alive man." One by one the newly arrived women left their lodges and walked in front of the man. He carefully looked at each one, but none was his wife.

The ghost chief then sent a messenger to the second and third camps, and the whole process was repeated without success.

"There is only one camp left," said the chief. "If she is not there, I can do nothing more for you."

The ghost chief and the Blackfoot stood as the women from the fourth camp walked by. First to pass before them was a group of four women. His wife was not among them. Then came three women. "There she is!"

cried the man, as he pointed to one of the trio. The ghost woman saw her husband, smiled, and went forward to kiss him. "Wait!" said the ghost chief. "Don't touch this man!" At the chief's instructions the man entered a lodge. The ghost chief took a pipe down from its place and told him that he was going to teach him the songs and ceremonies that went with it.

The next day the ghost chief invited all his friends to the lodge, where they went through a ritual to transfer the ownership of the pipe to the young Blackfoot. When it was over, the ghost chief raised the man to his feet in four stages—by the hips, the chest, the shoulders, and the head, just the way the ghosts had become visible. When this was done, he told the young man he should take the pipe back to his people and use its powers to help them. The pipe was covered with an owl skin and decorated with beaver claws and seven eagle feathers. With it were a fan made of crow feathers, a wooden bowl, and a rawhide container.

The ghost chief then invited the wife inside, where she and the pipe bundle were purified with the smoke of sweet pine. When she arose, the pipe bundle was placed on her back with a carrying strap. They went outside, and the man was told that his wife would follow him to the land of the living.

"On your way home," the ghost chief said, "don't look back. Don't look at your wife. Don't greet her or speak to her. Always face west, even when you're sleeping. At nightfall, your wife will place the bundle on a tripod and sleep beside it."

As instructed, the man began walking towards the west, his wife following a short distance behind. He did not look back, but he heard her footsteps as they left the Sand Hills. At night he did as he had been commanded, and in the morning he awoke facing west. He waited until he heard his wife shuffle around as she loaded the bundle on her back. When all was silent, he knew that she was ready. He did not look at her but continued to walk west.

On the morning of the fourth day, they arrived at a high hill overlooking his camp. When someone came up to see who they were, the man warned him away. "Run back and tell my father to put up four sweat lodges in a line from east to west," he said, "with the doorways opening to the east." When the lodges were ready, the man walked down the hill with his wife following behind, carrying the pipe bundle. It was placed on top of the first lodge, and the man went inside. After he had completed the sweat ceremony, the ground inside the lodge was covered with sand, filth, worms, and vermin. At the second and third lodges the amount of filth became less and less, and when the man came out of the fourth sweat lodge, it was completely clean. The man picked up the pipe bundle and went into his lodge, and when his wife entered, he turned and kissed her.

No one could remember the name of this first owner of the ghost medicine pipe. However, they do recall that the second owner was Bull Shakes His Head, another Blackfoot. When making the transfer, the first owner instructed each of the people in the camp to take an object from the new owner's lodge—a backrest, buffalo robe, liner—until it was completely stripped except for the ashes in the fireplace. After the ceremony those who had taken things replaced them with entirely new ones, so that the new owner of the ghost medicine pipe had new furnishings for his lodge. The symbolism was that the lodge was a new beginning for the owner, just as the pipe was a new beginning for the Blackfoot people, thanks to the generosity of the ghosts.

After Bull Shakes His Head, there were only seven other owners of the ghost medicine pipe. There were four Blackfoot—White Calf Sitting Down, Middle Calf, Big Snow Shoes, and White Nose. Then it went to three Bloods—Holy Walking Down, Holy Speaks, and Red Old Man. When Red Old Man died in the 1860s, the pipe was offered to his older brother, but he was afraid to take it. Then it was offered to his younger brother, and he too refused. The decision was made to place the medicine pipe beside Red Old Man's body, so his spirit could take it back to the Sand Hills from whence it came.

The belief in ghosts and stories about them did not end when members of the Blackfoot Nation settled on their reserves. If a person died in a house, no one would ever live in it again for fear of ghosts, and the building would have to be torn down. This was why a person near death was taken outside and placed in a tent. After he died the tent was folded away in the belief that the ghost would have no place to dwell and would leave for the Sand Hills.

People also continued to believe that the ghost of a person suffering a violent death was more likely to stay around than one who had passed away peacefully. An example of this occurred in 1907, when Tailfeathers, a Blood scout, learned that his youngest wife was being unfaithful. He decided to kill her, but as she was away at the time he chose to murder Day Chief, the head chief of the tribe, to use as his messenger to the land of the dead, then to kill his wife when she returned. However, he made the mistake of revealing his plans to a friend, who promptly passed the information along to the chief.

When Tailfeathers reached Day Chief's house, the leader was ready for him. The scout fired a shot at Day Chief, which severely wounded him, but the chief raised his revolver and shot and killed his attacker. Day Chief died a short time later.

Afterwards, Tailfeathers's oldest and favorite wife returned to her previous home on the Blackfoot Reserve, some one hundred and fifty miles away. While she was there, the widow was approached by a Siksika woman, Double Choosing, who inquired about her two children. Puzzled by the request, the widow asked the woman why she wanted to know. Double Choosing explained that she had been contacted by Tailfeathers's ghost, who had offered to be her advisor and said that he wanted to know about his children. For the next twenty or thirty years, everyone knew that Double Choosing had the power to find lost objects through the intercession of Tailfeathers.

Around 1931, Blood Indian Percy Creighton, who was working in the Blackfoot coal mines, was invited to Double Choosing's lodge for a meal. While he was seated on her couch, he heard a whistle outside. After it was repeated three more times, the woman said, "Oh, you are always asking for something to drink."[28] She picked up a cup, asked her grandson's wife to fill it with tea, then placed it behind a blanket. A short time later she reached over and picked up the cup. It was empty. Then Creighton heard the whistle again. She said, "Oh, you want something else," and told her grandson to fill a pipe and light it. She placed it behind the blanket, and soon Creighton saw smoke rising. Later she removed the empty pipe and said, "What next do you want?" At that moment Creighton heard laughter that seemed to come from nowhere, and he decided to leave.

The next day, he returned and asked if Double Choosing could find out how his own family was faring back home. The woman replied that Tailfeathers's spirit was down on the Blood Reserve, and she would find out when it got back. Creighton inquired every day, and on the third visit Double Choosing said, "Mrs. Crow Eagle [Creighton's aunt] is very sick." The following day, Creighton received a letter confirming that she was ill.

In another instance a man went to Double Choosing to see if Tail-feathers could find his team of horses. He had been searching for them for four days without success. The woman consulted the ghost and was told that the team was in a certain coulee. The man went to that place, and his horses were there.

There are many more stories about ghosts, such as that of the man who gathered some scattered human bones together and the grateful ghosts who led him to safety from a high cliff, or that of the man who had a beautiful female ghost prepare his food and fix his moccasins while he was on the warpath. But perhaps the best story is one told by Jack Low Horn about two brothers who killed each other at Rocky Mountain House in 1859. He said that "The people in the band put the two dead brothers in their own lodges and placed the two structures together, the entrances facing each other. 'Now you can fight all you want,' they said, and left them that way."[29]

8 Seen From Afar

Seen From Afar was considered to have been the greatest chief that the Blackfoot Nation ever had. He was greater than the legendary Scar Face, who brought the Sun Dance religion to the people, and greater than such nineteenth-century contemporaries as Bull Back Fat and Big Snake. He was greater than the brilliant peacemaker Crowfoot and his own nephew Red Crow. William F. Butler, who visited Fort Edmonton in 1870, described him as "a chief whose reputation for valor, capacity, and wealth, might favourably compare with that of any Indian leader from Texas to the great Sub-Arctic Forest."[1]

His Blackfoot name, Pee'naquim, has been translated in a number of ways, including Seen From Afar, Seeing From a Distance, Sees Afar, and Seen in the Distance. A native elder specializing in the finer points of the language believes that the name describes a man who could be seen from a great distance, hence Seen From Afar, and this has become the standard translation.

Regardless of the variations in the translation of his name, there is no question about his leadership. Seen From Afar was a fearless youth, a great warrior, and a wise chief who established a dynasty that lasted for more than a century. He was born about 1809, the son of Two Suns and Fine Charger. His father was a leader of his own clan and was one of the lesser chiefs of the Blood tribe. At the time of the boy's birth, Bull Back Fat, the head chief, carried out incessant warfare against the Crees, Flatheads, Crows, and other enemies. As a result Seen From Afar was raised in an atmosphere of conflict, where the protection of tribal hunting grounds and the destruction of enemies were the main preoccupations of the tribe.

The early warrior years of Seen From Afar are hard to pin down because of the multiplicity of Blackfoot names that were normally used by a person during his lifetime. A man was given a baby's name at birth, changed it for a young man's name when he went on his first raid, and then changed it again and again as he performed feats of valor. To add to the complicated procedure, when a man took a new name it was sometimes one that had been passed down from a relative, and when he abandoned an old name there was often a younger relative waiting to adopt it.

This was the case in the family of Seen From Afar. At birth Seen From Afar was given the name Tenderloin, or Osahko,[2] while as a teenager he was called Mad Wolf, or Siyeh.[3] Then he took the name Calf Rising in Sight, or Aponistai'nakoyim,[4] followed by Bull Collar, or Stamiks'ohkimi,[5] and finally, Seen From Afar. To add to the confusion for scholars, Seen From Afar's father had previously been named Seen From Afar.[6] It was only after he had given that name to his boy that he took the new name Two Suns. Later in life the father was called Father of Many Children, a common name that was as much a title of respect for a chief as it was a proper name. In descriptions of the early years of the boy's life, it is sometimes hard to tell whether events happened to the father or the son.

During his teens and into his twenties, Seen From Afar was establishing his reputation as a warrior. His fame was born early in his teenage years and grew rapidly because of his sheer audacity. Seen From Afar proved quickly that he was afraid of nothing. He was what the Blackfoot called *awatixkasi*, a man who would take wild and unnecessary risks that seemed foolhardy, and yet he did them with finesse and style. One elder said that "He acted crazy and did not know what was dangerous."[7]

Several such events that occurred while he was a teenager became part of Blackfoot folklore. One incident took place when Seen From Afar went on his first war party. When the warriors reached the Crazy Woman Mountains in southern Montana, they saw a huge grizzly bear on the other side of a creek, ambling along a trail. Seen From Afar said to his comrades, "I'm going to hide in the direction where he is going so that he'll walk nearly on top of me. If he's looking for something to fight, then I'll fight him."[8]

His companions tried to stop him, saying that the grizzly would surely kill him. But Seen From Afar paid them no heed; he took off all his clothes except his breechcloth and went to the trail armed only with a double-bladed Hudson's Bay knife. He chose an open spot and lay down on his back, his feet pointing in the direction from which the bear would come. Soon he heard the beast snuffing along the trail. It was downwind from him and soon picked up his scent.

Cautiously, the grizzly lumbered forward to the youth's feet. There it scratched one foot to see if the person would move, but Seen From Afar lay still. Then the bear scratched the other foot, but still the prone figure lay as if dead. When he did not move, the bear straddled him and put his snout close to Seen From Afar's face to see if he was breathing. Seen From Afar held his breath. Then, just as the bear raised a paw to place it on the Indian's chest, Seen From Afar jumped to his feet. According to one account, written in 1880, "At this moment the boy, with the quickness and agility of a cat, leaped upon the bear's back, catching a hold in the long shaggy hair with one hand, while with the other he plunged the deadly dagger into the heart of the grizzly, killing him almost instantly."[9]

The storyteller concluded, "This feat was witnessed with the greatest astonishment by all his companions. From a boy he had attained the rank of a warrior in a moment by the daring deed performed. Loudly were his praises sounded ever after, but the killing of that bear was the principal act of his life, which obtained for him the chieftainship over his people."[10]

On another occasion Seen From Afar left camp with some friends to hunt buffalo just after a blizzard had swept through the area. When they came to a coulee, they found a number of buffalo trapped in the deep snow. "I'll kill one of these bulls without using my gun," said the young warrior.[11] Armed only with his knife, he leaped from the edge of the coulee onto the back of one of the buffalo. Terrified, the animal jumped and whirled and broke out of its snowy trap. As it dashed across the open prairie, Seen From Afar stabbed it again and again until the animal dropped dead.

The young warrior repeated this feat during the summer, when he saw an old buffalo bull following a trail through the trees. He told his friends that he was going to have some fun and, despite their warnings, climbed a tree and waited for the beast. When it reached him, the bull stopped to scratch itself on the tree. Seen From Afar used this opportunity to drop onto the animal's back and, grasping the coarse hairs of its hump, he rode it like a wild bronco. The buffalo galloped out from the grove of trees, twisting, bucking, and jumping as it tried to dislodge its unwelcome guest. At last, tiring of the game, Seen From Afar nimbly jumped from the buffalo's back and laughed as it fled across the prairie.[12]

Another time the Bloods were camped on a river near a high cut bank, below which were the swirling waters of a whirlpool. Before anyone realized what he was doing, Seen From Afar removed his clothes, walked backwards toward the cut bank, and—just before reaching it—turned and jumped over the edge. He was knocked unconscious when he struck the lower slope of the bank, then rolled over and fell into the water. His body was caught in the whirlpool, spun around, sent through the rapids, and carried to a shallow place. When his friends rushed up to him, he was on his hands and knees, crawling out of the water. His skin was red from striking the cut bank and being punished by the water.

"Why did you jump?" his friends asked.

"I just wanted to know how fast I would fall," he replied.[13]

To show his contrariness and his belief in his own powers, Seen From Afar often performed acts that not only challenged wild animals and enemy tribes but also the world of the supernatural. This was almost unheard of. Everyone knew that the powers of the Sun, the Thunder, and the various other forces of Nature could help or harm a man. People were careful to pay proper homage to them, for even the benevolent ones could become angry if they were taunted or ignored. Yet Seen From Afar was not afraid to challenge the most powerful spirits of the Blackfoot people. For example, during a storm, when the Thunder spirit's voice was echoing across the prairie, Seen From Afar would go outside his lodge and begin shooting at the sounds of the thunder as though challenging its power. On one occasion, when reverent prayers were being given to the Sky People, he taunted the spirits by deliberately mixing up the words and saying them incorrectly. People waited to see him punished for this affront, but nothing happened.

The same situation occurred when the Bloods visited a sacred spring located just west of the present town of Vulcan. It was known as Stretches Out Spring, because it would bubble up, shoot a spray high into the air, and then settle down again. When the Blackfoot tribes visited the site, they would pray and leave offerings. An elder recalled, "All that pass by stop and take a bracelet or collar or earrings or piece of tobacco and give it to the spring, saying 'I want to see you stretch out.' Then the spring gushes out then comes out. It is colored like fur. It hears when it is spoken to."[14]

One day, Seen From Afar went with a number of Bloods to see the spring. The others offered gifts, spoke to the sacred waters, and waited for the spring to erupt. Then, as the water began bubbling up, Seen From Afar suddenly threw himself into the middle of the spring. Just as his feet touched the bottom, the water gushed out and he was thrown aside. Then the bubbling stopped. Never again did it shoot its spray into the air. As before, people predicted that calamity would befall the audacious Blood, but nothing happened.

These were the kinds of actions that made Seen From Afar the center of attention of his tribe, showing him to be fearless, resourceful, and high spirited. But he did not rely entirely on his own prowess to achieve success. In spite of his willingness to challenge the spirits, he still strongly believed in his Native religion and sought the guidance of his own spiritual helper. While he was still a teenager, he had a vision in which a king-bird came to him. It claimed that it could not be defeated by any other bird or animal and said, "I give you the same power for your protection."[15] The young man was instructed to wear a stuffed kingbird in his hair whenever he went to war. When Father Nicholas Point met him in 1846, he noted that the chief "carried his extravagant credulity so far as to believe the little black and yellow bird, whose winged carcass he wore on the top of his head, was nothing more or less than the master of life."[16]

Seen From Afar was also notable among his people for bringing sacred objects from the Mandan Indians. This occurred in 1833, when Prince Maximilian came up the Missouri River on a pleasure trip, traveling on the steamboat *Flora*. The boat was some distance below the mouth of the Marias River when it picked up Seen From Afar and his wife. According to historian Jack Holterman, "In the spring of the same year, just after the breakup of the ice, Seen-From-Afar and his wife had come down from the Blackfeet post on one of the boats, probably a mackinaw loaded with winter returns. They must have continued past Fort Union and on down to somewhere around Fort Clark. This would explain how they evaded all their potential enemies along their way."[17]

At Fort Clark, Seen From Afar and his wife visited the Mandan villages, and when they left, he carried with him a sacred pipe that the tribe had presented to him. It became known to the Bloods as the Mandan medicine pipe. Meanwhile, Handsome Woman had been invited to witness the Mandan women's buffalo dance. She noticed how similar it was to her own tribe's *Motokix* ceremonies. Before she left, she was presented with the leader's headdress and medicine bundle. When she returned to the Bloods, she incorporated the headdress and parts of the Mandan ritual into her own women's group ceremonies.[18]

With his daring and reckless nature, Seen From Afar soon gained the reputation of being a great warrior. After his first ventures on the warpath while he was a teenager, he continued to lead raids against his enemies and their horse herds long after he was married. Unlike his friends and others, he was unwilling to settle down to raise horses and protect their camp. Stated one elder, "When he went to war, Peenaquim [Seen From Afar] would go on raid after raid. Instead of returning to his home camp after making a successful raid, he would send some young boys back with his captured horses and give them to his wife to put in his herd."[19]

In one of his first major conflicts with Crow Indians, Seen From Afar was with a war party that became trapped on the Marias River; he and his men were surrounded by two hundred Crow Indians and battled for four days and nights. Seen From Afar fought like a tiger, and although he exposed himself to the gunfire of the enemy on many occasions, he was not even nicked by a bullet or arrow. "He saved the party," recalled an elder.[20]

He was also involved in a fight with the Crees in the eastern part of his hunting grounds. An elder said, "Down at Cypress Hills there were three big encampments of Crees where he went among them and made a battle with them. At the north side of Cypress Hill he came to another big encampment of Crees. He went among them and made a war with them. Further down the east side of the Cypress Hills there he came to another two encampments of the Crees. He went among them and made a war with them."[21] In each of the raids he was successful in decimating the enemy horse herds.

While most Bloods admired Seen From Afar for his courage and success, there were a few who were jealous of him. Among them was Big Snake, a prominent war chief of the Followers of the Buffalo band. Big Snake already had an enviable war record before Seen From Afar ever went on the warpath, and he resented the attention being paid to the young upstart. The trouble began when Big Snake permitted Seen From Afar to join a horse-raiding party that he had organized. As they approached a Crow camp, Big Snake announced that he wanted a white horse, and if anyone captured such an animal he must give it to him. During the raid Seen From Afar discovered a white horse tethered to its owner's tepee. It was saddled and had a gun attached to the saddle. Quietly, the young Indian cut the animal loose and led it from the camp.

When the Bloods assembled after the raid, Big Snake tried to claim the white horse, but Seen From Afar refused to give it up. During the dispute the war chief grabbed the gun from the captured horse's saddle, but Seen From Afar's comrades forced him to return it. As he handed the weapon back to the young warrior, Big Snake said, "If you don't give me that horse, you will forever be cursed with bad luck and you will never steal another horse."[22] But Seen From Afar was adamant; he had captured the horse and he would keep it.

A few weeks later, Seen From Afar set out on another raid, this time traveling with his close friend and companion, Rainy Chief. They were the same age and traveled together on many raids. In later years Rainy Chief became chief of the Hairy Shirt band, and in 1877 he signed the Blackfoot Treaty with the Canadian government. On this occasion the pair were unlucky and came back empty-handed. After this Seen From Afar went out on many raids but always had bad luck. He tried everything to overcome the curse. He prayed, he sought the advice of medicine men, and he slept on isolated hills to seek a vision, but nothing seemed to help.

Still hoping to break the chain of misfortune, Seen From Afar joined Rainy Chief in a war party that was going to raid the Crows. After three days of walking, Seen From Afar stopped to rest at sunset, and as he lay down he noticed two large black crows. One of them spoke to him, saying that if he would feed them some liver and fat, they would tell him how to get rid of Big Snake's curse. He fed the crows, and that night he had a dream in which the crow spirit came to him.

"See that tepee over there?" asked the crow.

Seen From Afar looked and saw a tepee that he recognized as one belonging to his own camp. As he watched, he saw Rainy Chief's sister, Holy Woman, or Nato'aki, push aside the flap and step outside. Her face was painted yellow, and she wore a buffalo robe beautifully decorated with porcupine quills. She walked over to the woodpile, gathered a load of wood, and returned to her lodge.

"Go back to your camp," said the crow. "She is the only one who can overcome the curse that is upon you."

When he awoke, Seen From Afar told his friend Rainy Chief what had he had dreamed, and after a brief discussion the two set out for home. Rainy Chief's sister was a spinster who had a scabby face and lived alone. When they arrived in camp, Seen From Afar took his favorite horse, put two blankets and two robes over it in place of a saddle, and took this as a gift for Holy Woman. As he entered her lodge, she said, "Ah, at last you have come. I've been expecting you for some time. I can cure you."

"Big Snake is a powerful medicine man," said Seen From Afar.

"He is nothing."

After praying to the Sun spirit, Holy Woman told the young man to make a sweat lodge. When it was ready, she sat beside the lodge with him, rubbed his body with sagebrush, and painted his face. When this was done, Seen From Afar was joined by a number of holy men, and they all took a sweat bath.

"Tomorrow," said Holy Woman, "you will go north on the warpath. As you go over a far hill you will see many elk. Among them is a white elk. Take it." Seen From Afar was puzzled for a moment, until he realized that she was using a religious expression and that "elk" meant "horses." She told him that as the war party was returning south they would meet Big Snake, who was on his way to trade at Fort Edmonton, and that he was to give the war chief the white horse.

Seen From Afar did as he was told. He found the white horse, a fine buffalo runner, and offered it to Big Snake. However, the war chief said he could not take such a fine animal on the long journey to Edmonton and asked him to put it in with his herd.

On his return from the north, Big Snake invited Seen From Afar to a feast. "You must go," Holy Woman told him. She said that Big Snake would offer him a weasel-tail suit but that he must not take it or the curse would not leave him. Just as she predicted, the suit was offered while they were eating pemmican. "I am glad to have this," said Seen From Afar, and continued eating. When he finished, he arose and said, "My elder friend. I was glad to get this suit but now I give it back to you. It is your suit and you look so fine in it when you announce in the camp circle that I cannot keep it." With that he left the war chief's lodge and the curse was broken.

At his next opportunity, Seen From Afar went with Rainy Chief to raid the Crows. This time they were able to take the best horses from the front of their owners' tepees and return safely to their own camp. In the following months there was no doubt that Seen From Afar was again the daring and successful raider and warrior of old.

Some time later, Seen From Afar led a war party that raided a Cree camp on the Bow River. When the enemy discovered their loss, four separate war parties were quickly formed and went in pursuit. When Seen From Afar saw them coming, he jumped off his horse and told the others to flee. As the Cree warriors approached, he fought them off and delayed them until his comrades made their escape.[23]

But perhaps Seen From Afar's most famous fight occurred when he actually invited his enemies to attack him. He was still a young man at the time and was using the name Bull Collar, while his friend Rainy Chief was known as White Wolf. On this particular raid, Seen From Afar and Rainy Chief were partners in organizing a war party in quest of Crow horses. All the others in their party were young teenagers. They traveled south to the Yellowstone country, where they found two large bands of Crows camping together to hold their Sun Dance. The camp was well guarded, and the Crows were obviously prepared to repel any attackers.

Seen From Afar and Rainy Chief watched from a nearby hill as the Crows put on a war dance. "It looks as though they want to fight," said Seen From Afar. "I'll flash my mirror to them so they'll come out to us."[24]

"No, my friend," argued Rainy Chief. "Let us not do this. We have with us young people who do not understand the art of war. We may lose some of them."

But Seen From Afar insisted. "No, we'll let the young men watch us. We alone will fight the Crows. The young ones can load our guns."

Then, while the Crows were still dancing, Seen From Afar took the spyglass that hung around his neck and used it to flash signals to the enemy camp. When the Crow leader saw this, he suspected a trap and warned his men not to respond.

"We are not women!" shouted a warrior. "We cannot let them flash lights at us. We must go out to investigate. If we pay no attention our enemies will make fun of us."[25]

So the Crows rode out to the hill where the Bloods had dug trenches. Seen From Afar and Rainy Chief stood separately, watching them advance.

Rainy Chief was tall and lithe, while Seen From Afar was short and looked like a boy. The Crows were surprised and, seeing an easy victory, they attacked the hill. At that time most of the Crows were armed only with arrows and spears, as there were very few guns in their camp. The Bloods, on the other hand, had Hudson's Bay Company muzzle loaders.

At the head of the Crows was a chief of one of the camps. Armed with a spear and shield, he rode up the slope, intending to run down Rainy Chief and kill him. But the warrior jumped aside at the last moment and shot the Crow chief dead. The Blood warrior then scalped him, took his weapons, and sent the horse back to the Crows.

Meanwhile, the leader of the other Crow camp attacked Seen From Afar, and he too was slain. As the Crows continued their assault, Rainy Chief and Seen From Afar stood in plain sight at the edge of some brush. Behind them were fortifications holding the young men. Each time the two Bloods fired their guns, they passed them to the others to reload. During this time an older Crow chief tried to lead another attack, but he too was killed, almost at the feet of Seen From Afar. As each warrior fell, one of the Blood leaders counted coup on the body and took the weapons. These were tossed into the trenches for the young men.

After suffering several losses, the Crows believed their enemy possessed supernatural powers and retreated down the hill. As they prepared to leave, a Crow using sign language asked them, "Who are you?"

"We are Bloods."

"What are your names that you act so brave?"

"We are White Wolf and Bull Collar," said Rainy Chief and Seen From Afar, giving the names they were currently using.

When the message was translated, the Crows knew that some strange powers were at work, for their two chiefs who had been killed were also known as White Wolf and Bull Collar. Rather than attack, the Crows set guards around the entire hill and prepared to besiege their enemies. Meanwhile, messengers were sent to a nearby Shoshoni camp for reinforcements so they could attack in force the following day.

Just before dark a Piegan who lived with the Crows called out to the Bloods. "You've killed quite a number," he said, "and the Crows have gone to the Snakes to ask for help. They are going to put up a big fight tomorrow and fight till you are all dead. I tell you this because I belong to your people. You see where I'm standing? Just below there is a coulee going to the river. When it is night, go down to the river by this coulee and go free."[26] Just before dawn, the Bloods found the unguarded coulee and successfully made their escape across the Yellowstone River.

According to a Blood elder, "When the warriors were all safely on the other side, they saw the enemy attack their trenches. When they found that the Bloods were gone, they cried and tore their hair they were so angry. We killed many of their warriors while none of the Bloods were hurt."[27]

Instead of fleeing back to their own hunting grounds, Seen From Afar and his party remained hidden in the district for several days, then they descended upon the same Crow camp at night and took a large number of their horses. Satisfied, they finally returned home in victory.

The audacious actions of Seen From Afar and Rainy Chief in exposing themselves to the enemy were told and retold around the campfires of the Blackfoot Nation. In honor of the event the young warrior's father gave him his own name, Seen From Afar, while he took the new name Two Suns. He also declared that his son was now chief of their band. This incident likely occurred in the 1830s, while the younger Seen From Afar was in his twenties.

On another occasion Seen From Afar and Rainy Chief went to raid the Crows, taking four young men with them. These were Medicine Calf, Kit Fox Head, and two others. Medicine Calf later became a chief of the Many Tumours band and signed treaties with the Americans in 1855 and with the Canadian government in 1877. Kit Fox Head was Seen From Afar's nephew.

This time they did not get away so easily after they had raided a Crow camp. Instead, they were pursued and had to take shelter on a bare hillock. Once the Bloods were surrounded, the Crows decided not to attack but to encircle them and wait them out. This occurred in the middle of summer, and there was no water anywhere on the hill. For two days and nights the Crows guarded the war party. On the third day thirst forced the Bloods to urinate onto a blanket, where the liquid was filtered and drunk. On the fourth day the Crows attacked, and although they were repulsed, Kit Fox Head was wounded and began to cry for water. That night, Rainy Chief and Seen From Afar scouted around the top of the hill and discovered an unguarded buffalo trail that led down a shallow coulee to the river. They went down the trail, each filled a water bag, and they then returned to the hill, where Kit Fox Head was the first to receive water. After the wounded man was refreshed, Rainy Chief and Seen From Afar led the Bloods down the secret trail and they safely made their escape.[28]

Some time after he had been made a chief, Seen From Afar took his followers into the foothills for the winter, not far from the Chain Lakes, west of the present town of Nanton. The tribe usually hunted near the Cypress Hills in the summer, traded with the Americans at Fort Benton or the British at Fort Edmonton in the fall, and then picked a protective campsite for the winter where they would not be too far from the buffalo herds. The favorite sites of the tribe were on the Red Deer River, along the Highwood, and in the region of the Belly and St. Mary's Rivers. Each area had plenty of trees for firewood and was close to the buffalo range. On this occasion Seen From Afar's followers fared well through the winter, but in the early spring the foothills were subjected to a series of savage blizzards that prevented them from leaving their camp. To make matters worse, the buffalo herds had already drifted out onto the prairie, so the Bloods were left to starve.

After several days some desperate families began to catch fish in the Chain Lakes. This action was almost unheard of, for the Bloods considered fish to be part of the Underwater People, who were evil. But desperation knows no limits, and soon everyone in the band was subsisting on fish. When the storms finally passed, the Bloods resumed their diet of buffalo meat, but from that time on the band was known as the Fish Eaters, or Mamyowi. It is a name that has stayed with them to this day and has been transformed from a term of mild derision to one that now reflects influence and power.

Seen From Afar came from a large family consisting of brothers, half brothers, and at least two sisters. Among his brothers and half brothers were Black Bear, Big Plume, Scalp Robe, Had a Big Chief, and Went With the Sun.[29] His sisters included Holy Snake and Antelope Woman. His brother Big Plume was much like Seen From Afar, wild and reckless, while Scalp Robe was a healer. But politically, the most important of his siblings was Holy Snake, a strong-minded woman whose actions would ultimately affect her brother's entire career. Her Blackfoot name was Natoyist'siksina, but traders shortened it to Natawista, or just plain Nattie. She was described by naturalist James J. Audubon as "handsome and really courteous and refined in many ways."[30]

In the autumn of 1840 the Fish Eaters band went on a trading expedition to Fort Union, at the confluence of the Missouri and Yellowstone Rivers. The chief factor there was Alexander Culbertson, a Pennsylvanian who had recently joined the American Fur Company and taken charge of the fort. There he became responsible for garnering the Blackfoot trade.

Culbertson had earlier married a Blackfoot girl, but she had returned to her people. Historian Jack Holterman believes she may have been a captive who had escaped from the Crows and turned up at his fort. If Culbertson wished to cement his relations with the Blackfoot, he knew that one way to accomplish this was to form an alliance with one of the leading families by marrying one of their women. When he saw Holy Snake, he knew she was the one. Artist Rudolf Kurz described her as "one of the most beautiful Indian women. . . . She would be an excellent model for a Venus."[31]

According to Holy Snake's great-granddaughter, "Culbertson, standing on the bastion of the fort, looked through his spy glass with more than ordinary interest. At thirty, he was in line to succeed Kenneth McKenzie as chief factor of the American Fur Company, but that day his interest was certainly more than commercial as the cavalcade galloped into view."[32]

Holy Snake was several years younger than Seen From Afar, so her older brother was responsible for any marriage arrangements. According to the great-granddaughter, "Culbertson, as soon as he saw the smoke drift up from the chief's lodge, sent a clerk from the fort with nine fine horses to tie to the door of Natawistacha-Iskana's elder brother's lodge. Apparently the presents and offer it implied were well received, if not expected, for on the following day nine horses of equal value were fastened to the door of the major's quarters. Shortly afterward the bride-to-be was escorted to Fort Union by her family and presented to the bridegroom."[33]

After this brief ceremony Holy Snake became known among whites as the "Major's Lady" and the "First Lady of the Upper Missouri," while Seen From Afar was often referred to simply as "Mr. Culbertson's brother-in-law." The relationship between Seen From Afar and the American traders was an ambivalent one, for the chief seemed to be genuinely fond of Culbertson, but at the same time he generally despised white people.

This hatred intensified in 1844, when two American Fur Company employees fired a cannon and killed several innocent people in a Blackfoot trading party. In retaliation the Blackfoot attacked Fort Piegan and burned it to the ground. Culbertson was able to calm the situation and built Fort McKenzie to replace the destroyed fort, but it did nothing to allay Seen From Afar's hostility against the traders.

This distrust was demonstrated in 1846, when the chief met Father Nicholas Point, a Jesuit priest who was laboring among the Flatheads and was trying to extend his ministries to the Blackfoot. When the opportunity arose, the priest accompanied an interpreter from Fort Lewis who was going to Seen From Afar's camp. Upon arrival Father Point went to the chief's tepee, which he described as follows:

> The lodge was equipped with everything it needed to be the lodge of a grand chief and medicine man of the first rank. Between the fireplace in the middle of the enclosure and the place farthest from the door, which was that of the master, there were a large crescent, a very elegant metal perfuming pan, all the material needed for the calumet, a basin full of water to quench the thirst of the smokers and, to make this more convenient, a goblet floating on the surface of the water. Above all this there was a richly decorated medicine calumet, a kind of scepter with a little bell on it, a feather bonnet, some boxes, arms, and receptacles of every sort.
>
> At the back of the lodge, opposite the opening, there was a bed of rich furs. To the right there was an elbow rest formed by a tripod. Beneath the tripod there was the living symbol of vigilance and nearby, the symbol of fidelity. That is, to the right and to the left of the chief were a cock and a dog.[34]

Seen From Afar was cool to his clerical visitor, but he invited a number of the leading men to his lodge so that they could hear his words. After they had smoked a pipe, Father Point made an appeal for peace between the Flatheads and Blackfoot and said it would be advantageous to the nation if he established a mission among them. Instead of his words being met with nods and mutterings of agreement, there was total silence. At last Seen From Afar turned to the interpreter and wondered aloud if the priest was telling the truth. "How is it," he asked, "that he tells the truth when the truth has never come from the mouth of a single white man?"[35]

The interpreter assured Seen From Afar that priests did not lie, and after some discussion the Blood leader permitted Father Point to baptize some of the children in the camp. Because of this concession, the priest believed that Seen From Afar had been "partly" converted to Christianity. Of course he was just fooling himself; the Blood leader had simply extended a courtesy to the visitor because of the recommendation of the interpreter. His general attitude towards whites was well known.

However, there can be no question that the marriage of Seen From Afar's sister to Culbertson was of great advantage to the chief. At that time the Bloods were divided into two main groups, one hunting in the northern part of their range, as far north as the Red Deer River, and the other in the southern range, south to the Missouri River. Bull Back Fat, chief of the Followers of the Buffalo band, was leader of the northern bands, while Seen From Afar of the Fish Eaters band had taken over the southern group. As trade with the Americans increased during the 1830s and 1840s, more of the northern bands gravitated to the south, and Bull Back Fat gained dominance over the entire tribe. But after the wedding of Holy Snake, Seen From Afar's fortunes began to rise. According to an elder, "One reason Peenaquim was chief was that his brother-in-law, Mr. Culbertson, used to give him all kinds of gifts and made him the richest warrior among the Bloods. He used to have whole rings of tobacco, bags filled with arrowheads, and many other things."[36]

With wealth came increased power and prominence, and by the 1840s Seen From Afar had surpassed Bull Back Fat in influence. The deference paid to him by the fur traders, his continued raids on enemy camps, and his reputation as a generous and lucky chief caused many Bloods to look to him for tribal leadership. At the height of his career Seen From Afar had ten wives and one hundred horses. He was rich enough to own two lodges and divided his wives between them. Handsome Woman was his favorite, or "sits beside him" wife, who sat next to him in their tepee. Another wife was responsible for the cooking, another for waiting on the chief, and yet another for looking after his medicine bundles.[37]

The chief was one of the few Bloods to own a tepee made of thirty buffalo skins, a huge structure reserved for the wealthy who had performed daring war deeds. According to James Bradley, "At Flatwood in 1848, Maj. C[ulbertson] saw a lodge of 30 skins owned by a Blood chief named Pe-in-ah Coo-yem [Seen From Afar]—the lodge poles were 35 feet long, and it contained two fires."[38] One of these fireplaces was used only for religious purposes. The tepee was so large that it was made in two pieces, each being a full load for a horse when the band moved camp.

This tepee was painted with a buffalo-head design that was given to the chief in a vision. Seen From Afar saw the tepee in his dream, and as he walked around it, the spirit owner called him inside. "I know you would like to own my tepee," said the spirit. "I give it to you as a present. I also have a medicine bundle that goes with this tepee. It is a bundle of buffalo stones and there are some horse tails that you will hang from each ear lap of this tepee."[39] When he awoke, Seen From Afar painted the buffalo-head design on his tipi. It was, according to Cecile Black Boy, "one of the oldest tipis the Blackfoot Indians ever had."[40]

When he traveled, Seen From Afar carried his own sweat lodge on a travois and made it available to anyone who wanted to use it. When the band went hunting, poor people came to him to borrow a good buffalo-running horse, and he never refused them. He also kept a supply of tanning tools, awls, knives, and other objects that he loaned to his followers.

By the early 1850s there was no doubt that Seen From Afar was the leading chief of the Blood tribe, if not of the entire Blackfoot Nation. When he went to Fort Benton, either to trade or to visit his sister, he was accorded the honors befitting a chief. For example, when he arrived at the fort in 1854, a scribe wrote, "A party of Blood Indians arrived for trade, headed by Mr. Culbertsons Bro in Law. Gave them a salute and hoisted our flag."[41]

The timing of Seen From Afar's leadership was fortuitous for the Bloods, for in 1853 the U.S. Congress appropriated $150,000 so that explorations could be made to determine the best railway route across the plains. One of these lines was from St. Paul, Minnesota, through Blackfoot country to Puget Sound. In order to explore this route, Isaac I. Stevens, newly appointed governor of Washington Territory, was selected to negotiate a treaty with the Blackfoot, Assiniboines, Crows, and other tribes in the area. To assist them, Alexander Culbertson was appointed special agent to the Blackfoot Indians. When the commissioners arrived to make the treaty, Seen From Afar and Bull Back Fat were in the north,

Seen From Afar, Peenaquim, was considered by the Blood Indians to have been their greatest chief. A fearless warrior, he was leader of the Fish Eaters band and signed the 1855 treaty with the American government. This sketch was made at the treaty grounds by artist Gustavus Sohon.
Courtesy Glenbow Archives, Calgary, AB, cat. no. NA-360-16

hunting near the Cypress Hills. When they were notified, they moved their camps to the mouth of Judith River in time for a meeting in mid-October 1855.

During the treaty discussions Governor Stevens emphasized two main points: that there should be peace among the tribes, and that all promises made by the white man at the treaty would be kept. The fact that the Indians would be surrendering a vast tract of land to the U.S. government was not emphasized. After some discussion the commissioners read sixteen clauses that constituted the "Articles of agreement and convention made and concluded at the council-ground on the Upper Missouri, near the mouth of the Judith River, in the Territory of Nebraska, this seventeenth day of October, in the year one thousand eight hundred and fifty-five."[42] They promised peace between the government and the Indian tribes and designated the location of the Blackfoot hunting grounds. In exchange for signing the treaty, the government promised payments of $20,000 a year for ten years.

When it was time for the Indians to speak, Seen From Afar was the only voice heard from the Blood tribe. He was concerned that the Crow Indians had failed to appear. "I wish to say that as far as we old men are concerned," he said, "we want peace and to cease going to war; but I am afraid that we cannot stop our young men. The Crows are not here to smoke the pipe with us and I am afraid our young men will not be persuaded that they ought not to war against the Crows. We, however, will try our best to keep our young men at home."[43] Bull Back Fat was silent at the hearings, and no one had any doubt that Seen From Afar was the leader of the entire tribe. Even the commissioner referred to him as "Head Chief of the Bloods."

When the document was prepared, Seen From Afar was the first to sign for his tribe. He did so under his name Calf Rising in Sight. After him came Father of All Children (or Bad Head), Bull Back Fat, Heavy Shield (or Many Spotted Horses), Medicine Calf (or Button Chief), and Calf Shirt.

Seen From Afar referred to himself as an old man who was seemingly not interested in war, yet he was only forty-six and just eight years earlier he had led a massive war party against the Assiniboines. About the same time he had also joined Old Sun, leader of the Siksikas, to raid Cree camps in the far north. When they reached the North Saskatchewan

River, they encountered a fleet of boats taking furs downstream from Fort Edmonton. Seen From Afar's nephew, Red Crow, was also a member of the war party. He stated, "The white men landed on our side, and we sat in a big circle and received many presents. There were three principal chiefs in our party, who took the goods and distributed to all. The white men told us that the gifts were to encourage us to trade with them. Blankets, tobacco, and goods of all kinds were given to us. In return some of the men took off their fancy dress, and presented them to the chief of the boat people."[44]

From there the war party proceeded along the river until they found a Cree camp. In the attack Seen From Afar saw a Cree chief named Handsome Man coming out of his lodge, so he shot and killed him.

On another occasion the Bloods were camped near the Sweetgrass Hills, with the South Piegans some distance away at Blue Lake. During the night nine Crees stole some Piegan horses and fled eastwards, not realizing that the Blood camp was ahead of them. The next morning was foggy, and the horse raiders passed so close to the Bloods that they were noticed by an observant scout. Seen From Afar immediately organized a pursuit and led his warriors along the clearly defined trail. When they were out on the open prairie, he divided the party, with Calf Shirt going directly to the Cypress Hills while Seen From Afar's men continued to follow the Crees' trail. A short time later Red Crow saw the Crees far ahead and used a mirror to signal his uncle. In the attack that followed, the entire Cree party was killed.

Now that he was rich, Seen From Afar may not have gone on horse-raiding expeditions, but he was quick to defend his camp and his hunting grounds. Nor had his general attitude towards white people changed. When Alexander Culbertson retired from the fur trade in 1858, the chief's only ally among the Americans was gone. And when Culbertson left the territory, his wife Holy Snake, the chief's sister, went to live like a white woman in Illinois.

After the promises made at the Judith River treaty, Seen From Afar soon learned that he could not trust the government agents any more than the fur traders. The $20,000 annual distribution of goods included such useless items as fishhooks and coffee, while the bolts of cloth were flimsy and inferior. In addition the discovery of gold in Montana Territory brought a rush of prospectors, who often ignored the treaty and encroached on tribal lands. The results were conflicts between the Black-foot and the intruders, with bloodshed on both sides. By 1866 the U.S. Indian agent was of the opinion that "The Bloods, Blackfeet and most of the North Piegans are at open war with the whites. . . . They live for the most part in the British possessions, and only come here to receive their annuity goods or to commit some depredations."[45]

One of those wishing to avoid trouble was Seen From Afar's old com-rade Rainy Chief, who stayed on the British side and took his trade to Fort Edmonton. In 1866 Seen From Afar decided that he would do the same, so he organized a trading party on the Belly River; as they traveled north they were joined by the Siksikas under Big Swan, their war chief. The Siksikas, who had always stayed on the British side, had suffered at the hands of Cree war parties and were glad to accompany the larger contingent of Bloods. While they were traveling north they were warned of a Cree ambush, so Seen From Afar sent a message to Fort Edmonton, asking the chief factor to send a trader out to meet them. The chief factor described what happened: "I accordingly sent out Mr. Cunningham 15 men & 30 Carts and oxen. When they got to Pene'quiems Tent or Camp they found all the Blackfeet there. Cunningham began to trade but had not done much when the Blackfeet began to pillage them & talk very badly."[46]

The problem was that the wagons were driven by Cree half-breeds, employees of the fort, and the Siksikas saw them as enemies. They threatened to kill them, but Seen From Afar and Siksika chief Crowfoot intervened and saw the traders escorted safely back to their fort. In gratitude the chief factor sent Seen From Afar a chief's suit of clothing and a gun.

As a result of this confrontation and the hostility of the Crees, Seen From Afar was obliged to return to the Americans to trade, but he con-tinued to live in British territory. Then, in 1868, he was persuaded to return to Montana for another treaty with the U.S. government. The 1855 treaty had a ten-year limit for providing annuities; when that passed and a proposed new treaty was never ratified, the distributions had ceased. The Blackfoot, not understanding the finer points of law, believed that the government had lied to them and was now cheating them. To resolve the problem the leading chiefs of the Blackfoot Nation were invited to Fort Benton to sign a new treaty. It drastically cut down the size of the reservation, threw the area open for settlement, and promised annuities for the next twenty years. This document was signed by Seen From Afar as well as such leading Blood chiefs as Calf Shirt, Father of Many Children, and Big Plume. However, it too was never ratified.

Seen From Afar and his followers returned from the treaty and went into a winter camp on the Oldman River, just south of the Porcupine Hills. There the chief directed the building of the last buffalo jump, or *piskun*, to be used by his people. John Cotton, a member of the Blood tribe, recalled the event:

> We had piles of stones or anything we could hide behind; these formed two V-shaped lines from the top of the cliff back out onto the prairie for quite a distance. When a herd had been sighted, the people hid behind the stones and waited for the men to call the buffalo. These two men were known as *awah'kix*, or buffalo chasers. They had a call—oh, oh, oh—an owl-like call, which made the buffalo bunch up. When the buffalo got within the outer parts of the V, the people hiding behind those stones jumped up and stampeded the herd. The frightened buffalo ran forward and each time they swerved to one side, the people hiding behind the stones jumped up and waved robes and blankets at them. When they got to the edge of the cliff, the buffalo couldn't stop because the rest of the herd was behind them. At the bottom of the cliff we had built a big corral of poles. At the place where the poles joined, they were bound together with rawhide. The first buffalo over the cliff were killed by the fall or were trampled to death by the others. As the rest of the herd came over the cliff, some were only wounded or were even unhurt, but these were killed by arrows.[47]

Under Seen From Afar's guidance, the buffalo were slaughtered and each buffalo was divided among six families. One took the heart and shoulder, another the loin and part of the guts, a third the flank and ribs, a fourth a hindquarter, a fifth the paunch and fat, and a sixth a hindquarter and the rest of the guts. When they butchered another buffalo, the same six families each took a different portion, until everyone had a fair share.

In the spring of 1869 the Bloods moved out onto the broad prairies west of the Cypress Hills, then in the fall they traveled to Fort Benton to trade with the Americans. While they were there, they learned that a smallpox epidemic was sweeping the British territory and the Bloods were dying like flies. While camped near the fort, Seen From Afar had a dream on four successive nights telling him that he would be safe as long as he did not try to cross the Milk River Ridge that divided the American territory from the British. However, the chief knew that his daughter, Mink Woman, who had married a Blood-Piegan chief named Running Rabbit, was camped on St. Mary's River far to the north. Mink Woman was a *mini'poka*, a favorite child upon whom the father had poured his love and affection. An elder recalled that when Mink Woman was younger, "She was such a great pet of his that whenever a camp was broken up, not a tipi was to be pulled down if Mink Woman was asleep."[48]

Seen From Afar was so worried about his daughter that he decided to defy his spirit helpers. Mounting his horse, he rode through the Blood camp, saying, "My people, my children, the Sun looks down upon me. I am going away. My dreams have told me not to cross the Milk River ridge. Four times I have been told. But I have no power to stay here. I must go to my daughter. My people, I may not see you again. Live good lives and do the best you can."[49]

Then Seen From Afar and his favorite wife packed their belongings and rode north across the Milk River Ridge. They found Mink Woman alive and well and, reassured, they headed back south with her. However, when they reached the ridge, Seen From Afar said, "I feel a pain in my back. I have the sickness. I will die today."[50] He lay down in his lodge and passed away later in the day.

His wife and daughter took his body back to the confluence of the Oldman and St. Mary Rivers and placed it inside his huge tepee, which was pitched beside a gnarled old cottonwood tree. With him were placed his personal possessions, including six revolvers and two rifles. Twelve horses were slain at the tepee door so they could accompany him to the spirit world.[51] According to a tribal member who visited the death lodge later, half the ground inside was painted red and the other half yellow. Scattered around were white plumes on the yellow side and red plumes on the red side. "When he died," he said, "all the people cried for him because they liked him."[52]

Seen From Afar's death occurred just as the whole world known to the Blackfoot was changing. American freebooters were soon to flood the Blood hunting grounds with whiskey from their trading posts on British soil. This would result in the coming of the North-West Mounted Police in 1874 to bring law and peace to the land. Seen From Afar had detested the Americans. Would his feelings have been any different for the red-coated Mounties? Whiskey trader John J. Healy did not think so. "Peen-na-quim was at one time the great Blood chief and a brother-in-law of Culbertson," he recalled. "He died in 1869–70 from smallpox—a good thing, as his death made the settlement of the north easier."[53]

The leadership of the Fish Eaters, and of the whole Blood tribe, was assumed by Seen From Afar's older brother, Black Bear. However, he too succumbed to the ravages of smallpox a few months later, and so the Bloods looked around for someone else to take his place. Their choice was a forty-year-old warrior named Red Crow, a younger son of Black Bear. Proving to be the right man to cope with the changing times, he took his tribe into the new life of Mounted Policemen and reservations without war or the loss of their pride and prestige. He was also the second generation of Fish Eaters to dominate the tribe, a dynasty that was to persist throughout the next century.

As for Seen From Afar, he is still remembered as the tribe's greatest chief. A warrior, holy man, and political leader, he feared nothing and let his tribe be subservient to no one during his long career. It was a solid base for the tribe to build upon during an uncertain future.

9 The Last Great Battle

The two protagonists in the great battle of 1870 near the present city of Lethbridge were lifelong enemies—the Assiniboines and the South Piegans. At the time the Assiniboines occupied a huge area of the plains of southern Saskatchewan and were supported in their offensive by their Cree neighbors from northeastern Alberta and central Saskatchewan. Meanwhile, the South Piegans made northern Montana their home, and in this battle they fought side-by-side with their allies, the Bloods. The fight took place near the confluence of the Oldman and St. Mary's Rivers—a place relatively foreign to both tribes. The South Piegans had been brought together there by a lust for revenge, a fear of the American cavalry, and the traditional empathy that existed between the two tribes.

A number of factors led to the confrontation. One was the attack on a peaceful band of South Piegans at the beginning of the year by the American army under Col. Eugene Baker. There had been some animosity between the Piegans and the Americans throughout the 1860s, after miners and settlers invaded the tribe's traditional hunting grounds. In the inevitable confrontations parties were killed on both sides, until local residents were referring to the incidents as part of a "Blackfoot war." Then, in 1869, a family dispute resulted in the death of Malcolm Clarke, one of Montana's leading citizens. He was murdered by his wife's nephew, a young man named Pete Owl Child, after the two had an altercation. The killer took refuge in the camp of Mountain Chief, one of the leaders of the South Piegans, so he and his followers were proclaimed to be "hostiles" for harboring the fugitive. In January 1870 Colonel Baker attacked the supposed "hostiles," but it turned out to be the wrong band. Instead of Mountain Chief's village, he virtually wiped out the peaceful camp of Heavy Runner, killing 173 people, mostly women and children.

The South Piegans were convinced that the American army was planning to slaughter the entire tribe, so many of them fled across the line to "British possessions," the common American term for Canada. They spent the winter along the Belly, Oldman, and St. Mary Rivers, where they hunted buffalo and traded the hides at Fort Whoop-Up for whiskey, trade goods, and repeating rifles. In August of 1870 the leading South Piegan chiefs sent a letter to Col. Alfred Sully, the Montana Indian superintendent, asking if they could safely return to their old hunting grounds. When they received no reply, most of them decided to stay in Canada for a while longer. By the autumn of 1870, after extensive hunting and trading, they were among the most well-armed Indians on the Canadian plains.

Meanwhile, the relationships between the various tribes on the western prairies were decidedly hostile. In 1867 the Piegans caught thirty Assiniboine men and women going to pick pine gum and killed them all. Later in the year, a battle took place between the Crees and Piegans in which the Piegans suffered great losses. A year later, a Piegan leader and six women were killed by Gros Ventres, and a short time later there was a pitched battle between the Kootenays and the Piegans. In 1869 the Blackfoot killed the great chief Broken Arm while he was on a peacemaking expedition, and the Crees retaliated by killing dozens from that tribe.

Although the South Piegans had been shocked by the slaughter of their people at the hands of the American army, they had not altered their determination to protect their hunting grounds from enemy Indians at any cost. These circumstances set the tragic scene that ultimately was to be played out near the present city of Lethbridge.

In the spring of 1870 the "peaceful" Piegan bands that had wintered on the American side of the line met with Mountain Chief's "hostiles" at the summit of the Milk River Ridge, just inside the Canadian territory, and planned for their summer hunt on the plains west of the Cypress Hills. But first they went to Fort Whoop-Up, at the confluence of the Oldman and St. Mary's Rivers, to make a peace treaty with the Kootenays. Afterwards, the two tribes camped together and hunted buffalo, which were plentiful in the area.

In early summer the South Piegans joined with their relatives, the North Piegans, and moved eastward to hold a Sun Dance at the edge of the Cypress Hills. While the ceremonies were being organized, a Piegan scouting party accidentally encountered a lone Assiniboine Indian. Armed only with a revolver, the man put up a fierce struggle but was finally killed by Heavy Shoe, after which Black Eagle took his scalp and Strangling Wolf his gun.

The Piegans realized that there must be an enemy camp nearby, so the next day they split their warriors into two groups and went searching for them. Their scouts soon determined that the Assiniboines had gone into hiding; in order to draw them out, one of the Piegan war parties acted as though it was attacking the other. From a distance it looked as though a small band of Assiniboines was being surrounded and would ultimately be killed. As expected, Assiniboine warriors dashed out from their hiding place in the hills to "rescue" their comrades, but they quickly found themselves facing a unified force of well-armed Piegans.

Many Tail Feathers, a South Piegan, recalled the event:

> I had been out hunting and when I came home I heard of the fight and rode to join them. When I got there, they were having a hard time with the enemy. I heard that Mountain Chief had been wounded in the foot. The Assiniboine who shot him had also shot Young Pinto Horse in the arm. Then Bull Chief shot the Assiniboine's horse out from under him. Red Old Man was the first one to kill an enemy. There was a very long line of fighting and many of the Assiniboines were afoot and soon the Piegans had the upper hand. After that they rounded up the Assiniboines and drove them like buffalo, and they killed, killed, killed.[1]

Many Tail Feathers and his friend Small Wolf pursued the fleeing enemy right into the forested slopes of the Cypress Hills but then retreated to avoid being ambushed. "We turned back," he said, "and found that only one Piegan had been slain, Small Person, but we had killed seventy Assiniboines."[2]

Because of the danger of retaliation, the Piegans abandoned their camp and moved to Elbow Creek, south of the present city of Medicine Hat, and there held a successful Sun Dance. "We were very happy," concluded Many Tail Feathers.[3]

Perhaps, but the Assiniboines were not. They had suffered a severe defeat at the hands of their most bitter enemy and had withdrawn to their hunting grounds in humiliation and anger. Later in the season, while camped in the Qu'Appelle valley, their leaders sent messages to other Assiniboine tribes in the Last Mountain Lake and Wood Mountain regions, asking them to form a huge revenge party to attack the Blackfoot tribes. Messengers also visited Piapot, leader of the Young Dogs—a group of mixed Assiniboine-Cree warriors—and Cree chiefs Big Bear and Little Pine, who were hunting north of the forks of the Red Deer River. All had suffered at the hands of the Blackfoot and were anxious to avenge the calamity that had occurred at the Cypress Hills during the summer.

There were three kinds of war parties among the Plains Indians. The most common was the raiding party, whereby a few young men set out to steal horses from their enemies. They were not out to kill anybody, but if the opportunity arose they did not let it pass. Another type was a war party organized to protect their hunting grounds and their camps. More than anything, this was a show of force to discourage enemy tribes from invading their territory or raiding their camps. The third type of war party was the revenge party. This was organized solely for the purpose of gaining satisfaction and honor by killing as many of the enemy as possible. If, at the same time, war honors could be gained by taking horses and other booty, warriors could do so, but this was not the main purpose of the campaign. This third type—the revenge party—was the one organized by the chiefs of the Assiniboines and Crees, with a massive force of some eight hundred warriors.

They gathered at the Red Ochre Hills on the South Saskatchewan River in late October, then traveled westward, passing the Cypress Hills and making their war camp at the mouth of Little Bow River. From there, scouts were sent out to find their enemies somewhere in the vicinity of Fort Whoop-Up. The revenge party and the scouts had no way of knowing that Mountain Chief's band and other South Piegans had

OPPOSITE PAGE   Piapot, a leader of the 1870 expedition against the Blackfoot, was chief of the Young Dogs, a mixed Assiniboine-Cree band. Armed only with a staff, he urged his men to fight against overpowering odds and then led them in a retreat to their own territory. Piapot later settled on a reserve in the Qu'Appelle valley, where he died in 1908.
Courtesy Glenbow Archives, Calgary, AB, cat. no. NA-532-1

decided to spend the winter near the fort; normally they would have been far to the south in Montana Territory.

At the time the scouts set out to reconnoitre, the Blackfoot tribes had already gone into their winter camps. The Siksikas were far away to the north in the region of the Bow River, while the North Piegans were nestled in the Porcupine Hills near the Rocky Mountains. The Bloods and South Piegans were the tribes near Whoop-Up; together they numbered more than four thousand people. The Bloods were camped along the bottomlands on both sides of the Oldman River for some fifteen miles, all the way from Fort Whoop-Up upstream to the smaller whiskey post of Fort Kipp at the mouth of the Belly River. The South Piegans were south of them and south of Fort Whoop-Up, along the St. Mary's River. At this time, stated historian George A. Kennedy, "The South Piegans were well armed with repeating rifles, needle guns and revolvers, the Bloods were not so well equipped, while the Crees and Assiniboines had only old muskets, Hudson's Bay fukes and bows and arrows to depend on."[4]

According to Mike Mountain Horse, when the Assiniboines and Crees arrived at the Little Bow, one of the leaders had a dream in which he saw his people trampled and killed by a buffalo with iron horns. Taking this as a bad sign, he urged the revenge party to turn back, but he was scorned by another leader who proclaimed, "My children, don't believe in a dream. Advance and capture the Blackfoot nations—womenfolk and children. The smallpox killed off most of their fighters, so we won't be opposed by any great numbers."[5] In the end a number of warriors returned east with the disaffected leader, while the remainder decided to continue with their raid.

The Assiniboine/Cree scouts located a Blood village on a river bottom, about three miles upstream from Fort Whoop-Up. Either through carelessness or impatience, they failed to search farther along the river, where the rest of the Blood camps were strung out for miles, or up the St. Mary's, where the Piegans were encamped for the winter. They probably took back a report that a small camp of the Bloods had been located on the Oldman River and would be an easy prey and an appropriate target for their revenge.

Just before dawn on or about November 1, the Assiniboines and Crees arrived at the brow of the hill overlooking the river.[6] Below them, in semidarkness, was a camp of eleven tepees of the Fish Eaters band under the leadership of Chief Mountain. The camp was on the northeast side of the river closest to the attackers, while a larger camp was across the river on the southwest side. The Assiniboines attacked the smaller camp, shouting "We are here!"[7] then firing into the tepees and killing one man and several women in the first onslaught.[8] A Blood named White Man Running Around, who was a boy of eleven at the time, remembered when the raid began. "The Assiniboines attacked us early in the morning before sunrise," he said. "Nine of the Bloods were killed and I was wounded."[9] The camp, although completely surprised, quickly responded and put up a spirited defence. One woman, Sinai'aki, killed three of the enemy with an axe when they entered her lodge, while at the same time some of the men used their modern rifles to hold back the raiders. Meanwhile, the noise of gunfire alerted the camp on the other side of the river, but in the darkness they could not tell what was happening. Several woman from the beleaguered village fled across the river, and one of them, Morning Star, gave news of the attack to Heavy Shield, leader of the Many Fat Horses band.[10] The Bloods quickly gathered their horses and raced across the river to rescue their comrades.

Some of the Assiniboines tried to round up the Blood horse herd, but they had to abandon the effort when the counterattack began. Two Crees, Day Horn and Medicine Rope, managed to mount one horse and ride away. The other men were surrounded and trapped. Piapot, leader of the Young Dogs, carried a curved staff as he rode among his men, urging them into battle.

When the first streaks of dawn colored the eastern skies, the Bloods became aware of the size of the huge revenge party they were facing. The Assiniboines and Crees also saw their enemies for the first time, and they were not what they had expected. Stated Mountain Horse, "At break of day warriors from the Blackfoot camps north and south could be seen approaching on horseback, in twos and threes, over hills and knolls, chanting their war songs in anticipation of battle."[11]

One of the rescuers was White Wolf, who recalled, "During the night I woke up and heard shots. At daylight we discovered who was attacking us. Just about daylight I jumped out of my tipi. I got on my horse and headed for the enemy with the rest of our [men]."[12] In preparation for war White Wolf had stripped to the waist, donned his red leggings and breechcloth, and placed his sacred feathers on his head. These were his

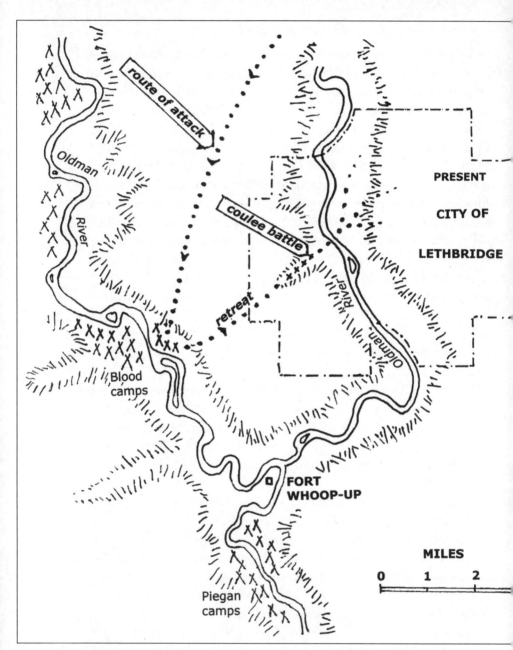

This map shows the route followed by the Assiniboines and Crees when they attacked Blood camps in 1870. In the subsequent battle they withdrew to a narrow coulee, where the fight continued for hours. Finally, the Assiniboines and Crees retreated, but they suffered great losses when they tried to escape across the Oldman River.

"medicine" to protect him from harm. He carried a shield and had a large knife and repeating rifle as his weapons.

As soon as the raid began, a messenger had been sent to the South Piegans for help. Mountain Chief, a twenty-two-year-old warrior, was in camp at the time. "The people were just getting up in the morning when the news came that the lower camp had been attacked by the Crees," he said. "I got my best horse; it was a gray horse. My father led his band in company with Big Lake who that summer had been elected a big chief. We rode up over the ridge while in the plain below the battle was raging. As we rode down the hill slope, I began to sing my war song. I carried the shield in my hand and this song that I sung belonged to that shield."[13] The song contained the words, "My body will be lying on the plains." Mountain Chief believed that his shield and song had the spiritual power to protect him from bullets.

When the Assiniboines saw how they had misjudged their enemy's strength, they must have been horror stricken; some became panicky and tried to flee. "Look at them coming over every hill," cried one warrior. "We are outnumbered. Let us retreat!"[14] The Assiniboines moved away from the valley onto the tableland that stretched for four miles across a wide bend in the Oldman River. They retreated to the northeast, fighting a rearguard action against the Bloods who were now streaming up from their camps along the river and the Piegans who were coming from the south. The Assiniboines finally reached a long coulee that extended out from the Oldman River; there, two of their men were killed just as they reached the hill leading down the slope. Once in the coulee, the others took up strong defensive positions. Their horses were tethered at the bottom of the coulee, while the men rimmed the coulee and shot at any attackers who ventured too close. Although the Assiniboines and Crees were armed only with muzzle loaders and bows and arrows, they were fierce fighters and kept the Bloods and Piegans at bay.

At great risk to their personal safety, some of the Bloods were able to occupy a short coulee immediately to the south of the Crees. The space between the two coulees was only thirty feet wide in places, so lead balls, bullets, and arrows were peppered back and forth across the line with great accuracy. These two coulees became the main focus of the battle for the next four hours. At one point two foolhardy Piegans tried to ride through the "no man's land" to ascertain the strength and locations of their enemy, but one was killed outright and the other was badly wounded after his horse was shot out from under him.

During this phase of the battle, about a dozen Assiniboines and Crees were killed. Bravery was shown on both sides, but the Piegans and Bloods also saw the fight as an ideal opportunity to earn personal war honors by performing heroic deeds. In fact so many were successful that the battle became known to the Blackfoot as "Many Deeds" or "Many War Victories."[15]

Running Crane, a South Piegan, was crouched in the narrow coulee when he was attacked by Crees who rushed his position. A Cree fired at Running Crane, but the South Piegan returned the fire and killed his opponent. Then, before he had time to shoot again, he was grabbed by another Cree and wrestled to the ground. In the melee Running Crane smashed his enemy over the head with his gun butt and killed him. "This deed was well known to our people," said a South Piegan.[16]

Big Wolf, a Blood, was only fifteen years old, but he too joined the fight. When an Assiniboine was killed, he and two other young boys rushed forward to strike the body (that is, count a coup) and take the scalp. The two other boys struck the body first, but Big Wolf was the one who scalped him. This was a great war honor for a young man who had never before been to war.[17]

When the young Piegan warrior Mountain Chief arrived at the scene of the conflict, he galloped right into the Assiniboine lines and then rode out again while bullets and arrows were whizzing about him. This was simply an act of bravado, a means to gain a war honor that could be recited at ceremonies for years to come. Emerging unscathed, he abandoned his horse and found a vantage point on the side of the hill. The battle was then at its height and, as he recalled, "I could not hear on account of the roar of the guns and could not see for the smoke."[18]

The Piegans and Bloods surrounded the coulee, but whenever young warriors tried to attack they were forced back by a shower of arrows and withering gunfire. At one stage the attackers even tried to throw large boulders into the coulee to dislodge their enemies. Finally, some Piegans gained an advantage when they got behind a small hill that commanded a view of the long coulee. This had a disquieting effect on the Assiniboines, who gradually retreated down the slope towards the mouth of the coulee. According to Kennedy, Jerry Potts, a mixed-blood scout, had

Big Wolf, a Blood Indian, was only fifteen years old when he scalped a slain Assiniboine at an 1870 battle near Fort Whoop-Up. He was about to scalp another enemy when the wounded man fought back, so Big Wolf shot him in the head and killed him. Big wolf is seen here in 1927.
Courtesy Glenbow Archives, Calgary, AB, cat. no. NB-21-1

joined the battle by this time. While Potts was reconnoitring around the edge of a ridge that faced the river, he saw the Assiniboines begin to slip away. Realizing that this was the beginning of a general retreat, he signaled his compatriots to charge the coulee. When they did, the withdrawal became a rout.

"I was on horseback when the [Assiniboines] attempted to escape," said Big Wolf.[19] The fifteen-year-old youth was still looking for war honors, so when he saw a Piegan shoot an Assiniboine, he ran to strike the body and collect a war trophy. He was the second person to reach the body; Weasel Fat was there ahead of him and took the man's bow and arrows. Big Wolf grabbed a coyote hide and was about to scalp the man when, only wounded, the Assiniboine tried to get up. "I shot him through the head and killed him," said the young warrior. "I took his scalp too, and that was the end of my first battle."[20]

Meanwhile White Wolf saw the enemy retreating, so he jumped from his horse and led the animal down the bank of the coulee on the dead run. There he caught up with a number of Assiniboines who were slowly making an orderly retreat. He confronted a man who fired two arrows at him, but in each case the Blood deflected them with his shield. As the enemy strung another arrow in his bow, White Wolf raised his gun and shot him dead. He took the man's scalp, his bow, and the ten arrows he still had in his quiver. Then, when another Assiniboine was killed beside him, he took that man's scalp too.

A Blood named Calf Shirt arrived just as the Assiniboines began their flight. He had been out hunting; as he approached his camp, he had heard the distant gunfire. He quickly changed into his war clothes and picked up his sacred Bear Knife, which was supposed to give him the power of a bear during battle. As he prepared to leave, his father said, "If

OPPOSITE PAGE   Jerry Potts, a mixed-blood scout, was staying at Fort Whoop-Up when the 1870 battle occurred. He joined the fight, later recalling that so many enemies were fleeing across the Oldman River, a person could shoot with his eyes closed and kill a Cree. In later years Potts became a scout for the North-West Mounted Police.
Courtesy Glenbow Archives, Calgary, AB, cat. no. NA-1237-1

you are killed, I will take your horse and clip its tail and mane. I will dress only in a breechcloth and lead your horse to a bluff overlooking the camp where I will mourn your death. But if you are not killed and are wounded by an arrow, do not let anyone else pull it out; come back to camp and let me remove it."[21]

Calf Shirt agreed, and as he left the camp he started to sing his war song. When he arrived at the scene of the battle, some of the Assiniboines were deserting the long coulee and fleeing towards the river, but a few stayed behind, putting up a stiff resistence. Calf Shirt saw two enemy warriors—one a tall man and the other wearing a calfskin robe—who were surrounded but had killed several Bloods who had tried to attack them. Calf Shirt approached them on foot with only his Bear Knife as a weapon. The tall enemy fired an arrow towards the approaching Blood; the arrow penetrated Calf Shirt's wrist but only pushed out the skin on the other side. Rushing his enemy, the Blood grabbed the bow with his wounded hand and hacked the man to death with his Bear Knife. The other man held his bow in readiness, waiting for a clear shot, but before he could fire, Calf Shirt grabbed his bow and stabbed him.

After the battle friends wanted to remove the arrow, but Calf Shirt replied, "No, my father will do it. He wants it as a trophy."[22] However, by the time he was ready to go back to his camp, his wrist and arm had become so badly swollen that he could no longer stay on his horse. At last he was placed on a travois and dragged back to his camp.

"By this time," said a Blood,

everyone was angry at his father for making such a foolish request to his son. Someone ran ahead to tell him and when he saw the crowd approaching, he became frightened and ran away. This cowardice made the people more angry and immediately steps were taken to remove the arrow. Makes Many Laws cut the shaft near the point and cut the skin where the arrow protruded. He then took a pair of brass tweezers and pulled the arrow through the wrist and cleaned the wound. After doctoring the wound four times, the swelling went away, the old skin peeled off of his arm and Calf Shirt was cured.[23]

Mountain Chief recalled that when the Assiniboines and Crees began to retreat, he mounted his horse and raced after those who were trying

During the 1870 battle near Fort Whoop-Up, White Wolf deflected two arrows shot at him by an Assiniboine then shot the man dead. He took the enemy's scalp, his bow, and ten arrows in his quiver. When another Assiniboine was killed, White Wolf took that man's scalp, too. The warrior is seen here as a blind old man in 1927. *Courtesy Glenbow Archives, Calgary, AB, cat. no. NB-21-17*

to cross the Oldman River. He ran down two enemy warriors on the trail, then dismounted to face a Cree armed with a spear who was starting to enter the water. Mountain Chief stabbed him between the shoulders with his own spear, took the man's weapon, and went back to his horse. There he ran over another enemy who was armed with a gun; the man grabbed the bridle, but the Piegan swung his horse's head around to shield himself then struck the man with the butt of his whip. As the Cree fell back, Mountain Chief jumped off his horse and killed him. "When I struck him," recalled the Piegan warrior, "he looked at me and I found that his nose had been cut off. I heard afterward that a bear had bitten his nose off."[24]

Mountain Chief jumped back on his horse and met an enemy horseman who was retreating towards the river. Both fired their guns, but both missed. As they slammed into each other, the Piegan grabbed his enemy's quiver of arrows, but the Cree took Mountain Chief by the hair and tried to stab him. When the knife struck, it became embedded in the Piegan's war bonnet and was wrenched out of the attacker's hands. Quickly, Mountain Chief pulled it loose and stabbed his opponent to death with it. By the time the fighting was over, the young South Piegan had taken nine enemy scalps.

In their haste to escape many Assiniboines fled over the point of a hill north of the coulee where a steep slope led to the river. According to Kennedy, "Over this pursuers and pursued both rushed headlong, horses and men tumbling over each other, the men fighting and struggling for dear life, until the bank was reached and the fight became a butchery."[25] The Assiniboines and Crees rushed into the river by the score, and the Piegans and Bloods stood on the banks, firing at them with their Winchester and Spencer repeating rifles until the river ran red with their blood. At this point the battle became a slaughter. "You could fire with your eyes shut and be sure to kill a Cree," said Jerry Potts.[26]

Although many of the fleeing Indians reached the opposite bank of the river, they had not escaped the fury and wrath of their enemies. Warriors rode across the stream and continued the slaughter. During the melee a Blood named Calf Chief stabbed a Cree warrior named Skinny to death. In another place a party of Assiniboines and Crees tried to make a stand, but they were surrounded and about fifty of them were killed. Among the dead were two mixed-blood sons of trader Hugh Sutherland. The two, named Yellow Hair and Curly Hair, had rejected the tedious routines of a fur trader for the more thrilling life of their mother's people. When someone had tried to dissuade the pair from going on the raid, Yellow Hair said, "I suppose I have relatives beyond the Big Water who would be sorry to see me leading this kind of life, but how can I help it?"[27]

Another group of ten men took refuge in a grove of trees. They dug trenches and tried to hold off the attackers, but their only firearm was an old revolver; even this was useless, because their powder got wet in the river crossing. Mountain Chief was among the attackers, but his father told him and the others that there had been enough killing and it was time to go home. "So we took pity on the tribe," he said, "and let them go so they could tell the story."[28] The only casualty among the beleaguered ten occurred when one accidentally shot another with an arrow. The rest were permitted to escape.

After the battle the Piegans and Bloods began to count the dead on both sides. According to John Cotton, "42 Bloods, Piegans and Blackfeet were killed. They thought this was a catastrophe but felt better when they found that 173 Crees had been killed."[29] Mike Oka, who was a boy at the time, commented, "I never saw so many scalps in all my life as on the next day in a victory war dance."[30] To commemorate the event, stone markers were placed at appropriate sites on the battlefield. In 1887 Charles Magrath noted "small cairns of stones which mark the places where the different heroes fell. More especially may these be observed along the brow of the ravine held in the commencement by the respective parties, also on the ravine down which the Crees were driven."[31] In addition a large stone was placed at the foot of the coulee to mark the place where the last enemy fell, and two cairns were placed to mark the place where the Sutherland boys died.

While the battle was remembered as "Many Deeds," the battlefield itself was named Asini'itomoht-saiya, or "The Assiniboines, where we defeated them."[32] And almost every winter count kept by the Blood, Piegan, and Siksika tribes recorded the historic event. The South Piegans noted it as "The Piegan fought the Cree on Belly River in Canada and killed one hundred of them."[33] The North Piegans recorded it as "When we beat the Crees at Lethbridge."[34] The Bloods had the following three winter counts: "*Assinay/itomotsarpi/akaenaskoy*—Assiniboines/when we defeated them/Fort Whoop-Up,"[35] "The Bloods had a big battle with the

- 131 -

Cree on St. Marys' river near Lethbridge & killed 250 Crees,"[36] and "At Fort Whoop-Up, Cree Indians attacked the Blood Indians camps along between two rivers, Old Man's river and St. Mary's river, and strong force of Bloods on war path. Crees retreated, killed about over 250 of them."[37] The Blackfoot, or Siksikas, recorded it as "Big Battle around Fort Whoop-Up"[38] and "Crees, killed them all."[39]

There never was any consensus as to the number of fatalities suffered during the battle. Besides Cotton's estimate of 42 Blackfoot and 173 Assiniboines/Crees, a trader writing a month after the fight said 52 Blackfoot and 93 Assiniboines/Crees had died.[40] Other estimates were: 200 to 300 Assiniboines and 40 Blackfoot killed;[41] 100 Assiniboines/Crees killed;[42] 135 Assiniboines/Crees killed;[43] and two estimates of 250 Assiniboines/Crees killed.[44]

Because of the proximity of the battle to Fort Whoop-Up, the question arises as to whether any of the American traders took part. Howell Harris admitted to have been an eyewitness to some of the battle but claims he was not actually a participant. American sources, on the other hand, state flatly that the whiskey traders did join the fray on the side of the Blackfoot. The first press report, published in a Montana newspaper in December 1870, stated, "There were about twenty white men encamped in the neighborhood and they joined in with the Bloods and Piegans."[45] Two weeks after the fight, A. J. Simmons, U.S. Indian Department official among the Assiniboines in Montana, wrote:

> The Blackfeet and Piegans were encamped near St. Mary's Lake across the line in the British possessions; about fifteen white men most from Fort Benton in this Territory were with them trading whiskey and other articles for robes and furs. About November first the camp was attacked by a war party of Assinaboines [*sic*], who fired into the lodges, killing it is said, fifty three men women and children belonging to the Blackfoot and Piegan camp. The white men now joined with the latter and together they killed about ninety of the Assinaboines, allowing but a very few to escape to tell the tale.[46]

Simmons was concerned that the actions of the traders would cause the defeated Indians to seek revenge. "The Assinaboines now declare hostility and vengeance on the whites generally," he said, "for the reason of this party having taken sides against them and in favor of their enemies. I think it will be hardly possible for you to maintain peaceful relations with those tribes so long as worthless irresponsible white men go among them, pass through their reservations to British territory, trade whiskey and participate in their warfares."[47]

From his own admission Jerry Potts took part in the fight, and at that time he was probably working for the traders at Fort Whoop-Up. Two other mixed-blood employees of the fort, Alex and Charles McKay, also joined in the fray.[48]

Hudson's Bay Company trader Isaac Cowie experienced no animosity when dealing with the Assiniboines after the fight. He simply stated, ". . . the news came in of a big battle at Belly River, in which the Crees and the Young Dogs belonging to the Touchwood Hills, with other Crees from Saskatchewan, and Assiniboines from Wood Mountain, had been defeated . . . by the Blackfeet. About twenty of the slain had book debts at Touchwood Hills, which I had to write off to profit and loss, with the explanation 'Killed by Blackfeet.'"[49]

Indian Department authorities in Montana tried to blame the fight on the liquor traffic. Two weeks after the battle, Montana Indian superintendent J. A. Viall wrote to his superior in Washington, D.C., that "I . . . have to report on investigation that the fight was the result of Whiskey, sent out I have no doubt by parties at Fort Benton."[50] However, there is no evidence that liquor was involved.

The earliest account of the battle was provided by Charles D. Hard, detective for the U.S. Indian Department at Fort Benton. On November 9, 1870, hardly a week after the event, he wrote that he had "just learned of a severe fight across the [line] near St. Mary's lake between the Assinaboine and Blackfoot Tribes."[51] The British, on the other hand, did not learn about the conflict until some two months later. On January 5, 1871, Chief Factor William Christie of Edmonton House wrote this somewhat garbled account: ". . . I have just had intelligence of a Fight which took place on Belly River, between the Crees, Piegans and Americans. It appears that a large War party of Crees stole Horses from the Traders & Piegans at Belly River, before leaving, the Crees foolishly fired on the Piegans Tents, were followed, Horses retaken, and 53 Crees killed (we wont miss them) 2 Americans and some Piegans killed."[52] The two "Americans" were probably the Sutherland brothers.

The first press report appeared in the *Helena Daily Herald* on December 2, 1870, a little more than a month after the occurrence. Although not entirely accurate as to the tribes and the events, it did record the fact that a major confrontation had taken place. It stated:

> We have advices from the north of a desperate battle that occurred a short time since, between contending Indian tribes, in the vicinity of the British line. A war party of allied Gros Ventres and Assinaboines made an incursion into the Blackfoot country, and attacking the Bloods and Peigans, defeated them, killing nine. There were about twenty white men encamped in the neighborhood and they joined in with the Bloods and Piegans the next day, attacked the Gros Ventres and Assinaboines and, it is said, killed every one of them, except one, whom they permitted to get off to tell the tale of disaster. The number of Assinaboines and Gros Ventres killed was about one hundred.

The first Canadian press report of the fight—a highly inaccurate one—was published in *The Manitoban*, in Winnipeg, on March 4, 1871:

> A novel battle took place between the Blackfeet and the Crees some two months ago, in which the latter were defeated with the loss of seventy braves. The Blackfeet, having been trading with the Americans, were armed with the best breech-loading rifles. A formidable body of their hereditary enemies, the Crees, determined to steal a march on the Blackfeet and approached their camp at daylight. While the Crees were yet a good and, they imagined, a safe distance off, out came the Blackfeet, the breech-loaders came into play and down went the poor Crees one after another, until seventy of the band had bitten the dust. The discomfited Crees were astounded, demoralized, on seeing their fellows shot down by footmen so far off and could not comprehend matters until one of the victorious chiefs called out, "You are fighting now against 'Long Knives.' We have their guns." The Crees did not wait for further information but skedaddled unanimously.[53]

The fight might simply have slipped into obscurity had it not been for several factors. First, it occurred next to a trading post and was witnessed (or participated in) by a number of Americans. Second, it proved to be one of the last major intertribal conflicts on the Canadian plains. Third, in 1887 Jerry Potts, one of the participants, was persuaded to tell his story to Lethbridge businessman Charles A. Magrath and to show him around the site. Magrath's notes were passed on to medical doctor George A. Kennedy, who, in 1890, published a detailed account of the battle in the *Lethbridge News*. Finally, and perhaps most importantly, the fight took place within what is now one of Alberta's major cities. Magrath exaggerated only somewhat when he stated that "in future Quebec with its Plains of Abraham will be a mere 'hole in the ground' as compared to [Lethbridge]."[54]

The site is commemorated today by Indian Battle Park on the east side of the Oldman River and by the naming of Indian Battle Coulee, where the main fighting took place.

10 The Prisoners

Blackfoot warfare during the nineteenth century included horse raids on enemy camps, revenge attacks to resolve affronts, and pitched battles to defend camps or hunting areas. The conflicts might involve as few as a dozen people or as many as five hundred, but they all had one thing in common: the defeat of an enemy. In these continuing struggles there was little room for sympathy or compassion. A woman was just as legitimate a foe as a man and could be just as deadly. Even children of an enemy tribe could be considered suitable prey if the circumstances were right. In particular, their deaths might occur when an enemy camp was attacked and it was important that no one should escape to seek help from other tribes.

But there were exceptions, both in taking prisoners and in showing compassion. The following was a typical situation. A Blackfoot revenge party descended upon an enemy camp at dawn, intent on killing as many people as possible. Some of the raiders secured the horse herd, while others swept into the village, riding over fleeing men, women, and children, shooting them or killing them with spears and knives. Although revenge was their main motive, each warrior was also intent on gaining war honors and in capturing booty for himself. The greatest achievements were touching an enemy during a fight, knocking down an enemy on foot, and snatching away war objects such as a gun or shield during the actual conflict. Once the village was overrun, warriors jumped from their horses and attempted to gain more war honors. They tried to be the first to strike a fallen enemy or to count a "coup." They tried to pick up such objects as guns, bows and arrows, knives, shields, and tepee flags. And they scalped all of the dead, both men and women. According to one elder, if a man captured a gun, he was permitted to wear a shirt trimmed with human hair. If he killed an enemy or took a bow and arrows, spear, shield, or scalp, he could wear a shirt trimmed with weasel tails.[1]

During this melee, any men found still alive were quickly dispatched. Women, on the other hand, might be killed or taken prisoner. Either way, they were initially treated like war trophies, warriors striking them with their clubs or whips to count a "coup" on them. The most dangerous time for female captives was the first few hours after the raid. Depending upon the whim of their captors, they might be spared and protected, sexually attacked and killed, or killed outright.

When the Blackfoot recounted their war honors, they spoke about women in a matter-of-fact way, considering them to be just another coup. Crow Chief described one of his battles. "One Sioux ran out of his lodge and I shot him and killed him first shot," he said, "also a Sioux woman, and killed her."[2] Wolf Eagle, who was in a fight with the Crows, recalled "killing a woman and two children who were left behind."[3] In other instances they told how they had captured an enemy. Boy Chief was raiding the Sioux near Wolf Point when he saw two small boys, "and I captured both of them."[4] Similarly, Mountain Chief painted his exploits on a canvas and part of them were interpreted as follows: "The Piegans killed all the Kootenais but one boy, which Mountain Chief captured and brought home with him. Below he is shown leading the boy by the hand."[5]

When the Blackfoot went to raid enemy camps for horses, the ideal situation was to enter enemy territory, capture as many horses as possible, and return to their own country without being discovered. But if the opportunity arose to attack a lone hunting party or travelers on the trail without fear of its developing into a major conflict, then the leader might seek scalps and booty rather than horses.

An example occurred when a large Blackfoot war party under Big Crow set out to wreak vengeance on the Crows in retaliation for an attack they had made on their camp. After traveling for some distance, a warrior named Tail Feathers Coming Over the Hill became dissatisfied with the way the leader failed to send out scouts, so he split off and organized a war party of his own. There were seven in his group: Tail Feathers, Flying Calf, Double Runner, Chief Bull, Spotted Fox, and two young boys. When they came to a high hill, they searched the open plains north of the Yellowstone River with field glasses and finally located two enemy hunters. Leaving the boys behind to keep watch, the others followed a coulee until they came close to the hunters then dashed forward to attack them as they were skinning an antelope. Both men began to run, but Tail Feathers shot and killed one on the spot, while the other man disappeared into a coulee. Quickly, the rest of the Blackfoot war party rushed forward to share in the war honors. Chief Bull took the dead man's antelope shirt, Double Runner took his bow and arrows, another got his scalp, and they all divided his clothes.

Meanwhile, one of the boys on the hill saw the other Crow and signaled the direction he had taken. The war party followed his trail, finding a lone tepee at the bottom of a coulee. Tail Feathers approached the lodge cautiously, pulled aside the door flap, then jumped inside. Instead of Crow warriors, he found two terrified women—the wife and the mother of the man they had killed. He touched them both with his gun barrel, indicating that he had captured them, and as the others came inside, he said, "Don't kill these women."[6] Then, while the spoils within the tepee were being divided, the leader took the women outside and, using sign language, he told the older one that she had nothing to fear. He took some charcoal from the fireplace, blackened her face, tied sagebrush around her wrists and head, and told her she was being offered to the Sun spirit. In this instance it meant that her life was being spared and that she was being sent home to her own people.

In gratitude the woman told Tail Feathers that her family had left the main Crow camp a short distance away to go hunting and also that there was a large Shoshoni camp nearby where the men were as plentiful "as blades of grass."[7] Fearing that the escaped Crow had gone for help, Tail Feathers decided to leave immediately and to take the younger woman with them. But when the woman fought the warriors and refused to go, Flying Calf shot and killed her. Tail Feathers was furious, for both women were his trophies, but there was nothing he could do, so he urged them to leave before the Crows or Shoshonis arrived. When they got to the hill where the two boys had remained on guard, some warriors wanted to stop and eat the dried meat and crushed berries that they had taken from the lodge, but Tail Feathers convinced them of their dangerous situation and they finally agreed to go. They returned north by a different route, safely reaching their own camps.

A similar incident occurred when a South Piegan leader named Heavy Runner formed a war party to raid the Crows. There were ten in the party: Heavy Runner, Little Dog, Yellow Wolf, Morning Plume, Flat Head, Many Butterflies, Bear Paw, Black Plume, and two others. They left their camp near Verdigris Coulee, just east of the present town of Milk River, then went south to Warm Spring Creek, and into the Judith Mountains. There they discovered a newly abandoned Crow camp, so they followed the trail all the way to the Missouri River. At daybreak they found the enemy village on a small island, and during the afternoon they noticed two riders coming along the river bottom toward them. As they approached, the Piegans saw that they were Crow women who seemed to be heading back to their old camp. Using trails at the top of the bank, the war party followed them, and when the women stopped at their old campsite, the Piegans attacked. There was a broad slough between the Piegans and the camp. By the time they had crossed it, the women had fled into the bushes, leaving their horses behind. Heavy Runner, the first man into the camp, struck the Crow horses with his whip, claiming them as his prize.

As Boy Chief recalled, "Both women ran and hid in the low brush. When Flat Head arrived he captured one of the women and gave her to Yellow Wolf. Flat Head then found the other woman and gave her to Heavy Runner. They learned that the women had come back for a lodge that was all rolled for packing."[8]

But no sooner were the women brought into the camp than Heavy Runner, leader of the war party, killed them both. The others were angry, particularly Yellow Wolf, who had wanted to take his woman home. But Heavy Runner was unmoved; his action had been taken entirely for revenge. "The Crows killed my brother and his wife," he said, "so I had to kill these two women."[9]

Even if women made it safely to the Siksika camp, there was no guarantee, particularly during the first few days, that they would survive. There was always a danger that some hothead would kill them during the aftermath of the raid or that a person who hated their tribe would simply take his revenge.

Such an incident occurred in the 1870s, when about half the Siksika tribe under Three Bulls was camped near the Bow River. The Crees had suffered a severe defeat the previous year, so a huge revenge party of more than a hundred men and several women set out to attack one of their enemy's camps. At that time the Siksikas were scattered all along the river, so the Crees approached a small, mixed camp of Siksikas and Sarcees that was off by itself. As they hid in a coulee waiting for dawn, a Siksika woman noticed a strange dog sniffing around and knew that enemies were near. She immediately told the chief, who sent messages to the Bloods and North Piegans camped a few miles away. During the night the Crees drove off the band's entire horse herd, and in the morning they attacked the main camp.

Warned by the errant dog, the Siksikas were ready for them. During the night one of the tepees had been fortified by putting rawhide cases around its base. All the women and children lay on the ground inside, while men with guns were able to shoot though holes they had cut in the sides of the tepee. In the first attack three Sarcees and one Cree were killed. A Siksika who could speak Cree then called out and warned the attackers that messages had been sent to nearby camps and that help was on its way. But the Crees did not believe him and continued their attack. A short time later, heavy clouds of dust could be seen from the west and the north as Siksika warriors converged on the camp.

Under the onslaught of superior numbers, the Crees retreated to a nearby coulee where they were quickly surrounded. They tried to build breastworks, but shots fired from the top of the coulee drove them into a trap where the last of them were slaughtered. When it was over, 104 men had been killed and 10 women captured. The women were claimed as trophies by Blood and Siksika warriors.

A young boy named White Backfat was in a Siksika camp when the victorious men returned. "When the battle was over," he said, "I saw the men coming back. Many carried scalps."[10] While the boy watched, his father came along with a young woman he had never seen before.

"This woman was taken by a young bachelor in the camp," said his father. "She will stay here for a while until she is ready to be taken to his place."[11] She was one of the ten captured Crees.

A short time later, another man came to the lodge and claimed that the woman was his. White Backfat's father refused to give her up and told the men to sort out the problem themselves. The newcomer was quick tempered, and when he failed to get the woman, he stalked back to his lodge. Meanwhile the other man, the young bachelor, went to his mother and told her to fetch the woman. White Backfat explained what happened next:

> The quick tempered man saw them going home and had on his blanket concealing a knife. He walked toward the women and stopped them and asked the older woman where she was taking the girl. He said, "I ought to have this girl. I got her." . . . The quiet man's mother started to argue and the quick tempered man drew his knife. When my mother looked out, the quick tempered man had already stabbed the Cree girl. . . . The Cree woman was trying to protect herself and dropped down. The mother held the Cree girl until she dropped, then she ran home. People ran out to see the fight. Some men tried to intervene but the quick tempered man cut off the girl's head and threw it after the mother, saying "Take the girl now."[12]

After the killing, the chiefs met in council to decide if any action should be taken. They learned that the quick-tempered man had been the first to capture the girl but had then decided that he did not want her. When he abandoned her, the young bachelor had claimed her. The council decided that if the quick-tempered man had wanted to kill the girl, he should have done so during the battle, but once she was in camp he should have left her alone.

The quick-tempered man was ordered to dress the dead girl in fine clothing and to bury her. He took a good blanket, a dress, and moccasins and went to the place where she lay. He spread the blanket on the ground, dressed the woman in the fine clothes, and wrapped the body and the head in the blanket. The bundle was loaded on a horse travois and taken to the trees, where it was placed on a burial scaffold. No further action was taken, and no payment had to be paid to the young bachelor for the loss of his woman.

When women were taken prisoner, it was usually to provide a wife for a young man or an additional wife for an older man. Cree wives were most common among the Siksikas, who lived closest to that tribe, while the Bloods and Piegans favored Crow women. One man was of the opinion that Crow women were popular because they were "good to sleep with."[13] Women from across the mountains—Kootenays, Flatheads, Nez

Perces—also appeared in Blood and Piegan camps. Eagle Ribs, a Siksika chief, saw such a girl in a Gros Ventre camp. When he learned that she was from across the mountains and had been captured by the Gros Ventres, he arranged to take her, named her Gros Ventre Woman, and gave her to a young man named Ikata.

Some names in the Blackfoot language indicate the origins of captive women. A few examples are Cree Woman, Nez Perce Woman, Last Captured Woman, Capturing Woman, and Snake Woman. The existence of these captives was noted by a number of fur traders and travelers. For example, in about 1819 trader Daniel Harmon stated that during an attack, the northern Plains Indians "labour to take as many of their women and children alive, as they possibly can, in order to carry them home as slaves. They never torture these captives; but keep them to perform the menial service about their tents, or dispose of them to others. Sometimes they are adopted into the families of their enemies, in the place of children that they have lost; and then they are treated with all the tenderness and affection, which would be exercised toward a near relation."[14] In 1841 Sir George Simpson, while visiting at Fort Edmonton, noted, "When a war party makes a foray into their enemies' lands, they cut off every human being that falls within their reach, without respect to age or sex, except in the case of some few girls whose beauty is their preservation, and who are made captives and introduced to the hareems of their victors."[15]

When a woman was captured, if the man taking her did not intend keeping her himself, she was often sexually abused. For that reason, men seldom gave captured women to their brothers or close relatives. Rather, they offered them to men in their warrior society or to poor young bachelors in their bands. They were not taken as slaves, Harmon indicated, but as spouses, with roles not unlike those of Blackfoot women. However, if they were taken as second or third wives, they were often abused by the older wives and were forced to perform the most arduous and difficult tasks in the lodge.

The husband had complete control over captive wives, just as he did over the wives from his own tribe. He could beat them, mistreat them, and even kill them in a fit of temper without fear of retribution. The only exceptions were those wives who came from large or influential families that might take offense and retaliate by killing the husband. But a captive wife had no such protection.

A Piegan named Has a Knife was a ferocious warrior whose wives, both Blackfoot and captive, stood in terror of him. One day he was sitting in his lodge when a comrade noticed the captive wife scurrying away to get water.

"That girl is terrified of you," said the friend. "Why don't you scare her."[16]

So the man hid along the trail, and when the woman came by, he jumped out and stabbed her to death. Has a Knife was the owner of the Bear Knife and, according to a Piegan, "he was tabooed from frightening anyone by his power, hence his comrade made a mistake in suggesting this. He had to go through with it."[17] But because she was a captive, nothing was done about the killing.

Another example of the mistreatment of a captive wife is told in a well-known story about Big Snake, a great Blood chief. He was with a war party in the 1840s that found a camp of Flatheads near the present town of Cardston. When they attacked, they killed everyone except an attractive young woman. Big Snake counted "coup" on her first and claimed her as his prize. When they returned to their camp, everyone expected the leader to offer the girl to a young bachelor, as he already had two wives. But because of her beauty, he decided to keep her for himself and called her Pretty Face. For the first few days, she was tied to one of the other wives at night, and during the day she had to collect firewood, carry water, cook, and tan hides. According to elder Joe Beebe:

> She proved herself willing and an expert in everything she did. But in spite of her skilful nature, Big Snake continually found fault with her, and made up petty excuses to ill treat her. One of his pet ways of torturing her was to burn her beautiful face with the flaming end of a stick from the fireplace. He also had a club whip which he used very frequently; her long fine hair also did not escape his rough snatches till she had hardly enough to braid. All this he did for no better excuse than because she was in his way when he came into his tepee, though busy she might be by the fireplace doing her cooking for him.

If his other women remonstrated at his brutality because they saw no reason for his doing what he did, they too would get a lash or two from the whip, so they quit interfering. As soon as one sore was about to heal on the little woman's face, Big Snake would have reason to burn her a fresh one, and always on the face, till her beautiful features were one mass of scars.[18]

About a year after her capture, Pretty Face had just left her tepee when Big Snake pursued her and knocked her down with a club. As she fell between two tepees, a neighbor woman grabbed an axe and stood over her to protect her from her husband's wrath. When Big Snake left, the woman took Pretty Face into her tepee. She then arranged for her to escape and for her son Calf Tail to escort her back to her own country.

They slipped away that night and crossed the mountains, and when they arrived at the Flathead camp, Pretty Face convinced the young man that he should come with her and receive gifts for having rescued her. But when they entered the village, the woman accused Calf Tail of being the person who had beaten her. When he realized that the Flatheads intended to kill him, the Blood warrior grabbed a knife and stabbed the girl's father. During the confusion he successfully made his escape and returned across the mountains. When Calf Tail came back to the Blood camp, Big Snake chided him for interfering and said, "A good thing for you that you were a brave man. You were very foolish. You ought to know that an enemy person, especially a woman, is not to be trusted."[19]

Meanwhile, Pretty Face's brother was suspicious about the woman's accusations and did not believe that Calf Tail had been guilty. Through some friendly Indians he learned that she had lied, and because this had caused their father's death, she was killed by her own people.

There were times when the Blackfoot showed compassion. A warrior in battle might suddenly spare a man's life or let a boy go if he was too young to put up a good fight. For example, Many Stars captured a Cree girl who was just a child. He became fond of her, and during a peace treaty he permitted her to return to her own people.[20] On another occasion the leader of a Piegan war party went ahead to search for enemies. He found two lone lodges, and when he looked inside one, he saw a beautiful woman. He hid near the camp, and during the night he crept into her lodge and made love to her. He returned to the war party the next day but told them nothing about the two lodges. The war party stayed in the district for several days, and each night the man slipped away to be with the enemy woman.

Soon he began to have mixed feelings about his situation. As leader of the war party, he knew he should tell his comrades about the camp, but he did not want to see the woman killed. He thought about taking the woman away and letting the war party kill the others, but that would make the woman sad. He knew he loved the woman, so at last he took everyone in the camp prisoner, went to the war party, and told his comrades that he had married the woman. He then invited the prisoners to become members of the Piegan tribe, and when they accepted, they accompanied the war party back to their camps as free men and women.[21]

Perhaps the most detailed account of a woman becoming a prisoner of the Blackfoot was provided by Watches All, a Gros Ventre woman. The story begins in the spring of 1867, when the Gros Ventres and Crows formed an alliance to get revenge for attacks they had suffered at the hands of the Piegans. After searching the eastern ranges of the Blackfoot hunting grounds, the scouts located a number of Piegan bands camped on Maple Creek, a few miles east of the Cypress Hills. Believing that they were few in number, the Gros Ventres and Crows set out to exterminate them. What they did not realize was that the lodges seen by the scouts had been augmented by a large influx of hundreds of North and South Piegans, bringing almost the entire tribe together.

When the Gros Ventres and Crows came close to the enemy camps, the weather was stormy, with a mixture of rain and sleet obscuring the scouts' view. However, they did see enough to know that the Piegans were still camped along the same creek. At dawn the next morning the war party captured Piegan head chief Many Horses and his wife, who were out on the prairie butchering a buffalo. Both of them were killed and scalped, their bodies left in a sexually explicit position.

A short time later in the Piegan camps, a scout called out, "Everybody get up and look. A great herd of buffalo is coming this way."[22] But as the "buffalo" came closer, the Piegans saw that they were the huge revenge party of Gros Ventres and Crows. Still unaware that there were other Piegans further along the creek, the Gros Ventres and Crows attacked a few lodges that their scouts had seen. As soon as the raid was underway, large numbers of Piegan warriors streamed in from the other camps. "I saw more people than ever before," said Watches All. "They came like ants."[23]

The Gros Ventres and Crows took shelter on a nearby ridge, but during the fight a number of them were killed. In anger, a Gros Ventre warrior waved a gun in the air and shouted, "Piegans, here is your great chief's gun. I have killed him and taken it."[24] This was the first time the Piegans knew that their head chief, Many Horses, had been slain. In response they rushed the Gros Ventre and Crow lines and forced them out of their defensive position. The enemy retreated along a coulee that led to the Cypress Hills, and soon their organized withdrawal became a rout. Mounted Piegans cut down dozens of men and women who were fleeing on foot and then pursued the enemy horsemen.

"I was riding behind another woman," recalled Watches All. "Our horse stepped into a hole, and pitched forward. The woman was thrown off, but I was thrown into the saddle. The horse started up again, but stepped on his bridle, which checked him. A Piegan rode up and struck me with his gun. Then he took my wrist, and I dismounted as he did." Watches All had become a prisoner of a Piegan warrior named No Chief.

Meanwhile, the slaughter continued. Piegan riders circled ahead and trapped Gros Ventres as they rushed down a steep bank; others were separated into groups of four or five and killed. The Piegans pursued the enemy for some eighteen miles before halting the carnage. When it was over, eight Piegan men plus Many Horses and his wife had been killed. According to the U.S. Indian agent at Fort Benton, the Piegans "killed some three hundred, capturing some three of their squaws and two children, besides taking from them nearly all their horses."[25] He was right about the number killed, but eighteen woman had been captured, not three. Among them was Watches All's mother, who was claimed by a chief and then given to another man.

While Watches All stood in fear, wondering what would happen to her, a Piegan rode up and struck her. Having counted his coup, he took her beaded necklaces and claimed them as his booty. With the battle over the Piegans returned victorious to their camp, and the women saw the bodies of their people scattered along the trail. All had been scalped.

"We came to the camp about noon," Watches All said. "Everybody struck me. All day they came and hit me, and one man hit me on the forehead and nearly killed me." Watches All had been wearing a fine buckskin dress covered with elk teeth. A Piegan woman demanded that she take it off and gave her an old dress to replace it. Then she and the other captive women were herded together and cross-examined to find out whether the Gros Ventres or the Crows had mutilated the bodies of Many Horses and his wife and placed them sexually together. The captives, all Gros Ventre women, persuaded their captors that their people would never do such a thing. Convinced, the Piegans returned them to their captors' lodges.

Meanwhile, an argument arose as to who had captured Watches All. The woman was taken to a council lodge, where a pipe and stem, knife, and gun were placed on an altar. In the lodge she saw No Chief and the other claimant standing before the chiefs in council.

"I pity this woman," said No Chief. "I will treat her well. Everyone all over the world hears it. I will take good care of her." Watches All was then asked which man had captured her. She described how her horse had stumbled and No Chief had captured her. She pointed to the other man, saying that he was the one who had taken her beads. As they left the lodge the other man tried to kill her, and she had to flee to her captor's tepee. There some women hid her, until the man finally went away.

"In the morning the Piegan broke camp," said Watches All. "I had no moccasins, no robe, and only one dress. No-Chief always rode around me, and protected me from the many people who wanted to kill me. He had taken me for his wife, and would not allow it."

The following day, a warrior who had lost a son in the fight announced that he intended killing the captured women. "Bring out all the captives," he announced. "I will put them on my son's grave." The captives were hidden by Piegan women, but four of them were found and put to death. This satisfied the grieving Piegans, and when people agreed that the tribe's losses had been satisfied, a great dance was held. Everyone gathered in the center of the camp to proclaim their victories and show off their spoils of war. This included the women, horses, weapons, scalps, and other objects, which were exhibited by their new owners, while others tallied how many Gros Ventres and Crows had been killed.

During the dance someone offered No Chief two horses for his Gros Ventre captive, and he accepted. She was given to her new captor and, like No Chief, he prevented others from killing her. The man treated her kindly. "I always took care of my husband's little boy," she said, "and did my work, and got along well."

A few weeks later, an American cavalry patrol came to the Piegan camp and tried to convince the chiefs to give up the prisoners. Some of the leaders agreed, and a crier rode through the camp saying, "Sell all the slaves. They will run off anyway. We cannot keep them." But when the soldiers left, they had only three women and two children; these were placed in a boat and returned to their tribe.

When Watches All had looked after her captor's boy for several months, the boy interceded on her behalf and begged his father to let her go. He replied that after she had tanned ten buffalo hides for him, she could go. During the winter the Piegans camped near the Sweetgrass Hills, where the buffalo were plentiful. The woman worked hard at her tanning chore, but by spring she still had not completed her ten hides. Meanwhile the Piegans and Gros Ventres kept raiding each other's camps, and each time a Piegan was killed, Watches All's life was in danger.

In the spring of 1868 the Piegans moved to Needle Nest, then to Big Rock, then on to White Wolf, where two Gros Ventre women escaped. Watches All explained what happened next:

> From there we went to another place. When we made camp I went for wood with my sister, a Piegan co-wife. Then my sister sent me to my mother, whose husband had just killed a buffalo. I went there and my mother's sister (co-wife) told her, "Cook something for your daughter." Then I brought back meat to my husband, but my mother's husband was stingy with his meat, and scolded her. Then his Piegan wife said to my mother, "You and your daughter are living poorly. You had better run off." So when I brought back the plates (on which the meat had been carried), my mother said she would escape with me that night. She said she would wait for me all night. She told me to leave my moccasins with her, and I left them.

But Watches All's husband suspected that she planned to flee, so he whipped her and ordered her to sleep sitting up straight all night. The man's other two wives watched her, but towards morning they both fell asleep and the Gros Ventre woman quietly slipped away. She met her mother, and together they ran through a chilling rain to a nearby creek, crossed a high hill, and continued running until daylight. Then they dug a hole, hid all day, and set out that night to find the Gros Ventre camps.

If her life with the Piegans had been an ordeal, Watches All's flight was equally grueling. She had only her dress, a pair of moccasins, and her robe. Her mother did not even have a robe to cover herself, and neither of them had food or weapons.

The next night was cloudy and dark, but mother and daughter made their way to the banks of Cow Creek. While traveling through the brush, the mother heard an owl hooting and said the bird was calling to them and would lead them to safety. They located the bird at daylight, but there were no Gros Ventre camps. Instead, they saw some people coming across the prairie and, suspecting they were Piegans, they ran into the bushes and hid until they passed. Watches All recalled:

> At night it rained again, and was so dark that we could see only by the lightning. I was walking with two sticks. We came to the mouth of Cow Creek, where the banks were high and steep, and slid down. I was thirsty, but could not reach the water, so my mother held my wrist while I scooped downward with the other hand and thus got a little water. Then we crossed Cow Creek at the very mouth, and on the other side of the stream found a piece of gunny sack. I took this for a robe and gave mine to my mother.

They began to see steamboats on the Missouri, but they were afraid to hail them as they might take them to Fort Benton, in the middle of Piegan territory, or downriver to the Sioux. Instead, they spent the next day traveling along the banks of the river, hoping to find a Gros Ventre camp. They made a wide circuit around a sleeping bear and stayed in the timber as much as possible. Watches All's moccasins were now worn out and, using the two sticks as canes, she had to travel slowly. They had not eaten since their escape.

When they heard a steamboat whistle, they hid in the bushes and were frightened when the boat stopped almost in front of them to pick up firewood. Then they saw some Crow and Gros Ventre women, so they ran to the boat and got on board. It took them about ten miles downstream and dropped them off at the Big Bend of the Missouri, a short distance from its confluence with the Musselshell. There the women found a store, a saloon, and a small camp of Crows. Said Watches All, "The Crow women pitied us and cried over us because we were so poor, and laid down many robes for us to sit on, and felt the sores on our feet. The storekeeper had a Gros Ventre wife. This man opened a keg and gave us whiskey. There was an officer (soldier-chief) at the Bend whose Piegan wife had run off to Fort Benton. He was leaving to go after her, and gave us sugar, cloth, blankets, and a sack full of meat."

While they were recovering, a Gros Ventre named Bull Lodge came to trade and agreed to guide them to their camp. There were six men and four women in the group. They boarded a passing boat and floated down to the mouth of Milk River. Watches All recalled:

> The next day we all went up Milk River on foot; only Bull-Lodge and his wife were on horses. We kept on the trail, and came to a recent camp-site. That evening Bull-Lodge and his wife went on, while the rest of us went to sleep where we were. Bull-Lodge travelled during the night and reached the Gros Ventre camp, where the old men were still awake smoking. He told my brother that my mother and I were behind and that he had better bring us and the others' horses. Then the people came and brought us, and all were glad to see us again.

So ended the adventures of Watches All. She survived the ordeal of her capture and was alive and well forty years later.[26]

Just as there were prisoners who were captured by the Blackfoot, so were Blackfoot women and children taken by enemy tribes. They might be captured during a raid on a camp, waylaid as they went for water, or even taken while they were members of a war party. Quite often these captive women married, had children, and stayed with the enemy even when they had a chance to return to their own people. A Crow named Pretty Shield said her tribe often captured Sioux and Piegan women. "And because they were treated well they never tried to get away. They had the same rights as Crow women, and worked no harder."[27]

About 1879, a Siksika woman was living with the Sioux during the time when Sitting Bull and his followers were refugees in Canada. In order to remain on the Canadian side of the border, they had made peace with the Bloods and Siksikas; they had not made peace with the South Piegans in Montana, however. One day, when the Siksikas under Many Swans were hunting near the Cypress Hills, they came upon a Sioux camp. The warriors from both sides quickly formed into two lines facing each other, ready to fight. Then the Siksika prisoner called out in her own language:

"My children, take courage and tell us where you're from, if you are Piegan or Sarcee or from the South Piegans. If you are from the South Piegans, do not say so. The people here are their enemies."[28] Many Swans shouted back that they were Siksikas, but the Sioux chief did not believe him. He thought they were South Piegans.

To resolve the matter the chiefs and headmen of the two tribes came together and sat in a circle to decide whether they would have peace or war. As a pipe was being passed around, the Sioux leader told the captive interpreter that he was sure the chiefs were South Piegan liars. Many Swans responded by sending for his pipe; he said he would smoke and tell only the truth. If the Sioux did not believe him, then they would fight. According to an eyewitness, when the captive saw an old woman coming with the pipe, she cried for joy because she recognized her as a friend of her family. "They shook hands and kissed each other," said the eyewitness, "and the woman interpreter asked if her parents and sisters were still living."[29] She was pleased to learn that they were very old and still alive.

"What are you saying?" asked the Sioux chief.

When the woman explained that the old woman knew her parents and that she was from the Siksika tribe, the chief was finally convinced that the people before him were Siksikas and his friends, not South Piegans. When they parted, the woman interpreter remained with the Sioux, for these were now her people.

In the 1830s three Blood warriors and a woman visited a trading post on the Missouri while they were on their way south to raid the Crows. They had traveled only a few miles from the fort, when they were suddenly attacked by a war party of thirty mounted Crows who had undoubtedly been lying in wait for them. Two of the Bloods were killed instantly, and the other was wounded. According to James Bradley:

> Though thus taken by surprise, his comrades killed by his side, and himself wounded, the surviving Blood warrior managed with such address, as the Crows dashed upon him, as to fell one from his horse with a single blow of his gun, leap into the seat, seize a lance in lieu of his own weapon which had fallen to the ground, and dash away in the direction of the fort. It happened that he had possessed himself of the best horse of the assailants, a swift and beautiful

animal, so that he easily distanced his pursuers, and arrived safely at the fort, leaving the squaw, his sister, a prisoner of the Crows.[30]

Several days later, the chief factor saw someone in the bushes on the other side of the Missouri. Curious, he took his skiff across and was surprised to see the woman who had so recently been captured by the Crows. "She was a sad sight," said Bradley, "being entirely naked except for the little protection afforded by bunches of sage-brush tied about her person, with feet lacerated by days of travel over stones and prickly pear, and worn down with exposure, fatigue and starvation."[31] She told the factor that she had been closely guarded during the day as they traveled south, and at night her clothes were taken away from her and she was obliged to sleep with "a lynx eyed" Crow woman. One night during a thunderstorm she managed to slip away and hide from her captors. For the next five days she traveled across the open plains with no moccasins, clothing, or food. She was almost ready to give up when she reached the Missouri and saw the American fort.

As might be expected, the Blackfoot had other heroic tales about their women and children escaping from the enemy. One such story involved a Piegan named Bad Young Man, or Paxka'panikapi, and his two wives. They were out hunting when they were suddenly attacked by Flatheads. All three fled, but the younger wife, Small Woman or Pokaki, had a slow pony and was captured. When the older wife saw what happened, she prayed that her co-wife would escape and vowed to receive one of the holy buffalo-tongue sacraments at the next Sun Dance if she was saved.

When Bad Young Man and his older wife got back to their camp, the Piegans immediately prepared to defend themselves against their enemy. The horses were driven into the middle of the circle of lodges, and next morning the chief split his followers into two groups, sending his best warriors ahead in the first section in case they were ambushed on the trail. When they reached their next campsite, they would set up defensive positions and the other group would join them. Bad Young Man and his wife were in the first group. When they came to a hill, they heard gunfire, so they immediately made a circle of travois in readiness for an attack. However, when the scout went to the top of the hill, he saw that the Flatheads were shooting at someone who was running away from them. It was Small Woman, Bad Young Man's youngest wife. Her husband and some other warriors quickly galloped to her rescue and brought her safely to the caravan. After she had recovered from her ordeal, she explained what had happened:

> My captor took me away to the enemy camp. He led me to a big tipi and called out a mourning couple, one of them a chief. I dismounted and was sent inside. My captor said to the couple, "Here is a daughter for you because you've lost one." Others rushed in to count a coup on me, but my new father said, "She is my daughter. Don't count coups on her any more."
>
> I was too scared to eat. My new mother said, "There is a Crazy Dog dance and we're going to it to tell the story of your capture. Don't be afraid. They won't do anything to you." We entered the dance tipi and there was another woman there, sent for to interpret. I was scared, hearing her talk Piegan. I asked, "What are you?" She said, "I was a Piegan, married here and though my husband is dead I have children here."[32]

The woman wanted to know how many Piegan camps were in the area and where they were located. Small Woman lied and said there were just a few of them, who had come to hunt near the mountains because the buffalo were scarce downriver. She knew the Flatheads were trying to find out if they had anything to fear from her tribe.

That night, her new father tied her up and made her sleep with her new mother. During the night Small Woman heard a member of her new father's all-comrades society come into the lodge and an argument take place. When the man left, Small Woman's new mother told her in sign language that the society members wanted to gang rape her and then kill her, but her new father had proclaimed again that the woman was his daughter and that no one would touch her. The new mother knew that the warriors would kill Small Woman when the first opportunity arose, so she went outside and pulled up the stakes of the tepee on the side where the Piegan woman was lying. Then, just before morning, she untied the ropes, gave Small Woman a pair of moccasins, and told her to crawl under the edge of the tepee and escape. She got only as far as a nearby coulee when she heard her new father shouting for her. Stopping only long enough to put on the moccasins, she ran toward the Piegan camp with the Flatheads in hot pursuit. That was when she was sighted by her Piegan husband and saved.

Another dramatic rescue occurred when a revenge party of Crows went north for the sole purpose of killing as many Blackfoot as possible. When they reached an enemy camp, they noticed a number of children playing in the nearby hills and saw them as an easy way of getting their revenge. They swooped down on the luckless group, and as the children fled in terror, they were struck down and killed by the attacking warriors. Only one boy was spared, and he was taken as a prisoner.

Some time later, the parents began to wonder why their children had not returned. When they went to investigate, they came upon the heart-wrenching sight of the bodies strewn over the hill. All the children had been scalped, even the youngest. As they ran from body to body looking for their loved ones, a beautiful woman saw that her little brother was not among them. When the sorrowful group returned to camp, she announced, "I will be the wife of whoever finds my brother."[33]

Only one man took up the challenge.[34] He followed the trail of the raiders to the Yellowstone River, and there he found two encampments of Crows. That night he saw a big Victory Dance being celebrated in one of the camps, so he boldly walked through the village, looking for signs of the missing boy. When he found nothing, he went to the other camp, and there he heard someone moaning. He followed the sound and discovered the boy tied to the top of a tall burial scaffold at the edge of the camp. The man waited until the dance was over. Towards morning he climbed the scaffold and released the child. He learned that he had been there for three days without food or water and that his legs had been bound together so tightly that he could not walk. The boy was being left there to die on the scaffold with the body of a Crow who had been killed by the Blackfoot. This was to be their revenge.

The man carried the boy out of the camp and safely made his escape, but because the child was gravely ill and could not walk, he had to carry him. They traveled, only by night, until the man became exhausted. On the third day he found a camp that he hoped was Piegan, but on closer examination he saw that it was Cree. He knew that the boy would die if he did not get help, so he decided to seek the assistance of this enemy tribe. Carrying the boy in his arms, he walked quickly through the camp and into the lodge of its chief. He knew that no one would touch them in there unless the chief agreed.

In sign language the Blackfoot explained what had happened. The Cree chief signed back, "Have no fear. You are safe in my lodge. We will call the medicine man to come and doctor your boy. When he is well enough you may go on, on your journey. No harm will come to you."[35]

After five days, while the boy was recovering under the care of the doctor, a young Cree entered the lodge and had a long discussion with the chief. After he left the chief explained that the man's father was dying, but he wanted to end his life with honor. He had challenged the Blackfoot to a duel, and the chief had accepted on his behalf. If the old man won, he would die knowing that he was a warrior. If the Blackfoot won, he was to be given horses and permitted to leave without interference and the old man would have perished in battle.

On the day of the fight, the two men walked toward each other from opposite ends of the camp. Both had been given rifles. As they approached the center, the Blackfoot raised his gun and shot the old man, killing him instantly. His adversary had made no effort to defend himself. Obviously he was there to die, not to fight. The Cree's son kept his promise; two horses were provided, and the man and boy safely returned to the Blackfoot camps. When they arrived, everyone was surprised, as they had thought that both of them were dead. The sister kept her vow and married the Blackfoot warrior, who later became a chief of his band.

The Blackfoot have related many other stories of bravery and cowardice, victory and defeat. There are accounts of men who spared the lives of their captives and adopted them into their families, either as wives or as daughters. There were others who admired the bravery of an enemy in battle and let him escape. But perhaps one of the strangest incidents occurred when a Blood war party captured a Cree. The man had been drinking at a stream when the raiders surrounded him. Instead of fighting, he just stood there. He wore tattered clothing and was so poor that he did not even have a knife. The Bloods did not kill him on the spot but took him prisoner until they had decided what to do with him. He could have been tortured and given a slow and excruciating death. He could have been turned loose and pursued like a fox chased by hounds. Or they could have simply killed him. But they did none of those things. In the end they painted his face black, told him that he was a gift to the Sun spirit, and released him. Was this an act of compassion? Red Crow, leader of the war party, said, "No doubt he wondered to what good circumstances he owed his really remarkable escape. I do not think he would ever have guessed the truth—that he was not worth killing."[36]

II His Name Was Star Child

In 1879 the North-West Mounted Police put a name down in their books as that of their "most wanted" man. He was Ku'katosi-poka, Star Child, a Blood Indian who was suspected of murdering the first member of the Mounted Police to die by human violence.

Star Child, the son of a Blood Indian named Weasel Child, was born about 1862. His mother, First to Enter, was a North Piegan, and the boy was raised in that tribe during his early years. When the Mounted Police came west in 1874, he was only twelve years old; he was a teenager when his father and others accepted a treaty with the Canadian government in which they surrendered their hunting grounds and promised to live in peace with their former enemies. As a result Star Child had been too young to participate in the exciting wars against the Crees, Assiniboines, and other enemy tribes.

In the two years following the treaty, the Blackfoot began to wonder about the pact. Three of their chiefs died within the year—a bad sign—and the promise of peace had caused their hunting grounds to be invaded by half-breeds and scores of their former enemies. Then, to add to their misery, the winter of 1877–78 had been a mild one with practically no snow. Across the line in Montana, commercial hide hunters set the prairies ablaze to prevent the buffalo from migrating north, and so the Blackfoot began to starve.

The Bloods, including Weasel Child and his family, followed the diminishing Canadian herds to the Cypress Hills and stayed there all winter, returning to the Fort Macleod area only to collect their treaty money. Then, in 1878 and 1879, they crossed the border into Montana each summer to hunt in the Judith Basin but followed the herds back to the Cypress Hills area for the winter.

By the autumn of 1879 their situation had become desperate. The Mounted Police shared their few rations, but it was not enough. A Montana newspaper observed that the Canadian government would be forced to "feed the starving reds, or increase the force of police sufficiently to carry on a constant and an effectual war with the desperate savages."[1] The newspaper also predicted dangerous times ahead, stating that "the scarcity of game in the North very materially changes the relations heretofore existing between the Indians and their Canadian protectors."[2]

By this time Star Child had turned seventeen and was no longer a boy. He huddled with the rest of the starving people and accepted the meager handouts of beef and flour issued at Fort Walsh. And it was there that the paths of Star Child and Constable Marmaduke Graburn first crossed. Graburn was a rookie on the force. He was the eldest son of Capt. Marmaduke Graburn, an employee of the Department of Marine and Fisheries in Ottawa. Young Graburn had joined the force as soon as he turned eighteen and was an avid hunter and sportsman. He had reached Fort Walsh on June 9 of that year and was considered to be a favorite of his comrades. He was described by one of his chums as "of most genial disposition, kind-hearted, truly brave, and honorable."[3] But for all his popularity, Graburn was apparently no friend of Star Child's. According to one report, the Indian hung around the fort, begging for food, and "gave a good deal of trouble, and in fact at one time Greyburn [sic] had strong words with him."[4] Mounted Police historian John Peter Turner claims that Graburn ordered Star Child out of the fort, calling him a "miserable dog."[5] If this is true, Star Child could well feel justified in killing the Mountie, for one of the worst insults that can be heaped upon a Blackfoot Indian is to compare him with a dog.

On November 16, 1879, Graburn was on duty at a horse camp about three miles from the fort. There, in the company of Payette, the scout, and Constable George Johnston, his comrade who had enlisted with him,

the young policeman watched over the Mounted Police horse herd. On that morning Johnston had received orders to go to their old camp about two miles away and recover a picket rope and an axe that had been left there in a hut. It was Johnston's turn to act as camp cook, so Graburn offered to perform the chore himself. Wearing his scarlet tunic, buckskin trousers, and a slouch hat, he picked up his carbine and ammunition, and at midmorning he rode off alone. As he disappeared along the winding trail near the creek, neither Johnston nor the scout realized that this would be the last time they would see Graburn alive.

He was expected back in an hour, and when he failed to appear, his comrades became anxious, fearing he may have met with an accident. However, this concern was allayed by the fact that his horse had not returned alone. When Graburn still had not shown up by midafternoon, the pair went to search for him. According to a policeman, "They left on foot, with their arms, and followed his tracks to the hut. They found the axe there, but the picket rope was gone. They noticed that he had, for some reason, gone on past the hut; most probably he found the rope had been taken and went further to look for it, intending to get the axe when he came back."[6]

They followed the tracks for another mile, and when they came to a gully, they fired shots in the air, hoping to attract his attention. By this time the daylight was dwindling and the snow that had been threatening all day began to fall, so the men returned to their camp. They checked the herd to make sure that Graburn's black trooper had not returned, then waited anxiously until dawn.

The next morning word was sent to Fort Walsh, and a mounted party joined the search. They retraced the steps taken by Johnston and Payette, crossed the gully, and about a hundred yards further on they came to a ravine that was almost impassable because of the dense brush along its banks. While they were searching for another path, the wind blew away some of the light snow that had fallen during the night, and the searchers saw that the area was spotted with blood and the snow was trampled as though there had been a struggle. Nearby, hanging on a bush, they found Graburn's slouch hat. "After an hour's searching," said a policeman, "they found the poor fellow lying dead in the gully, hidden about with bushes. He was lying on his face in a mass of blood."[7] A later autopsy showed that he had been shot in the back, just below his right shoulder blade.

By this time it was too late in the day to examine the death scene, so a guard was placed over the body. The following morning a wagon was sent to bring the frozen remains back to the fort. Jerry Potts, the Mounted Police scout from Fort Macleod, arrived at Fort Walsh and joined the officers the next morning when they went to examine the scene. They found cartridges scattered around on the ground, but the policeman's carbine was missing. Potts conducted his own search, and a short time later he found Graburn's horse wedged between two trees and shot in the head. A policeman reconstructed the scene as follows:

> Graburn had just crossed the creek and met two Indians, who had probably been watching him come along, and thought they had now a good chance to kill a white soldier. They stepped up to him to shake hands, and while one was pretending to pat his horse, but really holding it so it would not get away, the other stepped behind him and shot him through the back. He must have stayed on the saddle a few moments, as blood was found on it. The jumping of the horse probably threw him off on his face, as his nose was bruised by the fall. The Indians, knowing the horse would return to the herd and give the alarm before they could make their escape, took him to the bushes so as to be hard to find, and wedged him between two trees. One must have beat him behind and the other led him. They tied the halter rope to a tree in front of him so he could not move any way, and shot him with Graburn's rifle.[8]

Jerry Potts followed the trail of the two killers, one on foot and the other riding an unshod pony, but when their tracks entered the main trail, which led toward the Indian camps, the village, and the fort, all signs were lost. "We tried to track the murderer out on to the open prairie," said Supt. Sam Steele, "but a chinook had sprung up and melted the snow and, the ground being frozen, not a trace was left."[9]

At first there was no clue as to who might have fired the fatal shot, although there were a great many rumors. "There is no doubt but the foul deed was perpetrated by two Indians," stated North-West Mounted Police commissioner James F. Macleod in his report,

> but we have not been able to fix the guilt upon the murderers: I feel sure that they will be discovered, as when they are across the line

and think themselves safe, they will be certain to say something about it which will lead to their detection, and the other Indians will be sure to let us know. When the facts come out they will show that the atrocious crime was committed in revenge for some real or fancied injury done to the murderer or one of his family, not necessarily by a Policeman but by some white man.[10]

If the story of Graburn's calling Star Child a "miserable dog" was true, then the police commissioner had made a good guess. It was also possible, however, that the murderer had stolen the halter rope from the hut and that Graburn had followed his tracks and tried to apprehend him and his companion.

In the investigation suspicion pointed to Medicine Shield, a turbulent chief of the Siksikas, but there was no proof.[11] The police also checked into the activities of the Blood tribe and learned that Weasel Child, with his son Star Child and his friend Eagle Breast, had been camped in the vicinity and had departed for Montana immediately after the murder.[12] But again, there was no direct evidence linking them to the crime.

During the rest of the winter most of the Bloods stayed in Montana, hunting buffalo near the Bear Paw Mountains. A few remained in the Cypress Hills, where they lived off Mounted Police rations and what little game they could kill. The interpreters at the fort constantly asked new arrivals if they had heard anyone bragging about killing a redcoat. Friends of the police were urged to keep an ear open for any hint of the killer. Then, in midwinter, came the first clue as to the possible identity of Graburn's murderer; a tip was passed along to the Mounted Police that two Blood Indians who were at that moment in the guardhouse on suspicion of horse stealing knew something about the affair.

Supt. L. N. F. Crozier made discreet enquiries around the Indian camps and learned that the two men had been in the vicinity of the herd camp at the time of the killing. But as the investigation continued, the two prisoners received word via "moccasin telegraph" that they were being held for something more serious than horse stealing. The following afternoon, the two men, together with a Blood who was being held on another charge, were taken outside for their daily exercise. As soon as the trio and the two guards cleared the confines of the fort, the two Bloods made a daring break for freedom.

The third prisoner made no attempt to escape; he simply watched in astonishment as the two guards ran awkwardly in their long leather boots, trying to keep pace with the moccasin-clad prisoners. Then the third man also decided to escape and fled in the opposite direction.

The two Bloods raced to the large camp of their tribesmen nearby, where their wives were waiting with rifles and belts of ammunition. But the alarm had been sounded at the fort; a few minutes later a mounted party took off after the fugitives and trapped them before a shot could be fired. When they were returned to Fort Walsh, both Indians denied any involvement in the murder, but one man, Weasel Moccasin, claimed he had heard Star Child confess that he was the killer. "When they were down at Bear Paw, the latter made a confession to him," stated a reporter. "His story is a rambling and improbable one altogether, but it is not unlikely both he and Star Child may be proved to have had a hand in the crime."[13]

The police superintendent immediately sent a dispatch to Commissioner Macleod, who was in Fort Benton on business, asking if Star Child could be arrested at his camp in the nearby Bear Paw Mountains and brought back to Canada for questioning. Commissioner Macleod in turn made a formal request to the redoubtable sheriff of Choteau County, John J. Healy, and was told that the Mounted Police would have to put up five thousand dollars before he would try to make the arrest. The demand was turned down.

Not until May 13, 1881—a year and a half after the murder—was Star Child arrested. During the interim period he had stayed in Montana with the majority of the Bloods, attempting to kill enough buffalo to keep away the ever-increasing threat of starvation. In April of 1880 about half the Bloods returned to Canada under the leadership of Red Crow to collect their treaty money, but most left for Montana again in the fall. Only Red Crow and a few of his followers stayed in Canada, settling near the Belly River and building log houses to replace their worn lodges.

By the spring of 1881 even the most optimistic Blood had to admit there was little use hunting for an animal that had vanished from the prairies. The thundering herds were now reduced to a mere handful, and the whole Montana plains seemed to be devoid of game. So the Bloods moved westward to Fort Benton, but they were refused admission to the town to buy food. Instead, their camps were invaded by unscrupulous traders who sold them foul whiskey and took their few remaining horses and buffalo robes.

"While on the American side they had a good hunt," commented the Canadian Indian commissioner, "and had the whiskey traders kept away from them they might have returned in better circumstances than when they left; as it was, they were followed by the lowest class of thieves and whiskey traders who, in exchanging for robes, supplied the Indians with horses, then made them drunk, and while in that state drove their horses off."[14] Star Child was one of those Bloods who returned to Canada minus horses, robes, and food. On the verge of starvation, these Indians finally reached Fort Macleod and received rations from the government.

In early May 1881 interpreter Jerry Potts learned that Star Child was camped with some Siksikas at the mouth of the Little Bow River. When the Siksikas continued on to their reserve at Blackfoot Crossing, the young Blood decided to go to his own reserve at Standoff. On May 12 the interpreter was told that the wanted Indian was camped about eighteen miles from Fort Macleod. Corporal Pry Patterson, Corporal Wilson, and bugler George Callaghan, with scout Jerry Potts and a constable, left that evening and traveled all night, reaching the camp well before dawn. The plan was to close in on Star Child's lodge at dawn and take him without arousing the camp. However, Star Child—who claimed to have protective medicine—was not so easily captured. As the sun cleared the western sky the men closed in, but the wanted man suddenly stepped through the flap of his lodge, fully clothed and fully armed—his rifle pointed at Patterson's chest. The sergeant, thinking quickly, shouted an order to a nonexistent constable directly behind the Indian, telling him to grab Star Child's arms.

The Indian spun around, realizing too late that it was a ruse. There was no one behind him. Patterson hurled himself on the Indian, but in the struggle to gain possession of the rifle, it discharged and awoke the whole camp. In a few moments the small party of Mounties was surrounded by excited Indians who demanded the release of the handcuffed Star Child. Chiefs Red Crow, Strangling Wolf, and One Spot, however, quickly sprang to the aid of the Mounties and held back the hotheaded warriors while Patterson and his party galloped towards Fort Macleod. Several young Bloods dashed to their horses and followed a short distance behind, but they halted within sight of the fort.

Star Child was placed in the guardroom, where he languished for five months—through the rest of the spring, all summer, and well into autumn— as trial dates were set and postponed. A journalist who visited him in jail described what he saw:

> Star Child is a small and rather delicately-formed Indian, who looks wonderfully like a Chinaman, and the fact that he wears his hair in long closely-plaited braids rather strengthens his resemblance to the Mongolian family. When the door of his cell was opened he sprang from his bunk where he was lying (attired only in undershirt and drawers), and with a little nervous laugh shook hands with me. He is very quick and nervous in all his motions, but he has a weak look both in face and figure. From his appearance one would hardly suppose that he was the man either to plan or carry out the shocking crime with which he is charged.[15]

There was a rumor that he had confessed to the murder and was going to plead guilty, but this proved to be untrue. Yet time and again before the trial, he was referred to as the "murderer" of Graburn, and in the minds of most Mounties, he needed only a trial to see him hanged. Finally, on October 18, he was brought before a jury of six ranchers on a charge of murder. Stipendiary Magistrate James F. Macleod presided and was assisted by Supt. L. N. F. Crozier, Major J. H. G. Bray, and the crown prosecutor, Inspector Thomas Dowling.

In order to assure that the accused received a fair trial, virtually every civilian in the Fort Macleod area was summoned for jury duty, but even then, five of the six selected were ex-Mounties. These included Charles Ryan, trader; Daniel Horan, shoemaker; William Parker, ranch hand; Edward Maunsell, rancher; and one other. The only non-ex-Mountie was William S. Gladstone, a carpenter. The first witness was Weasel Moccasin, the Blood who had pointed the finger at Star Child in the first place. One of the jurymen later explained:

> He stated that Starchild told him that he had killed Grayburn [*sic*]. Asked if Starchild gave any reason for doing so, he replied that Starchild said that he and the policeman were riding together in the Cypress hills, that they came to a miry place and the policeman was afraid to cross it. Starchild then took the lead but his horse refused

to enter and the policeman struck him behind with a rope. This so annoyed Starchild that when they went some distance further he shot and killed the policeman.[16]

This evidence was less than convincing, considering that there had been snow on the ground and any "miry place" would have been frozen solid. As a reporter noted, he was not a credible witness, yet he was the only one to offer any direct evidence. Others were called only to confirm that Star Child had been in the Fort Walsh area at the time of the killing.

Magistrate Macleod then charged the jury, telling them to render a verdict based upon the evidence and not upon the rumors that had been circulating. If they had any reasonable doubt, they were to find in favor of the prisoner. According to Maunsell:

> The evidence that Starchild was seen round Fort Walsh did not help us much because there were several hundred Indians camped around there at the same time. We were reduced therefore to the evidence of the Indian who said Starchild had said he had killed Grayburn. [William] Gladstone was asked his opinion about this. Gladstone had lived mostly all his life amongst the Indians and knew their character thoroughly. He said that the Indians did not regard the killing of a whiteman or an Indian of a hostile tribe as a crime but rather as an achievement to boast about and that consequently it was possible that Starchild, especially as he was only a boy, might have lied and said he killed Grayburn. Gladstone was inclined to this opinion on account of the inadequate cause which Starchild was supposed to give as his reason for killing Grayburn.[17]

On the first vote, five were in favor of acquittal and only one was for conviction. The latter argued that this was the first murder of a Mountie in the Territories and that if Star Child was acquitted, the Indians would become arrogant and no settler would be safe from them. Then followed a full day of review and discussion, and in the end the verdict of not guilty was unanimous. The decision was unpopular, some angry police even accusing the jury of being afraid to convict an Indian because of possible reprisals. One policeman, Cecil Denny, could not believe that ex-members of the force could have willingly released the man. "It seems that five were for conviction and Gladstone for acquittal, who finally prevailed and he got off," he wrote. Of course, he was wrong. He was also in error when he added, "I am told that after he was let off, the Bloods openly said he had killed the man."[18] Similarly, Supt. Sam Steele was bitter about the verdict and stated, "There is no doubt that the jurymen who were for acquittal were afraid that the conviction would bring on an Indian war, or cause the Bloods to kill stock out of revenge."[19] But as juryman Maunsell stated, "As a matter of fact, it required greater courage to acquit Starchild than convict him."[20]

Although Star Child was free, he was not forgotten by the North-West Mounted Police. For the next two years, the *Fort Macleod Gazette*, run by an ex-Mountie, carried any news or rumors it heard about the young Indian's activities. In November 1882 the *Gazette* stated, "Star Child, the Blood Indian who was on trial here last fall for the murder of the policeman Graburn, is reported to have been shot last summer by the Assiniboines in the vicinity of the Bear Paw Mountains."[21] Two weeks later it reported, "The notorious Star Child, the murderer of Graburn, has at last met his just deserts. He was killed across the boundary line by a war party of Gros Ventres."[22] But Star Child was not so easily despatched. In the spring of 1883 the *Gazette* made a correction: "The rumor in circulation here some time ago that Star Child, the supposed murderer of Graburn, was killed by Assiniboines last fall, turns out to be untrue. He was wounded seriously but recovered and is at present at Badger Creek with the South Piegans. He spent the winter among the Crows at Yellowstone."[23]

The North-West Mounted Police watched his activities with interest. Below the boundary line he was out of their sphere of jurisdiction. But in Canada . . .

Star Child left his South Piegan friends late in June 1883 and headed north towards his home camp on the Belly River, taking with him some horses he had obtained in the United States. On July 5 a warrant was issued for his arrest on a charge of bringing stolen horses into Canada. A patrol made up of Sergeant Ashe, Constable B. R. Sleigh, Corporal Sam Derenzie, and Constable Bob Wilson, guided by Jerry Potts, traveled by darkness to the Blood Reserve, where a friendly Indian pointed out the shack in which Star Child was staying. Entering the building, they found the youth asleep, his rifle, revolver, and knife lying nearby. He was arrested without difficulty and lodged in the guardroom at Fort Macleod.

There was no five-month delay for Star Child's trial this time. The case came before Stipendiary Magistrate Macleod just sixteen days after his arrest, and he was sentenced to four years of hard labor in Manitoba's Stony Mountain Penitentiary. There can be little doubt that he was being tried a second time for the Graburn murder, as evidenced by the fate of his fellow horse thief, The Man with the Knife, who was given only six months in the Fort Macleod guardroom on the same charge. A newspaperman commented that Star Child was "the same Indian arrested over a year ago for the murder of Constable Graburn, but who escaped conviction for lack of evidence. The police, who have him in charge, are satisfied, however, that he is the party guilty of that crime."[24]

Star Child made the long trip to Stony Mountain Penitentiary in Manitoba, arriving there ten days after his conviction. And there he remained for two years, eleven months, and sixteen days from the date of his conviction. A year after entering the institution, Red Crow tried to get him released but was unsuccessful. But instead of dying of tuberculosis, as many Indians did at Stony Mountain, Star Child seemed to thrive on prison life. He became a favorite of the warden, Sam Bedson, teaching him Blackfoot while Star Child learned English. And his term at hard labor consisted of being a waiter for the Bedson household.

In June 1886 Star Child was visited by John Maclean, a Methodist missionary from the Blood Reserve, who wrote, "He is waiter with Capt. B. and is as smart, neat & clean a waiter as is to be found in any hotel in Winnipeg. Capt. B. has taken great pains to teach him. He can read words of three and four letters, understand all you say to him in English and is a genteel looking young man."[25] Maclean entered into a conversation with the Indian, which he recorded:

"Do you know me?"

Looking at my face, "Wait a little." Still gazing earnestly, "Where do you live?"

"At Belly River."

"Now I know you. I am very glad to see you. You have a good heart to come and see me."

"When are you going home?"

"Belly River used to seem a long way off. Now it does not seem far. . . . I am going to Belly River in three weeks. . . . You see me now, I am a chief, dressed like a white man. I want to do what is right."[26]

Star Child was pardoned on July 6, 1886, the third anniversary to the day of the time of his arrest. When he returned to his reserve, it was apparent that the changes had not just been happening to him. The unsettled conditions of the frontier had become a memory of the past, as cattlemen brought their great herds to feed on the same rolling prairies that had been the home of the buffalo. The Bloods were no longer wild and free warriors but were ragged mendicants obliged to line up for their weekly rations of beef and flour. A few were tending their gardens, while others were actively engaged in the religious life of the reserve. Medicine-pipe dances, the Sun Dance, and other festivals were the few escapes that they had from the depressed conditions on the reserve. A few men such as Big Rib and his cousin The Dog still went out on horse raids, but their chiefs discouraged these wild actions of a bygone era.

Star Child's attitude toward the North-West Mounted Police and their attitude towards him changed considerably after his release. Instead of confronting the authorities, the young Indian (he was still only twenty-four) at first seemed content to cooperate with them. In February of 1887, for example, he reported to his Indian agent that three young Bloods had returned to the reserve with a dozen horses stolen from ranchers in the Sweetgrass Hills area. Not only that, but he offered to round up the horses and put them in the government corral. The offer was accepted, and the horses were ultimately returned to their owner. "It would appear from this," said the Indian agent, "that Star Child's confinement in the Penitentiary has been beneficial."[27]

His efforts received the enthusiastic support of his chief, Red Crow, who was valiantly trying to attain some semblance of peace and order on the reserve. At that time the Bloods were angry over the killing of six Bloods by Gros Ventre and Assiniboine Indians a few weeks earlier, and all the chief's efforts were devoted to keeping his people at home until a peace treaty could be made with the Montana tribes.

In March Red Crow announced to the Indian agent that he and Star Child were leaving for the United States to meet with the Gros Ventres, seemingly further proof of the young Indian's complete rehabilitation. In fact it was simply an excuse for the young Indian to get away from the reserve and visit relatives on the Crow Reservation in southeastern Montana. The treaty trip was postposed, but Star Child left anyway, safely crossing the vast expanse of Montana prairies, where Indians were still in danger of being shot on sight. As a result Star Child was far away when the treaty was discussed, and he had no way of knowing that it had been successfully concluded. In his eyes the Assiniboines and Gros Ventres were still his enemies, as were the Crows even though he had relatives among the latter tribe.

In June 1887 a report was received by the Mounted Police that Star Child was back to his old way of life. When he left the Crow Reservation, he stole eight horses and traveled north with them to the wooded slopes of the Bear Paw Mountains. There the Crows caught up with him, and in a brief fight they recovered half the herd. Not satisfied with just four animals, Star Child swooped down on the reservation at Fort Belknap and took another four from the Gros Ventres and Assiniboines.

On June 27 Major Carrol, the U.S. commander at Fort Assiniboine, wired the Mounted Police, "Star Child and two others crossed line going north twenty miles east of Sweet Grass Hills on 22nd day of June with eight horses." Red Crow had just completed the pact of peace with the Gros Ventres and Assiniboines and, fearing that the raid might derail it, he personally intervened.

"On the 29th of June," stated Supt. Percy Neale of Fort Macleod, "Chief Red Crow came here with a number of minor chiefs. . . . He brought with him a Blood named Star Child, whom he surrendered and charged with bringing stolen horses into Canada, at the same time handing over three ponies said to have been taken from the Assiniboines."[28] The horses were placed in the police corral, and American authorities were notified to claim them and press charges against the horse thief. However, when it became evident that they would not be coming, Star Child was released for, as Supt. Neale stated, "beyond his own confession there was no evidence against him."[29]

That was Star Child's last brush with the law. A few months later, he was engaged as a scout by the Lethbridge detachment of the North-West Mounted Police. This was a job that Star Child filled to perfection. His quick wit, fearlessness, and determination made him one of the best scouts the North-West Mounted Police ever had on their payroll.

For example, on April 13, 1889, he found two white men with a ten-gallon keg of whiskey near the Indian camps at the river bottom below Lethbridge. When he took it away from them, the bootleggers tried to bribe him with free liquor. When that did not work, they tried to threaten him, but Star Child could not be dissuaded. He sent an Indian to fetch Sgt. Charlie Ross, and although the two white men fled, Star Child retained the keg. It was later taken to the barracks, where it was destroyed. For this singular action on the part of an Indian scout, Star Child's wages were raised from fifteen to twenty-five dollars a month. "I wish I could find another like him," commented his commanding officer. "This is the Indian who is said to have shot Graburn; whether or not, he is a man with a great deal of character, and is better employed as a friend than an enemy."[30]

Star Child's next major accomplishment occurred on April 22, when he informed his superintendent that Prairie Chicken Old Man and a party of Bloods had set out to raid the Indians in Montana. The American authorities at Fort Assiniboine were immediately notified, but it was too late. Shortly afterward, Col. Otis wired from Assiniboine that "three Bloods with stolen stock passed through Bear Paw Mountains on the 8th and there killed an Indian."

It turned out that the party, made up of five Bloods and one South Piegan, had taken about one hundred horses from the Crows but had dropped most of the poorer animals along the trail. In the Bear Paw Mountains they were attacked by Gros Ventres and Assiniboines, and in the ensuing battle an Assiniboine was killed. A Blood named The Scout took the dead man's horse, while Prairie Chicken Old Man lifted his scalp and kept his rifle. As the American cavalry appeared on the scene, the Bloods fled towards Canada, dropping all but five of their stolen horses. When they arrived safely at their reserve, the warriors were picked up then released with a caution. Meanwhile, Star Child was complimented by the police for his part in learning about the war party.

Some time later, while he was in a trading store at Standoff, Star Child passed on some information to Robert N. Wilson that offered a dramatic climax to the career of this resourceful Indian. "I have had a lot of trouble in my life," he said, "but I have come through very well. I think I have a charmed life because I have never taken a wife. If I ever marry, I will lose my 'medicine' and be like anyone else."[31]

So Star Child was not acting blindly when he committed his last outstanding deed. He had become famous as an accused murderer, a warrior, a horse raider, and a Mounted Police scout. Finally, he decided to defy his spiritual protector. His feat of courtship was no less spectacular and no less sensational than his other exploits. At that time many Indian women considered themselves fortunate if they could marry a white man. They received plenty of clothes and good food and had an easier life than their sisters who remained on the reserve. Therefore, an astonished murmur arose both among the Indians and the whites when it was learned that Star Child had courted the Indian wife of a white man and stolen her from beneath his very nose.

But this deed was Star Child's undoing. Soon after the incident he was dismissed from his position, and he died of tuberculosis within the year. As he had predicted, his "medicine" had left him when romance entered his life.

The final comment on Star Child was entered in the official reports of the North-West Mounted Police in 1889 by Supt. R. B. Deane. "Of the several Indian scouts that I have tried," he wrote,

> none have proved to be worth their salt but Star Child, and I am sorry to hear that he is dying of consumption. He did some good work for us and I do not expect to replace him. He was a determined rascal and the Indians were generally afraid of him. After he brought to a successful conclusion an intrigue in which he was much interested—no less than the enticing of a white man's Indian wife from him—he became less reliable and energetic and I was at last obliged to discharge him. I should be glad to get another native scout of similar calibre.[32]

And so ended the colorful career of a man who went from accused murderer to Mounted Police scout. For twelve years he led an almost charmed life through battles, starvation, and disease, only to die at the age of twenty-seven when he deserted his "strong medicine" for a dark-eyed girl.

Was he guilty of killing Constable Graburn? Probably. If either story is true, that is, that Graburn called him a "miserable dog" or that he was caught stealing a picket rope, the young Indian was daring enough to have committed the crime. No other person was ever brought to trial.

12 *Harrison's Horses*

If the Bloods were intent upon stealing horses, perhaps they should not have picked on Albert Harrison's herd. Most other Montana ranchers would have put the loss down to a bad experience with those "cursed" Indians from the Canadian side of the line, made a few threats about lynching, and then gone back to maintaining the rest of their herd. But not Albert Harrison. He wanted his horses back, and he wanted revenge.

In the summer of 1881 the Montana plains were overrun with horse thieves, both Indian and white. The near destruction of the last buffalo herds meant that Indians were leaving for their reservations (or reserves, if one is talking about Canada), while many hide hunters and other white men who had lived off the buffalo were now unemployed. For the Indians returning home, the idea of picking up a few stray horses seemed like a good idea, while to white horse thieves, the turbulent state of the Montana frontier was ripe for exploitation. So the Indians stole from Indians and white men, and the white men stole from everybody.

Before the Bloods returned to Canada in 1881, many of them had been robbed by bearded thieves who prowled the plains like hungry grey wolves. Even their head chief, Red Crow, had been a victim, as was Running Wolf, one of the war chiefs of the tribe. Yet the Montana press tried to lay all the blame for the unrest on Canadian Indians. One rancher in a letter to the *Benton River Press* exclaimed: "Let us rise up like men and defend our property, and teach these breech-clouted pets of the government that we have some rights which we will compel them to respect. Too long, already, have we submitted to outrages from them that we would not have tolerated for a single week if white men had been the perpetrators."[1]

The Indians were also angry, seeing themselves as victims rather than as perpetrators. As another Montana newspaper commented: "The Indians of the North complain of the whites, saying that they steal their horses and trade them whiskey. They do not wish trouble but they offered a camp of ponies if the whites would surrender Jim Morton to them. Morton, they say, is a horse thief and a whisky trader, and they want to kill him."[2]

When the Bloods got back to the Canadian side of the line, there were no more buffalo to hunt and there was nothing to do but hang around the camps and wait for the handouts of beef and flour. This was not exciting enough for the young men who had just returned from exhilarating times on the buffalo ranges of Montana. They had experienced the thrill of the hunt, the raiding of enemy horse herds, the protection of their camps from unscrupulous white men, and the challenge of surviving among the last buffalo herds, where they had often come in contact with enemies from the Sioux, Crows, Arapahos, and tribes from across the mountains.

Unwilling to give up this old way of life, a number Bloods decided to form a war party to raid the Crows on the Yellowstone River, some six hundred miles to the south. They were led by twenty-one-year-old Eagle Plume and Packs His Tail (full name: Packs His Eagle Tail Feathers on His Back), who was a year older. They organized secretly, for their chiefs had already decreed that no war parties should return across the border to the Montana Territory. The chiefs had been warned by the North-West Mounted Police that American ranchers were threatening to kill any Indians they found on their ranges, even if they were just passing through on the way to a reservation.

But Eagle Plume was an experienced warrior. To him, nothing had changed. The Crows were still camped on the Yellowstone River, and

OPPOSITE PAGE   Eagle Plume, a member of the Blood tribe, was a leader of the expedition that raided Albert Harrison's horse herd in southern Montana in 1881. During his career as a warrior, Eagle Plume took part in twenty-four raids against his enemies, killed seven men, and captured more than a hundred horses. He is seen here in 1927.
Courtesy Glenbow Archives, Calgary, AB, cat. no. NB-21-37

they still had plenty of fine horses. The white people—ranchers and cowboys in particular—were simply problems to be avoided.

Eagle Plume knew the south country well. He had been on a raid a few years earlier that had taken him right into the territory where they now planned to visit. He had been the leader of a party of nine that had traveled on foot to the Missouri River, then crossed it near the present city of Great Falls. There they had killed a fat buffalo cows, dried a supply of meat, and continued south to the Musselshell River. After crossing that stream, they had made for the sheltered slopes of the Crazy Woman Mountains, then followed Shield River, striking the Yellowstone River near the present town of Livingston. South of the river they had found a Crow camp. When they raided it, Eagle Plume and his companion were discovered, but they killed one of their enemy before he had a chance to sound the alarm. Then they took some of the finest buffalo-running horses in the camp and successfully made their escape.

Now, in 1881, Eagle Plume planned to return to the same territory. By the time the pair was ready to leave, their war party had expanded to at least ten people. Besides the original two, there were Hind Cow, Tongue Eater, Blue Owl, Rides Around the Dance Circle, Helps to Eat, Old Man Who Sidles at the Dance, Weak One, and Killed in the Night. Some of them were teenagers who had never been on a raid before. Their duty would be to tend the fires, look after the camp, and at night to build the wooden tepee-like structures that were their temporary dwelling places when they went to war. Such servants were not permitted to take part in the raid itself.

The men slipped away on foot from the Blood Reserve during mid-September 1881, with Eagle Plume leading the way. The journey was almost a replica of his earlier war venture, but this time they had to avoid any white settlements and ranches that had sprung up during the intervening years. Likely they passed east of the town of Choteau, then crossed the Sun and Missouri Rivers. By this time they were running out of the dried meat they had packed for the journey, so they killed a cow and took a few days to dry the meat. Their route took them through the wooded region of the Little Belt Mountains to the Crazy Woman Mountains and from there to Crow camps south of the Yellowstone.

But there were no Crow camps. Unknown to Eagle Plume and others in the war party, that tribe had been obliged to go to their reservation, seventy-five miles east, if they expected to receive rations from the government agent. A brief tour of the Livingston area indicated to the Bloods that their enemies had not been there for many months.

In hopes of finding camps farther east, the war party followed the Yellowstone downstream, and after about thirty miles they came to the mouth of Sweetgrass Creek. This too was barren of Crows. The Bloods crossed the river and went a few miles north to a lookout point where they had an uninterrupted view of the lands to the east. They could see a vast expanse of open prairie, with the Bighorn Mountains to the east and the Big Snowy Mountains to the north. There were eagles soaring high into the clear blue sky and a herd of antelope skittering away from a prairie wolf. But there were no Indian camps; just ranches. There were no buffalo; just cattle.

Packs his Tail could recall how the Bloods had been shamed when white men had stolen their horses as they camped along the Missouri River. His own chief, Running Wolf, had suffered such a loss. If the white man could take their horses, why could they not reply in kind? In Blood tradition if you were wronged by an enemy tribe, you did not have to seek out the actual person who had done the deed; revenging yourself upon anyone in that tribe would do. The same could apply here: the Bloods had been robbed by whites, so they in turn could get their revenge from anyone in the white tribe.

From their lookout point the Blood war party could see a number of ranches. Just east of them were a couple of small spreads, while to the south, at the mouth of Sweetgrass Creek, was a larger one. That night, October 6, 1881, Eagle Plume and the others walked east for a short distance until they came to Charles G. Brown's ranch on White Beaver Creek, where they picked up a couple of stray horses without going near the ranch house or the corrals. From there they went to the ranch of S. H. Murray, where they collected a few more horses until everyone was mounted.

From the hills they could see that the largest ranch—the one belonging to Albert Harrison—was to the south. As they approached it, they noticed that while a few horses wandered freely on the open prairie, the best ones were within a fence near the corrals. There were about forty of them, all good riding stock that had been broken to saddle. What the Bloods did not know was that Harrison and others were just starting their fall roundup of cattle, and these were the horses intended for the remuda—the stock from which horses would be selected for each day's work.

The gate was opened and the stock quietly herded along a trail to the north. As soon as they were out of earshot of the ranch buildings, the Indians cried *Hai-ya!* both in triumph for their successful raid and to spur the herd into a faster pace. The Bloods knew that in the morning the loss would be discovered and the ranchers might try to follow them. It was best to be far away before daybreak.

While traveling through Montana's ranching country, horse raiders usually moved by night and hid out during the day. This had not been necessary in the old days, when their only enemies had been the Crows and when two or three days of constant travel could bring them back to their own hunting grounds. Now they had to contend with cowboys who considered every Indian to be a menace, ranchers who saw them as horse thieves (even when they were not), and disreputable whites who were prepared to steal the horses the Indians had just acquired.

Eagle Plume and his companions pressed the horses hard for the rest of the night, until they reached the Musselshell River, where they found a good hiding place in one of the river bottoms. The next evening they crossed the open plains of the Judith Basin, and at the Judith Gap they veered west into the protective valleys of the Little Belt Mountains. Because of their constant hard riding, they lost fourteen horses along the way. The weaker ones had faltered and were abandoned, while a mare was stabbed to death when it resisted all efforts to keep up with the herd. In anger and frustration its rider had prodded it with his knife, but when it still refused to gallop, he killed it and left it on the trail.

The raiders relaxed once they were within the Little Belts, for there was little likelihood of their being accidentally discovered by a wandering cowboy. They slept most of the day, with only one guard remaining alert in case of trouble. He probably sat on a high ridge and watched for signs of trouble on the nearby prairies. But all he would have seen were a few deer, a coyote looking for its daily meal, and a flock of crows protesting his presence in a cacophony of squawks before flying off to pester someone else.

On their second day in the mountains, dark clouds began gathering to the north, swirling and rolling over the sky like some gigantic blanket. Soon the air turned from an autumn mild to a winter chill, and before noon the first scattering of snowflakes appeared. By early afternoon a full-blown blizzard had descended on the mountains and upon the raiders and their horses. It would have been foolish to travel in this weather, so the Bloods prepared a makeshift camp and settled down to wait out the storm. They were short of food, but it was an easy matter for a couple of the young men to slaughter a stray steer on the nearby prairies and bring the meat to camp.[3]

Three days later, with the storm gone and cold weather descending upon them, the raiders continued their journey, more leisurely now that there had been no signs of pursuit and their own trail had been wiped out by the snow. Following the edge of the Little Belts, they passed east of Tiger Butte then crossed the plains to the Missouri River near the Great Falls. From there it was an easy journey to the Teton River and the distinctive landmark known as The Knees. They passed Joe Kipp's trading post without stopping then camped near Henry Kennerly's ranch. The following day, within five miles of Willow Rounds, the party split, most of the Bloods continuing on north but a few deciding to visit relatives at the Blackfeet Indian Agency, located a few miles to the west.

The raiders were quite pleased. They still had more than thirty horses, and no one had bothered to follow them or intercept them along the way. At least that is what they thought.

The morning after the raid, Albert Harrison awoke with the news that his horses were gone. Incredulous, he stormed over to the field; sure enough, the gate was open and the animals had disappeared. The moccasin footprints in the dust left no doubt as to what had happened. A short time later, riders came from the Brown and Murray Ranches to say that they too had been raided. When the numbers were tallied, forty-eight horses were missing. All were branded with Harrison's Lazy H, Murray's Bull's Eye, or Brown's SO brand.

The cattle roundup was ready to begin, but Harrison was too angry to ignore the loss of his stock. Instead, he assembled the cowboys who had come to work and offered to put them on the payroll to recover his missing stock. Instead of fifteen dollars a month for riding the range, they would be paid the same wages to pursue a bunch of horse thieves and, if they were caught, to see them hanged. This might prove to be a lot more exciting than rounding up a bunch of bawling cows, so a dozen cowboys volunteered.

It took the ranchers a day to outfit the posse, but once on the road they had no difficulty in picking up the tracks of the rustled herd. Unencumbered by extra horses and with only a couple of pack ponies to carry their supplies, the cowboys made good time in their pursuit. They slowed down only to pick up the strays that the Bloods had abandoned, and by the time they reached Judith Gap they estimated that the Indians were only a day ahead of them. With good luck, they would catch up with them before they reached the Missouri River.

Then the blizzard struck. Harrison and the cowboys took refuge in a nearby ranch, but they knew the tracks of the raiding party would be completely obliterated. When the worst of the storm had passed, they fanned out across the prairie, hoping to pick up the trail in the new-fallen snow. They went as far as the Highwood Mountains, then they camped on the upper waters of Shonkin Creek before admitting defeat. Disappointed, Harrison, Murray, and Brown decided to send the cowboys back to the roundup without their ever having had a chance to make "a few good Indians," that is, to kill the raiders.[4] Meanwhile, the three ranchers continued directly northward to Fort Benton for help.

In 1881 Fort Benton, which was as far upriver as steamboats could go, was the major business center for the Upper Missouri River. The city of Great Falls did not exist (it would not be laid out as a townsite for another two years), and there was no other town for miles. Fort Benton was the seat for Choteau County and the headquarters for such major trading firms as I. G. Baker & Co. and T. C. Power & Bro. Its main street was lined with hotels, stores, saloons, boardinghouses, and transportation offices. Nearby were the docks, where dozens of steamboats disgorged their supplies of trade goods and mining equipment and took on furs, robes, and other wares.

The town was also the headquarters of John J. Healy, the sheriff of Choteau County. He had been a partner in the infamous Fort Whoop-Up, which, between 1869 and 1874, had sold whiskey and repeating rifles to the Blackfoot Indians in Canada. The fort had closed when the North-West Mounted Police came west; after that, Healy made the easy transition from whiskey peddler to lawman.

When he first ran for office in 1877, Healy told the electors, "don't vote for me if you plan on stealing any horses," followed by a threat to hang any miscreants.[5] He was a tough sheriff who knew the Indians well, particularly the Bloods, who had been his best customers in the whiskey-trading days. When Harrison reported the theft and his unsuccessful pursuit of the raiders, Healy immediately organized a posse to find the culprits. On October 16 Healy, accompanied by three deputies—Jeff Talbert, I. N. Clark, and Frank Goss—and the three Yellowstone ranchers, set out to pick up the trail of the war party. Wise to the ways of the Bloods, Healy led his men due west along the Teton River, looking for signs of horses having crossed the stream. He found what he was looking for at Timber Coulee, a tiny tributary of the Teton.

The sheriff reported that he "struck the trail of the stolen animals at the Knees; followed it to Kipp's Post . . . ; followed the trail from Kipp up to the Marias, to within five miles of the Willow Rounds, where a portion of this war party turned north with a large number of horses."[6]

The weather was cold and stormy, and although the signs were fresh, Healy knew there was little likelihood that he could catch the northern party before it reached the Canadian line thirty miles away. Instead, the posse continued west along the Marias River until the men came to the ranch of Sol Abbott, an ex–whiskey trader who lived there with his Piegan wife. There they found one of Harrison's horses in the possession of an elderly Blood woman who had received it as a gift. As Healy knew, the Bloods often gave a horse to the first tribesman they met when returning from a successful raid. In this instance the old woman had the luxury of the horse for only a couple of days before it was reclaimed by the Yellowstone rancher.

A short distance away, the posse visited the ranch of Henry Kennerly, another man with a Native wife. According to a newspaper report, the Blood horse raiders "camped one night near Henry Kennerly's ranch. Mr. Kennerly thought they were some cow boys and allowed them to go on unmolested. Next morning he saw on their camping ground war houses and other unmistakable Indian signs."[7]

During all this time the Bloods had no idea they were being pursued. When cowboys failed to follow them after their first night out, they likely thought they could far outdistance any later trackers. Then, when the blizzard struck, they probably believed there was no way that they could be found. The continuing bad weather made travel unpleasant if not dangerous for those not accustomed to the country, so the Bloods traveled at their leisure, without fear of apprehension.

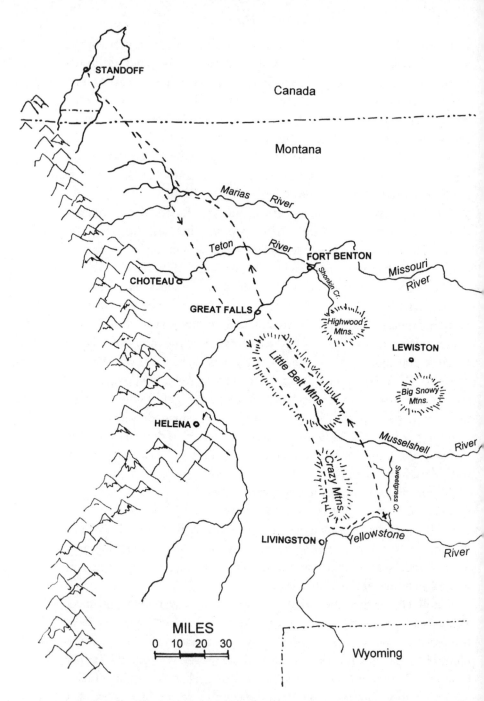

This map shows the route taken by Eagle Plume and his war party in 1881. They crossed the entire territory of Montana on foot and made their raid on the Yellowstone River.

On the following day Sheriff Healy and his posse rode into an Indian camp at the Blackfeet Agency and promptly arrested a Blood Indian named Bad Bull. The Indian did not have any stolen stock in his possession, but two of Harrison's horses were found in the camp, and the agent reported that Bad Bull had arrived at the agency a short time before. This was enough for the sheriff to have the Indian detained, even though he vigorously denied taking part in the raid.

Bad Bull, a son of Three Bulls, had a wife and three children. He had never been in trouble with the law, yet he was described in the Montana press as "an ugly customer who gave his captor no little trouble by resisting arrest and by his attempts at escape."[8] The sheriff knew that the Indian was not a member of the raiding party, so he never charged him with any crime. Rather, he simply made him a prisoner in an effort to get his fellow tribesmen to surrender the stolen horses. As a reporter commented, "It was not pretended that Bad Bull had anything to do with the stealing of the Yellowstone horses; it was not pretended that he had committed any offense for which he could be held amenable before the law. He was simply held as a hostage."[9]

Healy and his deputies spent the next few days searching the camps for horse thieves and missing animals. While this was going on, three Bloods who may have taken part in the raid heard about the apprehension of Bad Bull and fled across the line.

The Indian prisoner was kept in irons at the agency until Healy completed his search. By this time the sheriff had been on the trail of the raiders for more than a week, the three Yellowstone ranchers for close to three weeks. During that period they had located eighteen horses and detained one man. That was enough for Healy, his deputies, and two of the Yellowstone ranchers. But it was not enough for Albert Harrison. He insisted that the thieves be tracked all the way to Canada, and if no one else would accompany him, he would go alone.

Healy explained that Canada was out of his jurisdiction, but he did agree to arrange for a number of Piegan headmen to accompany Harrison. These included tribal chief White Calf, Fast Buffalo Horses, Big Plume, Calf Shirt, and four others. Healy also wrote a letter to the commanding officer of the North-West Mounted Police at Fort Macleod, which began, "The bearer, Mr. Harrison, a settler of the Yellowstone Valley, had in the neighborhood of fifty horses stolen by Blood Indians belonging to the Blood Reservation, on the Belly River, about two weeks ago." After describing the pursuit of the raiders, Healy continued, "for the sake of peace and good feeling between the settlers and the Piegans, I trust that some measures will be taken to recover the stolen animals and turn them over to Mr. Harrison and the Indians so that they may be brought here and turned over to their owners."[10]

If Healy had ended his letter on that amicable note, the matter would likely have remained a local one, not drawn to the attention of officials in Ottawa. But the ex–whiskey trader–whose business had been closed down by the Mounted Police–could not resist a little American saber rattling. He added, "Should this missive prove futile, serious consequences are liable to follow, as the people of Montana have tired of being harassed by the marauding hordes of the north, and will wreak vengeance upon all war parties caught this side of the line."[11]

In part Healy was echoing a threat being made by several ranchers and by the Choteau and Meagher Counties Stock Protective Association. Granville Stuart, a wealthy Montana rancher, called the Indians "lazy, filthy, brutal savages" and believed that the problem of horse stealing would be resolved "after we have converted a few of [these] breech-clouted pets into good Indians."[12] Similarly, a Montana newspaper editorial claimed, "At the present time the Mounted Police have lost control of the Indians. Warriors from the Blood, North Piegan and Blackfoot Agencies in the Northwest go openly to war on the white settlers of Montana and return with large numbers of white men's horses–horses having brands and harness marks upon them, and the Police dare not make proper efforts to seize these animals and return them to their owners."[13]

Sheriff Healy's letter–and threat–was passed on to Commissioner A. G. Irvine in Regina and ultimately to mandarins in Ottawa. Irvine concurred that Canadian Indians were causing problems in the United States, but he observed that the traffic was not all from north to south. He had affidavits that

> prove conclusively the many depredations committed on British soil by United States Indians. . . . the depredations on our side of the line have been quite as numerous as those said to have been committed in the United States. These depredations in almost all cases take the shape of horse stealing. A large proportion of the horses

stolen by our Indians in United States territory have been eventually recovered by the police and returned to their legitimate owners, while horses stolen by American Indians are, almost without exception, never returned.[14]

Superintendent L. N. F. Crozier, commanding a detachment at Fort Macleod, substantiated the views of his superior officer; "during the past summer," he noted, "there has scarcely been a ranchman or horse owner in this section of the country who has not lost horses by means of white thieves or half-breeds from the American side. In addition, as you are aware, a large and valuable herd of horses was stolen from the Police Farm by American horse thieves, and were only recovered after a great deal of trouble and considerable expense, in United States territory. The Indians here also say that they have lost a large number of horses by thieves across the line."[15]

While Canadians and Montanans were arguing about horse thieves and the efficacy of the Mounted Police, Albert Harrison was on his way north to find the rest of his horses. He and his escort of Piegans reached the Indian Agency at Standoff on October 25, and as soon as their complaint was heard, the agent instituted a search for the missing horses. To gain the cooperation of the Bloods, a meeting was held between the Piegan and Blood chiefs. As a result, two or three horses in miserable condition were produced. When the chiefs explained that these were the only white men's horses in their camps, Harrison went to the Mounted Police post at Fort Macleod and presented his problem directly to Inspector Crozier.

"They immediately sent out some Mounted Policemen," explained Harrison, "and by half-past ten o'clock they had brought in seven of the party—all that could be found—to the fort. A jury of twelve citizens was impaneled. The trial was held before Col. Macleod, the stipendiary magistrate. In less than two hours and a half the seven Indians were found guilty."[16] These were Eagle Plume, Hind Cow, Tongue Eater, Rides Around the Dance Circle, Weak One, Old Man Who Sidles at the Dance, and Killed in the Night. After the trial sixteen stolen horses and two colts were brought into the fort, and on the following day a party of Mounted Police rode to the mouth of the Little Bow River, where they succeeded in recovering two more horses and arresting one more raider. A second constable went to a ranch on the Oldman River, where another missing horse was found.

At first Harrison was extremely pleased with the results and spoke "in the highest terms of his treatment by the Macleod officials."[17] By the time he returned to Montana, the rancher had recovered more than half his horses after forty-four days of "the hardest riding I ever did."[18] The expedition had cost him five hundred dollars for salaries to his cowboys, payment to the Piegan chiefs, and other expenses. But it had all been worth it, because the horse thieves had been arrested and would feel the full weight of Canadian law.

But Harrison's gratitude later turned to fury when he learned that immediately after he was out of sight, the seven horse thieves had been lectured and released from custody. This had happened even though they had freely admitted their crime and a jury had found them guilty. The release had been authorized by Magistrate Macleod, who said that no Indians in the area had ever been convicted under this law, and "what they had done was not considered by them as offence in this country."[19]

Suddenly the Canadians were no longer nice guys. Harrison now complained that "as soon as I was gone, they went back on everything" and that the Mounted Police were cowards who were afraid to act because "there were more Indians than white men" in the area.[20] Instead of being grateful for getting some of his horses back, he now complained that all he had recovered were "a few of my poorest horses, sore-backed and run to death."[21]

His anger should have been mollified a short time later, when he was notified that sixteen more horses had been recovered by the Mounted Police. However, when he sent a couple of cowboys to collect them, he learned that the animals had been turned out to graze and now only seven could be found. To add insult to injury, Harrison had to pay $5.25 a head to get them back, as that was the amount the police had paid to friendly Indians for recovering them. Not only that, but two of the horses died on the way back to Montana.

Harrison was not a man to be trifled with. Probably no other rancher would have pursued his missing horses for forty-four days during one of the coldest autumns on record, spent more money in expenses than the horses were worth, and carried on a vendetta against the Mounted Police long after the events were past. But he was not a man to forgive or forget.

He was particularly incensed that the Canadians would release thieves such as Eagle Plume after they had admitted stealing his horses.

Four months after the incident, Harrison wrote an angry letter to the *Toronto Globe* "in order that the people of Canada may know how their Indian affairs are managed at Fort McLeod."[22] He gave his version of the incident, repeating his assertion that the Mounted Police were cowards, and implied that Canadians were paying the Indians to steal American horses. In reply to this diatribe, someone who signed himself "XYZ" (probably a Mounted Policeman) wrote to the *Fort Macleod Gazette*, commenting that Harrison "seems to have drawn on his imagination for most of its substance."[23] Regarding the release of the prisoners, the writer commented: "They were tried before Col. Macleod, and pleaded their ignorance that they could be punished on this side the line for stealing horses on the other, a fact of which not a few white men are as well ignorant. On this account, and in view of the good assistance which most of these very Indians had rendered in recovering the horses, Col. Macleod dismissed them with a severe caution."[24] As for the assertion that the Mounted Police were cowards, the writer called this "a most atrocious fabrication" and "is most absurd as well as utterly false,"[25] pointing to the many incidents in which desperate Indians had been arrested and imprisoned.

Meanwhile, what had happened to the innocent Bad Bull? When Healy and his posse returned to Fort Benton on October 28, they took the young Indian with them and placed him in the new brick jail. As a reporter commented: "Doubtless Bad Bull is a bad Indian; that he would steal a horse if a good opportunity were afforded we are ready to believe, but no charge of any kind was made against him except in a very general way."[26] Sheriff Healy admitted the Indian was innocent but said that "I intend . . . holding him for a reasonable time or until such time as the horses stolen from the whites this fall are returned."[27]

When Harrison returned from the north with some of his stolen horses, there was no longer any excuse to hold the Blood Indian as a hostage. But instead of simply releasing him, the sheriff decided to have "a little fun" at the Indian's expense. On the morning of November 7 Sheriff Healy, a newspaper reporter, and a dozen friends went to the jail to see the prisoner released. No sooner was he out of the cell, than he was pushed onto a chair and a sheet thrown over his shoulders. As he sat in fear and puzzlement, Bad Bull saw Charles Bryer, the local barber, walk into the room with his scissors and clippers.

He immediately realized what was happening, and "notwithstanding his protest and piteous appeals, his long black hair was soon clipped." The reporter added that "The Sheriff laughed. Everybody laughed. It was a brave deed!"[28] Healy then picked up three of the braids and gave them as souvenirs to his deputies.

When the incident was reported in the press, the response from Montanans was one of indignation and disgust. The act was described as "a foolish, blundering outrage,"[29] and the *Bozeman Courier* predicted that it would result in the revenge death of at least one settler. Everyone knew of the pride that Blackfoot men had in their hair and their disgrace if they lost it. Some men even wore their hair in topknots as a challenge to their enemies to try to take their scalps. In jail Bad Bull was reported to have spent many hours combing, grooming, and braiding his long black hair. Now he was bald and humiliated. And what was more grating was the fact that he was an innocent man who happened to be in the wrong place when the sheriff needed a Blood Indian hostage.

On the following day ex–whiskey trader Dave Akers sympathetically offered Bad Bull a place on his freight wagon on his return to Whoop-Up. It must have been a trip filled with anxiety and concern, for the Indian knew that the loss of his hair would make him subject to teasing and joking. And his worst fears were realized. A settler who witnessed the young man's arrival said, "The Indians indulged in considerable fun at Bad Bull's expenses, which fun that gentleman took very philosophically. But he swears by all that is binding among Indians that he is going to live among the south Piegans and in the spring, when Sheriff Healy is out on the lonely prairie, he will swoop down on him and wipe him off from the face of the earth."[30]

It was a brave promise, but it was not to be. Whether by humiliation, disease, or other cause, Bad Bull became ill and died a few months later without ever having had a chance to fulfill his vow of vengeance.

As for the leading horse raiders, Eagle Plume and Packs his Tail ultimately became respected members of the tribe, but not until they fulfilled their careers as warriors. By the time Eagle Plume settled down, he had been in twenty-four raids against his enemies, killed seven men, and captured more than a hundred horses.[31] He had three wives and at least ten children. As he got older he became a horse racer, and at the time of his death in 1936 he was one of the most respected patriarchs on the reserve. Packs his Tail became part of a notorious group of young men called the "Mule Outfit" who openly defied the Indian agent in the 1880s and tried to maintain the tribe's ancient traditions and practices. During this time he married Kit Fox Woman and they had two children. Then, in 1896, Packs his Tail found a new career as scout for the North-West Mounted Police. He was still a relatively young man when he died just after the turn of the century.

The adventure with Harrison's horses had been a mere sidelight in their careers, but it had a much greater impact upon Canadian-American relations. The Mounted Police were obliged to defend themselves against bitter attacks and to convince Montanans that their own citizens were guilty as well in providing sanctuary for horse thieves. The arrests resulting from the Harrison expedition also made it clear to the Bloods and Piegans that they could no longer raid across the line with impunity, for if the American cowboys did not get them, the Mounted Police would. As a result, the chiefs set up their own system of scouts to prevent young men from going out on war parties. The guards were not always successful, but they did well enough to ease tensions between the two nations.

The final word about the incident came from the *Chicago Times*, which commented early in 1882 on the unrest caused by the Canadian raiders. It stated:

> The tribes in particularly bad odor, from a record of deviltry that cannot be beat by any other redskins in the country, are the Northern Bloods and Piegans; but these scallywags are now conducting themselves with remarkable circumspection. That they should behave themselves is more than could have been reasonably expected, and that they should voluntarily constitute themselves a police force . . . is a freak without precedent in mountain history. Red Crow, the Blood chief, and Big Swan, the chief of the Piegans, have made their warriors patrol the northern border unceasingly for several weeks now, and as a result [Indian] riders from the queen's domains have been confronted at the line with a grim array of red robbers preaching an unwonted gospel of honesty, and ready to stop their progress southward at any cost. The Piegans and Bloods

express a determination to stop forever the horse stealing and cattle killing that have caused so much loss and annoyance to settlers in the past.[32]

Horse stealing and cattle killing were not completely controlled until the turn of the century, but the fuss created by Albert Harrison was the first step towards the elimination of a nomadic lifestyle that seemed to have no place in the sedentary life of the western tribes.

13   *Was Mary White Really White?*

A beautiful girl with blue eyes and light brown hair was born early in 1881, either on the Blackfoot Reserve to a Siksika family or somewhere in Montana, from which place she had been kidnapped from a white family. The search for the answer to that question caused an uproar that extended from Alberta to Ottawa to New York and all the way across the ocean to London.

The little girl, who was named Mary White or Spotted Woman, Kitsi-pimaiki, came to the attention of the public for the first time during the summer of 1883. Charles Kavanagh, manager for railway contractors Langdon & Shephard, reported to a Winnipeg newspaper that "Crow-foot, the Blackfeet chief, has in his possession a white female child about two years old. This little one has flaxen hair and blue eyes, and is a well-made pretty girl."[1] Kavanagh and a Canadian Pacific Railway train master tried to buy the girl from her mother for twenty dollars, but the woman refused and the matter ended there. Five years later, in the summer of 1888, a *Calgary Herald* reporter visiting the Blackfoot Reserve observed "a couple of interesting little white children, boy and girl, who, although possessing all the physical characteristics of white children are kept by one of the squaws as members of her family."[2] He described them as having blue eyes and fair hair and skin but dressed entirely in Indian fashion. He said there were two stories in circulation about them. One was that "the children were stolen some time ago from Fort Assiniboine, Montana, and that their father is an American army officer quartered there."[3] The other was a statement by her mother that the children were her own.

When the matter was investigated by Indian agent Magnus Begg, he reported that the children were not white but Native. Other government officials added that the little girl had been born during the winter of

Mary White, or Spotted Woman, became the center of attention when claims were made that she was a white girl captured by the Siksika Indians. She is seen here in an 1890 photograph taken by Trueman and Caple.
Courtesy Glenbow Archives, Calgary, AB, cat. no. NA-2357-1

1880–81 at Crowfoot's village. Her father was identified as Dog Child, Imita'kosi, a son of minor chief Weasel Calf, and her mother Handsome Gun Woman, Mutsina'maiaki, a daughter of Low Horn, also a minor chief. In a statement the Mounted Police said that "the child was born at the South Camp, Blackfoot Reserve" in the winter of 1880–81 and that "Crowfoot, Three Bulls, and Weasel Calf all state that they saw the child shortly after birth and there are a number of Indians who can testify to the same."[4] Dog Child himself, in one of his conflicting statements, said that Mary was born "at the time of the year when the ice was breaking up in the water" and that "the sun had risen only a few times when I sent for the priest and he baptized her."[5]

There are problems with these statements. For one, Crowfoot left Blackfoot Crossing in the autumn of 1879 to pursue the last buffalo herds into Montana and did not return to the reserve until August of 1881, so he was nowhere near the reserve in the late winter of 1880 or the early spring of 1881. Also, Dog Child did not appear for his treaty money when it was paid in the autumn of 1880, indicating that he was probably with the rest of the tribe in Montana. And finally, the current Roman Catholic missionary on the Blackfoot Reserve states, "After carefully checking all the records at the Mission Church here I cannot find any record of Mary White's baptism."[6]

As soon as the buffalo had become scarce in their hunting grounds late in 1878, the Siksikas had wandered east to the Cypress Hills, with only the old and the infirm remaining at Blackfoot Crossing to receive rations from the Mounted Police. In 1879, when the Canadian prairies were virtually destitute of buffalo, Crowfoot had been obliged to lead his people south to the Bear Paw Mountains of Montana and finally to the Judith Basin to join other tribes in their last great hunts. By the spring of 1881 the Blackfoot had to admit that the buffalo had been exterminated and there was nothing left on the Montana plains except ranchers and settlers, who hated Canadian Indians. A few Siksikas began to drift back to Canada as early as April, going first to Fort Walsh and then across the arid plains to Fort Macleod. The main party of Siksikas, under Crowfoot, arrived at the Mounted Police fort in July, rested for a few days, and reached the friendly confines of the Blackfoot Reserve at the beginning of August. Their years of wandering were over.

Dog Child had been a warrior in the days when there were still buffalo to be hunted. He had been a member of a war party that had killed and scalped four Nez Perces in the mountains of western Montana and had shot and scalped a Cree in another confrontation. He was also unique in that he was one of the few Siksikas who could speak some English. In the spring of 1875, he had been a witness to a murder when a Blood Indian named Bad Breast, Atsemoonikis, was accused of shooting his wife, Short Woman, near Fort Macleod. The sixty-four-year-old husband had fled before he could be questioned, but a year later he could not resist recounting his exploits when speaking to a group of Crees near Fort Walsh. He told how he had been a member of a war party about four years earlier that had wiped out a wagon train of Germans in the Porcupine Hills, killing three white women. He also claimed that he had slain thirteen people during his career, one of whom was his wife. The information was passed along to the Mounted Police, who immediately recognized him as the wanted man and arrested him.

There were no Courts of Queen's Bench in the West at that time, so any persons accused of capital crimes had to be sent all the way to Winnipeg—a thousand miles east—by wagon or horseback. Inspector Albert Shurtliff and an escort made that long trek with Bad Breast as their prisoner and Dog Child along as a witness. It was a new and wonderful experience for Dog Child, for to his knowledge no one from his tribe had ever traveled that far east before. As they ended their trek across the prairie and came to a line of trees, he was convinced that this was the edge of the world and they would fall off. When they got to Winnipeg, he could not comprehend the existence of so many buildings and "enquired if the houses were not tied together with a lariat."[7]

Once they arrived in the Manitoba city, they stayed there for several weeks waiting for the trial. When it was held, Dog Child testified that he had been a drummer at a dance in Stingy's lodge. About three in the morning, Short Woman was dancing with a young man, the two with a single blanket over their heads, when suddenly there were two shots and the woman fell dead with bullet wounds to the head. At first people thought the young man had shot her, but he showed that his revolver had not been fired. Then someone noticed a hole cut into the leather wall of the tepee and concluded that Short Woman's jealous husband had poked his rifle through the hole and shot her. Other witnesses said virtually the same thing, but no one had actually seen Bad Breast commit the deed, so he was found not guilty.

Dog Child and his wife, Handsome Gun Woman, were shown on the Blackfoot
rolls as the parents of Spotted Woman. Dog Child, nicknamed Winnipeg Jack, was a
scout for the North-West Mounted Police.

Courtesy Glenbow Archives, Calgary, AB, cat. no. NA-3730-1

During the time that he was in Winnipeg, Dog Child began to learn English, and when he returned to his own people he had picked up a working knowledge of the language. As a result, he was employed from time to time by the Mounted Police and Indian Department and was given the nickname "Winnipeg Jack."

Handsome Gun Woman was Dog Child's third wife, and he already had one son, False Takes the Gun, by one of his other wives. This boy was born about 1878 and when baptized was given the name Thomas White. After his sister Spotted Woman, or Mary, was born, there were two other children, a girl named Morning Star and a boy named Coyote. Within the reserve all were considered to be part of Dog Child's family.

While fair-skinned Mary may have been the subject of local gossip, her presence became an international issue in October 1889 during a visit of Canada's governor-general, Lord Stanley, and his wife. When the vice-regal couple went to the Blackfoot Reserve, they were accompanied by Frederic Villiers, an artist for the *London Graphic*. He wrote in the English newspaper: "A captive of one of the chiefs of the Blackfeet is a little white girl about nine years old. She was brought into camp on a pony, dressed in rich beadwork vestments, which ill became her fair hair and little white face. . . . I was told on good authority that she had been captured during a raid in United States territory, in which her father, an officer, was killed."[8]

The artist also made a sketch that accompanied the article, showing the girl sitting sedately on her horse. A few days later, when Villiers stopped in New York, he was approached by the *New York World* for more information about the "captive white girl." He stated that his source of information about her being kidnapped had come from the "Canadian fort," presumably the Mounted Police.

The New York newspaper knew a good human-interest story when it saw one, so it asked Villiers if he would write an article for them, providing more information about his experiences on the Blackfoot Reserve and, more particularly, about the little girl. The artist was pleased to oblige and recorded the following conversation he had had with a "reservation officer."

"Don't go away without sketching the Blackfeet white captive."

"No doubt, you mean," I replied with a smile, "the white captive with black feet; exactly what I go in for—studies in black and white."

"Joking aside," said my friend, "it's a fact. The Blackfeet have a little white captive. It's disgraceful in these civilized times that it should be so; but it is true. She was captured during a raid across the frontier, and the rumor goes that she is the daughter of an American officer killed in the fray."[9]

At Villiers's request, the girl was brought forward by Dog Child. She was riding a white pony that had a Mexican-type saddle covered in red leather and decorated with brass nails. She was dressed in a lavish Blackfoot dress decorated with a profusion of beads and looked to be about nine years old. She sat quietly on the horse while Villiers made his sketch, then slid to the ground and shook hands with him. She would not speak but held her head down and looked at the ground; as soon as the opportunity arose, she jumped back on her pony and disappeared into the crowd.

"I never saw a whiter girl in all my life," said Villiers. "There was no Indian blood in her veins. . . . Her little white face with small, regular features, and bright gray eyes stood out of a wealth of golden hair. Well, it would have been golden but for the alloy of dust and grit which besprinkled it."[10] He ended by expressing the hope that she would be returned to the people of her "own color, if not her own nationality."[11]

This was the kind of story that was designed to bring a sob to the throat of every mother and a burst of righteous indignation from every father. In short, it was a perfect attention-grabber for the sensation-seeking newspapers of the day. Not unexpectedly, the story was picked up by other newspapers all across the United States and Canada, and equally predictably, it brought a flood of letters to the editor. One example, directed to the *Macleod Gazette*, was from a man who felt the news "made one's blood boil" and said the girl should be rescued at any cost.[12]

Feelings were naturally high in Montana, and a Fort Benton newspaper commented that "If anybody in the country has lost a child or given one away, the River Press would be pleased to learn the particulars."[13] At Fort Shaw the commanding officer, considering the possibility that the story might be true, sent Lieutenant Ahern north to check it out. He got as far as Lethbridge, where Mounted Police authorities convinced him that Mary White had not been kidnapped from a U.S. military family. Meanwhile, Dog Child confused the issue by stating that Mary had not been taken after a fight with the army after all, but that she been given to him by a white woman after the father had died and the mother could not look after her.

Canadian officials knew that this matter could become a hot political issue and might end up on the floor of the House of Commons unless it could be refuted. Accordingly, both the North-West Mounted Police and the Indian Department were instructed to find out what had really happened.

Magnus Begg, the Blackfoot Indian agent, went with two policeman to interview Dog Child and received a signed statement from him, stating "that this child was born on the reserve and that I never told any person it was born any other place, and further that I never had a child given me by any person."[14] However, a few weeks earlier Dog Child had told a Mounted Policeman that "the reason he told Gladstone and others that the child was a white one and had been given to him in Benton was because he was always being bothered by people about her and he used to tell them the first story that occurred to him."[15] So Dog Child's depositions were at variance with each other and completely unreliable.

However, both the Indian Department and the Mounted Police were adamant that the child had been born to Handsome Gun Woman. Explained J. C. McIllree:

> The mother of the child (Winnipeg Jack's squaw) is not as dark as many Indians, and her hair is more brown than black. Jack states that this woman since he lived with her has had three children who were all white. The eldest was born South of the Line and died on the Reserve, the second one is the one in question, and the third is a girl about three years old, and she is if anything lighter in complexion than her eldest sister. Jack states that his squaw's mother was light complexioned, had light hair and was always taken for a half breed. I have inquired into this point and find it to be true as far as my inquiries have gone.[16]

McIllree was of the opinion that Handsome Gun Woman was the mother of Mary, but that Dog Child was not the father. He believed that the father was a white man named Joe Howard, an American trader who was now living on the Blackfeet Reservation in Montana. McIllree added that there were several Indian Department ex-employees, Mounted

Policemen, and Indians who could swear that they had seen the baby on the reserve "shortly after its birth."[17]

Meanwhile, the press was having a field day, with comments both for and against the idea that Mary White was indeed white. Those newspapers and letter writers close to the area tended to be sceptical, while those at a distance were more inclined to be angry and indignant. A. A. Vice, an old ex-whiskey trader, considered the story to be "the greatest hoax of the season."[18] He said the child was obviously a half-breed and "if the Canadian Government intend laying claim to all the children living in Indian camps who have light hair, blue or grey eyes and fair skins in the Northwest Territories, it will have its hands full."[19]

Similarly, Father Albert Lacombe, a famous Oblate missionary, felt that the story was ridiculous and the public was being misled by sensational reports. He said there were many boys and girls on the Blackfoot reserves of southern Alberta who had light-colored hair and European features, and that these were the offspring of Indian women and white men. "No, sir," he concluded, "the Indians do not want to steal white children; they have plenty of their own, born in camps."[20]

On the other hand, ex-Mounted Policeman C. R. Saffery, now living in New York, wrote to the *World* suggesting that an expedition be sent west to rescue the poor little white girl. The editors thought this was an excellent idea and awarded Saffery five hundred dollars as second prize in their "Idea Contest." Not only that, but they suggested that Saffery take part in the rescue.

Leading the expedition was Isaac Deforest White, one of the star reporters for the *New York World.* It is amazing how often the word or name "White" surfaced during this extravaganza. Mary White was probably given her name because her older half-brother was named Thomas White, the surname likely taken from Frederick White, comptroller of the North-West Mounted Police. It was a common practice of Indian agents and missionaries to name children after important figures. On the Blood Reserve, for example, there were Macdonalds in honor of Sir John A., Dewdneys after the Hon. Edgar Dewdney, Lacombes after the priest, and Wadsworths after the inspector of Indian Agencies. So 1890 saw Isaac White traveling west to see if Mary White, half-sister of Thomas White, was white.

Isaac White was the ideal man for the quest. Throughout his career he had been an adventurer who helped to fuel the sensationalism of his newspaper. At one time he was sent to the Yucatan to check a report that some American workers were being held in slavery. White managed to find sixteen witnesses who could prove that they had been shanghaied to Mexico by New York gang boss "Liverpool Jack" Fitzgerald. When the reporter tried to get the men on a ship, two of Fitzgerald's cronies had him arrested for anarchy. He was able to bluff his way out of the situation and later saw Fitzgerald convicted. Meanwhile, the *New York World* published sensation after sensation as the story unfolded. White also out-witted armed oyster pirates in Chesapeake Bay, identified a bomber who died while trying to extort money from financier Rufus Sage, and exposed conditions at Elmira Reformatory, which resulted in the dismissal of its superintendent.

White set out for the Canadian West "convinced that the little white-skinned girl described by Villiers was anything but an Indian child" and was "prepared to go to any extreme to gain possession of the little one and get her across the line to American soil."[21] In mid-January he met Saffery in Montreal to plan their strategy. The ex-policeman said he knew Jerry Potts, who lived at Fort Macleod, and that he would be the best person to assist them in interviewing the chiefs and Mary White's family. If they bought the girl, Saffery thought they might have to pay as much as fifty dollars for her, even though "an Indian will ordinarily sell any one of his children for from $10 to $25." If that did not work, they were prepared to kidnap her, and to this end they studied maps to find the various escape routes from the Blackfoot Reserve to the United States.

Once their plans were in place, they made a four-day journey on the Canadian Pacific Railway to Dunmore, just east of Medicine Hat, where they changed trains to take the tiny "turkey track" line to Lethbridge. From there they experienced a hair-raising trip on a stagecoach to Fort Macleod, dashing through snowdrifts while the thermometer hovered around thirty-five below (F). At the fort they were pleased to learn that the various trails south to Montana were still open in case they had to make a run for it. They were also successful in obtaining the services of Jerry Potts, and one of his first actions was to visit a Siksika Indian camped near the fort to ask him about Mary White. "The Indian knew of the girl," said White, "but had no idea of her parentage. He said that Dog Child had been across the border in Montana about the time the child must have been born if it were now nine years old." Potts also picked up a rumor "that there was a man in California who had had an infant stolen by Indians in Montana about the time that Dog Child was there."

Just as they were getting ready to leave, Potts became ill, so White and Saffery engaged the services of Ben DeRoche, an oldtime scout and interpreter. With some idea of conducting a pincer movement, White decided that he would take a stagecoach to Calgary then board a Canadian Pacific train to Gleichen, the closest station to the Blackfoot Reserve, while Saffery and DeRoche would retrace the route to Dunmore and close in on Gleichen from the east.

The trip north proved to be an ordeal for the New York reporter. Not only was it bitterly cold with a head wind, but the stagecoach had gone only a few miles when the snowdrifts became so deep that the driver had to stop and change to sleigh runners. They spent the night at Mosquito Creek (later Nanton), reaching High River at noon of the following day. North of there they lost the trail, and they were still on the open prairie after sunset. After searching for an hour they finally found the route again and reached Calgary late that night, with enough time for White to catch the train to Gleichen the following day.

As soon as the Mounted Police and the Indian Department learned that the New York reporter was in the area, they set to work to assure him that Mary was not a kidnapped white girl. Sergeant Todd met with White, while DeRoche slipped away to speak with people on the reserve. Before they had even seen the girl, Isaac White was persuaded by the police that Mary really was a Siksika Indian. He also believed that a schoolteacher and a cook employed by the Indian Department had misled Villiers into thinking that she was a white captive.

Having come this far, the reporter could not leave without actually seeing the girl, and Sergeant Todd was pleased to oblige. Traveling by sled, they reached Indian Agent Magnus Begg's home by noon and spent the night there. Doubtless, Begg took the opportunity to further convince White of the fruitlessness of his long journey. He was told that Mary had been born on the reserve a few weeks after Dog Child and Handsome Gun Woman had returned from Montana, that the government interpreter had seen her when she was only a few hours old and had registered her birth, and that the local Catholic missionary had baptized her. He was informed that several Indians were prepared to testify that Handsome Gun Woman was her mother.

Next morning, White was taken to a nine-foot-square shack that was Dog Child's living quarters while working as a scout for the North-West Mounted Police. Inside he found Mary White, her parents, and three other children. False Takes the Gun and Coyote were as dark as their father, while Morning Star was as fair as Mary. The reporter said the two young girls "looked as much out of place as two little chicks with a duck mother. They had on calico dresses, neatly fitted, but they wore the moccasins of the aborigines." He said that Mary was as fair as any American girl, her golden hair parted in the middle and braided on each side of her head and her eyes hazel grey. He described the meeting as follows:

> Her nose was aquiline, and an exact reproduction of her mother's. She had tiny brass earrings in her ears and snake-bangles of brass on either wrist. Her face was bright and cheerful and she had a very pretty way of dropping her eyelids when I looked at her. Once when I admired her bangles she smiled. . . . The little one could speak no English, but when she talked in her native tongue her voice was soft and pleasant to the ear. Although she seemed a very shy, gentle, little creature, and very much out of place in her grotesque surroundings.[22]

Convinced by what he was told by the Mounted Police and the Indian Department rather than by what he saw, Isaac White wrote a full-page article in the *New York World*, "Papoose After All," recounting his adventures and his meeting with the girl. Mary White, he said, "turns out to be of Indian extraction after all." With that article, the whole controversy ended as quickly as it started. Isaac White returned to New York to seek other sensational stories wherever they might appear. Dog Child and his family moved to a better house beside the Mounted Police barracks on the outskirts of Gleichen, and there the scout remained until his death five years later.

As for Mary White, she was sent to St. Joseph's Industrial School, just south of Calgary, but she cried so incessantly that her father picked her up and brought her home after just nine days. He doted on the girl, and in spite of pleas from the Catholic priest, he refused to send her away from the reserve. Instead, he enrolled her in the town school at Gleichen, where she attended day classes made up entirely of white students. However, immediately after Dog Child's death in 1895, Handsome Gun Woman agreed to place the girl in an Anglican boarding school that was located on the reserve. She was admitted on April 1 under the name Mary Dog Child.

The change of name was significant. There was tremendous competition between Catholic and Anglican missionaries for the bodies and souls of Indian children, and each time a child moved from one denomination to the other, every effort was made to expunge anything that would remind the family of what she had once been. The family name "White" had been adopted by the Catholics when False Takes the Gun went to school, so the Anglicans rejected it when they accepted Mary.

The likely reason for Handsome Gun Woman's placing the girl in the boarding school was that she was now fourteen and was already too much for her mother to handle. Whether they were white children from town or Indian children from the reserve, Mary was already running with the wrong crowd, so when her father died, her mother opted for the boarding school. However, the girl remained at the school for only three months before it was temporarily closed after a student died there.[23] When the school reopened, she did not go back.

In 1896 St. Joseph's Industrial School graduated one of its most successful students to date, Joseph Royal, Misam-onisi, a son of Crow Flag. He had learned carpentry at the industrial school, and when Gleichen merchant J. V. Beaupre offered to hire him to build a new store, the priests were elated. However, he had been on the job for only a few weeks when word was received by the priests that he had moved in with Mary White. Angrily, the principal of the school wrote to Beaupre, "I understand that Mary White, a girl of a questionable character, has been put into the young man's way and that he has been induced to marry her, after the Indian fashion."[24]

There were two strikes against Mary White in the eyes of the priests. First, she was "of questionable character"; perhaps worse, she was an Anglican. The priest wrote to the Mounted Police detachment at Gleichen:

The Department [of Indian Affairs] is very particular about the marriages of the pupils of the Industrial Schools, and has imposed certain regulations to comply with, one of them being the consent required from Head Office. The Dept. certainly will not admit of a pupil marrying after the Indian fashion. Joseph Royal being a

Catholic, I consider his Indian marriage as null. I will submit the whole matter to the Department, and in the meanwhile the young man should not be allowed to live with the girl.[25]

But the priest was too late. By the time the Mounted Police received the letter, Mary White was already pregnant. The Catholic missionary then wrote to the Indian Department, "Rev. Father Doucet, of the Blackfoot Reserve, informs me that Jos. Royal is quite decided to marry the girl Mary White with whom he is now living in the house of this girl's mother. In order to stop further scandal the Rev. Father Doucet tells me that he is instructing the girl, so as to marry them in a Christian and religious way, as soon as possible."[26]

The marriage—which took place on April 25, 1897—was a historic event, as it was the first Christian marriage performed in the Siksika tribe. Obviously, the participants were not of the missionaries' choosing, as the involvement of Mary did little to further the credibility of a good education. It was a necessary act, however, for less than six months later, baby Charles was born.

But the marriage itself was a failure. Joseph was only eighteen and his bride sixteen. Shielded from the temptations of teenage sexual life, Joseph was just reentering the Siksika community when he became entranced by the attractive and worldly Mary White. Their "Indian style" marriage, if left alone, would probably have lasted for only a few months. The fact that the two were now united in a legal marriage made no real difference, and they went their separate ways, while young Charles was usually left with his grandmother. "My mother mixed with the white people a lot and didn't like it on the reserve," Charles recalled. "She used to go to Gleichen and Calgary a lot and she talked good English."[27]

In 1899 the Indian Department recognized the split by issuing a separate treaty ticket to Mary. Hers was listed as Q50, issued to Mary Royal for one woman and one boy. From the separation it was downhill all the way. She began passing herself off as a half-breed in order to buy liquor, both for herself and for others, and drifted aimlessly between the Blood, Piegan, and Blackfoot Reserves as well as spending time in the adjacent towns and cities.

In the spring of 1905 she entered into an Indian-style marriage with Frank Bastien, a Piegan Indian, and the two moved to the town of Macleod, where she was accused of living off the avails of prostitution and providing bootleg liquor to other Indians. Bastien was sent back to his reserve with a warning that living with Mary was "very closely approaching committing bigamy," in view of her Christian marriage.[28] For her part Mary moved to a shack in Gleichen, on the outskirts of the Blackfoot Reserve, where her drinking and dissolute lifestyle continued to cause problems. The Indian agent asked for permission to tear down her shack, but he was advised to contact the Mounted Police "so that they can take such steps as are possible under the law to rid the town of her presence or prevent her continuing in the course described."[29]

But Mary White, alias Spotted Woman, alias Mary Dog Child, alias Mary Royal continued on her tragic path of self-destruction. It culminated in her contracting tuberculosis—a scourge of the Indian people at that time—and dying of the disease in 1910. She was only twenty-nine years old.

Was Mary the daughter of Handsome Gun Woman or was she a white child from Montana? Evidence would seem to favor the former, but there are many inconsistencies that leave the matter open to debate. The facts that her parents may still have been in Montana at the time she was born and that there was no baptismal certificate, the rumor that a California man had lost a baby girl in Montana, the inconsistencies in Dog Child's stories—all these points leave room for doubt.

Mary's only son told me, "The Blackfoot took my mother away when she was a baby. It was Dog Child who took her from some white people. This took place when the first settlers came out and she was stolen away from them."[30] But the story has less credibility with his addition, "My mother's sister was also stolen from the white people, but at a later date. I think she was born about 1886."

Another Siksika elder, Ben Calf Robe, said, "I have heard two stories about Mary White. One is that Winnipeg Jack had two wives and they lived close to town. One of these wives kept having sex with a white man and Mary was born. Someone said the storekeeper was her father. I also heard that Mary was supposed to have been kidnapped when she was a little girl. It could be true, too, for when I knew her she looked just like a white woman."[31]

Either way, she came to a tragic end early in her life. She was just too attractive to both Indian and white men, too vulnerable on the fringes of the white community, and too unprotected by her culture or her family to shield her from the temptations and realities of frontier life. If she was white, it was a tragic irony that she should die of a disease that was plaguing the Indians of western Canada. If she was Indian, it was simply a tragedy.

14 *The Bull Elk Affair*

Early in 1882 minor Siksika chief Bull Elk, Ponoka'stumik, was frustrated. He had gone to the ration house to buy a steer's head and some guts, and he was going home without either the food or his precious one-dollar bill. He had fired two shots at the local ration house, and now he was in danger of being arrested by the *Inaykiks*, the North-West Mounted Police.[1]

Bull Elk had been the leader of the Liars band since the early 1870s, when he took over from Middle Eater, who was going blind. Bull Elk had been on several raids against his enemies, mostly the Crees, but he had been among those who had welcomed the North-West Mounted Police in 1874. American whiskey traders had been wreaking terrible havoc among his people, and chiefs such as Bull Elk had been powerless to stop them. When the police drove the renegades away, the redcoats were treated as heroes. They also gained respect when Col. James F. Macleod, the senior officer in the area, told the chiefs that the police would be fair and honest in upholding the law.

"I . . . explained to them," said Macleod, "what the Government has sent this Force into the country for, and endeavored to give them a general idea of the laws which will be enforced, telling them that not only the white men but Indians also will be punished for breaking them, and impressing upon them that they need not fear being punished for doing what they do not know is wrong."[2]

Over the next several months the Mounted Police had lived up to their promises. Bull Elk was pleased to see whiskey traders arrested and jailed, and lawbreakers—whether Indian or white—given fair treatment. The police created such a bond of trust with the Blackfoot that when a treaty was presented to them in 1877, Bull Elk and others signed the document even though they did not understand it. The fact that Colonel

Macleod was one of the treaty commissioners was sufficient for the Indians to acquiesce.

During the period from 1874 to 1879, the Queen (actually, the government of Canada) was represented to Bull Elk's followers solely in the form of the North-West Mounted Police. They were the law officers, magistrates, jailers, customs officers, diplomats, and friends. And because of the wisdom and character of Colonel Macleod, the Indians were treated with compassion and understanding. The fact that there were less than two hundred Mounted Policemen in an area controlled by more than two thousand armed, independent, and self-sufficient Blackfoot warriors was perhaps another encouragement to treat the tribes with respect.

But whatever the reasons, the relationship between the Blackfoot Nation and the Mounted Police was one of mutual trust. In 1879, however, the situation changed drastically. On one hand, the rapid depletion of the buffalo meant that Bull Elk and his band either followed the last herds into Montana or they starved. All but the helpless and infirm chose the former. On the other, the Department of Indian Affairs took over all responsibilities for Indians in the North-West from the Mounted Police. Agents, ration issuers, farm instructors, clerks, and other positions were created to serve Indians who would soon be reservation bound. Henceforth, the police would simply be enforcers of the law.

The problem—for the Siksikas, at least—was that the Indian Department appointments were so wrapped up in patronage that many of the senior positions went to men who had few proven qualifications for the task. Within a short time the clerk for southern Alberta was arrested for fraud, while others in the West "prostituted their authority to the debauchery of young Indian women."[3] One of the men assigned to the Blackfoot Reserve during this period "had never seen an Indian before that month [and was] not capable to taking charge of them."[4] Some of the employees were ex-members of the Mounted Police, ranging from good men such as William Pocklington to questionable characters such as Edwin "Lying" Allen, a former police inspector who was ultimately fired by the Indian Department. Other employees were local residents, some of whom had been involved in the whiskey trade and probably still indulged in excessive drinking and perhaps some bootlegging on the side.

Bull Elk and most of the other Siksikas stayed in Montana until the summer of 1881, when the last buffalo herds were destroyed. As they slowly made their way back to Canada, they were a tragic sight. As Indian agent Norman T. Macleod commented, "Crow Foot arrived here [at Fort Macleod] on the 20th ulto with 1,064 followers, all in a most destitute condition. A large proportion of his followers consisted of old men, women and children. They were nearly all on foot."[5]

When they reached Blackfoot Crossing, they found that a ration house had been built on the north side of the Bow River at Blackfoot Crossing, while an old whiskey fort on the south side had become a Mounted Police outpost. An ex-policeman named John D. Lauder had been appointed the farm instructor, the most senior official on the reserve. His employees were a mix of ex-policemen and local westerners. Some may have been good men, but none seemed to have much sympathy for the hungry and disheartened Indians. As Lauder stated, the Indians "returned hungry and in bad temper, they had to eat their horses and dogs to keep alive; it was a hard job to keep them quiet."[6]

The rations consisted of a pound of beef and a half pound of flour per day per person. The flour issued to the western Indians was of questionable quality. In fact, just as the Siksikas came back into Canada, an Indian Department inspector said that the flour ration was "not quite unfit for food," and ordered it to be issued.[7] Other agents mentioned that the first flour rations were black, made from frozen wheat, while an ex–ration issuer complained that "part of the flour was musty with all the colours of the rainbow to look at. Many a time I had to take a hatchet to cut it to pieces, and then pulverise it."[8]

The beef ration included the bones, although the issuers tried to make a fair distribution so that everyone got an equal share of meat, fat, and bone. The cattle were mostly Montana range animals, tough and skinny. The agreement required that the cattle be delivered to the ration house, slaughtered, and weighed by the contractors. An arrangement was also made with the Indian Department that the contractors kept the hides, the heads, and the offal (the guts). The heads and offal were sold separately to the Indians, usually for a dollar.

Even though the government knew that the Siksikas would be returning from Montana, it was ill prepared to deal with them. There were no axes or other tools with which they could build houses to replace their worn out tepees; agricultural implements that were supposed to make them self-supporting had not been supplied; and the rationing system was haphazard at best. There was little or no game to be found near the Blackfoot Reserve, so the very lives of the Indians depended upon a steady supply of beef and flour.

Twice in October of 1881, Crowfoot went to the farm instructor to beg for more rations for his people. Instead of receiving a sympathetic hearing, he was accused of leading "a demonstration to try and intimidate the Instructor."[9] This was the chief's first experience in dealing with the Indian Department, and the results were decidedly unpleasant. A couple of weeks later Indian agent Norman Macleod arrived from his headquarters in Fort Macleod and lectured the chief about his conduct.

The situation with the Siksikas further deteriorated in November, when the contractors allowed the supply of beef to run short. The weather had been bitterly cold and stormy, and the rumor spread that the government intended to let the Indians starve to death. This was the second time the contractors had failed to supply beef on time, so the story created both anger and fear in the camps. Farm Instructor Lauder reported that the Indians had threatened violence if proper rations were not provided. In addition a number of starving Indians forced a passing party of government land surveyors to share their food with them. Instead of trying to correct the rationing procedures, the agent reported the unrest to the North-West Mounted Police, and arrangements were made to send a ten-man detachment to Blackfoot Crossing to reinforce the two men already stationed there.

If Bull Elk and the other Siksika chiefs expected that their old friends in the Mounted Police had come to help them, they soon learned differently. The officer chosen to head the detachment was Inspector Francis Dickens, a son of the famous novelist and probably the worst choice that anyone could have made to deal with such a delicate situation.

After receiving an education in Europe, Dickens had been appointed to the Bengal Mounted Police in 1864, largely through family influence, and spent the next seven years in India. When his father died, it took the son only three years to dissipate his inheritance. Then, in 1874, when he was broke and quarreling with his family, arrangements were made for him to receive an appointment to the North-West Mounted Police, probably to get him out of England.

He proved to be entirely incompetent and incapable of command. In 1880, for example, his commanding officer said, "I consider this officer unfit for the force. He is lazy and takes no interest whatever in his work. He is unsteady in his habits."[10] His biographer considered him to be "lazy, alcoholic, and unfit."[11] Yet this misfit became the representative of the queen's law to the Siksika Indians. Over the years they had come to expect honesty and fair play from the police; now they hoped that the redcoat officer would help relieve the desperate plight of the tribe.

However, as the days passed, nothing was done to correct the situation. The contractors and Indian Department employees were still officious and unsympathetic; hunger still stalked the camps; and the regular delivery of beef and flour was still uncertain. The Siksikas were angry, disillusioned, and fearful of the new type of existence that had been forced upon them with the loss of the buffalo.

Matters came to a head for Bull Elk on January 2, 1882. This was ration day, and a number of Indians had been employed by the contractors to help with the killing and butchering. Among them was Dog Child, one of the few Siksikas who could speak English; he was known to the whites as "Winnipeg Jack." He was assisted by Bull Elk, who had always been a willing worker.

Bull Elk's frustrations started when he said he wanted to buy an unborn calf that he thought was in a cow in the corral. However, when the animal was butchered, she had no calf. Disappointed, Bull Elk gave Dog Child a dollar for a cow's head that he had just removed during the slaughtering process. Dog Child, in turn, gave the money to William Barton, one of the contractors. Barton took the money, but after inspecting the head he said there was too much meat left on the neck, refused to release it, and gave the money back. Bull Elk argued unsuccessfully that he should be allowed to take the head he had chosen. Charles Daly, another contractor who was in charge of slaughter, saw the argument and jumped to the conclusion that Bull Elk had been caught trying to steal the head.

Then the chief's wife picked out a beef heart, lungs, and paunch and set them aside for the dollar. Barton looked at the pile but took away the heart and lungs and left only the paunch. This was far less than what most Indians got for their money, so the woman refused to take it.

Dog Child then picked out another head for Bull Elk, but while the chief was waiting to pay for it, someone else took it away. Bull Elk was getting angry and upset by this time, and when he complained, the head was returned to him. Satisfied, he gave the dollar to William Barton and prepared to leave.

Charles Daly, who had been busy with his own work, saw Bull Elk and his wife walking away with the head and again thought they were trying to steal it. He asked Barton if he had approved the sale of the piece, and Barton said he had not. In fact Dog Child had made the selection. Without investigating, Daly seized the head from Bull Elk's wife and threw it onto a pile. The chief stalked over, grabbed the head, and had walked several yards with it when Daly roughly grabbed him by the shoulder and snatched the head away.

This sketch shows the Blackfoot ration house where the trouble with Bull Elk occurred. The original drawing was made by missionary John Tims about 1881. *Courtesy Glenbow Archives, Calgary, AB, cat. no. NA-1033-4*

Francis Dickens, son of the famous author, was in charge of the Mounted Police at Blackfoot Crossing when the Bull Elk incident occurred. Dickens was considered to be incompetent and incapable of command, as demonstrated by his inept handling of this delicate situation. Artist unknown.
Courtesy Glenbow Archives, Calgary, AB, cat. no. NA-2483-7

Furious at the curt treatment he had received, Bull Elk stormed out of the area and went back to his lodge without either the head or his money. He grabbed his old flintlock gun and, approaching to within two hundred yards of the ration house, he fired two shots, one reportedly striking the lower logs of the building and the other going wild.[12] Barton and others at the ration house rushed to get their rifles, while Daly hurried to report the incident to the police. Meanwhile, Bull Elk's grandson talked the old chief into leaving the scene.

There seems to be little doubt that a confused and disorganized rationing system had caused the flare-up. Bull Elk may have purposely cut the first head for himself, leaving too much neck meat on it, for he showed no particular anger when it was taken away. However, Daly's actions in assuming that the chief was a thief created an untenable situation. Bull Elk became so thoroughly frustrated by his callous treatment at the hands of Daly that he vented his anger by firing his musket, either in the air or in the direction of the ration house depending upon whose evidence one wishes to believe.

When Daly reported the matter to the Mounted Police, he accused Bull Elk of trying to shoot him. Inspector Dickens made no effort to investigate the validity of the charge. Instead, he went across the river with Sgt. Joseph Howe and two constables to arrest the chief. When Bull Elk saw them coming, he ran out of his camp and up a steep hill to the place where the Siksika cemetery is now located. There he stood with his gun in a ready position. Howe pursued him, but as he drew near the base of the hill, a Siksika named Eagle Shoe interceded.

"Stop!" the Indian called to the policeman, "he will shoot you."[13]

Howe was going to continue, but Eagle Shoe went up the hill ahead of him and persuaded the chief to surrender. The police took the man into custody, but by this time the entire camp was aware of the arrest. They all knew of the events that had led to the altercation and were angry that no attempt was being made by the police to find out the facts. Sergeant Howe described what happened when they began to take Bull Elk away: "Constable Wilson took one arm and I took the other; we walked him on about 20 paces, when about thirty young Indians came running up from the camp and formed a half circle around us, calling out to the prisoner and to one another, 'Come, what are you afraid of, they are only four policemen.'"[14]

The police pushed their way through the crowd, but by the time they got on the ice of the Bow River, even old women and children had joined the mob. The officers were jostled and pushed, and an old woman snatched Bull Elk's gun out of the sergeant's hands. Howe continued with his report:

> I still held on to the prisoner with my left hand, while Inspector Dickens kept the Indians back in rear with his revolver; I could hear the young Indians loading their carbines, one of them discharged his carbine, and I heard the bullet whistle over my head. I then fired my revolver three times in the air, as I thought we had better get some assistance, this being a pre-arranged signal for the men at our quarters to double down; our strength all told was thirteen in number; we managed to get the prisoner to our quarters, all right.[15]

To the Siksikas, the ration-house shooting had simply been part of a larger problem in which they were the victims. The poor and inadequate rations, haphazard deliveries by the contractors, and callous treatment of the Indians by Daly and others were all seen as grievances that required attention. The situation called for the finesse of a diplomat who could enforce Canadian law and at the same time deal with the problems raised by the Siksikas. However, the officer on the scene was not a diplomat; he was Inspector Dickens.

Once the prisoner was safely in the detachment, the officer held an enquiry. He heard the evidence of Indian Department employee Charles Lefrance and contractors William Scott, William Barton, and Charles Daly, whose testimony included such blatantly false statements as "Bull Elk stole a beef head" and "the Indian was going to kill me."[16]

In their testimony Siksika chiefs Heavy Shield and Running Rabbit said that they had been midway between Bull Elk and the ration house and that no bullets had passed their way. Dog Child, also speaking for the accused, described the confusion that existed at the slaughter house. In his own defence Bull Elk said only that "I fired two shots, but did not fire at the men; I fired as I was going away."[17]

Although he did not testify, the senior Indian Department official, John Lauder, sided with the contractors. In his later recollections he said that Bull Elk had stolen "a good supply of beef," and that the chief was freed by "a hundred or more squaws."[18] His was a wholly inaccurate account that displayed no sympathy for the plight of the Indians under his charge. For his part Inspector Dickens made no attempt to probe more deeply into the matter. He saw it as a simple shooting incident and decided there was enough evidence to send Bull Elk to Fort Macleod for trial.

Meanwhile, the excited Indians had been milling around the detachment, isolating the warehouse and stables from the main building by their sheer numbers. A constable, writing in his diary, described the scene: "Just then a shout went up, and we could hear it repeated up and down the river. It was calling the camp to their assistance. Now they come in hundreds, build large fires around our hut, whoop and dance. They are even on the roof with axes ready for the word to commence."[19] More than seven hundred men, most of them armed, became such a threatening force that Inspector Dickens sent a messenger to Crowfoot for help.

The chief had always been a strong supporter of both the Mounted Police and the white man's laws. But no longer. When he arrived, Crowfoot was as angry as the rest of his people. As Dickens reported: "He said that he knew Bull Elk was innocent, that some of the white men had treated the Indians like dogs."[20] Together with his other chiefs, Crowfoot refused to permit the prisoner to be moved off the reserve. "Crowfoot said that he would hold himself responsible for the appearance of the prisoner, if the stipendiary magistrate or some magistrate came to try the case. As it was utterly impossible to get the prisoner to Macleod owing to the roads being completely blockaded, I told Crowfoot that I would let him take charge of the prisoner if he promised to produce him when required. This he said he would do, and I let him take the prisoner."[21]

The Siksikas were exuberant when they heard the news. According to the constable, "It was a glorious victory for them, they thought. What with the shooting off of their rifles and the whoops and yells. During all this I was standing outside. A young blood came up to me and rubbed the muzzle of his rifle he had just fired in my face. I could not do anything, but I have him marked."[22]

Inspector Dickens dispatched a messenger to Fort Macleod as soon as the Indians returned to their camps. When Superintendent Crozier received the news, he hurried to the scene with reinforcements of a further twenty men. Arriving at Blackfoot Crossing, he learned that the Indians were quiet, but he made no immediate attempt to contact Crowfoot or the other chiefs. Instead, he instructed Inspector Dickens to fortify the detachment in anticipation of a possible enemy attack. Sacks of oats and flour were piled against the walls of the building as a fortification, and loopholes were cut in the log walls. Bastions were built at two corners of the building. Holes were cut in the interior walls to facilitate movement from room to room. An old corral nearby was partially destroyed, and a supply of water was brought from the river in case there was an extended siege. When it was done, the police dubbed it "Fort Dickens."

Superintendent Crozier, whose report seemed more concerned with military defenses than negotiations with the Siksikas, was quite proud of his achievement. "The only weak points in case of an attack," he said, "would have been in the cover which would have been afforded to an attacking party by the river bank, and an old cellar."[23]

To the Siksikas the implications were clear. As far as they were concerned, Inspector Dickens had arrested Bull Elk without trying to determine the circumstances that led up to the incident or even whether the gun had been fired at the ration house. Then Superintendent Crozier had arrived and prepared for an armed confrontation with the Indians rather than speaking to them. "I . . . certainly fully determined to resort to extreme measures," admitted Crozier, "if any attempt was made to prevent my carrying out the law in the regular manner."[24] It must have made the Siksikas wonder whether there was indeed one law that applied equally to Indians and whites.

When Crozier was ready, he sent a messenger to Crowfoot, instructing him to produce Bull Elk for examination. The chief readily complied, and when he arrived, he found the military fortification facing him. Puzzled, Crowfoot asked the police officer if he had come there to fight. "Certainly not," was Crozier's grim response, "unless you commence."[25]

When the proceedings concluded at the end of the first day, Crowfoot again asked to take Bull Elk to his camp on his own recognizance. To his surprise the police officer refused and held the prisoner in the barracks overnight. The next day, after further examination, Crozier concluded that there was enough evidence for a trial and that Bull Elk would be taken to Fort Macleod to appear before a stipendiary magistrate.

Crowfoot was aghast. Bull Elk had been released into his custody by Inspector Dickens on the understanding that a magistrate would be brought to Blackfoot Crossing and the trial held there. First Crozier had failed to honor Crowfoot's custody arrangements, and now he was breaking a promise made by a fellow officer.

According to Crozier, Crowfoot fully agreed with the outcome of the examination, "endorsing perfectly what I had done, and had decided upon doing."[26] In fact Crowfoot could not help but feel concern about the belligerent stance of the Mounted Police and fear that they were only waiting for an excuse to launch an armed attack against the Siksikas. His failure to resist the police was probably more a result of his concern for the safety of his people than any endorsement of the police's actions.

Bull Elk was taken to Fort Macleod under heavy escort and was committed for trial. There, the fortunes of the Siksikas seemed to change, for the magistrate proved to be their old friend James F. Macleod. He had retired as commissioner of the North-West Mounted Police six years earlier and lived in nearby Pincher Creek. Two days after the prisoner arrived in Fort Macleod, the trial was held. At last the Siksikas had a chance to explain what had really happened; Magistrate Macleod was fully prepared to hear about all the rationing problems that Dickens and Crozier had ignored.

"The evidence was conflicting," said Indian agent Norman Macleod. "No intent of doing bodily harm could be shown. Harsh treatment and hard words were shown to have been used towards the Indians, giving them cause for complaint."[27]

In the end Magistrate Macleod sentenced Bull Elk to a paltry fourteen days in the guardhouse for using a weapon in a threatening manner. The sentence clearly reflected the fact that the Mounted Police had overreacted to a situation which in the end proved to be nothing more than a minor misdemeanor. If anyone appreciated the significance of the series of events, it was the magistrate. "It has been a nasty business," he wrote to his wife.[28]

The Indian Department also realized what a mess it had made in its rationing and administrative systems. Indian agent Norman Macleod was considered to be too old to maintain control of the entire region, so Treaty No. Seven was split into two areas, with Agent Macleod retaining the Bloods and Piegans in the south and former Mounted Police officer Cecil Denny assuming direction for the Blackfoot, Sarcee, and Stoney Reserves in the north. Farm instructor Lauder was dismissed and replaced by William Pocklington, and the entire procedure with the beef contractors was changed. Right off, they were obliged to have an adequate supply of beef and flour on hand at all times to remove any fears of enforced starvation. In addition, according to the Indian commissioner, "The Indians were finally quieted by the Department agreeing to take the heads and offal from the contractors at $1.00 per animal, and to distribute them as part of the rations. Axes and other tools were then given to the Indians, and they employed themselves industriously during the remainder of the winter in building houses, of which a great number were erected."[29]

The turmoil on the Blackfoot Reserve quickly subsided with the appointments of Pocklington and Denny, but some of the damage was already beyond repair. As Denny observed, the incident was "the first serious resistance shown towards the police since they had been in the country."[30] But more importantly, the confrontation had involved Crowfoot, who was one of the most influential chiefs in the North-West Territory.

With the insensitivity of Inspector Dickens and the heavy-handed reaction by Superintendent Crozier, the chief had become thoroughly disillusioned. He had ascribed to the Mounted Police a level of honor and compassion that previously had been fulfilled by officers such as Colonel Macleod. After the Bull Elk incident he treated them with caution and suspicion.

Within the next few years Crowfoot's changed attitude towards the Mounted Police was clearly evident. In 1883 he welcomed an emissary from Big Bear to hear about the possibility of holding a grand council that would consider the problems all Indians seemed to be having with the government. A year later he befriended a messenger from Louis Riel and challenged the Mounted Police when they tried to arrest him. When he was told that he was harboring a disturber of the peace, Crowfoot insisted on attending the man's trial and saw him acquitted of all charges. This further called into question the objectivity of the police.

All of this was a prelude to the North-West Rebellion of 1885. At the time of the outbreak the government desperately needed Crowfoot on their side, both for military and for political reasons. But by this time the chief had become so thoroughly suspicious of the government that he would have liked to join with the Cree insurgents. He was prevented not by any trust in the Mounted Police but by the strongly negative response from his closest ally, Red Crow, chief of the Blood tribe. Also, Crowfoot had been as far east as Winnipeg on the Canadian Pacific Railway and had some sense of the military power of the Canadian government. In the end his decision not to join the rebels was based on a realization that the rebellion was doomed to failure, rather than on any faith in those red-coated officers who had once "protected us as the feathers of the bird protect it from the frosts of winter." In one rash action in 1882, the Mounted Police had destroyed a faith that been an important part in the peaceful settlement of the Canadian West.

As for Bull Elk, he served his fourteen days and went back to the reserve. He then moved his band upstream to the North Camp Flats and set them to work to build houses, plant gardens, and dig root cellars. When he died in 1886, the *Calgary Tribune* gave him a sort of compliment, stating that "he was a very good Indian, as Indians go generally."[31]

15   *The Rise and Fall of White Calf*

By the spring of 1882 White Calf had been living peacefully on his reserve in southern Alberta for almost a year. This was not by choice, but with the buffalo gone he had the option of either accepting rations from the government or starving to death.

White Calf, or Onista'poka, was one of the war chiefs of the Blood tribe.[1] He was born about 1832 into the Followers of the Buffalo band. After he became a warrior he took the name Running Crane, then White Calf, and in the later years of his life he was known as Father of Many Children. He achieved an enviable war record, and on the basis of his leadership abilities he became chief of the Marrows band. In 1877 he was one of the Blood leaders to sign Treaty No. Seven with the Canadian government, bringing 107 followers with him.

Although he was said to have been an outstanding warrior, only one of his exploits was recalled in later years. He had gone on a scouting expedition with Eagle Head to find a Cree village, when they intercepted a man and woman on the trail. Although the man escaped, his wife was killed. Waving her scalp in the air, White Calf and Eagle Head returned to their camp with news of their discovery. The next morning the Bloods raided the enemy village; when the Crees tried to resist, they were "slaughtered like buffalo."[2]

In 1879 White Calf and fellow war chief Medicine Calf decided to follow the last buffalo herds into Montana Territory. At first there were plenty of buffalo, but the animals became scarce as the months passed, as hide hunters, Indians, and half-breeds slaughtered them by the thousands. In the summer of 1880 the Bloods held their Sun Dance at the confluence of the Yellowstone and Missouri Rivers. From there they traveled southwest, and when they arrived at the present site of Billings, they met a camp of Crows, their onetime hereditary enemies. John Cotton was twelve years old at the time, and he remembered the meeting. "Because we had promised in our treaty to live at peace with the other tribes and the Americans had stopped their Indians from going to war, we made a peace treaty."[3]

White Calf, Medicine Calf, and Bad Head sat in council with Crow chiefs Was Kicked and Pregnant Woman. Together they smoked a pipe, and the Crows invited the Bloods to stay with them. White Calf then pitched his camp about a half mile from the Crows. Later they were joined by Gros Ventres and Assiniboines who also made peace. At its peak there were more than a thousand lodges strung out along the Yellowstone River.

"From our big camp," said Cotton, "the Bloods and Crows would go hunting whenever the scouts located buffalo. Whatever tribe killed the first buffalo was in charge of that hunt. The Bloods, with their fast horses, were usually in charge." By the spring of 1881 the buffalo were gone from the Yellowstone range, and soon the Bloods began to starve. They could not expect any help from the Americans, so White Calf announced that they were leaving their Crow friends and going north to hunt. The hungry nomads were close to the Bear Paw Mountains, when one evening they heard a Blackfoot singing his buffalo song. From him they learned that a small herd of buffalo could be found at Hairy Cap in the Little Rockies. When they arrived there, the herd was soon sighted by their observant scouts.

"White Calf told us to prepare our buffalo horses," said Cotton. "When everybody was ready, he shouted the signal and we all rushed over the edge of a hill overlooking the creek. On the other side of Beaver Creek the valley was black with buffalo. Our horses rushed into the main herd and we were successful in killing many buffalo before the herd rushed away."[4]

The hunt was significant in that it was the last time White Calf's band found buffalo. Soon the Bloods were starving again and had no choice but to return to Canada. When they reached their reserve in the spring of 1881, they were tired, disillusioned, and hungry. Only the skimpy rations of beef and flour, supplemented by a few deer and prairie chickens they found along the Belly River, kept death away from their lodges. During this time White Calf kept the young men at home and would not let them to go to war. He was determined that he would honor the treaties made with the Crows, Gros Ventres, and Assiniboines.

White Calf was the second war chief of the tribe at the time. The paramount war chief was Medicine Calf, who was twenty years his senior. The two men got along well, but White Calf still had aspirations of ultimate leadership. He was described by a fellow Blood as "a great warrior who had much influence. He had a big voice and was a great orator."[5] During his early months on the reserve, he disdained farming and devoted his energies to protecting the camp and encouraging Native religious practices.

When the Bloods had left Montana early in 1881, only a few bands of Crees and camps of half-breeds continued to hunt south of the line. In the spring of 1882 the Americans decided to get rid of these unwanted "Canadian" hunters, so they mounted a military campaign, the Milk River Expedition, to clean out northern Montana. Soldiers rode into half-breed villages and burned down their cabins, then sent Cree bands scurrying back across the line with threats of confiscating their horses or worse.

In April Cree chief Big Bear, with about 150 lodges, arrived at Fort Walsh then went to join the 2,000 Crees and Assiniboines already camped near Cypress Lake, about twenty miles east. Little Pine, Foremost Man, Mosquito, Bear's Head, Thunder Child, and other chiefs had managed to keep their young men relatively peaceful and away from enemy horse herds. But Big Bear's warriors were fresh from the wild cesspool of central Montana, where there was little law for the white man and none for the Indian. Not satisfied to receive rations or hunt, these young warriors were looking for action and began raiding Montana ranches and the horse herds of the Blackfoot Nation. The presence of the newcomers was immediately noticed by the press. A reporter stated, "Big Bear, with an exceptionally large following of non-treaty and malcontent Indians, is now camped at a place known as 'the Lake,' about twenty miles from Fort Walsh. It is these Indians who have for years past been a firebrand in that portico of the Territories. During the past winter they remained south of the boundary line where from all accounts they led a rough and lawless life."[6]

In April Cree raiders began harassing the Bloods and driving off their horses. Traveling on foot across two hundred miles of barren plains, they preyed upon small camps that lined the banks of the Belly and St. Mary Rivers. During the night they swooped down on horse herds grazing on the nearby prairie, and by dawn they were halfway to the Cypress Hills with their booty. The frustrated Blood Indian agent, Cecil Denny, reported, "Our Indians in the agency have been very well behaved this spring, none of them having left their reserve to steal horses, but have been working hard on their farms. Since the Crees came back to Cypress, party after party have been up in this section, stealing horses. The Bloods have been to me continually with complaints."[7] The angry Bloods demanded action from the Mounted Police, or else they would seek their own vengeance. Agent Denny was an ex-Mountie. He knew how hard it was to catch small raiding parties who could easily hide from police patrols and disappear like grey wolves in the night. The Bloods wanted to recover their own horses, but the agent was also aware of how explosive that could be.

White Calf watched the situation with increasing anger. While he had not made a peace treaty with the Crees, he still expected that their common enemy, starvation, would be enough to keep them from each other's throats. As a tribal war chief he had specific responsibilities. As missionary John Maclean explained, "The duties of the war chief were to make arrangements for war, and to lead the warriors to battle. Virtually, he was supreme in the camp during a period of war."[8] To White Calf the constant raids on the Blood camps meant that they were already at war.

During this time an employee of the Indian agency acknowledged the frustration of the tribe, commenting that "The Indians are neglecting their farms to a certain extent, on account of the Crees from Cypress stealing their horses."[9] He suggested that if something was not done quickly, the Bloods would likely go on the warpath.

On May 17 the Crees again raided the Bloods, this time taking forty-five horses, including some of their prized animals. That was the limit. During the passing weeks war chief Medicine Calf had made no move to resolve the problem, so White Calf decided to act. He was determined to recover their horses, either with or without the help of the Mounted Police. The war chief gathered a few of his best men around him and went to see Agent Denny. When the chief insisted that he was going to pursue the raiders, the agent realized that nothing could stop him. So he informed White Calf that he must take only a handful of men with him and that they must go to Fort Walsh and let the police recover their horses rather than trying to do it themselves. The Indian agent then wrote him a letter of introduction to the commanding officer at Fort Walsh, stating: "This Indian, Se-ke-ma-ka, a Blood, has lost some horses,

In 1881, when Crees raided the Blood horse herds, Blood war chief White Calf led a force of two hundred armed men to Fort Walsh (seen here) in the Cypress Hills. When they were unsuccessful in recovering their horses, the Bloods attacked a small Cree camp near the fort and killed a man before returning to their reserve.
Courtesy Glenbow Archives, Calgary, AB, cat. no. NA-1060-2

stolen by Crees. He knows they are in the Cree camps, and is bound to go down to get them, although I have advised him otherwise, but as he is bound to go I thought it better to give him a note to you, so that you can keep your eye on him. He is after a good many horses stolen this spring, and goes down with tobacco to make peace with the Crees."[10]

With this paper in his hands White Calf invited all the young warriors of his tribe to join him. When they left the following day, instead of just a few companions, as Agent Denny had suggested, he had two hundred well-armed Bloods in his war party. On their way east they crossed the Whoop-Up Trail, where they encountered a wagon train hauling supplies from Fort Benton. The wagon master reported that "the band consisted wholly of warriors, all well mounted and armed to the teeth. They stopped the train line and insolently demanded a feed."[11] When the Bloods arrived at Fort Walsh the following day, the police also observed that they were well armed. According to an officer, they "all arrived with Winchester repeating rifles and a large supply of ammunition in two belts, one worn over the shoulder and the other round the waist."[12] True to his word, White Calf went directly to the fort and presented his letter to Supt. A. G. Irvine, the commanding officer. The war chief noticed that there was a small camp of Crees nearby, but he gave instructions that they were not to be molested. He wanted to visit the main camp at Cypress Lake and was willing to make a peace treaty with the Crees just as he had done earlier with the Crows, Assiniboines, and Gros Ventres.

The Bloods had traveled light and fast when they left their reserve. Like most war parties of the past, they carried little food and no shelter with them. Colonel Irvine agreed to give them rations, and as the weather had turned cold and nasty, he also loaned them a number of tents so they would have a dry place to sleep.

When Irvine and White Calf met, the police officer convinced the war chief that taking all the Bloods to the Cree camp would only invite trouble. Instead, he suggested that six Blood leaders be escorted to Cypress Lake by two Mounted Policemen, while the other Indians remained at Fort Walsh. When White Calf agreed, Inspector Edmond Frechette and a constable were detailed to accompany the peace party. On arrival at Cypress Lake the Bloods found the Crees to be in a surly mood. A few days earlier, two American ranchers with an escort of twenty-three redcoated policemen had visited the camp and demanded the return of horses taken by Big Bear's followers. Intimidated by the show of force by the Mounties, the Crees had reluctantly turned over thirty-two horses stolen from several ranches in Montana.

When the Bloods arrived, there was no impressive show of Mounted Police might, so the Crees were in no mood to cooperate. White Calf was there to make peace and hopefully to get the stolen horses back, so he ignored the scowls of Big Bear's warriors. On his instructions one of the Blood chiefs, Bull Back Fat, came forward with a gift of tobacco which, if it was smoked by both the Bloods and Crees, would cement a peace treaty between them. According to an observer, the Blood chief "made overtures of peace by offering the Crees some tobacco in exchange for stolen horses, but the Crees threw the tobacco in to a camp fire, accompanying the action with some remarks equivalent to the white man's go to h—l."[13]

White Calf must have regretted bringing only five men with him. Had his entire war party been there, the insult would have been quickly challenged or, more likely, would never have been made in the first place. As it was, the chief and his followers had to stand helplessly by while a cursory search was made of the Cree camp by the police. Only two horses were produced, in spite of the fact that—as White Calf later told Agent Denny—"they saw all their horses in the camp but they did not get any of them back, the Crees refusing to give them up."[14]

The inspector stated in his report, "I am satisfied that, with the exception of the two horses said to be still in the Cree camp, all the Bloods' horses have been stolen by Indians south of the line."[15] But he was wrong on both counts. Frechette had not recovered all the Blood horses, and the enemy tribes from Montana had been nowhere near the Blood Reserve. Besides, the trail that White Calf had followed from his reserve had led directly to the Cypress Hills. It was clear to the war chief that the escort of only two Mounted Policemen indicated that the police were not really concerned about the Blood horses—not like they had been when the horses of white ranchers from Montana had been involved.

Angrily, the six Bloods returned to Fort Walsh and immediately went to see Colonel Irvine. He reported to his superiors:

I had an interview last night with the Bloods. They appeared much disappointed at not getting their horses, the loss of which they persisted in laying at the door of the Crees. . . . The interview I mention having held, took place in my office, I having allowed some of the Indians (unarmed) into the Fort. They all expressed themselves in most friendly terms towards myself personally and the Police Force as well, however most bitter against the Crees. Although they promised me that they would return home that morning, I could see particularly among the younger men, that they felt humiliated at having to return without their horses, as that would make them appear in the eyes of their tribe as having accomplished nothing, notwithstanding the strength of the war party.[16]

One of the members of the war party was a twenty-two-year-old man named White Man Running Around. He recalled, "When the Bloods saw they would not get their horses, they held a council and decided to have war with the [Crees]. During the night we invaded the nine tepees [near the fort], but the tribe had all left the camp but one, and he was killed."[17] The Bloods had waited until after midnight, then slipped away from the tents and headed for the small Cree camp. These people were not actually the ones who had stolen their horses, but they were Crees, and the insults of the day had to be revenged. Suspecting that they might be under surveillance by the police, the Bloods left their campfires and candles burning in the tents, so that it looked as though they were still occupied.

It was a cold and stormy night, and the Bloods were able to approach the enemy camp without being observed. But when they made their attack, they were disappointed to find that the Crees had already fled and were taking shelter with some traders in the village. Only one man had stayed behind; he had not been as cautious as the others. For this he paid with his life. Venting their anger on the unfortunate victim, the Bloods shot him seven or eight times, stabbed him three times in the stomach, and scalped him. He was very dead.

Not satisfied, the Bloods pulled down the nine lodges and slashed them to pieces. Then they rummaged through the contents of the tepees and took anything of value. Meanwhile, another group from the war party found the Crees' horses and appropriated the entire herd.

White Calf's raid finally alerted the fort at 2 A.M., when Superintendent John Cotton reported that "there was some excitement in the Blood camp." Irvine and Cotton went to the bell tents and found them almost deserted. "The Indians had just gone," said Irvine. "A number of them had just ridden off towards the Fort Macleod road, and the few that still remained had their horses saddled. The Indians as they went, yelled and fired off their rifles, proving that they were in an excited state."[18]

When the police discovered the body of the dead Cree, they immediately became concerned about the eruption of a major conflict. A message was sent to an officer who was bringing new recruits to the fort, telling him to hurry. Another messenger was dispatched to Fort Macleod, but because he was afraid of angry Cree war parties, he took a circuitous route all the way south to Fort Benton, in Montana, then back north along the Whoop-Up Trail to Fort Macleod.

The Bloods returned to their reserve in triumph, in spite of the fact that they had not recovered most of their horses. More importantly, they had killed and scalped a Cree and had avenged the insult they received when Big Bear's followers had refused to smoke with them. The Bloods had a big Scalp Dance, and White Calf's reputation as the war leader of his people was well established. Without a vote or discussion he automatically became the leading war chief of the tribe, surpassing the aging Medicine Calf.

The Mounted Police feared Cree reprisals, but as it turned out, the Bloods were the ones who were still thirsting for war. Now that the Crees had rejected a peace treaty, White Calf saw no reason to keep his young warriors at home. With his blessing they could attack the Crees whenever they wanted to do so. A few weeks later, a Cree camp in front of Fort Walsh was besieged by Bloods. This time the raiders fired at the tents but made no direct attack. Their reluctance was well founded. As Irvine stated, "Knowing that lurking war parties had from time to time been seen in the vicinity, I had the Cree camp strongly guarded. Over the camp is placed nightly one officer and twenty men, and necessary steps taken to afford the Crees every protection. But for this, I have no doubt the Bloods would have made an attempt to annihilate the Crees."[19]

However, a number of other Crees heading north were not so lucky. When they were only a short distance away from the Cypress Hills, they were attacked by Blood raiders and most of their horses were taken. Many of the Crees had to complete the long journey to Battleford on foot.

In the end the conflict between the Bloods and Crees was not resolved by peace treaties or government diplomacy but rather by the closing of Fort Walsh early in 1883. The raids back and forth across the international boundary had created strained relations between the Canadian and American governments, and the Cypress Hills were proving to be too convenient a place from which to set out for the ranches in Montana. The Mounted Police tried to move the Crees and Assiniboines north to their allotted reserves, but as long as they could get rations from Fort Walsh, they were reluctant to leave. The authorities finally solved this problem by closing the fort, abandoning the area of the Cypress Hills, and leaving the Indians to starve or move. Once they were in the north, the Crees were too far away to cause any serious trouble and the raiding virtually ended.

As for White Calf, his actions gave notice to the government that he was not willing to conform meekly to the new way of life. He had no intention of becoming a farmer but was intent on preserving the free and warlike nature for which his tribe had become famous. He also had aspirations of becoming a political leader of the Blood tribe as well as being its war chief.

His opportunity came during the fall treaty payments in 1882, just four months after his Cypress Hills raid. When the treaty was signed in 1877, the government had permitted the Bloods to choose two head chiefs. One was Red Crow and the other an elderly leader named Rainy Chief. When Rainy Chief died a year later, Red Crow suggested that he be replaced by one of his own close relatives, a man named Running Rabbit. The position was filled without a vote, but Running Rabbit was chief for only a few months when he decided that he did not want it. He was part South Piegan and spent so much time with that tribe that he chose to live in Montana. This left the head chieftainship open, and this time, government regulations required that it be filled through a vote of all Blood males over the age of twenty-one.

When White Calf learned of the forthcoming election, he immediately tossed his headdress into the ring. Because of his recent victories, he proved to be such a popular choice that no one came forward to oppose him. Agent Denny, who was having a hard job getting the Bloods to settle down, concluded that he did not want White Calf to be a head chief. He preferred a replacement who would be pliable, inoffensive, and willing to follow his orders. When it was apparent that White Calf would not be opposed and would be a clear winner, he cancelled the vote and delayed it for a year. The following autumn, with obvious reference to White Calf, Agent Denny wrote, "Many of the old chiefs I find encourage the young men to go out horse stealing, and I intend to get a head chief elected this payment who will help us, and who is really a chief among the young men."[20]

During the intervening months Denny had picked out his own candidate, Calf Tail, a member of Wolf Collar's band who had no personal following of his own. Denny described him as "a very good man, and one who has been of great aid to me in taking stolen horses from Indians."[21] There was another reason for choosing him; he was White Calf's brother-in-law, and the agent obviously hoped to split the vote by having a relative running against the popular war chief. The Bloods' recollections of Calf Tail are negative; he was seen as a man without a war record or proven leadership capabilities. But he did have the endorsement of the government, and in the months prior to the election the Indian agent probably let the Bloods know what he expected of them.

Denny reported the results of the vote in September of 1883. "As a new chief had to be elected," he said, "I called a council of the tribe and put it to a vote. . . . Only two chiefs were voted for—White Calf and Calf Tail. Calf Tail was elected and the selection was a good one, he being really the only chief among the Band."[22] He went on to say that Calf Tail had stopped young men from going to war and had turned stolen horses over to the agency. Then, as if belying Calf Tail's exalted role, the agent asked permission to give him a wagon, as he was too poor to buy one of his own. Not only that, but as Calf Tail had no following, the Indian agent invited any Bloods to transfer to the new band that was being created. Many people saw the advantage of joining a band that was clearly being favored by the Indian agent, so they flocked to Calf Tail's side. When the treaty payments were finished, 272 Bloods had joined his band.

A member of the tribe explained what happened next. "When they were holding the election," said Harry Mills, "White Calf's brother-in-law, whom we called Great Chief, ran against him. When Great Chief won, White Calf told him he would not live long and put a curse on him."[23] Eight weeks later, Calf Tail was dead. No one in the tribe had any doubt that White Calf's curse had been responsible. This left Agent Denny without a pliable head chief and the new band without a leader. With a grim sense of humor, the Bloods named the band the Orphans because they had lost their father. Bull Horn was placed in charge as a minor chief, but the band's days of glory and influence were over before they had even started.

Agent Denny knew that if he called another election for the head chieftainship, no one would dare oppose White Calf. His solution was to leave the position vacant, and it remained that way for the next six years, until long after Denny had left. During the interim White Calf campaigned openly for the role of head chief. Not only did he believe he deserved the position, but he resented Red Crow's holding the sole leadership of the tribe. To him the Bloods always had two chiefs, a political chief and a war chief. And he was the undisputed war chief of the tribe.

Meanwhile, White Calf continued to play the role of tribal leader, and—regardless of the power or influence of the Indian agent—he was ready to oppose him whenever he believed it was in the best interests of the tribe. In the summer of 1884, as a cost-cutting measure, the agent attempted to issue bacon instead of beef. This was bad enough, but he tried to do it at a time when head chief Red Crow was away on an official visit to Ottawa. In response the Black Soldiers, a Blood warrior society, prevented any women from accepting the noxious meat, and White Calf demanded that no action be taken until Red Crow returned. When the head chief learned about the debacle, he immediately arranged for the beef ration to be resumed.

As war chief, White Calf counseled the young men to make war only against their enemies, such as the Crees, and was able to maintain peace with the Crows and Gros Ventres. In early March of 1885 White Calf's son, Never Ties His Moccasin Laces, joined three other young warriors in a raid on Cree camps in the Maple Creek area. They succeeded in running off seven horses but were apprehended as soon as they returned to the reserve. When White Calf tried to interfere with the arrest, he too was taken into custody and transported to the jail cells in Fort Macleod. He was released the following day, but Never Ties was charged with horse stealing.

A court appearance was held in Fort Macleod, but as no witnesses came forward to identify the horses, the matter was held over and the young man remained in jail. Meanwhile, Red Crow, White Calf, and other chiefs pleaded unsuccessfully for the warrior's release. "You have got the horses," said one chief, "give in the boy."[24] When the authorities refused, the disgruntled chiefs returned to their reserve.

"A reliable Indian has informed me," said Indian agent William Pocklington,

> that White Calf gathered the chiefs together and they settled that if after waiting two weeks the boy was not released, that they would send their old people away across the line and the younger men would remain and 'turn loose.' I scarcely think they will do this, but I am satisfied that if the excitement does not quiet down they will do or try to do a lot of mischief. . . . I think White Calf is at the root of all this. He is the great speaker of the tribe and has considerable influence over the young ones.[25]

A week later, mixed-blood forces under Louis Riel had a bloody fight with the Mounted Police in the Battle of Duck Lake and the North-West Rebellion had begun. Five days after that, all charges against White Calf's son were dismissed and the young man was released. The Bloods stayed out of the rebellion, but during the anxious weeks of conflict the government not only released Never Ties His Moccasin Laces but also increased rations, built a new ration house, and settled an outstanding land dispute.

In the summer of 1885, just after the rebellion, White Calf adopted the name of the recently deceased patriarch Father of Many Children and tried to unite several bands so that he could rightly claim the title of head chief. According to Agent Pocklington, "he asked me to let him take the whole of Hind Bull's band, also Father of Many Children's into his own, that Hind Bull was willing to give up his chieftainship and that Father of Many Children's son Wolf Bull would forego the chance of being made chief in his father's place."[26]

But Agent Pocklington had already experienced the threats and uncertainties offered by White Calf's unofficial leadership, and he was not prepared to sanction a change that would mean more trouble for the government. Like his predecessor, Pocklington wanted a "progressive" Indian who did what he was told, not a war chief who wanted to preserve the old ways. Missionary John Maclean described the chief perfectly when he said, "White Calf, the war chief of the Blood Indians, is a typical Indian, hating the language, customs and religion of the white man. As he sees the gradual decrease of his people and their dependence upon the government for support since the departure of the buffalo . . . he mourns the loss of the martial days."[27]

The matter came to a head at the treaty payments in November 1885, resulting in a direct conflict between White Calf and the Indian agent. At the payments Bull Horn and Wolf Bull both agreed to give up their minor chieftainships and let their bands be united under White Calf. This was undoubtedly a popular move, for it would bring together the old Followers of the Buffalo band, which had become fragmented on the reserve. Under White Calf it would be a counterbalance to the powerful Fish Eaters band, which was controlled by Red Crow.

Pocklington was adamant: there would be no union of bands under White Calf. "The fact is, being a great talker and no worker," said the Indian agent, "he is jealous of Red Crow having so large a Band, and thinks by having a large Band he would be more thought of by Departmental officials and the public generally. For my part I think it would be the worst possible thing that could happen, for being very much gifted as a talker, he would use his influence to put bad thoughts into the heads of the young men on the Reserve."[28]

When the Indian agent refused to consider the change, White Calf became furious. "He rose and talked, shouted and gesticulated like one bereft," reported Pocklington.[29] Then he hurled his treaty money back at the clerk, called government employees "dogs, liars, thieves, and goodness knows what," and stalked out of the meeting.[30] From that time on White Calf was viewed by the Indian Department as a "troublemaker."

At the same time White Calf's people still considered him to be one of their leading chiefs, and even Red Crow hesitated to take any action on important matters unless he was in attendance. White Calf was with Red Crow and was the chief spokesman in a meeting after a Blackfoot Indian was accidentally shot by a Mounted Police scout. He was also present with the chief when the size of the reserve was questioned and accompanied the surveyors when they pointed out the boundary markers. The Indian agent could not prevent White Calf from taking an active role in tribal politics, but he could deny him the head chieftainship and ridicule him at every opportunity. In correspondence with the Commissioner, the agent referred to White Calf as one of the "principal growlers,"[31] "the Old Talking Machine,"[32] and the "Prince of Grumblers."[33]

He also belittled White Calf among his own people, making it clear that the chief had little or no influence in the agency office. Finally, by 1889, Pocklington had eroded White Calf's influence to the point that it was possible to fill the head chief vacancy without fear that the war chief would be chosen. The successful candidate was Day Chief, a member of Red Crow's Fish Eaters band. He was just what Pocklington wanted—a man seen as progressive, willing to farm, and prepared to cooperate with the agency.

This ended any hope that White Calf might have held about becoming a head chief. In anger and frustration he abandoned the Blood Reserve in 1891 and moved to the South Piegan Reservation in the United States. There he was welcomed as a prominent member of the Blackfoot Nation and entered on the rolls of the Montana agency.[34] Pocklington, of course, was jubilant, saying his departure "will be a great blessing to the Reserve generally."[35] He suggested that White Calf be stripped of his minor chieftainship and his followers dispersed among the other bands. However, his superiors in Ottawa did not agree, and five months later the chief was back home after finding the American system just as bureaucratic as the Canadian one. According to the agent, on his return, "He made a speech in a very serious manner the import of it was that he should never give up his country & would return & settle here up the river. He has evidently lost a good deal of his influence."[36]

This petulant action on the part of White Calf virtually ended his role in Blood politics. People turned to another chief, Calf Shirt, as their war chief and to Running Wolf as the leader of the religious life of the reserve. This left White Calf with nothing but his own Marrows band. He still voiced his opinion in council meetings and spoke of the importance of unity, but the constant belittlement by the Indian agents had taken its toll. By the time he died in August of 1897, he was simply a relic of the past, a reminder of the warring days of the Blood tribe.

Would White Calf have been a good head chief? Probably not. His hatred of whites and his adherence to old ways and customs made it almost impossible for him to work with the various Indian agents. At that period of history Indian agents had almost life and death powers over their charges. They carried out policies designed to "civilize" the Indians by transforming them into self-sufficient farmers and forcing their children into residential schools. To disagree with the agent was to get the reputation of being a troublemaker, and White Calf filled that role almost from the beginning. As a head chief, he probably would have fought constantly with the agent over rations, cattle, farming, education, and all the other matters in which the wishes of the Indians themselves were of little consequence to the government.

There can be no question that White Calf was a strong and dynamic chief who had a devoted following. He was a magnificent orator with a vision for his people that offered them pride and dignity during the painful transition from a nomadic buffalo-hunting life to a life of farming and ranching. But his vision ran counter to the Indian Department's practice of exercising complete control at minimum expense while pursuing a policy of making the Indians self-sufficient as quickly as possible. White Calf's problem was that he was simply born a generation too late. As a war chief during the buffalo days he would have been magnificent, but during the reservation period he proved to be nothing more than an anachronism.

16 *Mike Running Wolf*

Mike Running Wolf was not considered by the authorities to be a problem, only an irritation. He was a product of the Old Sun Indian Residential School on the Blackfoot Reserve east of Calgary, and as a student he had never caused any difficulties. The only trouble in his early years concerned his name. He was entered into the treaty books as Mike Running Wolf while his brother, who had not attended school, was named Pretty Young Man. But when they were baptized, someone remembered that their father, Iron Shield, had been baptized years earlier and given the name of John Ham. The surname was likely "borrowed" from George H. Ham, a Winnipeg reporter who frequently visited the Blackfoot Reserve in the 1880s. Accordingly, when it came time for the two boys to be baptized, Mike Running Wolf became Jim Ham and Pretty Young Man was Joseph Ham. But most people continued to call them by their original names.

As a young man, Mike Running Wolf was "well liked by everyone"[1] and spoke good English. His only drawback was that he became argumentative and abusive when he was drunk, so people tended to let him alone if he had been overimbibing. However, he did gain the enmity of a fellow member of the tribe, Edward Costigan, and after that man was appointed a scout by the Royal North-West Mounted Police, there was sure to be trouble.

It happened at the Sun Dance on June 1, 1912, when the police received a report that Running Wolf had been drinking. He was not causing any trouble; according to a missionary, he was simply acting "slightly foolish, but nothing more."[2] When Scout Costigan arrived on the scene, he was urged by Running Wolf's friends to leave the man alone, as he was sitting peacefully in front of his tepee cutting some tobacco. They even promised to bring him in to the guardhouse at Gleichen when he was sober, so that he could be tried under the Indian Act for illegal consumption of liquor. At this time it was illegal for an Indian to drink liquor of any kind or to have it in his possession.

However, the scout had no intention of passing up this opportunity of punishing his old adversary. What happened next is described by the missionary: "The Indian Scout had just arrived to arrest Mike for obtaining liquor and spoke roughly to him. Mike was cutting either tobacco or a stick with his penknife . . . and said he would accompany the Scout presently, but was in no hurry. The Scout then caught him by the shoulders, whereupon Mike struck him with the open jack-knife in the leg, & the Scout fell back saying he was dead."[3]

During the excitement that followed, Running Wolf was joined by this brother, Pretty Young Man, and his brother's wife, Red Face. They were convinced the scout was dying, so they hitched up a bay and a black horse to a wagon and fled from the scene. Red Face had been looking after a young child named Edward Yellow Old Woman, so she brought him along as well. Meanwhile, Costigan was taken to the Gleichen hospital, where the wound was found to be a superficial one and no threat to the scout's life. His cry of being killed had been greatly exaggerated.

Once they were free of the Sun Dance grounds Running Wolf decided to go to Bassano, on the northeast edge of the reserve, to look for a bootlegger. When he had no luck, he broke into Robinson's Hardware and stole two rifles. The next day the group went to Brooks, a town about thirty miles away, to see if Running Wolf could find a bootlegger there. Presumably his philosophy was that as he was going to be hanged for killing the scout, he might as well enjoy himself while he still had his freedom and deal with anyone who got in his way. None of the usual rules of society now applied to him, for he could be hanged only once.

Pretty Young Man and Red Face were apprehensive about the new reckless attitude of Running Wolf, but neither was prepared to give up

OPPOSITE PAGE   Accompanying Mike Running Wolf on his journey of violence were his brother, Pretty Young Man, and Running Wolf's wife, Red Face, seen here in 1920.

the chance for a good drinking spree. They got to Brooks late that night and made camp about two miles south of town on the other side of the railway tracks. As soon as it was daylight, Running Wolf went to Brooks Hardware, where he bought two boxes of cartridges. From there he went to see a mixed-blood, Dick Larocque, who sold him three bottles of scotch whiskey. Before returning to the reserve, however, Running Wolf decided this was not enough and went back for another three bottles. Meanwhile, a Cree Indian named Many Shots had wandered into the camp, so Pretty Young Man opened one of the bottles to share a drink. By the time Running Wolf got back, Pretty Young Man was already drunk and the other Indian was gone.

Running Wolf was likely angry at his brother for dipping into his liquor supply, not because he wanted to keep it for himself but because he knew it was dangerous to drink so close to a white community. By this time he had had a chance to review his situation. He believed that the news of the Costigan killing would soon be circulated and that white people would be searching for him. His best course of action was to return to the reserve and hide out there until he could flee south, either to his fellow tribesmen on the Blood Reserve or perhaps across the line into Montana.

Realizing that a police patrol might come around to check their camp, he loaded his brother into the democrat and they set off for the Blackfoot Reserve. As soon as the town of Brooks was out of sight the bottle was produced, and all three began to drink. They had just finished the first bottle and were working on the second, when Pretty Young Man passed out and a bed was made for him in the back of the wagon.

They had gone about five miles when they caught up with a seventeen-year-old teamster named Emil Petersen who was walking along the trail, carrying a bundle of clothes. The Indians were not so drunk that Petersen saw any reason to be concerned, so he asked them for a ride and offered them twenty-five cents if they would take him a mile down the road to the railway siding of Cassils. Running Wolf asked for fifty cents, but when the teamster refused, he agreed to accept the lower figure. When Petersen counted out the money, the Indian saw that he still had another thirty-five cents, so when they got to Cassils, he said he would take him further for the rest of his money. As they drove along the trail, Running Wolf offered the young man a drink of scotch. At first he refused, but when this clearly annoyed the Indian, he reluctantly accepted.

They had gone a short distance past Cassils when Running Wolf asked the teamster to buy him some liquor at the next town. Petersen refused, giving as his reason that he was under age and the stores would not sell to him.

Angered by this further refusal, Running Wolf picked up one of his two rifles, pointed it at the young man, and told him to get out of the wagon. As Petersen recalled, "I got out and asked if I could have my clothes and while I was asking him he had a rifle pointing at my chest. He told me to get out of there."[4] Now frightened, Petersen had backed off about fifty feet when the Indian took a shot at him. As the teamster ran toward the protection of the railway grade and was about three hundred feet away, a second shot was fired. Once over the tracks, the young man threw himself down behind the grade and watched as the democrat continued on down the trail.

As soon as they were out of sight, Petersen went to the nearest railway siding and had the telegrapher contact the Mounted Police detachment at Bassano regarding the incident. That done, he continued his ten-mile walk towards his lodgings at Brandenburg's camp.

There were likely two thoughts tumbling through Mike Running Wolf's mind as the horses plodded along the trail. One was that he was wanted for murder, so it did not matter what he did. He could drink, steal, or kill if he wished. They could only hang him once. On the other hand the idea of escape rather than acceptance of his fate had become a clear alternative, so he needed to get to the reserve if he was to hide and ultimately make his dash to a safe haven. Depending upon his feelings at the moment, one or the other idea might predominate.

By midafternoon they were more than halfway to the reserve when Red Face, deciding that she had had too much to drink, took a place beside her husband in the back of the wagon. This left Running Wolf alone in the driver's seat when they caught up with Nicholas Klyne, a railway employee described as a "Galician."[5] As they drew within about thirty feet of the man, the Siksika called out:

"Hey! Wait, give me your blankets!"

"No, they're mine," Klyne replied.

Running Wolf raised his rifle and said, "I'll shoot you right now."[6]

Klyne ran for cover as five or six shots whistled past him. When he heard no more shots and felt he was safe, he turned and saw that the wagon was continuing on its way. The noise had awakened Pretty Young Man's wife, who had rejoined her brother-in-law on the seat. When Klyne checked, he found that one bullet had gone through his hat and two through the blankets he was carrying. Amazingly, he was unwounded. He quickly retraced his steps to Brooks, where he arrived "in a great state of excitement" and reported the matter to the local Mounted Police detachment.[7]

The Mounted Policeman on duty was twenty-three-year-old constable Francis Walter Davies, known to everyone in the area as Frank "Happy" Davies. Born in Hamstead, England, he had joined the Mounted Police in 1909; after completing his training he had been stationed at Gleichen and then at Cochrane, just west of Calgary. While at the latter place, he had been involved in gathering evidence for a prominent murder trial.[8] Early in 1912 he was transferred to Brooks, which he found to be "a pretty tough place."[9] Writing to his parents on March 25, 1912, he said, "at present I am engaged in teaching law and order to would be wild

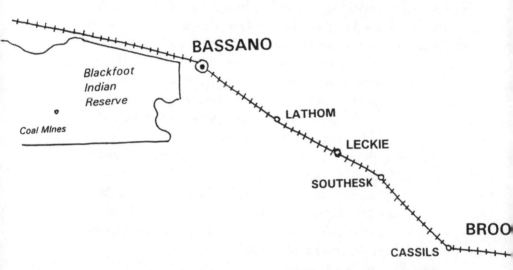

This map shows the journey taken by Mike Running Wolf in 1912 as he fled from the Blackfoot Reserve, believing he had killed a man. He went to a bootlegger in Brooks and, on his way back, shot at two men near Cassils and Southesk. He then shot and killed a Mounted Police constable near the siding of Leckie. When Running wolf returned to his reserve, he was captured by his own people.

and woolly Yankees—I find it rather exciting sometimes, but I always take my man—and that's our motto."[10]

Besides the Klyne complaint, Davies had received word from the Bassano detachment about the attack on Peterson and an incorrect report that the young man had been wounded. The policeman left late in the afternoon on the trail of the turbulent Indians. Whether by premonition or simply in the belief that he would not be back by nightfall, he left word with a friend to look after his dogs if he did not return. Dressed in his scarlet tunic, blue trousers, and white chaps, he set out on the well-worn trail that ran parallel to the railway tracks from Brooks to Bassano, a distance of some thirty miles. He passed a man with a load of telegraph poles about 7 P.M. and then caught up to Emil Peterson, who was still on the trail just past the siding of Southesk. He asked him if he was the man who had been shot at.

"Yes," he said.

"Where did they shoot you?"

"They did not shoot me, they shot at me."[11]

After leaving Petersen, Constable Davies' movements can only be surmised, for the next time he was seen by anyone other than his killer, he was lying dead on the prairie near the railway siding of Leckie.[12] Red Face gave her version of what happened, but this is suspect not only because she had been drinking heavily, but because she was a party to the crime. There were even those among the Siksikas who believed that she was the killer. Ed Yellow Old Woman, who was in the wagon at the time, denied it. "I guess it started because she was like a man," he said. "She was a good shot and could shoot targets with the men."[13]

According to Red Face, the sun was low on the horizon when Constable Davies caught up with the wagon and told Running Wolf to return to Brooks. When he refused, the policeman fired his revolver. "After the policeman shot," she testified, "his horse ran ahead and circled round the team and went to the left side of the rig and then Mike shot at him with a rifle. Mike fired the second shot. The first shot, the policeman sat on his horse, the second shot he fell off."[14]

Mike then handed the lines to Red Face, jumped down, and secured the policeman's horse. He stripped the body of its white chaps, belt, revolver, and hat and put these on. "Mike got on the policeman's horse and told me to drive on a little way and then Mike told me to stop, when he tied the policeman's horse to the team."[15] She did not mention it, but there can be little doubt that Running Wolf was singing a victory song while he paraded in the policeman's attire. This was a traditional way of showing that he had defeated an enemy in battle.

Questions were later raised in court regarding Running Wolf's sobriety at the time of the shooting. Yet he had no trouble holding the rifle and firing an accurate shot, just as he was probably playing with Petersen and Klyne when he shot close to them without hitting them. He was also sober enough to jump from the wagon, catch Davies' horse, don the policeman's accoutrements, and do a victory parade. The excuse of drunkenness is a logical and understandable one to explain the aberrant behavior of a man who had previously avoided violence. Yet placed in perspective with the events that had taken place before Running Wolf left his reserve, his state of intoxication probably had little or no bearing upon his actions. This was not a simple case of an Indian running amok, thus fulfilling all the stereotypes of the drunken savage. Rather, it was the action of a desperate man who wanted to avoid apprehension at all costs and to evade being hanged for the murder of Ed Costigan.

If that serious charge had not existed in his mind, Running Wolf was wise enough to know that he probably would have been given a short jail sentence for the trouble he had caused and for his infractions of the Indian Act. It was the threat of execution, not the alcohol, that caused him to kill Constable Davies on the open prairie on that warm summer evening in 1912.

After the murder Running Wolf wasted no time in seeking the sanctuary of his reserve. Meanwhile, Henry Walker, a homesteader from Berry Creek traveling with a companion, arrived at the murder scene about 8.30 P.M., shortly after the Siksika party had left. "There's a dead man," said Walker's companion. "No, it's a scarecrow," he replied.[16] When they investigated, they found Davies' body, still slightly warm, and sent word to the Mounted Police detachment at Bassano. Corporal Johnson immediately contacted coroner Dr. E. C. Harris, and the two drove to the murder site in his automobile, arriving at three o'clock on the morning of June 4. The Mounted Policeman had been killed by a single shot to the chest, and death had been instantaneous.

The news set off a massive manhunt. In Bassano, town police chief J. A. Clyne and two constables began a search of their area, while at

Gleichen, town policeman J. Roberts, a Mounted Police constable, and scouts Sun Calf, Turned Up Nose, and Dick Bad Boy organized a search party of some twenty men. Most were on horseback, but some traveled in automobiles supplied by Gleichen Garage. Indian Department inspector Glen Campbell arranged to have men guard all the bridges and ferries in the area "to prevent the escape of the murderers to the south."[17] Campbell also called all the chiefs to a meeting at the main bridge across the Bow River. There he was assured by the chiefs "that they were anxious that the Govt. should know that they deplored the crime [and] arranged to divide the country up & had scouts scatter to work it all from east to west in case the fugitives were in hiding."[18]

Meanwhile, Running Wolf and his party had reached the Blackfoot Reserve. The killer was feeling elated by his experience and began to drink more heavily, but as his sister-in-law testified, he had "enough to make him feel good, but he was not falling around."[19] The party approached a small village near the coal mines, and Running Wolf stopped at the first house—one belonging to Nice Cutter. When he learned that Vincent Yellow Old Woman's wife was there, he left the child then asked for directions to the tent of a Siksika named Keg.

At Keg's tent Running Wolf woke up Pretty Young Man, who had been sound asleep or unconscious in the back of the democrat during the whole episode. They went into the tent, where Running Wolf asked for breakfast and sat with two rifles under his legs and the policeman's revolver in his hand. Red Face recalled what happened next:

"Mike talked loud and wanted everybody to come into the tent. All the Indians came in, and Mike said, 'I want to see you now as you will not see me again because I am going away the first thing in the morning, because I killed a mounted policeman, and I am not going to let the police arrest me."[20]

When Pretty Young Man heard this, he felt sorry for his brother and started crying. As other Indians came into the tent, police scout Vincent Yellow Old Woman, father of Edward, quietly took a seat next to the killer. Another Indian named Buckskin stood behind them. At a moment when Running Wolf was distracted, the scout grabbed the revolver out of his hand while Buckskin pulled the rifles from under him. Two other Indians who were standing nearby with a rope lassoed Running Wolf, and in an instant he was completely overpowered. "They thought it was lucky that he got caught," said a Siksika. "If he ever got to the Sun Dance camp, he would have done a lot of damage."[21] Securely tied up, he was loaded in a wagon while Pretty Young Man and his wife followed willingly along. The Indians also took with them the policeman's gun, holster, chaps, and other accoutrements.

They immediately left for Bassano, and when town police chief Clyne learned of the capture he caught up with them on the trail. He took charge of the prisoners, locking up all three in the Bassano jail. While they were there, according to Red Face, she was threatened by Running Wolf and told not to admit to the killing. "Mike told me to say that the person who killed the policeman was the half-breed who gave him the whisky, the half-breed with the black moustache. I never saw this half-breed. Mike told me to say this after we were arrested."[22]

When the police were ready to transfer the trio to the Mounted Police lockup at Gleichen, scout Sun Calf was handcuffed between the two men and they were placed in a buckboard, Red Face seated behind them with a Mountie. "They got in," recalled a Siksika, "and there was a big crowd of people looking at them as they drove into the Mounted Police barracks. They cheered and waved their hats."[23] Within an hour or so of the arrest, the news was telephoned from Bassano to Gleichen, thirty miles away. But the Siksika Indians in the area already knew of it through their own mysterious "moccasin telegraph" and had spread the news.

In spite of the overwhelming evidence against him, Running Wolf claimed he was innocent. He said that the bootlegger, Dick Larocque, had murdered the policemen and given him the revolver, horse, and other objects. However, he could not explain the blood on his clothes nor the policeman's money in his pocket. In addition Larocque was able to provide evidence to show that he was in Brooks when the murder occurred. After a quick preliminary hearing Mike Running Wolf was charged with murder, while Pretty Young Man and his wife were held as material witnesses.

Larocque was charged with selling liquor to Indians and was given the maximum penalty of six months. There were some who believed that he was the indirect cause of the killing and should have stood trial as an accomplice. Meanwhile, Pretty Young Man was shown to have been help-lessly drunk during the whole escapade. He was useless as a witness and was sentenced to a month in jail at hard labor for being drunk in violation of the Indian Act.

Running Wolf was held in a Calgary jail until his trial three months later. Judge Sissons was the presiding magistrate, with James Short as prosecutor and Stanley Jones acting for the defense. After the opening statements of both lawyers, a medical examiner detailed the cause of death and Sgt. Thomas Irvine, a Mounted Policeman stationed at Gleichen, described the arrest of Running Wolf and his denial of killing Davies.

On the following day there was a whole parade of witnesses, including policemen involved in the arrest and Indians who had heard Running Wolf admit that he had killed the constable. Among the latter were Rabbit Carrier, Running Rabbit, and Tail Feathers, who told their stories through an interpreter. But the most damning testimony came when Red Face gave evidence against her brother-in-law. She described the trip to Brooks, the purchasing of liquor, and the fact that Running Wolf had shot and killed Constable Davies. The defense tried to pin her down as to whether the policeman had been shooting in the air as a warning or directly at them. She replied that "his revolver was pointed their way."[24] The day ended with testimony from Big Eye, who described the capture of Running Wolf at Keg's tent.

After all the witnesses had been heard, the two lawyers made their summations to the jury. The Crown prosecutor stated in part: "From the evidence given in the court there was very little doubt but that Running Wolf shot Davis [*sic*]. His written confession, and the fact that he rode into the Indian camp on Davis' horse, boasting that he had killed a policeman, was good evidence. There was one point, whether or not the accused was under the influence of liquor. Admitting that he was, that is no excuse for committing a crime."[25]

Speaking for the defense, Stanley Jones said that "the accused was in a frenzy for liquor. We all know the effect of liquor on Indians. It is so well known that a special law for Indians was necessary. The evidence showed that Ham [that is, Running Wolf] had consumed large quantities of liquor, and he did not know what he was doing. No man but an insane man would ride on the policeman's horse into camp and boast of having killed the policeman."[26]

He went on to point out that Davies fired the first shot and that until that time, the charges against Running Wolf were minor ones. He felt that the policeman's gunshot had been a provocation that Running Wolf had answered.

Interestingly, neither the Crown nor the defense raised the matter of the earlier incident that had resulted in the wounding of Scout Costigan and Running Wolf's subsequent flight from his reserve. Either the lawyers were unaware of the significance of the event or they could not see how the information would be important to their cases. In fact the Crown could have used it as an argument that the Indian believed he was fleeing from apprehension in a murder case, which would have made him a desperate man rather than a drunken one.

In his charge to the jury, Justice Sissons indicated that they had three choices. First, if the prisoner was "so utterly insane from intoxication that he was absolutely irresponsible for the act, not being aware of the purpose, intention and consequence of his act," then he should be acquitted.[27] Second, if he killed the constable "in the heat of passion and before the passion had time to subside," he should be found guilty of manslaughter.[28]

His third option was the most lengthy and would appear to have been the one most favored by the judge. He stated:

Did he shoot the policeman in an excited and intoxicated condition, but not so intoxicated as to be able to form an intention to shoot and kill the policeman? If he was capable, then the verdict would be one of murder. That he was more or less capable of forming an intention is shown by the fact that he took the chaps, belt, revolver and hat of the dead man. Having done this he caught the dead policeman's horse and, when he mounted it, instructed the squaw to drive the team, and rode the horse back to the reservation.[29]

The jury members must have been in a dilemma when they considered the facts of the case. They had no intention of acquitting the prisoner for killing a Mounted Policeman, so that ruled out the first option. But the option of manslaughter as presented by the judge seemed to be limited to an act performed in the heat of passion. To them it appeared that the deed had been done by a drunken Indian, but could that be defined as passion? On the other hand Judge Sissons' third option fitted the circumstances perfectly—yet they were reluctant to put a noose around the neck of an Indian who apparently had been so drunk that he was unaware of his actions at the time of the killing.

In the end they ignored the judge's charge and came back after an hour with a verdict of "guilty of manslaughter." Running Wolf was immediately sentenced to life imprisonment in the Edmonton Penitentiary. According to a reporter, "The prisoner took his sentence very cooly, and had nothing to say. This has been the result that he had hoped to achieve through his counsel, and there seemed to be a trace of satisfaction on the face of the aborigine as he was led from the dock."[30]

But the story does not end there. In 1919, at the urging of a number of Siksika Indians, missionary H. W. G. Stocken wrote to the Deputy Superintendent of Indian Affairs in Ottawa, asking for clemency for the prisoner. He wrote, "He has been in the Penitentiary for many years & has behaved in an exemplary manner as I have learned through Archdeacon Webb and others at Edmonton, who have visited him for time to time."[31] This letter, to which a long list of Siksika petitioners was appended, was forwarded without endorsement or support to the Remission Branch of the Department of Justice. The application was refused.

In 1922 Father J. L. Levern wrote to Ottawa on behalf of "a poor Indian detained in the penitentiary at Prince Albert, Sask., for the last ten years."[32] He indicated that the Indian agent favored Running Wolf's release and said that in the eyes of the Siksikas, ten years in prison was equivalent to a life sentence, as most Indians did not survive three- or four-year sentences. This time there was a letter of support from the Indian Department in Ottawa, which stated, "In view of the fact that this Indian has served ten years, and that his conduct while in the Penitentiary appears to have been satisfactory, the Department would be pleased if you would see your way clear to grant a ticket-of-leave."[33] On the basis of that recommendation, Running Wolf's sentence was reduced to twenty years and he was released on probation in November 1922.

Tom McMaster, a Siksika Indian, stated, "While Mike was in prison he dreamed that the next day he was going to get out. Mike had no knowledge that he was going to get out. He told some of the other prisoners about it and they told him he was crazy. But that day some men came and took Mike out."[34]

He returned to the Blackfoot Reserve and lived there quietly until his death in the mid-1930s. During those years after his release he turned to Native religion, joining the sacred Horn Society and becoming involved

in other religious activities. Those who knew him remembered him as a gentle and inoffensive man. Many were unaware of those few turbulent days in 1912 when Scout Costigan's cry, "I've been killed," sent him on a journey of mayhem, alcohol, and disaster.

During his early years Running Wolf had all the cards stacked against him—a lack of understanding of the law, the temptations of alcohol, and the warrior tradition of his people. All these factors had resulted in the death of an innocent Mountie. Like many of the Blackfoot of his time, Running Wolf's life had changed drastically from that of his parents and grandparents. Instead of coursing the plains in search of buffalo, he had been confined to his reserve, to the church mission school, and to the ration house. He was an outcast in a larger society that had overwhelmed his people. Succeeding generations would adjust, but for Running Wolf it was too late.

OPPOSITE PAGE   When Mike Running Wolf was released from prison after murdering a Mountie, he joined the religious life of the Blackfoot Reserve. He is seen here in the foreground during rituals of the Horn Society in the early 1930s. *Courtesy Glenbow Archives, Calgary, AB, cat. no. NA-739-13*

Notes

1 THE VENGEFUL WIFE

1. The date is based upon information provided to George Bird Grinnell that a daughter of one of the survivors of this incident married an employee of Edmonton House when that fort was built in 1795. See George Bird Grinnell, *Blackfoot Lodge Tales*, 49.

2. Ibid., 40.

3. Joe Little Chief, "The Story of Calf Looking," manuscript in Glenbow Archives, Calgary, M4394. Some editing of the manuscript was required.

4. Ibid.

5. Ibid.

6. Grinnell, *Blackfoot Lodge Tales*, 42.

7. Little Chief, "The Story of Calf Looking."

8. Grinnell, *Blackfoot Lodge Tales*, 44.

9. Little Chief, "The Story of Calf Looking."

10. Grinnell, *Blackfoot Lodge Tales*, 45.

11. Ibid., 46.

12. Little Chief, "The Story of Calf Looking."

13. Ibid.

14. "Woman's Revenge: A Legend of the Blackfeet," anonymous manuscript, written in an old Indian Department ledger book. Glenbow Archives.

15. Father Dugast, "Revenge of the Chieftain's Bride," trans. Helen Hibbard. *Montreal Daily Star*, July 11, 1885.

16. Grinnell, *Blackfoot Lodge Tales*, 48.

17. "Woman's Revenge."

18. Grinnell, *Blackfoot Lodge Tales*, 48.

19. Little Chief, "The Story of Calf Looking."

20. Adapted from Grinnell, *Blackfoot Lodge Tales*, 49.

21. Ibid.

22. Ibid.

23. Adapted from "Woman's Revenge."

24. John Maclean, *Canadian Savage Folk*, 312.

25. This tale has been recorded with some variations over the past 120 years. In one account the woman was from the Blackfoot tribe and the enemy was the Crow. In two other accounts the woman was Crow and the enemy was Blackfoot. In the account used here the chief was identified as Calf Looking, while in another he was identified as Running Elk. However, the general details of the original raid, the abandonment of the woman, the subsequent torture of her husband, the intervention of the old woman, and the wife's death by fire are all consistent. The writer has chosen the Blackfoot-Shoshoni version as the best documented and has selected those elements from various stories that are most consistent with Blackfoot practices.

2 PIPES AND FUR TRADERS

1. Crooked Meat Strings, Siksika Indian, interview by Lucien and Jane Hanks, August 2, 1941. Hanks Papers, Glenbow Archives.

2. Sleigh, Siksika Indian, interview by Lucien and Jane Hanks, c. 1939. Hanks Papers, Glenbow Archives.

3. Sylvia Van Kirk, "John Rowand," 779–80.

4. Ibid., 780.

5. Blackfoot winter counts indicate that at least part of this story took place in 1832. It is quite possible that the loss occurred in 1824, but the transfer ceremony described in the Native account did not take place until eight years later.

6. Hudson's Bay Company, Journal of Carlton House, 1824–25, entry for October 17, 1824.

Hudson's Bay Company records, B.27/a/14, Provincial Archives of Manitoba. Because of the multiplicity of Blackfoot names, it is possible that The Feather and Big Plume were the same person.

7. Many Guns, Siksika Indian, interview by Lucien and Jane Hanks, September 16, 1939. Hanks Papers, Glenbow Archives.

8. Hudson's Bay Company, Journal of Carlton House, entry for October 25, 1824.

9. Ibid., entry for December 29, 1824.

10. Ibid., entry for October 26, 1824.

11. Many Guns, interview, September 16, 1939. In their notes the Hanks refer to Rowand as "E" (an abbreviation of Ee'kaki) and Big Plume as "O" (an abbreviation of O'muhk-sapop). They will be referred to in this chapter by their proper names.

12. Ibid.

13. Ibid.

14. Ibid.

15. Hudson's Bay Company, Journal of Carlton House, entry for March 30, 1825.

16. Many Guns, interview, September 16, 1939.

17. Many Guns calls it a Union flag.

18. Many Guns, interview, September 16, 1939.

19. Adapted from Little Chief, "The Story of Calf Looking."

20. Based upon Many Guns, interview, September 16, 1939. Jim White Bull referred to the Blood as "Who's He?" (White Bull papers in author's possession), while Little Chief called the man "Mister Him."

21. Ibid.

22. Ibid.

23. Ibid.

24. Some accounts say that Humpback was a Cree, but Creighton's winter count states, "A man by the name of Hump Back killed a Cree enemy prisoner at a celebration at which there was dancing, etc. The enemy was scalped." Percy Creighton, Blood Indian, Winter count, Harry Biele Papers, Smithsonian Institution.

25. Today, the Sarcees use the Native term for themselves, Tsuu T'ina, so that they are called the Tsuu T'ina First Nation. However, as this is a historical account, I have used the more familiar name Sarcee.

26. Fur traders spoke Blackfoot when dealing with the Sarcees, because their own language was so difficult. In Blackfoot, Spotted Eagle was Peta'kihtsipimi, while Hanging Crow was Maistoi'tsista.

27. One account (Diamond Jenness, *The Sarcee Indians of Alberta*) identifies them as Sarcees named Spotted Eagle and Cut Knife or Crow Flag; another as Sarcees named Spotted Eagle and Hanging Crow (Pretty Young Man manuscript, "Stories about long ago," told by Tonny Pretty Young Man, Sarcee, in the early 1940s. Accession #992, Glenbow Archives); and a third as Bloods named Black Eagle and Broken Knife (Bobtail Chief interview).

28. Jenness, *The Sarcee Indians of Alberta*, 81.

29. He was identified by Bobtail Chief (interview) as John Rowand (Short Man), but the events described in the story likely occurred in the 1860s or 1870s, long after Rowand's death.

30. Jenness, *The Sarcee Indians of Alberta*, 81.

31. Pretty Young Man "Stories about long ago."

32. Jenness, *The Sarcee Indians of Alberta*, 82.

33. Adapted from Pretty Young Man, "Stories about long ago."

34. Jenness, *The Sarcee Indians of Alberta*, 81.

35. Ibid., 82.

36. Adapted from Pretty Young Man, "Stories about long ago."

37. Jenness, *The Sarcee Indians of Alberta*, 82.

38. Ibid.

39. Adapted from Pretty Young Man, "Stories about long ago."

40. Ibid.

41. Jenness, *The Sarcee Indians of Alberta*, 82.

42. Ibid., 80.

3 MASSACRE AT SUN RIVER

1. As there are four versions of this story, none being entirely complete, it has been necessary to select the details that appear to provide a running account. One of these sources, which is used sparingly, is a semi-fictional article by James Willard Schultz, "Indians Battle on Sun River in 1833," which appeared in the *Great Falls Tribune*, September 5 and 12, 1937.

2. Split Ears, South Piegan Indian, grandson of Bear Chief, interview by James Willard Schultz, August 6, 1915. Schultz Papers, Montana State University. Unless otherwise stated, all direct quotes come from this source.

3. Split Ears, interview.

4. Ibid.

5. Ibid.

6. *Sun River Sun*, December 25, 1884.

7. Pete Eagle, South Piegan Indian, interview by Claude Schaeffer, June 10, 1952, Schaeffer Papers, Glenbow Archives, Calgary.

8. Split Ears, interview.

9. Ibid.

10. *Sun River Sun*, December 25, 1884.

11. Ibid.

12. Ibid.

4 THE REVENGE OF BULL HEAD

1. Elliott Coues, ed., *New Light on the Early History of the Greater Northwest*, 2:723–24.

2. Hugh A. Dempsey, ed., *The Rundle Journals, 1840–1848*, 263.

3. Dick Sanderville, South Piegan Indian, interview by Claude Schaeffer, May 21, 1952. Schaeffer Papers, Glenbow Archives.

4. James Doty, "A Visit to the Blackfoot Camps," 17.

5. Hugh A. Dempsey, ed., *Heaven is Near the Rocky Mountains*, 30–31.

6. Ibid.

7. "Fort Benton Journal, 1854–56," 69.

8. "Report of commissioners Alfred Cummings and Isaac I. Stevens on the proceedings of the council with the Blackfeet Indians," Montana Historical Society Archives, SC-895.

9. Charles J. Kappler, ed., *Indian Affairs. Laws and Treaties*, 1:737.

10. Annual report of Gad E. Upson, United States Indian Agent, September 1, 1864. SC810, Montana Historical Society.

11. John J. Healy, "Frontier Sketches, Number Thirty-Three," *Benton Weekly Record*, November 8, 1878.

12. DeMarce, Roxanne, ed. *Blackfeet Heritage*, 182.

13. James Bradley, "Blackfoot War with the Whites," 253–54.

14. *Montana Post*, April 28, 1866.

15. Nicholas Sheran later settled at Lethbridge, where he became Alberta's first coal miner.

16. John J. Healy, "Frontier Sketches, Number Thirty-Three."

17. Report of Hiram D. Upham, April 20, 1866. U.S. Interior Department, Bureau of Indian Affairs Records. Montana Historical Society, SC895.

18. *Montana Post*, "Helena Letter," May 19, 1866.

19. Report of Hiram D. Upham.

20. Letter, Sully to the Commissioner of Indian Affairs, January 3, 1870. *Piegans. Letter from the Secretary of War.* 41st Cong., 2nd Sess., HR, ex.doc. 269, 1870, 36.

21. Report of Hiram D. Upham.

22. Pat Bad Eagle, North Piegan Indian, interview by Hugh A. Dempsey, April 1, 1961. In author's posession.

5 THEY ACTED LIKE WOMEN

1. Fish Wolf Robe, South Piegan Indian, interview by Claude Schaeffer, July 20, 1965. Schaeffer Papers, book 3, folder 4, box 17, Glenbow Archives.

2. Claude E. Schaeffer, "The Kutenai Female Berdache: Courier, Guide, Prophetess, and Warrior," 222.

3. Ibid.

4. Mollie Arrow Top, South Piegan Indian, interview by Claude Schaeffer, August 18, 1965. Schaeffer Papers, book 3, folder 4, box 17, Glenbow Archives.

5. John Ground, South Piegan Indian, interview by Claude Schaeffer, September 30, 1950. Schaeffer Papers, box 17, book 7, folder 2, Glenbow Archives.

6. Henry Angelino, interview by Charles L. Shedd, *American Anthropologist* 8 (1955): 125. Cited in *Oxford English Dictionary*.

7. Eli Guardipee, South Piegan Indian, interview by James Willard Schultz, January 1929. Schultz Papers, Special Collections, Montana State University Library, Bozeman, Mont.

8. Ibid.

9. Ibid.

10. Ibid.

11. Ibid.

12. Many Tail Feathers, South Piegan Indian, interview by James Willard Schultz, August 4 and 5, 1922. Schultz Papers, Special Collections, Montana State University Library, Bozeman, Mont.

13. Crooked Meat Strings, interview by Lucien and Jane Hanks, July 27, 1939. Hanks papers, box 300, folder 11, Glenbow Archives.

14. Marie Small, South Piegan Indian, interview by Claude Schaeffer, August 18, 1965. Schaeffer Papers, box 17, book 7, folder 2, Glenbow Archives.

15. Fish Wolf Robe, interview.

16. Crooked Meat Strings, interview.

17. Dog Chief, Siksika Indian, interview by Lucien and Jane Hanks, August 1, 1939. Hanks papers, box 300, folder 27, Glenbow Archives.

18. Crooked Meat Strings, interview.

19. Ibid.

20. Dog Chief, interview.

21. Ibid.

22. Ibid.

23. Ibid.

24. Ibid.

25. Apioh'suk, Siksika Indian, interview by Lucien and Jane Hanks, June 18, 1941. Hanks papers, box 300, folder 47, Glenbow Archives.

26. Ibid.

27. Francis Black, Siksika Indian, interview by Lucien and Jane Hanks, June 1938. Hanks papers, box 300, folder 3, Glenbow Archives.

28. See Oscar Lewis, "Manly-hearted Women Among the North Piegan," 173–87.

29. James Willard Schultz, *Running Eagle, The Warrior Girl.* Schaeffer described the book as being written "in a novelistic vein," and he cited it "with some reluctance." Schaeffer, "The Kutenai Female Berdache," 227.

30. Statement of Weasel Tail in John C. Ewers, "Women's Roles in Plains Indian Warfare," *Skeletal Biology in the Great Plains*, ed. D. W. Owlsey and R. L. Jantz, 328.

31. One Gun, Siksika Indian, interviw by Lucien and Jane Hanks, July 24, 1939. Hanks papers, box 300, folder 45, Glenbow Archives.

32. Ewers, "Women's Roles in Plains Indian Warfare," 328.

33. Ibid., 329.

34. Ibid.

35. John Rowand, letter to Donald Ross, December 21, 1844. M936, City of Edmonton Archives.

36. Joe Beebe, Blood Indian, interview by Esther S. Goldfrank, January 8, 1939. Goldfrank papers, Glenbow Archives.

37. Ibid.

38. Fish Wolf Robe, interview.

39. George First Rider, Blood Indian, interview by Claude Schaeffer, January 10, 1961. Schaeffer papers, box 17, book 16, file 3, Glenbow Archives.

40. One Gun, interview.

41. Ibid.

42. Ewers, "Women's Roles in Plains Indian Warfare," 329.

6 THE BATTLE AT ELKWATER LAKE

1. Account told by Many Tail Feathers, South Piegan Indian, to James Willard Schultz, August 4 and 5, 1922. Schultz Papers, Special Collections, Montana State University Library, Bozeman, Mont. This story was collected by Schultz and is in his collection as abbreviated interview notes. I have expanded the notes into narrative form. Any conversations used here are the words of Many Tail Feathers, taken directly from his account.

2. Ambrose Gravelle, Kootenay Indian, interview by Claude Schaeffer, July 17, 1969. Schaeffer Papers, box 17, book 5, folder 4, Glenbow Archives.

3. Ibid.

4. Ambrose Gravelle, Kootenay Indian, interview by Claude Schaeffer, July 10, 1969. Schaeffer Papers, box 17, book 3, folder 4, Glenbow Archives.

5. Many Tail Feathers, interview.

6. Ibid.

7. Clark Wissler, *The Social Life of the Blackfoot Indians*, 46.

8. Ambrose Gravelle, Kootenay Indian, interview by Claude Schaeffer, July 8, 1969. Schaeffer Papers, box 17, book 4, folder 1, Glenbow Archives.

7 GHOSTS

1. Charlie Pantherbone, Blood Indian, interview by Hugh A. Dempsey, August 2, 1960.

2. Claude E. Schaeffer, *Blackfoot Shaking Tent*, 13.

3. Father J. L. Levern, "Notes et Souvenirs Concernant les Piednoirs." Translation from French. Microfilm in Glenbow Archives.

4. Ibid.

5. Grinnell, *Blackfoot Lodge Tales*, 273.

6. Interview with Pretty Young Man, Siksika Indian, interview by Lucien and Jane Hanks, 1941. Hanks Papers, Glenbow Archives.

7. Ibid.

8. The leader is identified as Heavy Collar by Grinnell (*Blackfoot Lodge Tales*, 70), as Crow Eagle by Walter McClintock (*The Old North Trail* [Lincoln: University of Nebraska Press, 1992], 145), as Many Feathers on the Head by Willie Whitefeathers ("Reminiscences," *Prairie Patchwork* [Lethbridge: Southern Alberta Writers' Workshop, 1980], 231), and as Long Hair by Cecil Black Plume ("Longhair," *Outlook* [Lethbridge Jail, April 1973]).

9. McClintock, *The Old North Trail*, 147.

10. Grinnell, *Blackfoot Lodge Tales*, 72.

11. Ibid.

12. Ibid., 74.

13. Whitefeathers, "Reminiscences," 232.

14. Ibid., 233.

15. Mrs. Takes the Gun Himself, Siksika Indian, interview by Lucien and Jane Hanks, July 28, 1940. Hanks Papers, Glenbow Archives.

16. Ibid.

17. Grinnell, *Blackfoot Lodge Tales*, 274.

18. Ibid.

19. Cecil Denny, *The Riders of the Plains*, 118.

20. Ibid., 119.

21. Ibid.

22. Levern, "Notes et Souvenirs Concernant les Piednoirs."

23. Old Bull, Siksika Indian, interview by Lucien and Jane Hanks, September 7, 1940. Hanks Papers, Glenbow Archives.

24. Ibid.

25. Personal communication from Fran Fraser, 1963, based upon interviews with Stump and Joe Good Eagle.

26. Hugh A. Dempsey, *The Blackfoot Ghost Dance*, 12.

27. Jim White Bull, Blood Indian, interview by Hugh A. Dempsey, June 5, 1954. Unless otherwise stated, all quotations relating to the origin of the ghost medicine pipe are from this source.

28. Joe Beebe, interview.

29. Jack Low Horn, Blood Indian, interview by Hugh A. Dempsey, December 29, 1954.

8 SEEN FROM AFAR

1. William F. Butler, *Red Cloud: The Solitary Sioux.* While the book itself is fiction, Butler has used a number of accurate descriptions based upon his western experiences.

2. Percy Creighton, Blood Indian, interview by Hugh A. Dempsey, July 17, 1954.

3. Yellow Kidney, South Piegan Indian, interview by Claude Schaeffer, November 25, 1948. Schaeffer Papers, Glenbow Archives.

4. Jack Holterman, *King of the High Missouri: The Saga of the Culbertsons,* 212.

5. Charlie Pantherbone, Blood Indian, interview by Hugh A. Dempsey, July 24, 1954.

6. DeMarce, *Blackfeet Heritage,* 180.

7. Paul Little Walker, Siksika Indian, interview by Lucien and Jane Hanks, August 5, 1941. Hanks Papers, Glenbow Archives.

8. Ibid. Little Walker included this conversation in his story.

9. *Benton Weekly Record,* January 9, 1880.

10. Ibid.

11. Frank Red Crow, Blood Indian, interview by Claude Schaeffer, May 1948. Schaeffer Papers, Glenbow Archives.

12. Yellow Kidney, interview.

13. One Gun, Siksika Indian, interview.

14. Ibid.

15. Ibid.

16. Joseph P. Donnelly, ed., *Wilderness Kingdom: Indian Life in the Rocky Mountains, 1840–1847. The Journals & Paintings of Nicholas Point, S.J.,* 117.

17. Holterman, *King of the High Missouri,* 34.

18. There is no way of knowing whether this trip was made by Seen Far Afar, who was only twenty-three years old at the time, or by his father, who had once carried the same name. Blood elders believed that the traveler had been the younger Seen From Afar.

19. Percy Creighton, interview.

20. Eagle Feathers, South Piegan Indian, interview by James Willard Schultz, undated. Schultz papers, Montana State University.

21. Ibid.

22. Charlie Crow Eagle, North Piegan Indian, interview by Oscar Lewis, August 9, 1939. Lewis Papers, Smithsonian Institution.

23. Ibid.

24. Charlie Pantherbone, grandson of Rainy Chief, interview. Unless otherwise stated, all quotes for this story are those given by Pantherbone.

25. Ibid.

26. Paul Little Walker, interview.

27. Harry Mills, Blood Indian, interview by Hugh A. Dempsey, December 27, 1953.

28. John Cotton, Blood Indian, interview by Hugh A. Dempsey, December 26, 1953.

29. DeMarce, *Blackfeet Heritage,* 180.

30. James J. Audubon, *Audubon and His Journals,* 2:112.

31. Rudolf Friedrich Kurz, *Journal of Rudolf Friedrich Kurz, 1846–1852,* 115.

32. Dabney Taylor, "The Major's Blackfoot Bride," *Frontier Times,* 43:1 (December–January 1969), 27.

33. Ibid. James Willard Schultz gives a highly romanticized account of this wedding and courtship that is more a testament to the writer's imagination than to fact. See his *Signposts of Adventure,* 112–17.

34. Donnelly, *Wilderness Kingdom,* 114–15.

35. Ibid., 116.

36. Percy Creighton, interview.

37. John Ground, South Piegan Indian, interview, September 30, 1950.

38. James H. Bradley, "Affairs at Fort Benton, From 1831 to 1869."

39. Statement of Cecile Black Boy, accompanying paintings of Blackfoot tepee designs. Glenbow Archives.

40. Ibid.

41. Anne McDonnell, ed., "The Fort Benton Journals, 1854–1856," 26. Entry for March 25, 1855.

42. Charles J. Kappler, ed., *Indian Affairs. Laws and Treaties,* 1:736.

43. "The Blackfoot Indian Peace Council," 10.

44. S. H. Middleton, ed., *Indian Chiefs, Ancient and Modern*, 156.

45. Report of Hiram D. Upham.

46. Letter, W. J. Christie to Richard Hardisty, November 2, 1866. Hudson's Bay Company Archives, B.60/b/2.

47. John Cotton, Blood Indian, interview by Hugh A. Dempsey, January 4, 1957.

48. Joe Beebe, interview.

49. John Cotton, interview.

50. Ibid.

51. William F. Butler, *The Great Lone Land*, 314.

52. Paul Little Walker, interview.

53. Tappen Adney, "John J. Healy and the Bloods." Manuscript in Tappen Adney Papers, Montana Historical Society Archives.

9 THE LAST GREAT BATTLE

1. James Willard Schultz Papers, Montana State University Special Collections, Bozeman. Adapted from shorthand notes of interview with Many Tail Feathers.

2. Ibid.

3. Ibid.

4. *Lethbridge News*, April 30, 1890. See also Carlton R. Stewart, ed., *The Last Great (Inter-Tribal) Indian Battle*, 10–13.

5. Mike Mountain Horse, *My People the Bloods*, 50. Mountain Horse, a Blood Indian, obtained this information from a Cree named Iron Horn, from the Fort Belknap Reserve, who was a member of the revenge party.

6. Kennedy gives the date as about October 25, but A. J. Simmons states a month after the event that "About November first the camp was attacked . . ." Letter, A. J. Simmons to Jasper Viall, November 30, 1870," Letters Received by the Office of Indian Affairs, 1824–81, Montana Superintendency, 1864–1880," roll 490, U.S. National Archives.

7. Mountain Horse, *My People the Bloods*, 50.

8. Kennedy identifies the man as a brother of Red Crow, the head chief of the tribe, but this relationship was not known by Blood informants. Personal communication from various elders.

9. White Man Running Around, war record, 1927. Printed broadside. Fort Macleod Museum.

10. Mike Mountain Horse, interview, *Lethbridge Herald*, July 27, 1940.

11. Mountain Horse, *My People the Bloods*, 50.

12. White Wolf, war record, 1927. Printed broadside. Fort Macleod Museum.

13. Joseph K. Dixon, *The Vanishing Race*, 112–15.

14. Mountain Horse, *My People the Bloods*, 51.

15. Adam White Man, South Piegan Indian, interview by Claude Schaeffer, November 22, 1950. Schaeffer Papers, Glenbow Archives.

16. Ibid.

17. Big Wolf, war record, 1927. Printed broadside. Fort Macleod Museum.

18. Dixon, *The Vanishing Race*, 112–15.

19. Big Wolf, war record. In the text the interpreter has mistranslated *Assiniboine* as *Sioux*. Although of the same origin, the Assiniboines had separated from their parent tribe many years earlier.

20. Ibid.

21. Jim White Bull, Blood Indian, interview by Hugh A. Dempsey, December 29, 1955.

22. Ibid.

23. Ibid.

24. Dixon, *The Vanishing Race*, 112–15.

25. *Lethbridge News*, April 30, 1890.

26. Ibid.

27. James F. Sanderson, "Indian Tales of the Canadian Prairies," 14.

28. Dixon, *The Vanishing Race*, 112–15.

29. John Cotton, Blood Indian, interview by Hugh A. Dempsey December 29, 1955.

30. Mike Oka, "A Blood Indian's Story," 13.

31. Stewart, *The Last Great (Inter-Tribal) Indian Battle*, 9–10.

32. George Dawson, "Blackfoot Names of a Number of Places in the North-West Territory, for the Most Part in the Vicinity of the Rocky Mountains," *Report of Progress, 1882– 83–84.* Ottawa: Geological and Natural History Survey and Museum of Canada, 1885, 159. Dawson spells the word "assini-etomotchi."

33. Mountain Chief in Wissler, *The Social Life of the Blackfoot Indians,* 49.

34. Bull Child in Paul M. Raczka, *Winter Count: A History of the Blackfoot People,* 63.

35. Bad Head in Hugh A. Dempsey, *A Blackfoot Winter Count,* 15.

36. Percy Creighton, Winter count, Harry Biele Papers.

37. Jim White Bull, "Records by the Blood Indians and Blackfoots." Typed copy of manuscript in possession of the author.

38. Many Guns, Siksika Indian, interview by Lucien and Jane Hanks, August 31, 1938. Hanks Papers, Glenbow Archives. Many Guns wrote "Fort Whoop-Up" as "Ft. Hooper." He added, "Blkft, 2 Piegan tribes, Bloods wintered at Ft. Hooper; Crees, Assiniboines et al. warred. Crees, Assiniboines didn't know there were so many tipis. Bft. Confederation tipis were stretched along a river. 10 outlying tipis attacked; message went up and all attacked. Many drowned. A tremendous victory for Bft. Confederation. Hundreds killed."

39. Houghton Running Rabbit, Winter count, Glenbow Archives.

40. Letter, Charles D. Hard to J. A. Viall, November 9, 1870. "Letters Received by the Office of Indian Affairs, 1824–81, Montana Superintendency, 1864–1880," roll 490, U.S. National Archives.

41. Dr. George A. Kennedy in *Lethbridge News,* April 30, 1890.

42. Mountain Chief in Clark Wissler, *Social Life of the Blackfoot Indians,* 49.

43. Isaac Cowie, *The Company of Adventurers,* 414.

44. Winter count by Jim White Bull, typed copy in possession of the author; Percy Creighton, Winter Count, Harry Biele

Papers.

45. *Helena Daily Herald,* December 2, 1870.

46. Letter, Simmons to Viall, November 30, 1870.

47. Ibid.

48. Sanderson, "Indian Tales of the Canadian Prairies, 14.

49. Cowie, *The Company of Adventurers,* 414.

50. Letter, J. A. Viall to E. S. Parker, November 14, 1870. "Letters Received by the Office of Indian Affairs, 1824–81, Montana Superintendency, 1864–1880," roll 490, U.S. National Archives.

51. Letter, Charles D. Hard to J. A. Viall, November 9, 1870. "Letters Received by the Office of Indian Affairs, 1824–81, Montana Superintendency, 1864–1880," roll 490, U.S. National Archives.

52. Hudson's Bay Company Archives, B.239.c.20, cited in Stewart, *The Last Great (Inter-Tribal) Indian Battle,* 23.

53. *The Manitoban,* Winnipeg, March 4, 1871. Cited in Stewart, *The Last Great (Inter-Tribal) Indian Battle,* 21.

54. Stewart, *The Last Great (Inter-Tribal) Indian Battle,* 10.

10   THE PRISONERS

1. Sleigh, interview.

2. Untitled manuscript in Glacier National Park Archives, West Glacier, Montana.

3. Eagle Calf and Heavy Breast. *Picture Writing by the Blackfeet Indians of Glacier National Park Montana,* 4.

4. Untitled manuscript in Glacier National Park Archives.

5. Eagle Calf and Heavy Breast, *Picture Writing by the Blackfeet Indians of Glacier National Park Montana,* 20.

6. Running Rabbit, Siksika Indian, interview by Lucien and Jane Hanks, July 12, 1939. Hank Papers, Glenbow Archives.

7. Ibid.

8. Boy Chief, South Piegan Indian, interview by James Willard Schultz, August 7, 1913. Schultz Papers, Montana State University Library.

9. Ibid.

10. Apioh'suk, interview.

11. Ibid.

12. Ibid.

13. Crooked Meat Strings, interview.

14. Daniel Williams Harmon, *Sixteen Years in the Indian Country*, 222.

15. Hugh A. Dempsey, ed., "Simpson's Essay on the Blackfoot, 1841," 8.

16. Sanderville, interview.

17. Ibid.

18. Joe Beebe, "Justice Among the Indians Before the White Man's Law Came." Manuscript in Beebe Papers, Glenbow Archives.

19. Ibid.

20. Crooked Meat Strings, Siksika Indian, interview by Lucien and Jane Hanks, September 13, 1938. Hanks Papers, Glenbow Archives.

21. Clark Wissler, *Blackfoot Mythology*, 162.

22. George Bird Grinnell, *The Story of the Indian*, 135.

23. A. L. Kroeber, *Ethnology of the Gros Ventre*, 217. Unless otherwise stated, all quotations by Watches All are from this source.

24. Grinnell, *Blackfoot Lodge Tales*, 137.

25. Letter, George B. Wright to Secretary of the Interior, July 5, 1867. Montana Indian Superintendency Papers, Montana Historical Society.

26. Ibid.

27. Frank Bird Linderman, *Pretty Shield: Medicine Woman of the Crows*, 173.

28. Apioh'suk, interview.

29. Ibid.

30. James Bradley, "Affairs at Fort Benton from 1831 to 1869," 69.

31. Ibid.

32. Mrs. Axe, Siksika Indian, interview by Lucien and Jane Hanks, July 24, 1941. Hanks Papers, Glenbow Archives.

33. Cecil Black Plume, "Children Massacred," *Kainai News*, March 15, 1953.

34. As stated by Black Plume, "This story was handed down to us from our old ancestors and we forgot the name of the hero."

35. Jim Black, "Rescue of the Captured Boy," *Siksika Nation News*, August 1998.

36. S. H. Middleton, ed., *Indian Chiefs, Ancient and Modern*, 154.

II HIS NAME WAS STAR CHILD

1. *Benton Weekly Record*, September 12, 1879.

2. Ibid.

3. *Winnipeg Daily Times*, December 20, 1879.

4. Denny, *The Riders of the Plains*, 198.

5. John Peter Turner, *The North-West Mounted Police*, 1:496.

6. *Winnipeg Daily Times*, December 20, 1879.

7. Ibid.

8. Ibid.

9. Samuel B. Steele, *Forty Years in Canada: Reminiscences of the Great North-West with Some Account of his Service in South Africa*, 147.

10. *Report of the Commissioner of the North-West Mounted Police Force, 1879*. Ottawa: Queen's Printer, 1880, 18.

11. J. H. McIllree, Diary, entry for May 7, 1880. Microfilm M-473, Glenbow Archives.

12. W. H. Williams, *Manitoba and the North-West; Journal of a Trip from Toronto to the Rocky Mountains*, 133.

13. Ibid.

14. *Annual Report of the Department of Indian Affairs for the Year Ended 31st December, 1881*, xxxvii.

15. Williams, *Manitoba and the North-West*, 133.

16. Letter, E. H. Maunsell to J. F. Price, May 29, 1922. Elizabeth Bailey Price Papers, M1002, f.1, Glenbow Archives.

17. Ibid.

18. Letter, Cecil Denny to Edgar Dewdney, November 1, 1881. Indian Affairs file 29506, National Archives of Canada (hereafter NAC).

19. Steele, *Forty Years in Canada*, 151–52.

20. Letter, E. H. Maunsell to J. F. Price, May 29, 1922. Elizabeth Bailey Price Papers, Glenbow Archives.

21. *Fort Macleod Gazette*, November 24, 1882.

22. Ibid., December 4, 1882.

23. Ibid., March 14, 1883.

24. *Manitoba Free Press*, July 31, 1883.

25. John Maclean, letter to his wife, June 8, 1886. Maclean Papers, United Church Archives, Toronto.

26. Ibid.

27. Letter, William Pocklington to Indian Commissioner, February 3, 1887. Blood Reserve letter-books, Indian Department Records, NAC.

28. "Annual Report of Superintendent P. R. Neale, 1887," *Report of the Commissioner of the North-West Mounted Police Force, 1887*, 48.

29. Ibid.

30. William M. Baker, ed., *Pioneer Policing in Southern Alberta: Deane of the Mounties, 1888–1914*, 21.

31. Turner, *The North-West Mounted Police*, 2:433.

32. "Annual Report of Superintendent R. B. Deane," *Report of the Commissioner of the North-West Mounted Police Force, 1889*, 41–42.

12   HARRISON'S HORSES

1. Granville Stuart in *Benton River Press*, August 31, 1881.

2. *Benton Weekly Record*, October 13, 1881.

3. While none of the participants left a detailed account of their travel, the route described is the most direct one along a path indicated by press reports. The blizzard, too, was recorded in the press.

4. *Benton River Press*, October 19, 1881.

5. Joel Overholser, *Fort Benton: World's Innermost Port*, 272.

6. *Report of the Commissioner of the North-West Mounted Police Force, 1881* (hereinafter *Report of the Commissioner, 1881*), 15.

7. *Benton Weekly Record*, October 27, 1881.

8. Ibid., November 3, 1881.

9. *Benton River Press*, November 9, 1881.

10. *Report of the Commissioner, 1881*, 15.

11. Ibid.

12. Letter, Granville Stuart to M. E. Milner, November 3, 1881, reprinted in *Benton Weekly Record*, November 17, 1881.

13. *Benton Weekly Record*, November 10, 1881.

14. Ibid., November 14, 1881.

15. Ibid., November 16, 1881.

16. Ibid., November 10, 1881.

17. Ibid.

18. *Manitoba Free Press*, May 12, 1882.

19. *Report of the Commissioner, 1881*, 16.

20. *Manitoba Free Press*, May 12, 1882.

21. Ibid.

22. Ibid.

23. *Fort Macleod Gazette*, July 16, 1882.

24. Ibid.

25. Ibid.

26. *Benton River Press*, November 9, 1881.

27. *Report of the Commissioner, 1881*, 15.

28. *Benton River Press*, November 9, 1881.

29. Ibid.

30. *Benton Weekly Record*, December 22, 1881.

31. James Willard Schultz and Jessie Louise Donaldson, *The Sun God's Children*, 217.

32. Reprinted in the *Manitoba Free Press*, January 13, 1882.

13   WAS MARY WHITE REALLY WHITE?

1. *Winnipeg Daily Times*, July 31, 1883.

2. *Calgary Herald*, July 25, 1888.

3. Ibid.

4. Letter, J. C. McIllree to the Commissioner, February 19, 1890. RCMP papers, NAC.

5. *New York World*, February 9, 1890.

6. Letter, Father M. McMahon to Hugh A. Dempsey, October 12, 1971. In author's possession.

7. *Manitoba Free Press*, September 27, 1876.

8. Cited in *New York World*, January 5, 1890.

9. Ibid.

10. Ibid.

11. Ibid.

12. *Macleod Gazette*, February 6, 1890.

13. *Benton River Press*, February 12, 1890.

14. Statement by Dog Child, February 28, 1890, in letter, Magnus Begg to Hayter Reed, March 1, 1890. RCMP papers, NAC.

15. Letter, J. C. McIllree to the Commissioner, February 19, 1890. RCMP papers, NAC.

16. Ibid.

17. Ibid.

18. *Winnipeg Free Press*, February 24, 1890.

19. Ibid.

20. *Macleod Gazette*, May 1, 1890.

21. *New York World*, February 9, 1890. Unless otherwise stated, all further quotations are from this source.

22. Ibid.

23. For a full account of this incident see Hugh A Dempsey, "Scraping High and Mr. Tims," in *The Amazing Death of Calf Shirt and Other Blackfoot Stories*, 186–209.

24. Letter, Father A. Naessens to J. V. Beaupre, January 22, 1897. St. Joseph's Industrial School letter-book, vol. 4, 305, Glenbow Archives.

25. Letter, Father A. Naessens to Sgt. J. J. Marshall, January 22, 1897. St. Joseph's Industrial School letter-book, vol. 4, 301, Glenbow Archives.

26. Letter, Father A. Naessens to Indian Commissioner, February 16, 1897. St. Joseph's Industrial School letter-book. vol. 4, 355, Glenbow Archives.

27. Charles Royal, Siksika Indian, interview by Hugh A. Dempsey, April 15, 1959.

28. Letter, P. C. H. Primrose to Blackfoot Indian agent, April 28, 1905. RG 10, vol.1154, no.225, NAC.

29. Letter, Assistant Commissioner, RNWMP, to Blackfoot Indian agent, July 3, 1905. RG 10, vol. 1154, no. 230, NAC.

30. Charles Royal, interview.

31. Ben Calf Robe, Siksika Indian, interview by Hugh A. Dempsey, March 25, 1972.

14 THE BULL ELK AFFAIR

1. This account is an adaptation of Hugh A. Dempsey, "The Bull Elk Affair," 2–9. Since then, additional information has come to light, which is included here.

2. Report, James F. Macleod, December 1, 1874, in *Report of the Commissioner of the North-West Mounted Police, 1974*, 66.

3. *Stratford Beacon*, June 26, 1885.

4. Hugh A. Dempsey, *Crowfoot, Chief of the Blackfeet*, 146.

5. Ibid., 134.

6. John D. Lauder, "Arrest of Blackfoot Indian Chief Bull Elk." Manuscript in RCMP Archives, Ottawa.

7. Dempsey, *Crowfoot*, 135.

8. Hugh A. Dempsey, *Big Bear, The End of Freedom*, 121.

9. Letter, N. T. Macleod to Indian Commissioner, December 10, 1881. Blood letter-books. (These letter-books are now in the National Archives of Canada, Ottawa, but were consulted by Hugh A. Dempsey while they were still in storage at the Blood Indian Agency.)

10. Letter, A. G. Irvine to Minister of the Interior, November 17, 1880. RCMP Papers, RG-18, vol. 12, file 460, NAC.

11. R. C. Macleod, "Francis Jeffrey Dickens," in *Dictionary of Canadian Biography* 11:261.

12. Head chief Heavy Shield and minor chief Running Rabbit, who were standing

nearby, claimed that Bull Elk had not been firing at anyone and that both shots went wild.

13. *Report of the Commissioner, 1881*, 53.

14. Ibid.

15. Ibid.

16. Ibid., 51.

17. Ibid.

18. Lauder, "Arrest of Blackfoot Indian Chief Bull Elk."

19. *Manitoba Free Press*, April 13, 1882.

20. *Report of the Commissioner, 1881*, 50–51.

21. Ibid.

22. *Manitoba Free Press*, April 13, 1882.

23. *Report of the Commissioner, 1881*, 54.

24. Ibid., 55.

25. J. G. A. Creighton, "The Northwest Mounted Police of Canada," 257.

26. *Report of the Commissioner, 1881*, 55.

27. Letter, N. T. Macleod to Indian Commissioner, January 12, 1882. Blood letter-books.

28. Turner, *The North-West Mounted Police*, 1:631. In his report of the incident, Turner, RCMP historian, said that Bull Elk had been charged with attempted murder and had been given a stiff sentence. Neither statement was true.

29. Report of the Commissioner, *Annual Report of the Department of Indian Affairs for the Year ended 31st December, 1882*, xvii.

30. Denny, *The Riders of the Plains*, 159–60.

31. *Calgary Tribune*, December 3, 1886.

15 THE RISE AND FALL OF WHITE CALF

1. The translation of the chief's name has always been a puzzle. It was constantly shown in Blackfoot as Onista'poka, which, according to elders, means Calf Child, but it was always translated as White Calf. The name White Calf would be translated as Onista'ksiksinum or perhaps A'ponista. Yet various chiefs who have held this name, including the head chief of the South Piegans, always had the term translated as White Calf.

2. "The Life History and Adventures of Red Crow," in Middleton, *Indian Chiefs, Ancient and Modern*, 163.

3. John Cotton, interview.

4. Ibid.

5. Harry Mills, Blood Indian, interview by Hugh A. Dempsey, December 27, 1953.

6. *Saskatchewan Herald*, Battleford, May 27, 1882.

7. Letter, Cecil Denny to Indian Commissioner, May 21, 1882. Blood Agency letter-book, NAC.

8. John Maclean, "Social Organization of the Blackfoot Indians," *Transactions of the Canadian Institute*, 252.

9. Letter from the Blood Agency, June 16, 1882, in *Fort Macleod Gazette*, July 1, 1882.

10. Letter, Denny to Indian Commissioner, May 17, 1882. Blood Agency letter-book, NAC. Denny has used White Calf's other name, Running Crane, in the letter.

11. *Benton Weekly Record*, June 15, 1882.

12. Letter, A. G. Irvine to Comptroller, May 21, 1882. RCMP Records, RG 18, B3, vol. 2186, 626–36, NAC.

13. *Benton Weekly Record*, June 22, 1882.

14. Letter, Denny to Indian Commissioner, June 4, 1882. Blood Agency letter-book, NAC.

15. Letter, Irvine to White, May 21, 1882.

16. Ibid.

17. Information sheet in the Fort Macleod Museum.

18. Letter, Irvine to White, May 21, 1882.

19. Letter, A. G. Irvine to Comptroller, July 5, 1882. RCMP Records, RG 18, B3, vol. 2186, 728–30, NAC.

20. Letter, Denny to Indian Commissioner, September 5, 1883. Blood Agency letter-book, NAC.

21. Letter, Denny to Indian Commissioner, July 28, 1883. Blood Agency letter-book, NAC.

22. Letter, Denny to Indian Commissioner, September 28, 1883. Blood Agency letter-book, NAC.

23. Harry Mills, interview.

24. Letter, William Pocklington to Indian Commissioner, March 18, 1885. Blood Agency letter-book, NAC.

25. Ibid.

26. Letter, Pocklington to Indian Commissioner, November 9, 1885. Blood Agency letter-book, NAC.

27. John Maclean, *Canadian Savage Folk*, 555.

28. Letter, Pocklington to Indian Commissioner, November 9, 1885. Blood Agency letter-book, NAC.

29. Ibid.

30. Ibid.

31. Letter, Pocklington to Indian Commissioner, April 4, 1891. Blood Agency letter-book, NAC.

32. Letter, Pocklington to Indian Commissioner, October 31, 1891. Blood Agency letter-book, NAC.

33. Letter, Pocklington to Indian Commissioner, May 30, 1891. Blood Agency letter-book, NAC.

34. Letter, Pocklington to Indian Commissioner, July 1, 1891. Blood Agency letter-book, NAC. Pocklington was also told that White Calf would be accompanying other Piegan chiefs to Washington, D.C., but the information was incorrect. The man invited to the capital was also named White Calf, but he was a recognized chief of the South Piegans.

35. Letter, Pocklington to Indian Commissioner, May 30, 1891. Blood Agency letter-book, NAC.

36. Letter, Pocklington to Indian Commissioner, October 30, 1891. Blood Agency letter-book, NAC.

16 MIKE RUNNING WOLF

1. Canon H. W. G. Stocken, letter to D. C. Scott, July 14, 1919. Copy in George H. Gooderham papers, Glenbow Archives.

2. Ibid.

3. Ibid.

4. Report of Supt. R. Burton Deane in *Report of the Royal Northwest Mounted Police, 1912*. Ottawa: King's Printer, 1912, 42.

5. *Calgary Herald*, October 15, 1912.

6. Report of Supt. R. Burton Deane in *Report of the Royal Northwest Mounted Police, 1912*, 43.

7. *Calgary Herald*, June 4, 1912.

8. See David Bright, "The Murder of John Middleton," 3–12.

9. Richard Goss, "Death of a Mountie," 3.

10. Ibid.

11. Report of Supt. R. Burton Deane in *Report of the Royal Northwest Mounted Police, 1912*, 42.

12. Ed Yellow Old Woman, who was an infant in the wagon at the time, claimed he remembered the incident (interview by Hugh A. Dempsey, January 10, 1981), but his account is so garbled and at odds with documented information that it is likely he heard stories about it when he was older.

13. Ed Yellow Old Woman, Siksika Indian, interview by Hugh A. Dempsey, January 10, 1981.

14. Report of Supt. R. Burton Deane in *Report of the Royal Northwest Mounted Police, 1912*, 44.

15. Ibid.

16. *Calgary Herald*, June 6, 1912.

17. Letter, Glen Campbell to Ottawa, May 5 [sic], 1912. RG 10, vol. 7468, file 19104-2 pt. 1, NAC.

18. Ibid.

19. Report of Supt. R. Burton Deane in *Report of the Royal Northwest Mounted Police, 1912*, 44.

20. Ibid.

21. Howard McMaster, Siksika Indian, interview by Lucien and Jane Hanks, July 27, 1938. Hanks Papers, M8458, box 64. Glenbow Archives.

22. Report of Supt. R. Burton Deane in *Report of the Royal Northwest Mounted Police, 1912*, 44.

23. Howard McMaster, interview.

24. *Calgary Herald,* October 16, 1912.

25. *Calgary Albertan,* October 17, 1912.

26. Ibid.

27. *Calgary News-Telegram,* October 16, 1912.

28. Ibid.

29. bid.

30. Ibid.

31. Letter, Canon H. W. G. Stocken to D. C. Scott, July 14, 1919. Copy in George H. Gooderham papers, Glenbow Archives.

32. Letter, J. L. Levern to Department of Indian Affairs, August 30, 1922. RG 10, vol. 7468, file 19104-2, pt. 1, NAC.

33. Letter, Duncan C. Scott to Remissions Branch, November 2, 1922. RG 10, vol. 7468, file 19104-2, pt. 1, NAC.

34. McMaster, interview.

Bibliography

UNPUBLISHED MATERIALS

Correspondence

Christie, W. J. Letter to Richard Hardisty, November 2, 1866. B.60/b/2, Hudson's Bay Company Archives. Public Archives of Manitoba, Winnipeg, Manitoba.

Maclean, John. Letter to his wife, June 8, 1886. John Maclean Papers. United Church Archives, Toronto, Ontario.

McMahon, Father M. Letter to Hugh A. Dempsey, October 12, 1971. In author's possession.

Maunsell, E. H. Letter to J. F. Price, May 29, 1922. M1002, Elizabeth Bailey Price Papers. Glenbow Archives, Calgary, Alberta.

Naessens, Father A. Letter to Indian Commissioner, February 16, 1897. St. Joseph's Industrial School Papers, vol. 4, 355. Glenbow Archives, Calgary, Alberta.

———. Letter to J. V. Beaupre, January 22, 1897. St. Joseph's Industrial School Papers, vol. 4, 305. Glenbow Archives, Calgary, Alberta.

———. Letter to Sgt. J. J. Marshall, January 22, 1897. St. Joseph's Industrial School Papers, vol. 4, 301. Glenbow Archives, Calgary, Alberta.

Rowand, John. Letter to Donald Ross, December 21, 1844. M936. City of Edmonton Archives, Edmonton, Alberta.

Stocken, Canon H. W. G. Letter to D. C. Scott, July 14, 1919. George H. Gooderham Papers. Glenbow Archives, Calgary, Alberta.

Interviews

Apioh'suk. Siksika Indian. Interview by Lucien and Jane Hanks, June 18, 1941. Hanks Papers. Glenbow Archives, Calgary, Alberta.

Arrow Top, Mollie. South Peigan Indian. Interview by Claude Schaeffer, August 18, 1965. Claude Schaeffer Papers. Glenbow Archives, Calgary, Alberta.

Axe, Mrs. Siksika Indian. Interview by Lucien and Jane Hanks, July 24, 1941. Hanks Papers. Glenbow Archives, Calgary, Alberta.

Bad Eagle, Pat. North Peigan Indian. Interview by Hugh A. Dempsey, April 1, 1961. In author's possession.

Beebe, Joe. Blood Indian. Interview by Esther S. Goldfrank, January 8, 1939. Esther Goldfrank Papers. Glenbow Archives, Calgary, Alberta.

Black, Francis. Siksika Indian. Interview by Lucien and Jane Hanks, June 1938. Hanks Papers. Glenbow Archives, Calgary, Alberta.

Boy Chief. South Peigan Indian. Interview by James Willard Schultz, August 7, 1913. James Willard Schultz Papers. Special Collections, Montana State University Library, Bozeman, Montana.

Calf Robe, Ben. Siksika Indian. Interview by Hugh A. Dempsey, March 25, 1972. In author's possession.

Cotton, John. Blood Indian. Interviews by Hugh A. Dempsey, December 26, 1953, December 29, 1955, and January 4, 1957. In author's possession.

Creighton, Percy. Blood Indian. Interview by Hugh A. Dempsey, July 17, 1954. In author's possession.

Crooked Meat Strings. Siksika Indian. Interviews by Lucien and Jane Hanks, September 13, 1938, July 27, 1939, and August 2, 1941. Hanks Papers. Glenbow Archives, Calgary, Alberta.

Crow Eagle, Charlie. North Peigan Indian. Interview by Oscar Lewis, August 9, 1939. Oscar Lewis Papers. Smithsonian Institution, Washington, D.C.

Dog Chief. Siksika Indian. Interview by Lucien and Jane Hanks, August 1, 1939. Hanks Papers. Glenbow Archives, Calgary, Alberta.

Eagle, Pete. South Peigan Indian. Interview by Claude Schaeffer, June 10, 1952. Claude Schaeffer Papers. Glenbow Archives, Calgary, Alberta.

Eagle Feathers. South Peigan Indian. Interview by James Willard Schultz, n.d. James Willard Schultz Papers. Special Collections, Montana State University Library, Bozeman, Montana.

First Rider, George. Blood Indian. Interview by Claude Schaeffer, January 10, 1961. Claude Schaeffer Papers. Glenbow Archives, Calgary, Alberta.

Fish Wolf Robe. South Peigan Indian. Interview by Claude Schaeffer, July 20, 1965. Claude Schaeffer Papers. Glenbow Archives, Calgary, Alberta.

Gravelle, Ambrose. Kootenay Indian. Interviews by Claude Schaeffer, July 8, 10, and 17, 1969. Claude Schaeffer Papers. Glenbow Archives, Calgary, Alberta.

Ground, John. South Peigan Indian. Interview by Claude Schaeffer, September 30, 1950. Claude Schaeffer Papers. Glenbow Archives, Calgary, Alberta.

Guardipee, Eli. South Peigan Indian. Interview by James Willard Schultz, January 1929. James Willard Schultz Papers. Special Collections, Montana State University Library, Bozeman, Montana.

Little Walker, Paul. Siksika Indian. Interview by Lucien and Jane Hanks, August 5, 1941. Hanks Papers. Glenbow Archives, Calgary, Alberta.

Low Horn, Jack. Blood Indian. Interview by Hugh A. Dempsey, December 29, 1954. In author's possession.

McMaster, Howard. Siksika Indian. Interview by Lucien and Jane Hanks, July 27, 1938. Hanks Papers. Glenbow Archives, Calgary, Alberta.

Many Guns. Siksika Indian. Interviews by Lucien and Jane Hanks, August 31, 1938, and September 16, 1939. Hanks Papers. Glenbow Archives, Calgary, Alberta.

Many Tail Feathers. South Peigan Indian. Interviews by James Willard Schultz, August 4 and 5, 1922. James Willard Schultz Papers. Special Collections, Montana State University Library, Bozeman, Montana.

Mills, Harry. Blood Indian. Interview by Hugh A. Dempsey, December 27, 1953. In author's possession.

Old Bull. Siksika Indian. Interview by Lucien and Jane Hanks, September 7, 1940. Hanks Papers. Glenbow Archives, Calgary, Alberta.

One Gun. Siksika Indian. Interview by Lucien and Jane Hanks, July 24, 1939. Hanks Papers. Glenbow Archives, Calgary, Alberta.

Pantherbone, Charlie. Blood Indian. Interviews by Hugh A. Dempsey, July 24, 1954, and August 2, 1960. In author's possession.

Pretty Young Man. Siksika Indian. Interview by Lucien and Jane Hanks, 1941. Hanks Papers. Glenbow Archives, Calgary, Alberta.

Red Crow, Frank. Blood Indian. Interview by Claude Schaeffer, May 1948. Claude

Schaeffer Papers. Glenbow Archives, Calgary, Alberta.

Royal, Charles. Siksika Indian. Interview by Hugh A. Dempsey, April 15, 1959. In author's possession.

Running Rabbit. Siksika Indian. Interview by Lucien and Jane Hanks, July 12, 1939. Hanks Papers. Glenbow Archives, Calgary, Alberta.

Sanderville, Dick. South Peigan Indian. Interview by Claude Schaeffer, May 21, 1952. Claude Schaeffer Papers. Glenbow Archives, Calgary, Alberta.

Sleigh. Siksika Indian. Interview by Lucien and Jane Hanks, c. 1939. Hanks Papers. Glenbow Archives, Calgary, Alberta.

Small, Marie. South Peigan Indian. Interview by Claude Schaeffer, August 18, 1965. Claude Schaeffer Papers. Glenbow Archives, Calgary, Alberta.

Split Ears. South Peigan Indian. Interview by James Willard Schultz, August 6, 1915. James Willard Schultz Papers. Special Collections, Montana State University Library, Bozeman, Montana.

Takes the Gun Himself, Mrs. Siksika Indian. Interview by Lucien and Jane Hanks, July 28, 1940. Hanks Papers. Glenbow Archives, Calgary, Alberta.

White Bull, Jim. Blood Indian. Interviews by Hugh A. Dempsey, June 5, 1954, and December 29, 1955. In author's possession.

White Man, Adam. South Peigan Indian. Interview by Claude Schaeffer, November 22, 1950. Claude Schaeffer Papers. Glenbow Archives, Calgary, Alberta.

Yellow Kidney. South Peigan Indian. Interview by Claude Schaeffer, November 25, 1948. Claude Schaeffer Papers. Glenbow Archives, Calgary, Alberta.

Yellow Old Woman, Ed. Siksika Indian. Interview by Hugh A. Dempsey, January 10, 1981. In author's possession.

Manuscripts

Adney, Tappen. "John J. Healy and the Bloods." Tappen Adney Papers. Montana Historical Society Archives, Helena, Montana.

Beebe, Joe. "Justice Among the Indians Before the White Man's Law Came." Glenbow Archives, Calgary, Alberta.

Creighton, Percy. Blood Indian. Winter count. Harry Biele Papers, 1939. Smithsonian Institution, Washington, D.C.

Gooderham, George H. Papers. Glenbow Archives, Calgary, Alberta.

Hudson's Bay Company. Journal of Carlton House, 1824–25. B.27/a/14, Hudson's Bay Company Records. Provincial Archives of Manitoba, Winnipeg, Manitoba.

Lauder, John D. "Arrest of Blackfoot Indian Chief Bull Elk." RCM Police Archives, Ottawa, Ontario.

Levern, Father J. L. "Notes et Souvenirs Concernant les Piednoirs." Microfilm. Glenbow Archives, Calgary, Alberta.

Little Chief, Joe. "The Story of Calf Looking." M4394. Glenbow Archives, Calgary, Alberta.

McIllree, J. H. Diary, 1880. Microfilm. Glenbow Archives, Calgary, Alberta.

Pretty Young Man, Tony. Sarcee Indian. "Stories about long ago." Accn.#992. Glenbow Archives, Calgary, Alberta.

Running Rabbit, Houghton. Winter count. Glenbow Archives, Calgary, Alberta.

Schultz, James Willard. Papers. Montana State University Special Collections, Bozeman, Montana.

Untitled manuscript. Glacier National Park Archives, West Glacier, Montana.

White Bull, Jim. "Records by the Blood Indians and Blackfoots." Typed copy in possession of the author.

"Woman's Revenge: A Legend of the Blackfeet." Glenbow Archives, Calgary, Alberta.

NEWSPAPERS

Benton River Press, August 31, October 19, November 9, 1881; February 12, 1890.

Benton Weekly Record, November 8, 1878; September 12, 1879; January 9, 1880; October 13 and 27, November 3, 10, 14, 16, and 17, December 22, 1881; June 15 and 22, 1882.

Calgary Albertan, October 17, 1912.

Calgary Herald, July 25, 1888; June 4 and 6, October 15 and 16, 1912.

Calgary News-Telegram, October 16, 1912.

Calgary Tribune, December 3, 1886.

Fort Macleod Gazette, July 1 and 16, November 24, December 4, 1882; March 14, 1883; February 6 and May 1, 1890.

Helena Daily Herald, December 2, 1870.

Lethbridge Herald, July 27, 1940.

Lethbridge News, April 30, 1890.

Macleod Gazette, May 1, 1890.

Manitoba Free Press, Winnipeg, September 27, 1876; January 13, April 13, and May 12, 1882; July 31, 1883.

The Manitoban, Winnipeg, March 4, 1871.

Montana Post, Virginia City, April 28 and May 19, 1866.

New York World, January 5 and February 9, 1890.

Saskatchewan Herald, Battleford, May 27, 1882.

Stratford (Ontario) Beacon, June 26, 1885.

Sun River (Montana) Sun, December 25, 1884.

Winnipeg Daily Times, December 20, 1879; July 31, 1883.

Winnipeg Free Press, February 24, 1890.

GOVERNMENT DOCUMENTS

Canada. Annual Reports of the Commissioner of the North-West Mounted Police Force, 1874–1912. Ottawa: Queen's Printer.

——. *Annual Reports of the Department of Indian Affairs, 1881–89.* Ottawa: Queen's Printer.

——. "Annual Report of Superintendent P. R. Neale." *Report of the Commissioner of the North-West Mounted Police Force, 1887.* Ottawa: Queen's Printer.

——. "Blackfoot Names of a Number of Places in the North-West Territory, for the Most Part in the Vicinity of the Rocky Mountains," George M. Dawson. *Report of Progress, 1882–83–84.* Ottawa: Geological and Natural History Survey and Museum of Canada, 1885.

——. Letter, Assistant Commissioner, RNWMP, to Blackfoot Indian Agent, July 3, 1905. Indian Department Papers, RG 10, vol. 1154, no. 230. National Archives of Canada, Ottawa.

——. Letter, Magnus Begg to Hayter Reed, March 1, 1890. RCMP Papers, RG 18, vol. 40, file 217-1890. National Archives of Canada, Ottawa.

——. Letter, Glen Campbell to Ottawa, May 5 [*sic*], 1912. Indian Department Papers, RG 10, vol. 7468, file 19104-2, pt. 1. National Archives of Canada, Ottawa.

——. Letter, Cecil Denny to Edgar Dewdney, November 1, 1881. Indian Affairs file RG-10, 29506. National Archives of Canada, Ottawa.

——. Letters, Cecil Denny to Indian Commissioner, May 17, May 21, and June 4, 1882; July 28, September 5 and 28, 1883. Blood Reserve letter-books, RG-10. National Archives of Canada, Ottawa.

——. Letters, A. G. Irvine to Comptroller, May 21 and July 5, 1882. RCMP Papers, RG 18,B3, vol. 2186. National Archives of Canada, Ottawa.

——. Letter, A. G. Irvine to Indian Commissioner, May 17, 1882. Indian Department Papers, RG 10. National Archives of Canada, Ottawa.

——. Letter, A. G. Irvine to Minister of the Interior, November 17, 1880. RCMP Papers, RG 18, vol. 12, file 460. National Archives of Canada, Ottawa.

——. Letter, J. L. Levern to Department of Indian Affairs, August 30, 1922. Indian Department Papers, RG 10, vol. 7468, file 19104-2, pt. 1. National Archives of Canada, Ottawa.

——. Letter, J. C. McIllree to the Commissioner, February 19, 1890. RCMP Papers, RG 18, vol.40, file 217-1890. National Archives of Canada, Ottawa.

——. Letters, Norman T. Macleod to Indian Commissioner, December 10, 1881, and January 12, 1882. Indian Department Papers, RG 10. National Archives of Canada, Ottawa.

——. Letters, William Pocklington to Indian Commissioner, March 18, November 9, 1885; February 3, 1887; April 4, May 30, July 1, October 30 and 31, 1891. Blood Reserve letter-books, RG-10. National Archives of Canada, Ottawa.

——. Letter, Insp. P. C. H. Primrose to Blackfoot Indian Agent, April 28, 1905. Indian Department Papers, RG 10, vol. 1154, no. 225. National Archives of Canada, Ottawa.

——. Letter, Duncan C. Scott to Remissions Branch, Department of Justice, November 2, 1922. Indian Department Papers, RG 10, vol. 7468, file 19104-2, pt. 1. National Archives of Canada, Ottawa.

——. United States. Annual Report of Gad E. Upson, United States Indian Agent, September 1, 1864. SC-810. Montana Historical Society Library, Helena, Montana.

——. Interior Department, Bureau of Indian Affairs Records. Report of Hiram D. Upham, April 20, 1866. SC-895. Montana Historical Society Library, Helena, Montana.

——. Letter, Charles D. Hard to J. A. Viall, November 9, 1870. Letters Received by the Office of Indian Affairs, 1824-81, Montana Superintendency, 1864-1880, roll 490, National Archives and Records Administration, Washington, D.C.

——. Letters, A. J. Simmons to Jasper Viall, November 9 and 30, 1870. Letters Received by the Office of Indian Affairs, 1824-81, Montana Superintendency, 1864-1880, roll 490. National Archives and Records Administration, Washington, D.C.

——. Letter, Alfred Sully to Commissioner of Indian Affairs, January 3, 1870. Piegans. Letter from the Secretary of War. 41st Cong., 2nd Sess., HR, ex. doc. 269, 1870.

——. Letter, J. A. Viall to E. S. Parker, November 14, 1870. Letters Received by the Office of Indian Affairs, 1824-81, Montana Superintendency, 1864-1880, roll 490, National Archives and Records Administration, Washington, D.C.

——. Letter, George B. Wright to Secretary of the Interior, July 5, 1867. SC-895. Montana Historical Society Library, Helena, Montana.

——. "Report of commissioners Alfred Cummings and Isaac I. Stevens on the proceedings of the council with the Blackfeet Indians." SC-895. Montana Historical Society Library, Helena, Montana.

BOOKS AND PAMPHLETS

Audubon, James J. *Audubon and His Journals.* 2 vols. London, 1899.

Baker, William M., ed. *Pioneer Policing in Southern Alberta: Deane of the Mounties, 1888-1914.* Calgary: Historical Society of Alberta, 1993.

Butler, Francis F. *The Great Lone Land.* Toronto: Musson, 1924.

———. *Red Cloud: The Solitary Sioux.* London: Sampson Low, Marston and Co., 1896.

Coues, Eliott, ed. *New Light on the Early History of the Greater Northwest: The Manuscript Journals of Alexander Henry, Fur Trader of the Northwest Company, and of David Thompson, Official Geographer and Explorer of the Same Company.* New York: Francis P. Harper, 1897.

Cowie, Isaac. *The Company of Adventurers.* Lincoln: University of Nebraska Press, 1993.

DeMarce, Roxanne, ed. *Blackfeet Heritage.* Browning, Mont.: Blackfeet Heritage Program, 1980.

Dempsey, Hugh A. *The Amazing Death of Calf Shirt and Other Blackfoot Stories.* Norman: University of Oklahoma Press, 1994.

———. *Big Bear: The End of Freedom.* Vancouver: Douglas and McIntyre, 1984.

———. *The Blackfoot Ghost Dance.* Calgary: Glenbow Museum, 1868.

———. *A Blackfoot Winter Count.* Calgary: Glenbow Museum, 1965.

———. *Crowfoot, Chief of the Blackfeet.* Norman: University of Oklahoma Press, 1972.

———, ed. *Heaven is Near the Rocky Mountains: The Journals and Letters of Thomas Woolsey, 1855–1869.* Calgary: Glenbow Museum, 1989.

———, ed. *The Rundle Journals, 1840–1848.* Calgary: Historical Society of Alberta, 1977.

Denny, Cecil. *The Riders of the Plains.* Calgary: The Herald Co., 1905.

Dixon, Joseph K. *The Vanishing Race.* New York: Doubleday and Co., 1913.

Donnelly, Joseph P., ed. *Wilderness Kingdom: Indian Life in the Rocky Mountains, 1840–1847. The Journals and Paintings of Nicholas Point, S.J.* New York: Holt, Rinehart and Winston, 1967.

Eagle Calf, and Heavy Breast. *Picture Writing by the Blackfeet Indians of Glacier National Park Montana.* St. Paul: Great Northern Railway, c. 1920.

Grinnell, George Bird. *Blackfoot Lodge Tales.* Lincoln: University of Nebraska Press, 1962.

———. *The Story of the Indian.* New York: D. Appleton and Co., 1895.

Harmon, Daniel Williams. *Sixteen Years in the Indian Country.* Toronto: Macmillans, 1957.

Holterman, Jack. *King of the High Missouri: The Saga of the Culbertsons.* Helena, Mont.: Falcon Press, 1987.

Jenness, Diamond. *The Sarcee Indians of Alberta.* Ottawa: National Museum of Canada, 1938.

Kappler, Charles J., ed. *Indian Affairs. Laws and Treaties.* 2 vols. New York: AMS Press, 1971.

Kroeber, A. L. *Ethnology of the Gros Ventre.* New York: American Museum of Natural History, 1908.

Kurz, Rudolf Friedrich. *Journal of Rudolf Friedrich Kurz, 1846–1852.* Bulletin 115. Washington, D.C.: Smithsonian Institution, 1937.

Linderman, Frank Bird. *Pretty Shield: Medicine Woman of the Crows.* Lincoln: University of Nebraska Press, 1972.

McClintock, Walter. *The Old North Trail.* Lincoln: University of Nebraska Press, 1992.

Maclean, John. *Canadian Savage Folk.* Toronto: William Briggs, 1896.

Middleton, S. H., ed. *Indian Chiefs, Ancient and Modern.* Lethbridge: Lethbridge Herald, 1951.

Mountain Horse, Mike. *My People the Bloods.* Calgary: Glenbow Museum, 1979.

Overholser, Joel. *Fort Benton: World's Innermost Port.* Helena: Falcon Press, 1987.

Raczka, Paul M. *Winter Count: A History of the Blackfoot People.* Brocket, Alberta: Oldman River Culture Centre, 1979.

Schaeffer, Claude E. *Blackfoot Shaking Tent.* Calgary: Glenbow Museum, 1969.

Schultz, James Willard. *Running Eagle, The Warrior Girl.* Boston: Houghton Mifflin, 1919.

——. *Signposts of Adventure.* Boston: Houghton Mifflin, 1926.

——, and Jessie Louise Donaldson. *The Sun God's Children.* New York: Houghton Mifflin Co., 1930.

Steele, Samuel B. *Forty Years in Canada: Reminiscences of the Great North-West and with Some Account of His Service in South Africa.* London: Herbert Jenkins Ltd., 1915.

Stewart, Carlton R., ed. *The Last Great (Inter-Tribal) Indian Battle.* Lethbridge: Lethbridge Historical Society, 1997.

Turner, John Peter. *The North-West Mounted Police.* 2 vols. Ottawa: King's Printer, 1950.

White Man Running Around. War record, printed broadside. Fort Macleod Museum, Fort Macleod, Alberta.

White Wolf. War record, printed broadside. Fort Macleod Museum, Fort Macleod, Alberta.

Williams, W. H. *Manitoba and the North-West: Journal of a Trip from Toronto to the Rocky Mountains.* Toronto: Hunter, Rose and Co., 1882.

Wissler, Clark. *Blackfoot Mythology.* New York: American Museum of Natural History, 1908.

——. *The Social Life of the Blackfoot Indians.* New York: American Museum of Natural History, 1911.

ARTICLES

Black, Jim. "Rescue of the Captured Boy." *Siksika Nation News,* August 1998.

"The Blackfoot Indian Peace Council." *Frontier and Midland* 17, no. 3 (1937).

Black Plume, Cecil. "Children Massacred." *Kainai News,* March 15, 1953.

——. "Long Hair." *Outlook,* Lethbridge Jail, April 1973.

Bradley, James. "Affairs at Fort Benton, From 1831 to 1869." *Contributions to the Historical Society of Montana* 3 (1900): 201–87.

——. "Blackfoot War with the Whites," *Contributions to the Historical Society of Montana* 9 (1923): 252–58.

Bright, David. "The Murder of John Middleton." *Alberta History* 46, no. 4 (Autumn 1998): 2–12.

Creighton, J. G. A. "The Northwest Mounted Police of Canada." *The Western World* (November 1893): 254–57.

Dempsey, Hugh A. "The Bull Elk Affair." *Alberta History* 40, no. 2 (Spring 1992): 2–9.

——, ed. "Simpson's Essay on the Blackfoot, 1841." *Alberta History* 38, no. 1 (Winter 1990): 1–14.

Doty, James. "A Visit to the Blackfoot Camps." *Alberta Historical Review* 14, no. 3 (Summer 1966): 17–26.

Ewers, John C. "Women's Roles in Plains Indian Warfare." In *Skeletal Biology in the Great Plains,* edited by D. W. Owlsey and R. L. Jantz, 325–32. Washington, D.C.: Smithsonian Institution, 1994.

"Fort Benton Journal, 1854–56." *Contributions to the Historical Society of Montana,* vol. 10. Helena, Mont.: Neagle Printing, 1940.

Goss, Richard. "Death of a Mountie." *Alberta History* 46, no. 2 (Spring 1998): 2–9.

Hibbard, Helen, ed. "Revenge of the Chieftain's Bride," by Father Dugast. *Montreal Daily Star,* July 11, 1885.

Lewis, Oscar. "Manly-hearted Women Among the North Piegan," *American Anthropologist* 43 (1941): 173–87.

McDonnell, Anne, ed. "The Fort Benton Journals, 1854–56." *Contributions to the Historical Society of Montana*, vol. 10, 1–99. Helena, Mont.: Neagle Printing, 1840.

Maclean, John. "Social Organization of the Blackfoot Indians." *Transactions of the Canadian Institute* 4, part 2, no. 8 (December 1895): 249–60.

Macleod, R. C. "Francis Jeffrey Dickens." *Dictionary of Canadian Biography*, vol. 11, 261–62. Toronto: University of Toronto Press, 1982.

Oka, Mike. "A Blood Indian's Story," *Alberta Historical Review* 3, no. 4 (Autumn 1955): 13–16.

Sanderson, James F. "Indian Tales of the Canadian Prairies." *Alberta Historical Review* 13, no. 3 (Summer 1965): 7–21.

Schaeffer, Claude E. "The Kutenai Female Berdache: Courier, Guide, Prophetess, and Warrior." *Ethnohistory* 12, no. 3 (Summer 1965): 193–236.

Schultz, James Willard. "Indians Battle on Sun River in 1833." *Great Falls Tribune*, September 5 and 12, 1937.

Taylor, Dabney. "The Major's Blackfoot Bride." *Frontier Times* 43, no. 1 (December–January 1969): 26–29, 46–48.

Van Kirk, Sylvia. "John Rowand." *Dictionary of Canadian Biography*, vol. 7, 779–80. Toronto: University of Toronto Press, 1988.

Whitefeathers, Willie. "Reminiscences." *Prairie Patchwork*. Lethbridge, Alberta: Southern Alberta Writers' Workshop, 1980.

Index